S0-ABC-978

MADE FOR EACH OTHER

"You want McKenzie Station, Robin, and the only way it can be yours is if I marry you!" Kate hissed.

"Hell, Kate, I had no idea your father would hatch up this scheme! Why should McKenzie Station be mine if you refuse to marry me? I never considered any other option. We both know we don't belong together."

"Don't play games with me. You know well enough that Father is so set on our marriage that should I refuse he threatened to leave McKenzie Station to you and name you my guardian until I marry. You talked Father into this, and now I want you to talk him out of it."

"Am I so repulsive that you can't stand the thought of me touching you?" The words hissed from his throat with such ferocity that they frightened Kate. "I recall a few kisses we shared that you seemed to enjoy. Do you think me unworthy of your dainty hand?"

Other *Leisure* and *Love Spell* books by
Connie Mason:
VIKING!
SURRENDER TO THE FURY
FOR HONOR'S SAKE
LORD OF THE NIGHT
SHEIK
PROMISE ME FOREVER
ICE & RAPTURE
LOVE ME WITH FURY
SHADOW WALKER
FLAME
TENDER FURY
DESERT ECSTASY
A PROMISE OF THUNDER
PURE TEMPTATION
WIND RIDER
TEARS LIKE RAIN
TREASURES OF THE HEART
THE LION'S BRIDE
SIERRA
BEYOND THE HORIZON
TEMPT THE DEVIL
CARESS AND CONQUER
PROMISED SPLENDOR
WILD IS MY HEART
MY LADY VIXEN
BRAVE LAND, BRAVE LOVE
BOLD LAND, BOLD LOVE

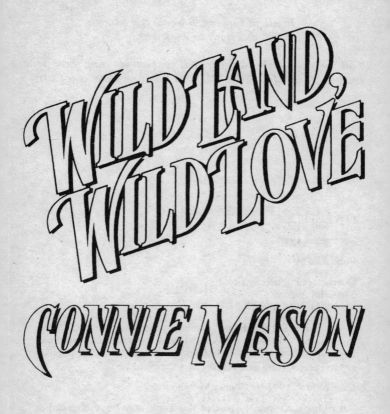

WILD LAND, WILD LOVE

CONNIE MASON

LOVE SPELL BOOKS   ✦   NEW YORK CITY

*To Alicia Condon, a wonderful editor
and a joy to work with.*

To all my readers, whose letters tell me I am pleasing them, especially a group of Raleigh, NC, fans who love Dave and Casey.

LOVE SPELL®

September 1998

Published by

Dorchester Publishing Co., Inc.
276 Fifth Avenue
New York, NY 10001

ISBN 0-505-52278-0

The name "Love Spell" and its logo are trademarks of Dorchester Publishing Co., Inc.

Printed in the United States of America.

Prologue

Aboard the Southern Star *Somewhere in the Pacific Ocean, 1812*

"I'm sorry, Kate, when we left England I never imagined the hardships you'd have to endure. Nor thought I'd not live to see the end of our journey."

The words no sooner left his mouth than William McKenzie's gaunt body was beset with a bout of coughing so severe it left him drenched in sweat and so weak that just breathing sapped his limited strength. The terrible, debilitating illness taking so great a toll on McKenzie's body had struck without warning, leaving him a mere shadow of his former robust self.

"Don't talk like that, Father," Kate chided with

9

gentle encouragement. "You'll be on your feet again in no time."

"I hate to disappoint you, Kate," William gasped, struggling for breath, "but you heard the ship doctor. Lung fever, he called it. And more likely than not 'tis weakened my heart. Even if by some miracle I reach New South Wales alive I won't live long. Ah, Kate, I'm sorry it has to end this way. I had such grand hopes for us in New South Wales. My deepest regret is that you've no man to take care of you once I'm gone."

"You're going to get well, Father," Kathryn McKenzie insisted obstinately. Though her words were fervent they lacked conviction.

William McKenzie had been desperately ill and near death many times since they'd set sail from England over five months ago. His tall frame was thin and gaunt, and he peered at Kate through dull blue eyes sunk deep in their sockets. The violent storms they had encountered only added to William's woes. He slept a great deal, ate little of the indigestible ship's fare, and his mind often wandered back to happier times.

"You're a beautiful liar, Kate," William said, managing a weak smile. "But we must be prepared to face reality. You're a woman, you can't possibly run a sheep farm in a penal colony inhabited by killers, rapists, and thieves. If you had a husband like most young women your age you wouldn't be alone when I—pass on. Lord knows you've had plenty of offers."

"No one suited me, Father," Kate said with a

hint of reproach. "Being a spinster isn't the worst thing in the world. I'm only twenty-six. I'd rather spend my life alone than accept a proposal from a man I could neither respect nor love."

"I've spoiled you, my dear," William sighed bleakly. He was growing weary and his voice shook from the effort of speaking. "Many young women never know their husbands until they marry. You're far too willful and much too independent for most men. More's the pity, but I selfishly let you have your way after your mother passed on. I should have found you a good husband years ago."

"I'm not looking for a husband," Kate declared stoutly. "If I wanted a husband I would have remained in London with Aunt Eudora."

"You're so beautiful, Kate, so very beautiful. 'Tis a pity you've found no one you could love."

Kate, a nickname only her father was permitted to use, was indeed a lovely young woman. Her heart-shaped face was dominated by huge violet eyes framed by thick black lashes. But those weren't the only intriguing features Kate McKenzie possessed. Equally intriguing were full lips that seemed to be perpetually red, long thick hair as dark and shiny as a raven's wing, and a flawless peaches-and-cream complexion. She was slim, a shade taller than average, and full-busted. She was also somewhat haughty, argumentative, stubborn, and independent. If there was a man somewhere who wanted her, she would undoubtedly find fault with him. William McKenzie despaired of ever bouncing a grandchild on his knee.

11

"I told you, Father, I don't need a husband," Kate reiterated firmly. "A man would only complicate my life."

"When my brother Thad died and left me McKenzie station in New South Wales, I'd hoped we'd be starting a new life and you'd find someone to your liking. Now I'll not live to see it." A thin sigh, half regret and half weariness, slipped past his colorless lips.

"Why don't you rest, Father," Kate urged, pulling the blanket over his cadaverous form. "You'll feel much better when you awaken. I know how disappointed you've been in your business dealings, but New South Wales *will* be a new beginning for us. You've too much to live for. I won't let you die."

Kate tiptoed from the tiny airless cabin and carefully made her way to the pitching deck above. She stared bleakly into the swirling black water, spindrift joining the tears sliding down her cheeks. If Father died now, she'd be left alone to manage McKenzie station, she reflected sadly. She could always return to England and live with Aunt Eudora, but that thought offered little comfort. Her elderly aunt wouldn't rest until she saw Kate properly married. It was a sobering thought. One that made Kate more determined than ever to remain a spinster and carry on in New South Wales with or without her father.

After her cousin Mercy McKenzie Penrod died of pneumonia in 1809 in New South Wales, poor Uncle Thad had returned to England a broken man and had neither the will nor inclination to recover

12

from his beloved daughter's untimely death. He died soon after of a broken heart and left his prosperous sheep farm to his brother William, Kate's father and Thad's only living relative. With great anticipation William made plans to travel with his daughter to Australia to inspect his property, never dreaming he'd fall desperately ill a few weeks out of England.

Was the entire McKenzie family cursed? Kate wondered glumly. First her mother had been taken in the flu epidemic five years ago. Then Cousin Mercy had died tragically, followed by Thad. Now she was in grave danger of losing her own father.

"No!" Kate shouted, her words stolen by the wind and tossed out to sea. "I won't let you have him—I won't!"

Chapter One

New South Wales, Australia, October 1812

"Don't tell me who to marry, Dare," Robin charged, scowling at his friend.

"It's for your own good," Dare returned, annoyed that Robin would think he'd offer unsound advice. "Serena is a beautiful woman, but she's not for you."

"You've already taken the only woman worth having in New South Wales," Robin contended sourly.

Dare Penrod did not take offense at Robin Fletcher's startling words. He was well aware of his friend's love for Casey O'Cain Penrod, Dare's cherished wife. Nor was Dare jealous, for no man could wish for a better friend than Robin Fletcher. Robin had forfeited his own freedom and lost everything he had sweated and toiled for in order to help Casey. On several occasions Dare and his father, Roy, had petitioned Governor Macquarie for Robin's freedom, but the long-anticipated pardon had yet to be granted.

"If you plan on marrying Serena for her money, I've told you time and again I'd gladly give you whatever you need."

"Bloody hell, Dare, I'm not looking for a handout." Absently Robin ruffled his sandy brown hair with a callused hand, his vivid blue eyes troubled. "Once I'm pardoned I'll settle on the thirty acres allotted to me by law and try to forget about the land I was stripped of when I lost my freedom. Serena's money will allow me to buy more land and sheep and plant crops."

They were seated in the den of the comfortable new home Dare had built for Casey when they returned from England. With the money Dare had inherited from his English grandfather he'd purchased a large tract of land on the Hawkesbury River and now owned a prosperous sheep farm that surpassed any in New South Wales, including his father's.

"I'm not going to argue with you, Robin," Dare sighed. "Just remember I'm willing to help you in any way I can."

Superbly fit and aggressively handsome, Dare Penrod rested his slate gray eyes pensively on his friend. Nearly the same height as Dare, Robin was lean and sinewy, his sandy brown hair shot with streaks bleached blond by the brutal sun. Robin's

quickly intelligent blue eyes, which used to twin-
kle with good humor and warmth, were now
somber. Thick, ropy muscles corded his tanned
torso and broad chest, rippling down his back as
he clenched and unclenched his fists. The months
spent toiling in the coal mines had changed Robin
Fletcher from a fun-loving, easygoing man into a
man who had been cheated out of all the pleasures
of life. A smile no longer came easily to his lips,
and his bright blue eyes held a glimpse of the pain
and disillusionment life had dealt him.

Convicted of poaching and transported to New
South Wales, Robin Fletcher had earned his freedom once and lost it when, as a favor to Casey, he
aided an escaped convict wounded by the "Rum
Corps" during a daring escape. As a result he'd
been sent to toil in the coal mines. Later Robin was
given a "ticket of leave" to work where he wanted
for whomever he pleased.

"Thanks, mate."

The corners of Robin's mouth tilted into a rare
smile despite his somber mood. The past few years
hadn't been kind to Robin. He'd lost his land and
his freedom; he'd had to watch the woman he
loved marry his best friend and bear his children.
He had learned to live with life's disappointments,
for time had a way of healing grievous wounds. But
it had also robbed him of warmth and humor, and
replaced it with a hard-edged, cynical bitterness.

"I've always known I could count on the
Penrods." Robin's words implied that the subject
was closed.

"The McKenzies are due to arrive any day now," Dare said, honoring Robin's unspoken request. If Robin didn't want to talk about Serena Lynch, that was fine with him.

"I know," Robin replied thoughtfully. "They'll be pleased at how well you've taken care of McKenzie station for them."

"Lord knows I have my hands full with my own farm, but I didn't have the heart to refuse when Thad asked me to look after the place in his absence. Since I *was* married to his daughter, Mercy, he more or less expected it of me. I fully expected him to return one day."

"Mercy's death was hard on Thad," Robin said slowly.

"Aye, but if it wasn't for your taking over management of McKenzie station when it became burdensome for me, the place wouldn't be in such good shape today."

"What do you suppose William McKenzie and his daughter are like?"

"We'll find out soon enough," Dare said. "I'm hoping you'll meet them in Sydney in my stead. There's always so much to do at shearing time."

"Thought I'd take the dray to Sydney tomorrow and wait until their ship arrives."

"Good idea. I'll give you the key to Casey's house in town so you'll have a place to stay."

"Did I hear my name mentioned?"

Pert, red-headed Casey O'Cain Penrod lit up the room with her vibrant beauty. Robin was struck anew by his loss and his friend's good fortune.

"I'm not interrupting, am I?"

"Never!" Dare refuted, rising and slipping an arm around her slim waist.

Despite two children—three-and-a-half-year-old Brandon and Lucy, nearly two—Casey remained reed slim, supple and sweetly fashioned. Robin turned away as Dare planted a kiss on her freckled nose, unwilling to intrude upon so private a moment. Whenever Dare and Casey were together it was as if no one existed but the two of them. If their love were a beacon it would light the world. Robin envied the closeness they shared, and knew he'd never be so fortunate as to find a woman like Casey. He supposed there would always be a part of him that loved her.

"What were you two discussing so seriously?" Casey asked, smiling at Robin in genuine welcome.

"Serena Lynch," Dare said sourly. "And Robin's pardon, which is taking longer than any of us would like. I don't know why Governor Macquarie is moving so slowly on this."

"Give him time," Casey advised. "The governor has worked wonders since the Rum Corps was disbanded and sent back to England. When are the McKenzies due to arrive?" she asked Robin.

"I'm going to Sydney tomorrow to wait for their ship. Word has it that the *Southern Star* will arrive at any time."

"You don't know how much I appreciate your going in my stead," Dare repeated. "My leaving now would create a hardship."

"I don't mind," Robin said. "It sure beats the coal mines. Besides, I've enjoyed managing Mc-

Kenzie station. I'll miss it when Thad's brother takes over the reins."

"He'll need help, Robin. As a 'ticket of leave' man you can work for whom you please," Dare reminded him.

"I hope to have my own farm before long," Robin replied. His voice betrayed some of the anguish and frustration he felt at having been stripped of everything he owned by Lieutenant Governor Johnson after Governor Bligh had been ousted from power.

"And a wife?" Casey teased.

Robin searched her lovely upturned face. Serena was beautiful, but she couldn't compare with Casey's radiant beauty. "Perhaps," he said evasively.

Suddenly Brandon Penrod burst into the room with the fury of a whirling tornado. Hard on his heels was a tiny replica of Casey. Dainty and ladylike, Lucy Penrod was the exact opposite of her boisterous brother.

Robin was a favorite of the children, and it was some time before he could take his leave. When he did he carried the hope that one day he would find just one-tenth of the happiness shared by Dare and Casey.

When the *Southern Star* sailed into Sydney Cove a few days later, Robin was on the quay as the passengers debarked. It was a typical spring day, warm and breezy. Dressed in flannel shirt open at the neck, moleskin trousers, and wide-brimmed hat, Robin carefully scrutinized the passengers as they walked down the gangplank. There weren't many. Several men, quite possibly speculators, several families with children, a few husbands and wives, most young, and of course, more convicts. The wretched creatures, ill-clothed and pale, looked dazed and sick as they were prodded down the gangplank. Robin shuddered, remembering well the hopelessness he'd felt when he first set foot in New South Wales.

The stream of passengers had all but stopped, and Robin frowned, wondering what had happened to the McKenzies. According to the letter Dare had received a few weeks ago, the McKenzies were sailing on the *Southern Star*. Had they decided to take another ship? Robin wondered. His thoughts strayed for a moment, then skidded to a halt as a beautiful but somewhat distraught young woman appeared at the railing.

She was tall and reed slender; wispy tendrils of jet black hair had worked loose from the rather prim bun fastened at her nape and blew about her memorable heart-shaped face. She clutched the rail, unaware of the beguiling picture she made with the breeze molding her dress against her lush curves. Robin stared appreciatively at long slim legs and full breasts suddenly thrust upward as she lifted her arms to shield her eyes against the merciless glare of the sun.

Kathryn McKenzie searched the quay anxiously. Thad McKenzie had spoken glowingly of poor Mercy's husband, Dare Penrod, and Kate hoped the letter telling of Thad's death and their intention of sailing to New South Wales aboard the *Southern Star* had reached him in time. Having someone meet them certainly would be a comfort, especially since her father was so desperately ill.

By some miracle William McKenzie still lived, barely. Reduced to mere skin and bones by his illness, William clung stubbornly to life. It was almost as if he refused to die until his beloved daughter's future was settled. His fear of leaving Kate alone and unprotected on a convict island had given William the strength to prolong his stay on earth, though the effort cost him dearly and he suffered untold anguish.

Kate's eyes swept the quay, then came to rest on the tall, sandy-haired man staring up at the ship. The upward tilt of his head pulled taut the olive skin of his powerfully virile face. Broad-shouldered and slim-hipped, he stood with legs apart, arms folded across his massive chest. Kate wondered if the man could be Dare Penrod, her dead cousin's husband, and called out his name, gesturing wildly. The wind ripped the words from her mouth and blew them away before they could reach the man's ears.

Robin started up the gangplank. Clutching the rail, Kate waited, finding much about him to admire. He moved with the rolling gait and confidence of a man accustomed to vigorous exercise. His deep tan hinted at long hours spent beneath the broiling sun, and his rippling muscles suggested that he was no stranger to hard work. Once again Kate wondered if the man was Dare Penrod.

Her next thought came hard on the heels of her first. Had he remarried? Kate couldn't recall when she had seen a man as intriguing as the sandy-haired stranger walking toward her.

Robin's steps faltered as he got his first good look at the woman standing at the ship's rail. He gazed into her eyes and felt himself drowning in a sea of violets. The shock sent his pulses racing wildly.

"Are you Dare Penrod?"

Her voice was as softly hypnotic as her eyes, but Robin somehow found the wits to reply.

"I'm Robin Fletcher. Are you Miss McKenzie?"

"Aye. Where is Dare Penrod?" Kate asked sharply. "I hoped he'd be on hand to meet our ship." Her voice edged up a notch, giving Robin the impression that she hovered on the brink of hysteria.

"I'm here in Dare's stead," Robin informed her. "Where is your father?" Robin thought it strange that William McKenzie was absent, and he frowned as he searched the deck behind Kate.

Kate's full lips quivered, but she'd held up thus far under the burden of her father's illness and wasn't going to crumble now. The future of McKenzie station depended on her strength and courage to cope with any adversity. At least until her father recovered enough to manage his own affairs. She refused to consider the possibility that William McKenzie might never recover.

"Father is ill—desperately ill," Kate said, swallowing the lump rising in her throat. "Thank God you've come. I don't think I could have gotten him off the ship alone."

"I've been in Sydney several days waiting for the *Southern Star* to arrive," Robin informed her. "I've brought the dray for your trunks; we can make a place for your father to lie down."

Relief churned in Kate. She was grateful to transfer temporary responsibility to this capable man, whoever he was. There would be time enough after her father was made comfortable to learn who and what Robin Fletcher was. If Dare Penrod trusted him, she could do no less.

"Father is still in his cabin. I'll take you to him." Kate whirled, treating Robin to the sight of trim ankles beneath a froth of white petticoats. Gathering his wits, he hurried after her.

The cabin was small, dim, and smelled of sickness. Adjusting his eyes to the reduced light, Robin searched the cramped room for William McKenzie and found him reclining on the bunk. He was fully dressed, the clothes hanging loosely on his wasted frame. Robin was appalled at the condition of the man, and when William started to wheeze and cough, Robin realized something that Kate had refused to acknowledge. William McKenzie was dying. Robin approached the sick man and knelt beside him.

"I'm Robin Fletcher, sir. I've come to take you to McKenzie station. Welcome to New South Wales."

William managed a weak smile. "Thank you, son." His voice was thin and labored, the effort sending him into another spasm of coughing. "I see you've already met my daughter Kate."

"Kathryn," Kate corrected as she offered Robin a cool hand. "Kathryn Molly McKenzie."

"Pleased to meet you, Kathryn Molly McKenzie," Robin drawled with a hint of amusement. Something told him there was more to Miss McKenzie than a beautiful face and well-turned figure.

Obviously she wasn't a young girl in the first blush of youth, and there was no indication that she was a widow. She was wonderfully mature and poised, and Robin couldn't remember being so fascinated by a woman since that day he first set eyes on Casey O'Cain. Kate's small slim hand was nearly swallowed by Robin's larger one, and he hung on to it a moment longer than courtesy demanded. A warm flush worked up his wrist, spreading through his entire body. Kate frowned, feeling some of those same vibrations and becoming confused by them.

Reluctantly Robin dropped her hand and turned back to William. "Are you able to walk, Mr. McKenzie?"

"I—don't know," William gasped.

"No matter." Robin grinned, trying to hide his dismay over William's pitiful condition. Then he bent and lifted the emaciated man in his arms as if he were weightless. "Lead the way, Miss McKenzie. I'll follow with your father and then arrange to have your trunks carried off the ship."

"I—feel—so helpless," William sighed.

"No need, Mr. McKenzie, you'll be on your feet

again in no time," Robin said cheerfully. In his heart he knew William McKenzie would be lucky to live long enough to see McKenzie station.

"Be careful," Kate said anxiously as Robin carried William down the gangplank and settled him in the bed of the dray. With blankets he'd thoughtfully brought along, Robin helped to make him more comfortable, hoping he'd be able to withstand the rigors of the trip to McKenzie station.

Robin left them to see to their trunks, and when he returned Kate was already seated in the wagon bed next to her father.

"You'll be more comfortable up here on the seat, Miss McKenzie," Robin advised. "We'll need room for your trunks in the back with your father."

At first Kate thought to protest, but when the trunks arrived she realized Robin had spoken the truth. After murmuring a few soothing words to her father, she climbed onto the seat next to Robin. Then the lumbering vehicle jerked to a start. Kate grasped the seat and hung on, glancing worriedly back at her father wedged in between two trunks.

"Sorry, Miss McKenzie, these bullocks aren't the most graceful creatures."

"Are there no horses here in New South Wales?" Kate remarked dryly, unaware of how close to the truth she came.

"Very few," admitted Robin. "Bullocks are far more practical. Some of the more prosperous farmers own horses, and of course, Governor Macquarie."

"Didn't Uncle Thad own horses?"

"There are two excellent horses at McKenzie station, but I hated to hitch them to the dray when bullocks would do just as well."

Robin turned down George Street, and Kate stared in horror at the gallows and whipping post prominently displayed in the center of the block.

"Do—do they still use those?"

"Upon occasion," Robin allowed. "Convicts outnumber settlers three to one. But Governor Macquarie has done wonders since his arrival in 1809. His first act was to disband the Rum Corps and establish legal tender instead of rum in exchange for goods."

He pointed out a newly constructed building. "That's the new hospital. Around the corner is St. James Church, still unfinished but coming along nicely with the help of convict labor. Rumor has it that Macquarie intends to appoint an ex-convict as magistrate. The exclusionists and 'pure merinos' are up in arms over the prospect, but I reckon Macquarie will have his way. It's about time, if you ask me. Exclusionists believe time-expired convicts belong in a permanent lower class."

"If they were first-class citizens they wouldn't be convicts, or find themselves transported like cattle to a strange land," Kate sniffed somewhat haughtily.

Robin eyed her narrowly but withheld comment. At least until he knew Kathryn Molly McKenzie better. Funny, he wouldn't take her for a snob, but he should have expected as much. Both Thad and Mercy McKenzie had been "pure merinos" and exclusionists, so why should Thad's brother and niece be any different?

Chapter Two

"Why are we stopping?" Kate asked as Robin pulled up in front of a small house close to the center of town.

"I'm going to borrow more blankets and pillows so your father can travel in comfort."

"Who lives here?"

"The house belongs to Casey, Dare Penrod's wife. It was left to her by her first husband. I've been staying here while waiting for the *Southern Star* to arrive."

"Dare Penrod has remarried?" Kate asked. "Uncle Thad spoke of him often. Were he and Mercy terribly in love? Her death must have devastated him, just as it did Uncle Thad. I'm surprised he remarried so soon."

Robin avoided her eyes, unwilling to apprise

Kate of Mercy's true nature or the real reason Dare married her when it was Casey he loved—always Casey.

Kate waited in the wagon with her father while Robin went into the house for bedding. He was gone a long time, and when he emerged he carried a basket on one arm and a blanket and pillow tucked under the other.

"Thought you might be hungry," he explained as he set the basket on the seat between them, then cushioned William's head with the pillow and tucked the extra blanket beneath him to cushion his frail bones.

"Sorry to be so much trouble, son," William apologized.

"Is there a doctor in Parramatta?" Kate asked worriedly. "If not perhaps we should consult a doctor in Sydney before continuing our journey."

"There is a doctor in Parramatta now," Robin said. "We even have a decent road to Parramatta, thanks to Governor Macquarie, who used convict labor to build roads and public buildings."

"A doctor can't cure me, Kate," William said gently. Robin recognized resignation in William's voice and added his own mute agreement. Kate, however, disagreed vigorously.

"I won't have you talking like that, Father! You'll be on your feet in no time."

Soon Sydney lay behind them as the bullocks plodded steadily forward. Kate stared in awe at the thick impenetrable bush growing on either side of the track, consisting of dozens of species of eucalyptus and undergrowth of wattle, vines, and scrub. Some of the trees were ancient, growing forty feet high with willowlike leaves so sparse that grass grew lush on the forest floor beneath them. The first time Kate heard the jungle cry of a kookaburra she started violently. But soon she was so enchanted by the brilliant array of wildflowers she no longer had time to worry over strange sounds.

"I've never seen anything like it," Kate said, her violet eyes wide with wonder.

"'Tis like no place in the world," Robin agreed.

"Tell me about McKenzie station," Kate urged, anxious to learn all about her new home. "Do you live nearby?"

"I thought you understood. I'm a 'ticket of leave' man."

A terrible suspicion took hold of Kate and refused to let go. "What is a 'ticket of leave' man?"

"A 'ticket of leave' man is allowed to work wherever he chooses," Robin explained, unaware of the way Kate was edging away from him on the seat or the whiteness forming around her mouth.

"My God, you're a convict!" Kate gasped. She clutched her throat in a defensive motion, as if she expected Robin to turn on her with his next breath. "Is Dare Penrod mad, trusting someone like you in Sydney on his own?"

"Someone like me?" Robin repeated, his sandy brows rising several notches. "I'm sorry if my presence offends you, but obviously Dare trusts me enough to get you to McKenzie station safely. He entrusted me with the welfare of McKenzie station in Thad's absence, and you'll find everything in perfect order."

His handsome features hardened to stone, his blue eyes narrowed and darkened, giving Kate a fleeting glance at a man who could be a formidable foe if he chose. And here she was, alone, in the middle of nowhere with a sick father, at the mercy of a vicious convict. It was common knowledge that the scum and dregs of society were transported as punishment for crimes too despicable to mention. Robin Fletcher might well be a murderer or rapist. Just the thought of all the crimes he might have committed left Kate weak and shaken.

"I hope Dare Penrod knows what he is doing," Kate muttered, unconvinced. "How—how many other convicts are there at McKenzie station?"

"Forty," Robin returned, scowling furiously. "I've been station boss for two years, ever since Dare moved to his own land and could no longer devote the time needed to McKenzie station. As a 'ticket of leave' man I'm free to work where I choose. I was with Roy Penrod, Dare's father, before I moved over to McKenzie station. I'll go back now that you've come to claim your property, so you no longer need worry about me."

"Forty convicts!" Kate gulped, wondering how in the devil she'd be expected to control men lacking in every social grace. Rough, vicious men so crude and uncivilized England could no longer hold them. And Robin Fletcher was one of those men!

Robin watched the expression on Kate's face

change from open friendliness to fear and disgust, and it rankled to think she was just like her cousin Mercy. Mercy had been cold, calculating, manipulative, and sly. She had also been a beautiful woman, just like Kathryn McKenzie. At least Serena Lynch didn't look down her nose at him or consider him less than human.

Kate grew silent as she contemplated life amongst convicts. Of course she'd known New South Wales was a penal colony but somehow it hadn't occurred to her that she'd be the one to deal with them on a day-to-day basis or that convicts would play so large a role in her life. The thought that she had mistaken someone like Robin Fletcher for an upstanding citizen like Dare Penrod completely unnerved her. She sat in silent rumination until a wallaby came crashing out of the bush, startling her. She shrieked in alarm and without conscious thought slid close to Robin. Robin grinned, his good humor suddenly restored.

"'Tis only a wallaby, Kate, a common sight here in the bush. They're quite harmless."

Kate flushed, embarrassed by her lack of knowledge and her sudden awareness of the heat emanating through Robin to the side of her body where they touched. She jerked away, stunned by her reaction to a man she barely knew. A man who could very well be a murderer—or worse.

"My name is Kathryn," she returned haughtily. She was more than a little annoyed by Robin's familiarity and vowed to speak to Dare Penrod about him when she finally met the man who had been Cousin Mercy's husband.

"I like Kate better," Robin returned cheekily.

Was he deliberately goading her? Kate wondered. She gnashed her teeth and stared straight ahead, trying her best to ignore Robin. She failed miserably. Not only was she very much aware of him as a man, she was annoyed by her unaccustomed response to a man she should treat with the utmost contempt. In an effort to conceal her confusion she turned back to see to her father's comfort.

"How is he faring?" Robin asked, genuinely concerned.

"He's dozing," Kate answered in a hushed voice. "He does a lot of that lately." A frown worried her brow. "I'm terribly concerned about him."

"If you'd like, we can stop in Parramatta and let Dr. Proctor take a look at him."

Kate brightened. "Oh, yes, please. The ship's doctor said there was nothing he could do, that Father—that he . . ." her voice caught on a sob, "that his heart is weak. He offered little hope."

Her voice was low and trembling, her emotions close to the surface. Aware of her fragile control, Robin placed a big hand over her closed fists resting in her lap. Kate stiffened, his callused palm oddly stirring against the smooth flesh of her hands. Mistaking her response for revulsion, Robin quickly removed his hand, scowling as he concentrated on the dirt track winding through the forest.

An uneasy silence prevailed until Robin halted the dray beside the Hawkesbury River that ran parallel with the track.

"Why are we stopping?"

"Are you hungry? 'Tis a good place to stop and eat."

Robin jumped to the ground, then reached up and swung Kate down to stand beside him before she could protest. His hands lingered on her slim waist a moment longer than necessary, then abruptly he let them fall and turned away.

"See to your father," he said gruffly, "while I set out the food."

Kate knelt beside William, helping him to sit up in the wagon bed. The effort was nearly too much for him, and he sat back weakly, panting. When he caught his breath, he said, "Robin Fletcher seems like a capable young man."

"He's a convict, Father," Kate stressed. "Lord only knows what vicious crime the man committed."

William seemed startled by Kate's revelation. He had been dozing in the dray and hadn't heard the conversation concerning Robin's status.

"If Dare Penrod sent the man, that's good enough for me," William contended.

"You're much too trusting, Father," Kate chided. "This is a wild country with strange customs, and Dare Penrod—" Suddenly Robin walked up to the dray and Kate fell silent.

Robin slanted Kate a quizzing glance, a glance that made her lower her eyes guiltily.

"How are you feeling, Mr. McKenzie?" Robin asked solicitously.

"Don't worry about me," William gasped, managing a tepid smile. "How much further?"

"We're about halfway to McKenzie station. I've fixed you a plate of food."

"Nothing for me," William said, turning away from the sight of Robin's offering.

"Father, please try to eat something," Kate urged. "There's a doctor in Parramatta, I've asked Mr.—er—Robin to take us there first." Somehow it didn't seem right to address a convict as mister.

"No, Kate, I want to go home first—to McKenzie station. The doctor can come out later if you'd like, but I seriously doubt there is anything he can do."

"Father—"

"Your father is right, Kate—excuse me—Miss McKenzie. Once he's settled in at McKenzie station, I'll send for the doctor." He turned his attention to his own plate of food but paused when William laid a hand on his arm.

"Tell me about McKenzie station. Thad led me to believe it's a prosperous enterprise. I owe Dare Penrod a great deal for managing the property in our absence. I hope I'll be able to thank him in person."

"I'm certain both Dare and Casey will be calling on you soon."

"Casey?"

"Dare's wife."

"He's remarried then. Is it someone he met in England during his visit?"

"No," Robin said, hesitating a moment before adding, "Casey is an ex-convict."

Kate gasped, shocked to the core by Robin's

startling revelation. How could a man of breeding marry a woman convicted of a crime vile enough to earn transportation? she wondered. Kate hoped she wasn't expected to befriend a woman of such questionable morals and reputation. What in the world had ever possessed Dare Penrod to marry such a woman after having a sweet, refined wife like Cousin Mercy?

William was startled by Robin's words, but unlike his daughter he gave no indication, preferring to waive judgment until he met both Dare and Casey. He liked Robin Fletcher despite his background and he was anxious to judge for himself how well McKenzie station had prospered under Robin's guidance. God willing, he'd live long enough to see that Kate inherited a prosperous business. William was all too aware that his desire to see to Kate's future had kept him alive these long weeks.

Then Robin began telling William about McKenzie station and his attention sharpened. Kate listened also, dismayed and vaguely uncomfortable at the note of pride in Robin's voice. To Kate, Robin sounded much too possessive of a property that didn't belong to him and never would. But William heard only Robin's fierce love of the land, his confidence in his ability and pride in his accomplishments. William had no idea what crime Robin had committed but instinctively felt the punishment had been unnecessarily harsh.

"It sounds as if McKenzie station has prospered in Thad's absence, and I have you and Dare Penrod to thank for it," William said gratefully.

"I was but doing my job," Robin said tightly. "A 'ticket of leave' man is free to work where he wishes, and I couldn't ignore Dare's plea for help when he asked me to step in as station boss at McKenzie station."

"It seems to me that Dare Penrod could have found someone other than a convict to see to the welfare of McKenzie station," Kate interjected with a toss of her well-shaped head.

"Kate!" William admonished sharply as he launched into a fit of coughing that greatly sapped his flagging strength. "Where are your manners?"

Accustomed to disparaging remarks from exclusionists and "pure merinos," Robin merely smiled grimly. His blue eyes were shot with shards of ice, and Kate shivered, his glacial stare chilling her to the bone. The man was dangerous, she reflected, far more dangerous than she had originally thought. She silently vowed to speak to her father about Robin Fletcher once they were alone and urge him to banish Robin from McKenzie station. But now, seeing William weakened from his bout of coughing, Kate shoved all thought of Robin aside as she bent solicitously over her father.

"I'm sorry, Father, I don't know what possessed me to speak like that." Deliberately she refrained from looking at Robin, for he'd know immediately she wasn't sorry at all. Being in close contact with criminals and felons would take some getting used to, and she wasn't certain she could ever learn to like it, or treat them with any degree of courtesy.

Aware of William's distress, Robin curbed his anger. The poor man couldn't help it if his daughter was an outspoken little termagant with an acid tongue and a vile disposition. Obviously William had allowed his daughter too much freedom to vent her spleen. A woman her age should be married with several children hanging on to her skirts.

"It's time we were on our way, sir," Robin said as he gathered up the remnants of their picnic. "I'm anxious to reach McKenzie station before dark. There are still too many bushrangers about for comfort. That's not the kind of welcome I'd wish for you." He hoisted himself onto the dray without first offering a hand to Kate. She flashed him a disgusted look, then climbed clumsily into the seat beside him.

"What are bushrangers?" she asked as she twitched her skirt primly into place about her long legs.

"They're escaped convicts who live in the wild. They live off the land, stealing cattle and sheep as needed and carrying out daring bail-ups. No one is safe on the track as long as bushrangers roam free."

Kate glanced around nervously, imagining all manner of depraved characters hiding in the bush to ambush them. "Are you carrying a weapon?"

Robin laughed harshly. "I'm a convict, remember?"

"I—of course, how silly of me." Kate's face glowed a dull red. Would she ever reconcile herself to this wild, uncivilized country? She turned away, exclaiming over the wizened face of a koala smiling down at her as he munched calmly on eucalyptus leaves.

Farther on she spied a kookaburra in a pepper tree and gave it her full attention, relieved to find something other than the intimidating presence of Robin Fletcher to concentrate on.

It amazed Kate to think that in England it would be fall while in Australia it was spring. Flowers abounded everywhere in wild profusion. It had startled her to learn, when she held a bloom to her nose, that it had no fragrance. Robin had informed her that, while beautiful, most flowers in Australia were devoid of scent.

Though it was only fifteen miles from Sydney to Parramatta, the trip to McKenzie station took several hours.

"Ahead is Penrod station," Robin pointed out as they drove past a large, neat house set well back from the track. "It belongs to Dare's father, Roy. McKenzie Station is beyond the bend in the river. Dare's land lies due west of McKenzie station and encompasses nearly all the land along the Hawkesbury River stretching to the foothills of the Blue Mountains."

"The river is high," Kate mentioned conversationally.

"Spring runoff," Robin replied. "We've had a tremendous amount of rain this spring. Runoff comes down from the Blue Mountains and fills the river and streams. Some years it causes flooding so severe all crops are lost. Then there's drought to contend with," Robin continued. "Summers are hot and dry, and you'll grow so sick of heat and dust you'll wish for winter.''

"Does Australia have no redeeming qualities?'' Kate asked, wondering if it had been a mistake to come to a place so lacking in everything she knew and loved.

Robin's thick brows slanted upward and his blue eyes grew dreamy as he looked beyond Kate to where the Blue Mountains rose tall and majestic in the west.

"Redeeming qualities?'' he repeated, dragging his eyes away from the far horizon to stare at Kate. "This land is so vast, no mortal has conquered its dimensions. It's wild, untamed, and uncivilized. The flora and fauna are so different from what we know, each day is a new experience. Once I'm emancipated I'll never leave. I want my children to be a part of the taming of Australia. I'd give anything to be the first to find a route across the Blue Mountains.''

Kate stared with open curiosity at Robin as he spoke. His passion for a land meant to be his prison stunned her. His words were so stirring, Kate fell silent in order to contemplate the wonders of which Robin spoke.

"There it is, McKenzie station,'' Robin said, halting the dray to allow Kate an unrestricted view of the house and surrounding land. Larger than Penrod station but smaller than Dare's farm, McKenzie station was an impressive sight to behold.

"I . . . I never dreamed it was so big,'' Kate said, awed by what she saw.

Wild Land, Wild Love

The land surrounding the house was largely cleared of brush as far as the eye could see. A white fence surrounded the sprawling rectangular house of two stories. Close by stood stables, cow sheds, convicts' huts, and a blacksmith's shop. The entire farm appeared well cared for and prosperous, attesting to Robin Fletcher's ability as station boss. In the distance Kate could see green paddocks with grazing cattle in the meadows and sheep on the hillsides. Chickens scratched in the yard in the dappled shade of several large gum trees.

When Kate had looked her fill, Robin set the dray into motion. Several convicts greeted Robin and stared curiously at Kate as they entered the yard. Robin returned their greeting with a careless wave while Kate squirmed uncomfortably and tried to ignore their pointed stares.

"Relax, Kate," Robin said, reverting to her nickname and earning a frown for his familiarity. "'Tis only natural that the men are curious about their new master and mistress."

Robin drew up before the front door and leaped down from the dray. Kate scrambled down before Robin could lend her a hand and went immediately to her father's side.

"We're here, Father."

Suddenly a strange occurrence diverted their attention. When they had driven into the yard it was still daylight. Then, in the brief span of a heartbeat, the azure sky turned indigo as the sun dropped below the horizon. It all transpired so quickly, Kate was stunned by the startling phenomena. In England, as in most parts of the world,

41

daylight was followed by dusk that gradually turned into night. In New South Wales a black velvet curtain descended without warning to blot out the light. It was truly an odd occurrence, one that would take some getting used to.

Briefly Robin explained what they had just experienced, and by the time he finished two women appeared in the doorway of the house to greet them. According to Dare's instructions, Robin had engaged the services of two women convicts to serve William and Kate at McKenzie station. He had sent them ahead with orders to ready the house for their master and mistress. He turned to greet them now and introduce them to the McKenzies.

Kate looked to Robin for an explanation, for she had no idea who the women were. One looked to be about forty, not unattractive, with brown hair starting to turn gray at the temples and pulled back into a neat bun. She was of medium height, her body softly rounded and pleasing to the eye. The second woman was much younger and more flamboyant, with dark red hair, deep blue eyes, and a flirtatious smile. Her figure was stunning; high breasts, slim waist, and long legs were put together in such a fashion as to demand immediate attention. She smiled at Robin in a way that grated on Kate's nerves.

"This is Maude," Robin explained, gesturing toward the older woman. "Maude will act as cook and housekeeper." Maude bobbed her head. "And this is Lizzy. Lizzy does general housecleaning and whatever chores you deem necessary. They are convicts assigned to work for you. If you have any complaints about their work you need only tell Dare and he'll have them replaced.''

"Convicts," squeaked Kate. She'd had no idea she'd be surrounded by convicts inside her house as well as outside. Was she to be safe nowhere? She spared a glance at Robin and saw that he was scowling at her, expecting her to make some reply or at least acknowledge the two servants. "I—I'm sure we'll get on famously," she said for want of a more intelligent reply.

"This is Miss McKenzie," Robin continued as he addressed the two women. "You will both take your orders from her. At the present time her father is ill, and you will be expected to see to his needs until he is back on his feet."

Only then did Maude and Lizzy discover William lying in the bed of the dray. "Oh, the poor man!" Maude exclaimed, looking at William with sympathetic brown eyes. Lizzy merely stared. "I'll prepare a room for him immediately. Come along, Lizzy." Reluctantly Lizzy followed, obviously content to stand there and stare at Robin.

When they disappeared into the house, Robin lifted William from the dray and preceded Kate into the house. He headed directly up the stairs and paused before the master bedroom. Maude and Lizzy were just turning down the bed. Very carefully Robin set William down on the feather mattress, and stepped back to allow Kate access to her father.

"I'll fix you something nourishing," Maude said as she got her first glimpse of William's emaciated frame.

"Thank you," Kate replied, grateful for the woman's concern. Surely Robin was mistaken, this gentle woman couldn't be a convict. Seeing that Lizzy hung back, Kate quickly dismissed her. That one she wasn't sure about. There was something sly about her that Kate didn't like.

"If there is nothing more I can do for you, I'll leave," Robin offered when he noted that William appeared to be dozing.

Suddenly William opened his eyes. "Don't leave yet, Robin, I'd like to speak with you privately. After I rest a bit."

"I'll see to the luggage," Robin said, turning to leave.

"You'll come back?" William asked hopefully.

"Aye, I've nowhere to go tonight." Robin nodded at Kate, then left father and daughter alone.

"What do you want with Robin?" Kate asked curiously.

"I've need of a good man at McKenzie station," William said. "I'm going to ask him to remain as station boss."

"Is that wise, Father? I—the man is dangerous. I don't trust him. Find out what crimes he's committed before asking him to remain."

"Trust me, daughter, I believe I'm a better judge of character than you are. You have nothing to fear from Robin Fletcher."

Nothing to fear! Kate screamed in mute appeal. Dear God, didn't Father realize that this man was a

44

danger to her? Didn't he care that her very soul was at risk? Robin Fletcher made her *feel*. He made her feel things a twenty-six-year-old woman had no business feeling, let alone thinking. Why now? she cried out in silent supplication. And why a man so totally unfit? Robin Fletcher—God help her. She needed all the help she could get if he remained at McKenzie station.

Chapter Three

Kate settled into her room, which obviously had been Mercy's for it was definitely a woman's room, decorated in soft pastels and sporting dainty furniture. When Lizzy showed up to help with her unpacking, she declined her offer, sending her instead to help Maude with supper. When Lizzy lingered, Kate asked, "Is there something you wished to speak to me about?"

Lizzy fixed Kate with an impertinent look and asked, "Is Robin Fletcher going to remain at McKenzie station as station boss?"

"I don't see as how that's any of your business, Lizzy," Kate said. "You may go now."

Lizzy slanted Kate a sullen glare, then turned abruptly and left. Kate returned to her unpacking, having no idea why Lizzy's innocent question

46

should irritate her. It didn't matter to her how many conquests Robin made.

Meanwhile, Robin had seen to the luggage and returned to William's room. He found William awake and struggling with a tray of food Maude had just sent up to his room. He looked up at Robin and forced a grin. "Ah, Robin, you're here. Please take the tray, I find I have little appetite these days."

Robin looked at the uneaten food and frowned. "Maude will feel slighted if that's all you eat of her cooking."

"'Tis all I can manage. Please don't tell Kate, she's so set on my recovering."

"As we all are. How can McKenzie station thrive without its owner?"

"That's what I wanted to talk to you about, Robin," William said. His eyes were dull from weariness, but he was determined to get this settled tonight, before Robin left. "I want you to remain at McKenzie station. I need you, Robin. You've done a marvelous job here, and I'd like you to continue as station boss."

Robin hesitated so long, William added, "You are free to work where you please, aren't you?"

"Aye," Robin said slowly. "Have you talked this over with your daughter?"

"Kate is headstrong and stubborn, but in her heart she knows she can't handle the farm on her own. I certainly am no help, and it's not going to get any better. You're an experienced sheep man; I trust your judgment."

"You don't even know me," Robin persisted.

"Dare Penrod seems to think highly of you, since he put you in charge here."

"Dare and I have been friends a long time, since we first arrived in New South Wales. But there is a difference between us. Dare is a settler and I am a convict."

"Why are you deliberately trying to discourage me, Robin?"

"Your daughter neither likes nor approves of me, sir," Robin said. Though his voice was solemn, his eyes danced with an amusement that wasn't lost on William.

"Does that bother you?" William asked. "Kate has never dealt with convicts; she is too new to a convict colony to judge people. Let me handle Kate. Besides," William said slyly, "I have the feeling that you and Kate are much alike, both stubborn and proud. That's why—never mind, Kate has much to learn."

"Kate is not a child, Mr. McKenzie."

"Aye," William admitted sadly. "She's had her way far too long. What she needs is a husband she cannot rule; a man who will give her children and allow her to make her own decisions while keeping a firm upper hand."

"Were there no such men in England?"

"Many," William observed, "but none Kate would have. But enough of my daughter. Will you stay, Robin?"

"Before I answer I should tell you that the Penrods have petitioned the governor for my freedom. Should it be granted soon, I will want to settle on my own land. 'Tis time I settled down."

"Do you have a woman in mind?" William asked sharply.

"Perhaps," Robin hedged.

William seemed satisfied with his answer. He was about to question Robin further when Kate walked into the room. She spared Robin a brief glance before spying the virtually untouched tray of food that had been set aside.

"Father, you must eat if you are to get well."

"Perhaps my appetite will return tomorrow," William offered lamely.

"I think you should rest now. Are you finished with Robin?"

"Not quite. I have yet to receive an answer from Robin concerning my offer."

Kate shot Robin a fulminating look, as if warning him to have a care for her father's health. "Can't it wait until tomorrow?"

"No, daughter, this can't wait."

Robin stared at Kate. At her beautiful face tilted at a defiant angle, at her tempting body stiff with disapproval, at her violet eyes narrowed with contempt, and the answer to William's question came easily. "Aye, I'll stay, Mr. McKenzie, for as long as you have need of me."

A tremulous sigh slipped past William's lips, and he closed his eyes, exhaustion and illness taking their toll.

"Father," Kate cried, dismayed by the turn of events. "Just because I'm not a man doesn't mean I'm incapable of seeing to McKenzie station. I'm a quick learner. I'll manage on my own just fine until you're on your feet again."

"Please don't defy me on this, Kate," William said tiredly. "I'm not too ill to know what is best for McKenzie station and my own daughter. Please leave me now, I'm too weary to argue with you."

"Of course, Father," Kate said guiltily, kissing William on the cheek. "Maude has supper ready and I'm famished."

"Sup with her, Robin," William insisted, unaware of Kate's horrified look. "I'll talk with you tomorrow."

"If you say so, sir." The corner of Robin's mouth tilted upward, not quite a smile but enough so that it made Kate spin around and stomp from the room in a flurry of petticoats and whirling skirts. Robin caught up with her easily.

"I'm not so bad once you get to know me."

"I have no intention of getting to know you any better than I do now."

"Is it just me you have an aversion to or convicts in general?"

Kate halted in her tracks and Robin came up hard against her, nearly bowling her over. Seeing her teeter, he grasped her, pulling her close. The moment their bodies touched a scalding heat shot through Robin. It was almost as if they were bound together by a flaming band of invisible heat. Kate gasped, her violet eyes wide with shock. Robin groaned. It was a curiously unsettling sound, but it brought Kate abruptly to her senses.

"Take your hands off me!"

"Ah, Kate, you do try a man. Can't you feel it?"

"I feel nothing," Kate denied hotly, "but your filthy hands on me."

Wild Land, Wild Love

The skin on Robin's face grew taut and his white teeth flashed dangerously in a parody of a smile. "You're a liar, Kathryn Molly McKenzie. Do you want me to prove it to you?"

Kate blanched, suddenly frightened of this man she knew nothing about. There was no one else in the house except two women servants and a sick father to come to her aid. And of course forty convicts on the property, no doubt all as depraved and vicious as Robin Fletcher.

"Please," she whimpered.

"Aye, you do please me, Kate. A bit long in the tooth and haughty for my tastes, but still pleasing." His voice was low, his breath uneven as he felt the soft contours of her body pressed so intimately against his own rigid hardness.

Suddenly he saw the whiteness of her face, the terror in her expressive eyes, and realized that she was truly frightened of him. Did she expect him to attack her like a wild animal?

Then he knew.

That was exactly what she expected from a convict. Suddenly, taunting the haughty Miss McKenzie no longer was appealing to him. Abruptly he released her and stepped back.

"I find I have urgent business in the convict hut, Miss McKenzie. You will excuse me, won't you? Enjoy your supper." He was down the stairs and out the door before Kate could catch her breath.

She stood for a long time, staring at Robin's departing back, puzzled by his abrupt exit. The man was an enigma. He took such delight in taunting her, yet when he was with her father his eyes were filled with a compassion few men possessed. What were his crimes? she wondered. He appeared capable, her father seemed to trust him—yet—yet—she couldn't help but be leery of a man who dared to . . . Dared to what? Touch her? Taunt her? For a moment she'd thought he meant to kiss her!

Then a strange thing happened. Out of the blue Kate's thoughts took her on a forbidden journey. She touched her lips, wondering what it would feel like to be kissed by Robin Fletcher, touched by him, caressed in places . . . She groaned, shocked by her wanton thoughts, frightened by the intensity of the feelings Robin aroused in her. She was no young miss smitten by her first man. But then, Robin Fletcher was no ordinary man.

"Is something amiss, mistress?"

Kate started violently, surprised to find Lizzy standing beside her.

"N—no, everything's just fine. Is supper ready?"

"Aye, Maude sent me to find you." She glanced around the dimly lit hallway. "Is Robin still about?"

"No, he's gone back to wherever it is he goes when his work is done," Kate said brusquely.

"He's missed supper. Is it all right if I take him out something to eat?"

"Do what you like, Lizzy, I couldn't care less," Kate replied, flouncing off.

Dismayed, Lizzy stared after Kate, her mouth working wordlessly.

* * *

Two days later Robin still hadn't decided what it was about Kate McKenzie that made her different from any other woman he'd known. She was no schoolgirl, but neither was she so old as to be undesirable. Perhaps that was what bothered him about Kate. He wanted her. It had taken him two days to admit it, but he bloody well did want her. Perhaps he should take time out to go to Parramatta and see Serena, he considered. Her tempting little body never failed to perk up his spirits or take his mind off things he had no business thinking about—like Miss Kathryn Molly McKenzie.

During the past two days he'd seen blessed little of Kate, and that was fine with him. When they were together he was too often on the receiving end of her sharp tongue. Robin knew Kate thought herself as capable as any man, but he'd like to see her control forty convicts and work them to the benefit of McKenzie station. If it weren't for William and his desperate need of him, he'd leave and see how fast McKenzie station would fall to ruin. At times the little shrew made him angry enough to spit nails.

At that moment the object of Robin's thoughts was hurrying out of the house in search of him. A worried frown marred her smooth brow, and her violet eyes were clouded with anxiety. Robin was in the cow shed when he saw her coming and went out to meet her.

"Is something wrong, Kate?"

"It's Father." Robin noted the slight tremble of her hands and the catch in her voice, and his heart skipped a beat. Had the end come already for William?

"Is he worse today? How can I help?"

"You mentioned the doctor in Parramatta. It's time we summoned him. I don't care what Father says, I won't give up on him."

"Aye, I'll go for him myself," Robin offered.

"Robin, take the horse, it's faster."

Dr. Daniel Proctor left William McKenzie's room shaking his head. True to his word, Robin had brought him to McKenzie station within an hour after Kate's request. He stood with Kate outside William's door now as Dr. Proctor quietly shut the door behind him and approached them. The doctor's face was solemn, his eyes grim.

"How is he, doctor?" Kate asked anxiously. She had spoken little while the doctor was with William, merely walking back and forth, wringing her hands.

"Not good, Miss McKenzie, not good. I can merely concur with the ship doctor that your father's heart is severely damaged."

"Is there nothing we can do? Surely some medicine . . ."

"Nothing known to man will cure your father of his ailment," the doctor said as gently as possible. He didn't believe in giving hope where none existed. "Make him as comfortable as possible until the end and see that he avoids all stress."

"Dear God," Kate said shakily. "I had hoped . . . I prayed that he'd recover." A tear slipped from the corner of her eye and slid down her cheek. "Can I go in to him now?"

"By all means, just see that he has plenty of rest and eats properly, though his appetite will be lacking as his weakness progresses."

Kate nodded, thanked the doctor, and slipped into her father's room.

"How long does he have, Dan?" Robin asked once Kate was out of sight.

A rather handsome man of thirty-five, Dr. Dan Proctor was well acquainted with Robin. Since Dr. Dan had delivered Casey's daughter and been befriended by the Penrods, the Penrods' friends became his friends. And Robin Fletcher, though he was still technically a convict, was a good man to have as a friend. Dr. Dan was a settler, having arrived in New South Wales about the same time as Governor Macquarie. A plea for doctors was what originally had brought him to Australia, but he soon grew to love the country and intended to stay forever. That he hadn't yet found a wife was lamentable, but he hadn't given up hope. In fact, the moment his twinkling brown eyes settled on Kate McKenzie, he was smitten.

"William McKenzie is a very sick man," Dan hedged.

"That's obvious. Can't you be more specific than that?"

"Only God knows when a man will die, but in William's case I'd venture to guess that he won't be with us much longer. A month perhaps, maybe two."

"Bloody hell! What a damn shame."

"I assume you're talking about the daughter.

What will she do once her father passes on? Too bad she never married."

"Lucky for the bloke who would have married her," Robin muttered. "She's a sharp-tongued vixen who thinks she can run McKenzie station by herself."

"She looks capable enough," Dan observed. "Quite pretty, too."

"Don't get any ideas, Dan, Kate isn't for you."

"Kate is it?" Dan said, raising a finely arched eyebrow. "So that's how the wind blows. What about Serena? Last I heard, you and Serena planned to marry as soon as your pardon was granted."

Kate stood poised in the doorway, having quietly opened the door while Dan and Robin were talking. She had emerged just in time to hear Dan's last sentence about Robin and some woman named Serena and their plans to marry. Before Robin could answer Dan's question he spotted Kate, leaving whatever he was going to say unsaid.

"How is he?" Robin asked as Kate emerged into the hallway.

"He wants to talk with you."

"Now?"

"Aye. I'll speak with Dr. Proctor while you're with Father."

"Keep it brief, Robin," Dan warned. Then he turned to Kate. "Come along, Miss McKenzie, you look as if you could use a cup of tea, and I know I can."

Robin watched them walk away, then turned into William's room. He approached the bed gingerly, not wanting to awaken him if he had fallen asleep.

"It's all right, Robin, I'm awake. Have you spoken with the doctor?"

"Aye."

"Then you know I haven't much longer."

"Mr. McKenzie, I . . ."

"Let's not fool ourselves, Robin, we both know my time is limited. Kate might not want to admit it, but we're both man enough to recognize the truth."

"Kate loves you, sir."

"Aye, and I love her. I'm worried about her, Robin. After I'm gone she'll have no one. And it would please me if you call me William."

"Has Kate no relatives in England, William?"

"No one but an elderly aunt. But you know Kate, she's stubborn enough to remain at McKenzie station and go it alone. She's strong, Robin, but not that strong."

"Headstrong, you mean," Robin remarked.

That brought a chuckle from William's emaciated frame.

"Aye, that too."

"Why are you telling me this?"

"Because—because—God, I don't know. I'm so very tired. Perhaps we can talk about this another day."

"Aye, another day, William. Don't worry about anything right now. All is going smoothly, and there is cash available should Kate need it. Dare will be here soon and he'll apprise you of the financial status of McKenzie station. He sent word that he and Casey will be around tomorrow. They wanted to give you a day or two to rest before visiting."

Seeing that William's eyes were closed, Robin tiptoed from the room. Dr. Dan was just leaving.

"I'll be back in a few days, Kate, but if you need me sooner you have only to summon me."

Kate? He was already calling her Kate? Why should that bother him? Robin asked himself. Dan was an unattached, attractive man, and Kate was certainly old enough to form her own friendships.

"Thank you, Dan, I feel much better with you caring for Father."

Dan? Kate was acquainted with him well enough to call him Dan? Bloody hell, what was wrong with him! What did it matter that Kate and Dan were calling each other by their first names despite the fact that they had just met?

"What did Father want?" Kate asked once the door was closed on Dan.

"I don't rightly know," Robin said thoughtfully. "We never finished the conversation. He grew tired and I left."

"It's just as well," Kate decided. "Dan said stress is bad for Father. From now on if any problem arises concerning the farm, please consult with me and I'll make the decision whether or not to present it to Father."

"Why don't you ask Dare to handle matters for you, Kate? I'm sure he'd help if you'd ask him."

"Are you suggesting that I'm not capable?" Kate bristled. "And how many times have I told you my name is Kathryn? *You* may call me Miss McKenzie."

"I'll bloody well call you what I please," Robin declared hotly. "I'm damn tired of that haughty attitude of yours. One day soon I'll be as free as you and a property owner."

"But you'll always be an ex-convict," Kate tossed back. She was aware that she was being deliberately cruel but seemed unable to stop herself.

She was hurting.

Hurting because her father was dying and she was alone. Hurting because she wanted to pour out her misery to Robin but was too proud to do so.

Robin winced, stung by Kate's deliberate insult but by now aware of what drove her. No one should be alone at a sad time like this. He knew, for there were times when he'd needed someone and had had no one to turn to.

"Kate," he said softly, ignoring her taunts. "It's all right to reach out to someone. There are times when even the strong need someone."

"I—don't need—anyone," Kate refuted. Her words were strained and disjointed as they slipped past the lump in her throat. Then she turned her back on him, unwilling for him to see the tears glistening in her eyes.

"Kate," Robin said, grasping her shoulders and turning her around to face him. He lifted his hand and traced her cheek, feeling the wetness there. When he reached her chin he lifted it so she was forced to look at him. "It's all right to cry."

She shook her head vigorously.

"You little fool, can't you bend enough to accept comfort when it's offered?"

"I—don't need comfort from you."

"Aye, perhaps you don't. Perhaps 'tis something else you need. Something to take your mind off your father."

Before Kate sorted through the meaning of his words, Robin lowered his head and touched her lips with his. Kate's first thought was that his lips were as warm as the sun. With a queer sense of detachment she remained still in his arms, letting his lips taste hers, finding it odd that she felt no disgust, only a pleasant sensation she found vaguely disturbing. Then suddenly the kiss deepened and she found herself pressed intimately against the hard wall of Robin's chest, his lips moving on hers, his tongue prodding her lips apart.

Robin was lost. Lost the moment his lips touched Kate's. Lost the instant he touched her. No longer was he offering comfort. He was kissing Kate because he wanted to, because he needed to, and because he had never enjoyed anything more in his life. Against his will his hands began stroking her gently, finding the tiny indentation of her lower back strangely erotic despite the layers of clothes separating them. His hands slid lower, lower still, curving around the sweet mounds of her buttocks and bringing her closer—closer, until she could feel the hard thrust of his desire straining between them.

Anger!

Raw, black anger.

Never had Kate been so angry at another human. Never had she allowed a man to manhandle her like Robin was doing. Was she mad to allow him such liberties? No, she decided, just numb with grief over her father's grave condition. And Robin Fletcher, convict and Lord knows what else, was taking advantage of her confusion and grief. With a sob she wrenched out of his grasp, the angry color draining from her face, leaving it waxen with shock and blank with disbelief.

"How dare you take advantage of me in such a vile manner!"

Suddenly aware of how completely he was losing control, Robin flushed guiltily. Kate was right. She might be a vile-tongued, ill-tempered shrew but she was entitled to more respect than he was showing her. Just because she considered him an animal didn't mean he had to act like one. What was it about Kate McKenzie that made him lose every ounce of restraint he'd ever possessed? God knows she was attractive, but he'd seen women more beautiful. Her body was made for loving, but so was Serena's. Yet some unknown force drew him to her, made him want to discover what devils drove her, what made her so different from other women. Only one other woman in his life had the power to move him in that way. Casey O'Cain Penrod.

"I won't say I'm sorry, Kate, 'cause I'm not. You have to admit I did take your mind off your problems for a brief time. I'll get back to my duties now. If you need me you know where to find me."

Robin turned and walked away. Abruptly he paused, then whirled back to face Kate. "Kate, I truly am sorry about William."

Kate watched him walk away, undecided whether to lash out at him or thank him for his concern. In the end she said nothing. Her feelings were too confused to form a coherent answer.

Dare and Casey Penrod arrived the following day with their children. They stopped first to speak to Robin, who informed them that William was dangerously ill and unlikely to recover. Kate saw their wagon lumbering down the dusty lane and stood on the porch waiting for them. Brandon was the first to scramble out of the wagon, jumping up and down as he waited for the slower members of his family to follow. Little Lucy soon joined him, and Kate's first thought was that she'd never seen a pair of toddlers more adorable than the Penrod offspring. Then she got her first glimpse of Dare and Casey and she knew from whence came their good looks.

My God, she's beautiful! Kate thought, awed. Casey's hair was like a living flame, somewhere between a brilliant red and burnished copper. Instinctively Kate knew Casey's eyes would be green and she wasn't disappointed. Then she turned her attention to Dare and realized that he was beautiful too. Not just handsome, but shamefully beautiful in a male, rugged way. His slate gray eyes were laughing down at Casey now, but Kate hadn't the slightest doubt that those same mesmerizing eyes could turn as cold as ice given sufficient provocation. The love they shared was so palpable, so blatantly obvious, it was like a kick to Kate's gut.

Dare held out his hand. "I'm Dare Penrod. This is my wife, Casey. And these two little imps are Brandon and Lucy. Robin told us your name is Kate. Welcome to New South Wales."

Kate almost corrected Dare concerning her name but thought better of it as she grasped Dare's hand. Her first impression was that she'd always have a friend in Dare Penrod. She wasn't quite so sure about Casey, after all she'd heard about the woman. Casey didn't look like a felon, but looks were often deceiving. However, when Casey added her own words of welcome, Kate let herself be drawn into the woman's warm embrace.

"Please come in," Kate invited. "Robin said you'd be here today, so I've been expecting you."

"Had we known your father was so ill we'd have been here sooner," Dare said. "We want to help in any way we can." Kate didn't doubt his sincerity.

"Thank you. Uncle Thad said you were the best thing that ever happened to Mercy." Suddenly Kate realized what she'd said and turned a becoming red. "Oh, I'm sorry."

"Nothing to apologize about," Casey added quickly, then changed the subject. "At least Robin is here with you. He's a good man to have around."

Kate bit her tongue to keep from tossing out a scathing retort. When she was sufficiently calm, she asked, "Have you known Robin long?"

"Nearly all my life," Dare laughed. "Or so it

seems. We've been through some rough times together, but I won't bore you with them. Is your father up to company?"

"He knows you were coming today and is anxious to meet you. If Casey doesn't mind waiting, I'll take you up to him."

"Go ahead," Casey urged. "I'll check on the children while you're gone. Hard telling what kind of mischief they're getting into."

Casey walked outside, relieved to see that Robin had both Brandon and Lucy in tow. She waved and hurried over to where Robin was showing the children the newest calf.

"Don't let them give you fits, Robin," Casey laughed.

"I'm glad you brought the little imps. I've missed them."

They stood talking while the children ran off to investigate some other miracle, unaware that Kate was standing on the porch, watching. Suddenly Casey spied her, said something to Robin, and walked back to the house. Still Kate watched, but it wasn't Casey who had her attention, it was Robin. The tilt of his head, the look on his face as he spoke with Casey, the special way his eyes followed her trim figure. It was almost as if—as if he loved her!

My God, he did love her!

Kate should have known by the tenderness in Robin's voice when he spoke of Casey, the reverent look on his face whenever he mentioned her name, that he harbored more than friendship in his heart for his friend's wife.

Her next thought tumbled from her mind before

she could stop it. How horrible it must be to love your best friend's wife! Close on the heels of that thought came another. Does Dare know?

"The children are fine," Casey said when she stood beside Kate. "Shall we sit out here so I can keep an eye on them? I'm sure Robin has more important things to do than watch my children."

For a time they talked of trivial things, England and the changes time had wrought. Then they spoke of William and his illness. All the while they spoke, Casey had the uneasy feeling that Kate McKenzie was uncomfortable around her. It was as if the woman didn't want to form a friendship with Casey. Casey knew there was plenty of gossip about her in Sydney and Parramatta, but it seemed unlikely that Kate would have heard it yet. And she knew Robin wouldn't spread rumors.

Just then Brandon ran up to the porch, asking if he and Lucy could accompany Robin to the stables.

"He certainly is a big boy for his age." Kate smiled, admiring the sturdy little lad. "He's the picture of his father." Kate knew Mercy had only been dead a little over three years, so Brandon couldn't be over two and a half, perhaps nearly three.

"I'm almost four," Brandon said proudly. "And Lucy is nearly two."

The smile froze on Kate's face. "Four?" she repeated stupidly. "You're almost four?"

Casey knew exactly what Kate was thinking and chose to ignore it. It was no one's business when Brandon was conceived. Though everyone knew

Dare had been married to Mercy at the time and Casey had been wed to Drew Stanley, no one doubted that Dare was Brandon's father.

"I'm nearly four and Papa is going to buy me a pony," Brandon continued blithely. "Lucy is too little. May I go with Uncle Robin?"

"Of course, dear, don't get in the way," Casey replied, aware that Kate was staring at her strangely.

"Kate, I want us to be friends. There aren't many women here on the Hawkesbury and what few there are should be able to depend on one another."

"Were you and Cousin Mercy friends?" Kate asked. Lord, why was she pursuing this? she asked herself. What did she hope to gain? Obviously Casey O'Cain was a husband stealer as well as a felon. Was she also an adulteress?

Casey thought about her answer for several long moments before replying, "No, Mercy and I were never friends."

Chapter Four

Casey's answer did little to endear her to Kate. According to Uncle Thad, Mercy had been a paragon of virtue and could do no wrong.

Casey realized she and Kate were starting off on the wrong foot and sought to make amends. "You must realize, Kate, that I was a convict and had little contact with your cousin."

"Robin told me you were a convict, Casey," Kate said thoughtfully. "But I know your crime couldn't have been too serious or Dare would never have married you."

Casey drew in a ragged breath, uncertain whether or not to reveal the nature of her crime. After all, it was common knowledge, and Kate was bound to find out sooner or later. In any event, Casey thought it should come from herself since she was the only one who knew the truth. A very honest person, Casey decided nothing could be gained by lying to Kate. "I killed a man."

The color drained from Kate's face, leaving her white as a sheet and thoroughly shaken. Instinctively she drew back. Casey recognized her fear and shock and quickly added, "It was an accident, Kate. I could never harm another living soul. Evidently the governor believed me, for I was soon pardoned."

Somehow Kate couldn't think past the word "kill." Then the fact that Casey was a loving wife and mother somewhat eased her mind and she was able to think more calmly. But before she could comment, Dare returned and suggested they leave.

"I had a long talk with your father, Kate, and I assured him I'd help whenever you needed me. Just send for me and I'll be here. But with Robin around you're in good hands. There is nothing he doesn't know about raising sheep and farming."

He turned to Casey. Kate saw his eyes darken to smoky gray and realized immediately that a special love existed between Dare and his wife, one that was hard won and would last forever. "Shall we take our little imps home, love?" Dare asked, draping an arm around Casey's slim waist.

"If we can get them away from their Uncle Robin," Casey laughed up at Dare. She turned to Kate. "I'm so glad we've met, I hope we can become good friends. It does get lonely out here on the Hawkesbury. Ben used to come and visit often but he joined the group charting a course across the Blue Mountains and we haven't seen him in ages."

"Ben?" Kate asked curiously.

"Ben is my younger brother," Dare explained. "An adventurer if I ever saw one. I'll leave all the exploring to him since I much prefer remaining home with Casey and the children. Bloody hell," he chuckled, "I sound like a doddering old man. But I must admit, life is never dull with Casey."

I'll bet not, Kate thought but did not say.

"I don't think Kate likes me," Casey mused thoughtfully as they rode home.

"You're imagining things, love," Dare scoffed. "She's a bit shy, but I find her delightful. Knowing that her father is so ill must be terribly difficult for her. William is worried about what will happen to her and McKenzie station after his death. He's afraid Kate will try to manage on her own and lose everything."

"'Tis a pity she never married."

"That's what William says. She's had offers enough, it seems, but no one suited. At twenty-six she's already considered a spinster and unlikely to wed."

"She's very beautiful," Casey observed.

"So are you, love," Dare said softly. "Put the children to bed after we get home and I'll show you how much I appreciate you."

Casey's eyes twinkled with helpless mirth. "Dare Penrod, you're incorrigible! Thank God you've never changed."

* * *

Kate lingered on the porch after the Penrods left, trying to come to terms with all she had learned today. Finding out that Dare hadn't been faithful to Mercy was bad enough, but learning that Casey was a convicted killer shocked her. And if all that wasn't enough, the knowledge that Robin was in love with Casey Penrod was totally unexpected, although she should have suspected it.

"What did you think of Dare and Casey?" Kate was so lost in thought she hadn't seen Robin approach. When she looked up at him, the thought struck her that he was every bit as good-looking as Dare Penrod.

"Dare seems like a wonderful man," Kate hedged, deliberately refraining from including Casey. "I'm certain he'll be a good friend to Father and me."

"You can depend on it," Robin concurred. "Did you and Casey have a nice visit?"

Kate sighed, seeing no help for it but to voice her feelings. "It was very—enlightening."

"Exactly how do you mean that?"

Damn, this wasn't going to be easy! "I learned some things today that—well—that shocked me."

"Such as," Robin persisted doggedly.

"If you must know, I learned that Dare was unfaithful to Cousin Mercy. Brandon was conceived while Dare and Mercy were still married."

Suddenly Robin was at a loss for words. If Casey had wanted Kate to know the whole story she would have told her. "Is that all?"

"Is that all? Isn't that enough? If I were married, my husband damn well better be faithful to me."

"I pity the man who marries you," Robin returned, his temper flaring. How dare Kate judge Casey and find her lacking? "At least Casey knows how to be a wife."

"I'm sure you wish she was yours," Kate tossed back.

"Damn right!" Suddenly Robin realized what he had just said and fell silent.

Robin's words only confirmed Kate's suspicion. "I know you love Casey Penrod. All one has to do is look at you when Casey is around and it's visible for the whole world to see. Does Dare know you covet his wife? How far has it gone?"

Anger exploded in Robin's brain. He grasped Kate's shoulders and gave her a shake that nearly sent her head flying from her shoulders.

"You acid-tongued little witch! If you haven't anything good to say about a person, don't say anything. Casey is one in a million. She'd never do anything to dishonor Dare. She and Dare were meant for one another. Few people are blessed with a love like theirs."

"Are you saying you don't love her?"

"Of course I love her. Like a friend, not a lover."

Kate merely smiled. That made Robin angrier, and he gave her another vicious shake.

"Take your hands off me!" she said between chattering teeth.

"Just keep your vile tongue off Casey," Robin warned ominously.

Suddenly Kate realized she was acting like a fool. She was being judgmental and unfair. Normally she wasn't like that. It was true she had little use for convicts, knowing their vicious natures, but hadn't Casey said the killing had been accidental? And as for Robin loving Casey, that was his business. The one thing Kate couldn't forgive Casey for was her sin against Mercy.

"Robin, I'm sorry. I'm sure Casey is a wonderful woman. She and Dare seem very happy together. Many people love where there is no hope of reciprocation."

Robin's hold on her slackened. "You do know how to rile a man, Kate. But you also know how to apologize prettily. I'm sorry if I hurt you. 'Tis strange how we seem to rub each other the wrong way. All that energy should be directed in another direction." His eyes were like shards of blue glass, sharp and piercing, and Kate felt as if he had reached into her soul and dragged forth an emotion she had yet to discover.

"I don't know what you are talking about. If you would kindly unhand me, I'll go to Father now. It's time for his medicine."

Robin made no move to release her, instead drawing her closer until she felt his warm breath brush her cheek. "You do try a man, Kate McKenzie. I'd like to teach you how to be a woman."

"I know how to be a woman," Kate retorted hotly. Why was she trembling? Why were her knees weak and her heart pounding?

"No, there are so many things you don't know. Things I'd like to teach you. If only—" His sentence ended abruptly, the need to lower his mouth and taste her lips too potent to resist.

Kate saw his mouth descending but made no effort to resist, mesmerized by the sensuous fullness of his lips, the moist corners of his mouth and the tip of his tongue as it flicked out to trace a line across her closed lips.

"Kate . . ." Her name was an anguished groan as it slipped from his throat. "You do tempt a man."

Then he was kissing her. Not a subtle meeting of lips but hard and hungry. Demanding and so full of need and want, Kate felt consumed by his devouring hunger. She had been kissed many times in her life but never with such overwhelming intensity or powerful craving. Robin's kiss gave her a taste of heaven and a glimpse of hell. When his tongue parted her lips and slipped inside, she felt a surge of heat rush through her body.

And it frightened her.

Never in her life had Kate been so fearful of losing her identity—her soul—all that made her Kate McKenzie, twenty-six-year-old spinster! And she didn't like it. It had to be stopped before she made a fool of herself. Marshaling her wits, she bit down hard on Robin's tongue. He yelped and thrust her aside so abruptly she nearly fell, finally managing to right herself and slant him a satisfied smile.

"Bloody hell, Kate, you do try a man! Haven't you ever been kissed before?"

"Not like that and certainly not by a convict," Kate declared with a toss of her ebony curls. "From now on please keep your hands to yourself and your remarks confined to business concerning your duties." She whirled and flounced off in angry indignation.

Robin watched her leave, his mouth taut, his eyes as cold as shards of blue ice. But despite his anger he couldn't help but admire her. So proud, so haughty, so—so—damn infuriating! All he had to do was look into the mesmerizing pools of her violet eyes and he forgot everything but how much he'd like to see those eyes turn dark with passion. Passion for him and all the wonderful things he'd like to do to her and with her. Kate had no idea how very beautiful she was. That she had remained unmarried this long was a mystery, unless one took into consideration her sharp tongue. Her body was made for loving. A long-in-the-tooth virgin, he thought, chuckling to himself.

Suddenly Robin's laughter died. Was Kate McKenzie a virgin? Had no man moved her enough in her twenty-six years to make a woman of her? His thoughts took him onto dangerous ground, and he shook his head to clear it. Any man who was brave enough to make love to Miss Kathryn Molly McKenzie took his chances on being unmanned. She would probably demand equal time and want to call the shots. Come to think of it, that wouldn't be all bad, Robin decided, shaking his head as he pictured all the ways Kate would want him to love her.

Several days later Kate had another visitor, this one quite unexpected. During that time she had spoken to Robin only briefly concerning his duties, allowing nothing of a personal nature. He'd been up to see William a time or two, but Kate kept her father's visitors strictly regulated, determined to follow the doctor's orders concerning stress. Robin was nowhere in sight when a man riding a fine-looking horse entered the yard. He dismounted, tossed the reins around the porch railing, and approached the front door. Kate answered the door on the third knock. She was somewhat startled to find a stranger standing on her doorstep.

In his mid-thirties, he was tall and slender with brown hair, light blue eyes, and a slim mustache gracing his upper lip. He was rather pleasant looking, though not as ruggedly handsome as Robin. He greeted Kate with a warm smile.

"I'm Ronald Potter. We're almost neighbors. I came to pay my respects. I knew your uncle quite well and was sorry to hear of his death. He never quite got over his daughter's tragic death."

"Won't you come in, Mr. Potter," Kate invited, opening the door so Potter could step inside. "Father is sleeping right now but he'll awaken soon and I know he'll want to see you." She led the way into the parlor. Potter waited politely until she was seated, then took a seat opposite her.

"You say we are neighbors?" Kate asked conversationally.

"In a manner of speaking. After the 102nd Regiment was disbanded I bought land and settled on the Hawkesbury."

"You were in the Rum Corps?" Kate asked, recognizing the name.

"Yes indeed." Potter's chest puffed up, pleased that Kate had recognized the name.

"What made you settle in New South Wales?"

"It's a land of opportunity," Potter said slyly. "I was able to buy a prime piece of land on the Hawkesbury and felt it was time I settled down."

"You should have brought your wife to visit, Mr. Potter."

"I have no wife, Miss McKenzie, but I'd certainly not be averse to taking one should I find someone who pleases me." His eyes told Kate he found her eminently pleasing. "I've bought more land in addition to my original purchase of Fletcher station and hope to expand until I own one of the largest sheep stations in New South Wales."

"Fletcher station?" Kate asked sharply. "Did I hear you right? Are you referring to Robin Fletcher?"

"Aye, your station boss. His land was confiscated when he was convicted of aiding an escaped convict. I bought the station. I hope the man isn't giving you problems. Watch out for him, Miss McKenzie. Robin Fletcher is a troublemaker."

"I—I'll try to remember, Mr. Potter."

"Please let me know if you have any trouble with Fletcher. I carry a lot of clout in the territory and I can have his 'ticket of leave' revoked. Who knows, maybe I can get him sent back to the coal mines." His smile was so cold, so utterly devoid of warmth, Kate shuddered.

"It appears you hold no love for Robin Fletcher," Kate probed innocently.

Wild Land, Wild Love

"The man is a convict, and I try to have as little to do with convicts as possible. Now Governor Macquarie wants to appoint time-expired convicts as magistrates. It's a grave mistake, if you ask me. There should be two societies in New South Wales. One for settlers and one for ex-convicts, and never the twain shall meet."

"You have strong feelings concerning convicts, Mr. Potter. What about people like Dare Penrod's wife, Casey? Surely there are many like her who have become useful citizens and cause no further trouble."

"Casey O'Cain," Potter said bitterly. The name invoked a multitude of memories, most of them bad. "I could tell you much about Casey. I knew her even before she went to Penrod station as a servant. She killed a man in cold blood, did you know that? Dare Penrod couldn't keep his hands off her, not even when he married Thad's daughter. It's no secret that their son was conceived while Dare was married to Mercy McKenzie. Casey was nothing but a whore. She tried to seduce me as well as every other man she came in contact with. She slept with all the Penrod men. She even seduced Robin Fletcher. Ask him. I'm sure he'll not deny they were lovers."

What Ronald Potter didn't say was that he'd tried his damnedest to keep Dare and Casey apart. He had been instrumental in having Robin sent to the coal mines. He nearly raped Casey and would have if the Penrods hadn't arrived at a most propitious moment. Vindictive, mean, and vicious, Ronald

Potter had never forgiven Casey or the Penrods for foiling his plans. But the "Rum Corps" had made him rich, and one day he'd find a way to claim revenge.

Kate was stunned. It seemed as if Casey's crimes were common knowledge, as well as the relationship between her and Robin. Yet both Robin and Casey claimed they were merely friends. Whom was she to believe? Suddenly the front door was flung open and Robin stomped into the room. His eyes were wild as they searched the room and found Potter.

"What in the hell are you doing here, Potter?"

"Are you screening Miss McKenzie's visitors?" Potter asked snidely. "If you must know, I've come to pay my respects. We're neighbors, you know."

"How could I forget? You bought my land for a pittance after it was stolen from me. I suggest you leave."

"Robin!" Kate gasped, shocked by his audacity. "This is my house, you have no right to treat Mr. Potter in so despicable a manner."

"You don't know the man, Kate. You don't know what he's capable of or how his mind works."

"Kate?" Potter repeated, looking at Kate with a new boldness. "You let a convict address you in such a familiar manner?"

"I allow nothing," Kate bit out, wishing Potter would leave. "Robin does as he pleases. Father seems to trust him, and I trust Father's judgment. Perhaps Father is awake now, Mr. Potter. If you'll wait here, I'll see if he's up to company." She sent

Robin a fulminating glance, then left the room.

"Keep away from Kate, Potter," Robin rounded on him the moment Kate was gone. "I won't have you corrupting her."

"Any fool can see she's past the age where protection is required." Potter smiled derisively. "Are you telling me she's an innocent? Remarkable, given her age. Besides, who appointed you her guardian? I heard her father is ill and unlikely to recover. Miss McKenzie will need someone to guide her once her father is gone. Why not me?"

"Because you're the last person in the world Kate needs advice from. Any advice you give her will benefit only yourself. I haven't forgotten how you treated Casey or those long months I spent toiling in the coal mines."

"Still protective of Casey O'Cain, are you? I always knew she was a whore."

The words were barely out of Potter's mouth before Robin reacted. Hauling Potter out of the chair, Robin let loose a left jab that sent Potter reeling. Robin's fist reared back and would have struck again if Kate hadn't come rushing into the room and stopped him.

"Robin! Stop! How dare you attack my guest? Mr. Potter has done nothing to warrant such treatment. He's been courteous and charming. I won't blame him if he never comes back after this. What makes you my keeper? I'm perfectly capable of taking care of myself and choosing my own company. Please leave."

Her words were like a dash of cold water, and

Robin reluctantly released Potter. "All I can say is that you have poor taste, Kate," Robin said sourly. "If you don't believe me, ask Dare. Or Casey. They can tell you volumes about Lieutenant Ronald Potter. None of it good." Whirling on his heel, he slammed out of the room.

"I'm sorry, Mr. Potter," Kate apologized. "You must think me a poor hostess. I'll hope you'll not hold Robin's outburst against me. Robin makes his own rules."

"I'd feel much better if you called me Ronald. And I shall call you Kate. We are neighbors, after all."

"If you'd like, Ronald. Father is awake now and would be happy to see you. Don't stay too long, he's very weak."

"Of course, Kate, my visit will be short."

"How dare you, Robin Fletcher! How dare you accost my company? Do you think I'm a child that needs protecting?" Immediately after Potter left, Kate went in search of Robin, determined to vent her spleen on him.

"Is he gone?" Robin asked lazily. Kate had finally found him in the stables, grateful that she'd be able to confront him in relative privacy.

"He's gone, but I'm sure he'll come back. He seems a pleasant enough man."

"You're a terrible judge of character, Kate," Robin challenged.

In order to blow off steam that had been building since he'd seen Potter, Robin grabbed a pitchfork and began pitching hay into the stalls. Kate couldn't take her eyes off his bulging biceps slick with sweat or the thick ropy muscles of his thighs bulging beneath his moleskin trousers. For a breathless moment her eyes strayed to dangerous territory, then when she realized she was staring at the bulge where his legs met, her eyes shot upward. Robin saw where she was looking and chuckled. So the high and mighty Miss Kate McKenzie wasn't as unmoved by him as she thought, he grinned with devilish amusement.

For the life of her, Kate couldn't remember what Robin had said. "What? What did you say?"

"I said you shouldn't stare at a man like that. It's likely to get you in trouble."

Flame touched Kate's cheeks. I—I wasn't staring. I was merely—uh—."

"Come here, Kate."

"No."

"I said come here."

Kate was shocked when her legs obeyed. They carried her to within mere inches of Robin. She could smell the sweet, masculine odor of sweat and hay and horses, and a scent that was his alone. Instinct told her it was the musky scent of male arousal, and she wasn't immune to it.

"I'm going to kiss you, Kate."

"No."

"Then I'm going to put my hands on you. On your breasts—they're lovely, you know. Full and round and sweetly curved. I'll bet your nipples are—"

"My God, you're—you're outrageous! Why are you doing this to me? If you're trying to shock me, it won't work. Your words mean nothing to me."

"Don't they? I know you're aware of me as a man."

"You're a convict who works for me," Kate refuted in stubborn denial.

"Shut up, Kate, so I can kiss you."

Abruptly her mouth closed, and Robin took advantage of the silence as his mouth came down hard on hers. His kiss was challenging, daring her to resist, begging her to respond. Against her will, she succumbed to the forceful domination of his lips, allowing his tongue to invade the sweet warmth of her mouth. His kiss sang through her veins, and Kate wondered briefly if she'd ever been truly alive before. Her lips burned like fire, her stomach twisted into a wild swirl, and her knees felt like jelly.

She hated it. She hated the way Robin Fletcher made her feel.

When his lips left her mouth to press gentle breathless kisses into the softness of her neck, Kate breathed a sigh of relief, suddenly able to think again. Then his hands found her breasts, doing all the things he'd told her he'd do, fondling, molding, rolling the nipples between finger and thumb. It felt so good, Kate knew she had to either hit Robin or demand more. She chose to hit him. Doubling her fist, she pulled back and let it fly into his gut.

"Whoooosh! Bloody hell, Kate, why did you do

that when you know you were enjoying it?"

"Do you think I enjoy being mauled by a convict?" Kate screamed, thoroughly shaken. "If Father didn't need you so badly, I'd insist you be sent back to the coal mines."

Robin's eyes narrowed dangerously. "What do you know about the coal mines?"

"I know that Ronald sent you there for committing a crime after you were pardoned. Ronald said if you proved troublesome he'd see that you were sent back."

"Ronald, is it. You've grown chummy in a short time. I don't know why I bother trying to protect you. Why do you insist on believing someone like Potter when you have only to ask Dare or Casey for the truth?"

"Perhaps I will ask them," Kate returned shortly, "although Ronald told me things about Casey that were far from flattering."

"I'll bet. Did you believe him?"

"I—I don't know what to believe."

Suddenly Robin's eyes drifted beyond Kate to the doorway, and Kate whirled to see what he was staring at. The figure of a woman stood framed in the opening, the sun at her back outlining the generous curves of her figure. It was Lizzy. She was staring at Kate and Robin in a peculiar manner. With a start Kate realized she was standing so close to Robin their bodies were touching. Cursing beneath her breath, she stepped back, but it was too late; Lizzy had already drawn conclusions.

"Were you looking for me, Lizzy?"

"Aye, your father wants you, mistress," Lizzy said, shifting her gaze to Robin.

Kate nodded and started forward, brushing past Lizzy and out the door. When she glanced back she saw that Lizzy had sidled next to Robin, smiling up at him in a most beguiling manner. Kate snorted derisively. What did she care? Women could fall all over Robin Fletcher for all of her.

Days passed and still William McKenzie clung to life with a tenacity that surprised Dr. Proctor. After his first visit he could have sworn William wouldn't last a week. But days later William was still hanging onto the fragile thread of life, fighting death with a stubbornness that his daughter had inherited. Dr. Dan had been a frequent visitor to McKenzie station, and it wasn't just because of William. He liked Kate and enjoyed her company.

Dr. Dan wasn't Kate's only visitor during that time. Ronald Potter showed up more often than Robin would have liked. But since Kate had soundly berated him for insulting her company, he conveniently disappeared whenever Potter arrived. Since that day in the stables Robin steered clear of Kate. Deciding he needed a woman to stop him from thinking of Kate, he visited Serena twice. But each time he couldn't bring himself to make love to her. Nor could he stop his mind from picturing Kate spread beneath him, her incredible eyes glazed with passion, her ebony hair spread around her like a halo. Bloody hell, was he mad? Kate wasn't for him. They couldn't stand each other. Two minutes in each other's company and they were at one another's throats. If Kate thought of him at all it was with revulsion.

One day Dare showed up, his face wreathed in smiles. He made directly for Robin, waving a paper in his hand. "It's here, Robin! Your pardon. You're a free man." Dare's mood was jubilant and he slapped Robin on the back until Robin nearly lost his breath.

Reverently Robin took the document from Dare's hand and read it slowly and thoroughly. He had waited for it so long it seemed like a miracle. Free! Free at last. No longer could Kate call him a convict. No longer could she look down her nose at him. God, it felt good. Words of gratitude tumbled from his lips, but Dare refused to hear them.

"No one is more deserving of freedom than you are, Robin," Dare said, grinning from ear to ear. "I must tell William. He'll be as pleased as I am at your newly acquired freedom, though I doubt not he'll be unhappy if you leave his employ. He is still in desperate need of your services."

"Aye, William does need me even though his daughter thinks otherwise."

"Still at loggerheads with Kate?" Dare teased. "I thought by now you'd have her eating out of your hand."

"If I offered that contrary female my hand she'd bite it," Robin grumbled sourly.

"Tell her of your pardon, Robin. Perhaps she'll change her attitude."

"I'm the same man whether I'm free or not," Robin said. "A piece of paper won't change me, nor will it change how Kate feels about me.

Besides, mate, it matters little to me what Miss Kathryn Molly McKenzie thinks of me."

Dare eyed him shrewdly. "Perhaps Miss Kathryn Molly McKenzie is more woman than you give her credit for. Perhaps she's more woman than Serena Lynch."

Chapter Five

It took Robin several days to come to the realization that he was truly and finally a free man. He had but to go to Sydney to receive his pardon from Governor Macquarie and select his thirty-acre land grant. He chose a track of land near Parramatta that had limited access to the Hawkesbury, but by this time land was becoming scarce, due to speculators who bought up prime property and time-expired convicts who were given their thirty acres as dictated by law. When he got back from Sydney it was immensely comforting to confront Kate on an equal footing, which Robin did almost immediately upon his return to McKenzie station.

Robin found Kate in the kitchen giving instructions to Maude about William's lunch. The poor man barely touched his food these days and seemed to be growing weaker by the hour.

"Kate, I'd like to speak with you a moment, in private," Robin added, seeing the interested look on Maude's face.

Kate frowned, but followed Robin to the small room off the parlor set aside for an office. "Is there something you'd like to discuss with me, Robin?"

Kate knew what Robin wanted; he was going to tell her he was leaving to settle on his own land. She couldn't blame him, and even welcomed the news. She had congratulated him briefly on his newly acquired status but other than that had kept her distance. Her temper had a way of exploding whenever she was with Robin Fletcher. He was the most outrageous, exasperating man she'd ever met. No other man had the ability to scramble her brains and turn her insides to mush, and she hated the feeling. Besides, she felt perfectly capable of running the farm without outside help.

"I just wanted you to know I won't leave you and your father stranded until I find someone capable to take my place."

"That won't be necessary. I know what has to be done. I'm also aware of how anxious you are to settle down on your own land. Please feel free to leave whenever you wish."

"I'm thinking of your father, Kate. It would cause him much anguish to leave you in charge, and you know what the doctor said about stress. I know how you feel about me, but I won't leave your father in a bind."

"How thoughtful of you," Kate mocked. "Do you have anyone in mind?"

"Yes, that's why I'm here. I want you to accompany me to Parramatta. I've heard of a 'ticket of leave' man looking for work. I thought you might like to interview him before asking him to come out to talk with William."

Kate thought about that for a moment and decided she had nothing to lose. She knew as long as her father lived he'd insist on a competent station boss. "When will you leave?"

"Can you be ready in an hour?"

"Of course. Father will sleep most the afternoon, and I should go to Parramatta for supplies anyway."

Robin nodded. "I'll hitch the dray and wait outside. Wear a bonnet. December is one of our hottest months and the sun is brutal."

An hour later Robin boosted Kate onto the unsprung wagon seat and hopped into the driver's seat beside her. He slapped the reins on the backs of the two lumbering bullocks and they plodded forward. It took nearly two hours over rutted track to reach the thriving city of Parramatta. More and more businesses were cropping up in Parramatta and capitalists had moved into town, expanding the growing economy, which now boasted a doctor, a bank, and many stores selling goods necessary for survival.

"Do your shopping, Kate," Robin instructed, "while I find our man. I heard he's working in one of the stores. If I'm not back by the time you finish, wait for me in the dray."

Robin lifted her down from her high perch, but even before his hands left her waist a woman came rushing from one of the stores, calling Robin's name. She threw herself into Robin's arms, nearly bowling Kate over in the process. She was small and voluptuous with clouds of silver-blond hair floating around her exquisite face. China blue eyes as big as saucers smiled up at Robin as she greeted him with an enthusiasm that left a bad taste in Kate's mouth.

"Robin, we've heard your good news! No one is more deserving of freedom than you." To lend emphasis to her words she stood on tiptoes and planted an exuberant kiss on Robin's lips.

Robin laughed, grasping her waist and twirling her about, sending her skirts flying about her shapely ankles. Kate thought the display revolting.

"It is quite wonderful, isn't it, Serena," Robin concurred happily.

"What are your plans?" Serena hinted slyly. "I've been hoping they include me."

Robin's face gave away nothing of his thoughts and whether or not his future included Serena Lynch. A few short weeks ago he had been ready to propose to Serena the moment his pardon was granted. With her dowry he proposed to buy land from ex-convicts who had been given land grants and then fallen deeply in debt. When they were forced to sell, most of that land went directly into the hands of capitalists, but Robin intended to snare a portion of it for himself. He still wanted land, but since meeting Kate, Serena no longer seemed as appealing. Serena was so lovely, it wasn't as if Robin were her only chance at marriage. No indeed, Serena wouldn't be long without male companionship. In fact, Robin was certain he wasn't the only man Serena was seeing. She wasn't the type to sever relationships until she was certain they would no longer be useful.

"I haven't decided yet what I'm going to do or how soon I'll settle on my own land," Robin explained. "I've saved most of my wages so I'll be able to build a fine house. But I can't possibly leave McKenzie station until I find a replacement. William McKenzie is gravely ill, and I won't leave him in a bind."

For the first time since she'd approached Robin, Serena turned the intensity of her blue gaze to Kate. Nothing she saw seemed to impress her.

"Serena, this is Kate McKenzie. Kate, meet Serena Lynch. Serena's father owns the bank."

Kate gritted her teeth in annoyance. What must she do to impress upon Robin that her name was Kathryn? "Pleased to meet you, Serena."

"Are you the wife of the new owner of McKenzie station?" Serena asked.

"No, I'm his daughter."

"Daughter! His *single* daughter?" Serena stressed. The inflection in her voice told Kate exactly what Serena thought about a woman still unmarried at her advanced age no matter how lovely she might be.

A strange noise was coming from Robin, and Kate whirled to stare at him, suddenly aware that he was chuckling. She scowled at him fiercely, but it only made his eyes dance with amusement.

"I'm sorry to disappoint you, Serena, but I am unmarried and quite happy with my present state.

Now if you will excuse me, I have shopping to do." Her lips pursed thoughtfully, Serena watched Kate walk away.

"Ugh, what an unpleasant woman," she said, promptly relegating Kate to the realm of spinsterhood. "'Tis no wonder the woman never married, she's as plain as an old shoe."

Plain? Kate? Somehow Robin never thought of Kate as plain. And he could personally attest to the fact that she was all woman, soft in all the right places and wonderfully fashioned.

"Did you come to town to see me, Robin?" Serena asked coyly. "No one is home right now and we could be alone." Her eyes promised delights Robin was well aware of, having sampled the ample charms of Serena Lynch often enough in the past.

Though not yet twenty, Serena Lynch knew all about pleasuring a man. From the first time they made love, Robin knew she wasn't a virgin, but was too much of a gentleman to mention it. It really didn't matter how Serena lost her virginity, for he was no innocent either. Dare had warned him that Serena was often seen with other men, and snippits of gossip were bandied about concerning the beautiful blond. But Robin preferred to think that the gossip was merely the result of rejected suitors. Not that Robin held any false expectations concerning Serena. She was a flirt, knew how to please a man in ways he'd never taught her, and probably would only remain faithful as long as Robin kept her home and pregnant. He had no idea why she wanted him.

"I'd like nothing better than to spend time alone with you, Serena." Lies—all lies. "But I have business in town. I promised William McKenzie I'd find someone to replace me. And Kate is depending on me to get her back home before dark. You know how dangerous the road is after dark."

Serena peered at Robin through incredibly long lashes, aware of the potent message she was conveying. Only this time it didn't appear to be working. Robin seemed preoccupied, glancing several times in the direction in which Kate had just disappeared. A totally preposterous thought popped into Serena's head. She promptly dismissed it. It was too ludicrous to think that Robin was interested in a dried-up old spinster when she, Serena, was more than willing to grant his every desire. There were other men Serena could have, but, perversely, she wanted Robin. He was a wonderful lover, always generous in his desire to please her, handsome and virile. It had mattered little that Robin was a convict, for she knew that his influential friends, the Penrods, had petitioned the governor in his behalf and a pardon would eventually be granted.

"Will you come visit me soon, Robin?" Serena asked, clearly disappointed. "We've been seeing a lot of each other lately, and Papa likes you. I would seriously consider a proposal from you if one were offered."

Marriage to Serena? Suddenly the prospect sounded dismal. Perhaps Dare was right. Perhaps he wasn't thinking clearly. Dare had generously offered to lend him the money he needed, and Robin knew Dare was sincere in his offer. Robin fully intended to take a wife one day, but he wasn't sure Serena was the woman he wanted.

"I'll try, Serena," Robin promised halfheartedly. She looked at him hopefully, expecting more. "As for offering for you, we'll talk about that later." It was a lame excuse but it would have to suffice.

"Make it soon, Robin, make it soon." Then she pressed herself up against him and kissed him soundly on the lips. "That's so you'll know what my answer will be when we finally discuss your 'plans.'"

Kate happened to glance out the store window when Serena was kissing Robin and she snorted in disgust. The little hussy, Kate thought uncharitably. Doesn't she know what a spectacle she is making of herself? How could Robin want a woman so lacking in control? A thought came unbidden to her mind. Perhaps, since Robin couldn't have Casey Penrod, he had settled for Serena.

"I found the man I was looking for," Robin said when he met Kate back at the dray a short time later. "His name is Gil Bennett. Here he comes now."

Kate turned and watched as a short, stocky man with thinning hair approached the dray. The moment she set eyes on him, she knew she didn't like him. His eyes were shifty, refusing to look at her straight on, and his lip curled in a way that made her skin crawl. He also swaggered when he walked.

"You Miss McKenzie?" he asked, raking Kate

from head to toe in a manner that suggested contempt for the female sex in general. "Fletcher said ya needed a station boss."

"Perhaps," Kate hedged, slanting a glance at Robin to see if he concurred in her opinion of Gil Bennett. He did. "Where did you work last?"

Bennett hesitated for a moment, then said, "I was station boss over at Parton station for a spell."

Suddenly bells rang in Robin's head. Parton station. There was gossip just recently of the Partons' daughter and one of the convict laborers. The man had seduced the young girl, then when the girl became pregnant he tried to abort her and she bled to death. Since the girl hadn't lived to name the guilty party, the man had remained unknown. Could Bennett be the man who had cruelly snuffed out a young girl's life? Could Robin take the chance of allowing someone like that around Kate? The answer came quickly.

"I don't think you're the man the McKenzies are looking for," Robin said. Kate breathed a sigh of relief. If Robin hadn't come out and said it, she would have.

Instinctively Bennett knew Robin had heard the gossip concerning Betsy Parton. "Listen, Fletcher, I need the work," Bennett whined. "I'm not the man responsible for what happened to Parton's daughter."

Kate had no idea what Bennett was referring to but she voiced her own opinion. "Robin is right, Mr. Bennett. I don't believe you'll do."

Bennett's face grew red and his eyes narrowed dangerously. "Ain't I good enough for ya? Perhaps

95

you want a handsome bloke like Fletcher who will lift yer skirts for ya whenever ya get an itch. If that's what it takes, I'm yer man. I ain't had no complaints yet."

Kate gasped, sidling closer to Robin. The man was crazed.

"Get out of here, Bennett. You heard Miss McKenzie. You may or may not be responsible for killing Parton's daughter, but I don't want you anywhere near Miss McKenzie."

"I heard old man McKenzie is like to die any day now," Bennett snarled. "There ain't a man alive willin' to take orders from a woman. She'll need someone like me to keep the convicts in line."

"I disagree. Most of the convicts working at McKenzie station aren't troublemakers," Robin contended. "Besides, our minds are made up. We don't need you at McKenzie station."

"Can't the woman speak for herself?"

"I agree wholeheartedly," Kate said.

"Damn uppity bitch," Bennett grumbled, turning away. "She'll get her comeuppance one day."

"What was that all about?" Kate asked once the man had stomped off down the street in a huff. "I don't understand what you were saying about the Parton's."

"I'll tell you on the way home. Are you ready to leave?"

"More than ready," Kate said.

Kate shuddered. "What a despicable man! That poor girl." They were on their way back to McKenzie station and Robin had just told Kate what had happened at Parton station and why he didn't trust Bennett.

"Nothing has ever been proved against him, Kate, but I don't think we should take that risk. Had I known he worked for the Partons I never would have suggested you talk to him."

"I didn't know men like that existed."

"This is a convict colony. Men like Gil Bennett are more common here than honest men. But not all convicts are like Bennett; some have been transported for crimes barely worth mentioning," Robin explained. "Take Maude, for instance. Her crime was stealing a loaf of bread to feed her dying husband. Lizzy was convicted of prostitution. Not everyone is a pickpocket, thief, rapist, or killer."

"What about you, Robin?" Kate asked with slow deliberation. "What was your crime?"

"Does it matter? Can't you judge me on the kind of man I am instead of on the nature of my crime? Perhaps my years as a convict have changed me. Perhaps I'm not the same man I was when I arrived in New South Wales."

Annoyed, Kate retorted, "Maybe I'm just trying to understand you, Robin.

"I defy understanding, Kate. I meant it when I said my years as a convict have changed me. I was young when I arrived, too trusting, and much too easygoing. Experience has taught me to trust no one, except perhaps the Penrods. I no longer take the simple pleasures of life for granted or look for the inherent good in people. I've learned to be hard and tough and—yes, dammit, even ruthless."

Kate sucked her breath in sharply, seeing a

Robin she never knew existed. She'd already discovered he was harsh and demanding, but what she never suspected was how badly life had treated him and how deeply it had affected him. For a brief moment she had a glimpse into the inner man, and it frightened her. Yet there were times she had pierced that tough facade and discovered quite another man. Which was the real Robin Fletcher? Not that it mattered. Robin would be gone soon and her life would once again be free of male arrogance.

Kate fell silent, content for the moment to savor the unique scenery and absolute serenity of the forest. She was able to recognize many different varieties of trees now. Black wattle that produced pods, the bottle tree, resembling bottles with trunks that grew seven feet in diameter, the grass tree, gray mangrove, she-oak with its needle like branchlets that served as leaves, and of course the stringy bark eucalyptus. Every now and then a wallaby burst from the bush and crossed their path. So engrossed was Kate in the intriguing Australian scenery that she didn't realize Robin had stopped the dray.

"Don't be alarmed, Kate."

"What!" She looked up at Robin, startled by the intense look on his face. "What is it?"

"Bushrangers. It appears as if we're going to be victims of a bail-up." He said it so calmly, Kate wasn't certain whether to believe him.

Then Kate saw them. Five men, all armed with makeshift weapons ranging from thick clubs to knives, had appeared as if by magic from the forest and now stood before them. "Dear God."

"Don't panic and let me do the talking," Robin hissed. "I understand these men, their desperation, their hopelessness."

Kate gulped noisily, attempting to swallow the fear rising in her throat.

"Well, mates, what 'ave we here?" one of the men called out. He looked pointedly at Kate, his lip curled in a sneer. "Looks like we 'ave us a good time tonight."

Robin cursed the fact that he had no weapon as he wondered how in the world he was going to get Kate out of this mess.

One of the men came close to the side of the dray, reaching out for Kate. She screamed and Robin kicked out, knocking him away with his booted foot. Suddenly all five men rushed the wagon, and though Robin fought valiantly, he was soon overpowered and dragged to the ground. Held securely by one of the bushrangers, Kate was mute with terror as she watched Robin being struck down. Men were surging into the bed of the dray now, rummaging through all the supplies Kate had purchased in Parramatta.

"Take everything and let us go," Robin panted as he tried to rise to his feet but failed. "At least let the lady go. Don't you realize I'm a convict myself and you're attacking one of your own?"

"You ain't one of us, mate. If ya are a convict yer a 'ticket of leave' man and the next thing to free. We'll never be free. We takes our food and our women where we finds 'em."

"Aye," chorused his mates, ogling Kate lewdly.

Kate cringed, her eyes wild with panic. She knew these depraved men intended to kill Robin, then rape and kill her. She looked around, desperately searching for help she knew was nonexistent.

Then she saw him.

He came crashing out of the forest, a giant with a chest as wide and immovable as a wall, immense shoulders, and bull-like neck. He was bearded, and both his facial hair and exposed body parts were covered in rust-colored hair. His legs were as sturdy as oaks and his arms corded and bulging with muscles. The sight of him rendered Kate speechless and she would have fainted on the spot if Robin hadn't picked that moment to chuckle aloud. Bug-eyed, Kate stared at Robin as if he had lost his mind, thinking him crazed to laugh at the towering giant, a man who could easily crush him in one hand.

"'Tis Big John," one of the men shouted out. "Come see what we found, mate."

"Aye, Artie, 'tis Robin Fletcher and a lass. But I'm thinkin' you've made a mistake this time." There wasn't a man in New South Wales who had lived there in Governor Bligh's time that didn't know of Robin Fletcher, the Penrods, and Casey O'Cain. "Let Fletcher up." The other men obeyed instantly. No one argued with Big John.

Big John offered a huge gnarled hand and Robin grasped it gratefully, struggling painfully to his feet. He was bruised and aching in places he hadn't known existed. Since he'd left the coal mines, Robin had met Big John on several occasions. The towering giant seemed to appear from nowhere when one least expected him.

"Who's the lass?" Big John asked, jerking a thumb toward Kate, who by now was well past hysteria and just plain numb.

"Kate McKenzie," Robin informed him. "Her father is the new owner of McKenzie station. She's also my boss."

For some reason that remark brought a collective guffaw from the bushrangers.

"McKenzie," Big John said, his brow wrinkling in concentration. Suddenly his brow cleared. "You mean she's related to the woman who tried to do Casey in?"

"Kate isn't like Mercy," Robin assured him.

"You say the lass is yer boss?"

"Aye. Her father is too ill to see to business, so Kate runs the station with my help."

"Is she yer woman?"

"Aye," Robin lied, ignoring Kate's gasp of protest.

"I hear you've been pardoned," Big John said.

"Aye," Robin grinned. "Free as a bird."

"I wish ya luck, Robin Fletcher. With yer freedom and with yer woman. By the looks of her you'll have yer hands full." Big John's booming laugh reverberated through the surrounding forest, jerking Kate from her frozen state.

"I am not—"

"Be quiet, Kate," Robin hissed sharply. "For once do as I say." To Big John, he said, "Are we free to go?"

"No harm will come to you and yer woman, Robin Fletcher."

Robin nodded. "Take the supplies, Big John. We can get others."

"Now wait a minute," Kate began. Her angry tirade was brought to a skidding halt by Robin's warning glance.

Big John motioned to his friends, and together they managed to carry away everything Kate had purchased that day. Fuming in impotent anger, she forced herself to stand helplessly aside while the bushrangers stole everything of value and melted back into the forest. Big John was the last to leave.

"How fares Casey?" he asked. Kate was startled by the tender look on the big giant's face. Did everyone love Casey Penrod?

"She and Dare are as much in love as the first day they met," Robin said. "They have two children now."

Did his voice hold a note of sorrow? Kate wondered. Was there a hint of sadness in his eyes?

"Tell her Big John sends his regards. Tell her if she ever has need of him, he'll come." Then he turned and was soon lost in the shadow of a tall eucalyptus.

"Climb in the wagon, Kate. Let's get out of here. I don't trust one of those men without Big John to control them."

Kate needed no further urging, and soon they were plodding down the track as fast as the bullocks would go.

"What did Big John mean when he said Cousin

Mercy meant Casey harm?" Kate asked. "Uncle Thad never mentioned anything about that."

"It's not my place to tell you, Kate. If Casey wanted you to know she would have told you."

Kate chewed on that for a while, then said, "I fear there is much I don't understand, and I fully intend to get to the bottom of it one day."

Robin didn't respond, and a few minutes later they were home. "See to your father while I unhitch the dray. I'll be up in a few minutes and explain why we're so late. I don't want to alarm him, but he should be told of the danger that exists in a convict colony."

A short time later Robin entered William's room. The poor man looked sicker with each passing day, if that was possible. His skin was sallow, his eyes sunken into their sockets, and his cheeks hollow and gaunt. Kate was bending over him, fluffing his pillow and gently reprimanding him for not eating the tray of tempting food Maude had prepared for him.

"Leave off, Kate," William said wearily. "You're late, I expected you back hours ago." Then he saw Robin and bade him enter. "Come in, Robin. Did you find the man you were looking for?"

"Aye, but he wasn't what I expected. We'll find another."

William sighed. "Are you so set on leaving, then?"

"Eventually I must, William." Robin glanced at Kate, then said, "Did you tell him about the trouble we had on the road?"

"No, perhaps—"

"What kind of trouble?" William asked, his interest clearly aroused.

"I want William to know the dangers that exist for a woman in a convict colony, Kate," Robin persisted. "When I'm gone you can't be wandering off by yourself. We were waylaid by bushrangers, William. We lost our supplies but luckily escaped with our lives."

"Bushrangers!" William's face grew red with alarm—the first color he'd shown in weeks. "What happened?"

Robin told a terse version of the bail-up.

"Thank God for Big John. It seems that you and the Penrods have some useful friends." Then he turned to Kate. "You're not to go out on your own, daughter. What happened today only reinforces my belief that you simply cannot manage here alone after I'm gone."

"You're going to get well, Father—"

"Kate, Kate, face reality, I'm never going to get well. It's a miracle that I'm still alive. Leave us, daughter, I want to speak to Robin privately."

"Must you?"

"Aye, be a good girl and do as I say. Just keep in mind I'd never do anything to hurt you."

His strange choice of words caused a frisson of apprehension to race along Kate's spine. But not wanting to cause her father further distress, she quietly left the room, tossing an angry glance at Robin as she shut the door. If he hadn't insisted on telling Father about the bail-up, William wouldn't have been so upset.

Wild Land, Wild Love

"I thank you for telling me what happened today, Robin," William said. "Kate is precious to me. I want her to be safe always, even after I'm gone." He looked at Robin squarely, wanting no misunderstanding concerning his next words. "I've been giving the situation considerable thought and after much soul-searching I've come to a decision.

"You're a good man, Robin, a damn good man. I'd trust you with my property and with my daughter. Kate needs someone, someone who can handle her. I believe, given the right man, she'll make a wonderful wife and mother."

Robin held his breath. He knew. He *knew* what was coming, and he didn't like it. William had no right to ask.

"I want McKenzie station to be yours after I'm gone, Robin. I'm asking you to marry Kate."

Chapter Six

Robin chose his words carefully. He didn't want to hurt William, but neither did he wish to be pushed into something he'd regret the rest of his life. McKenzie station was indeed a temptation. Robin couldn't hope to amass so much land in his lifetime. But if two people didn't belong together, it was he and Kate. Robin wasn't certain he could survive the constant barrage of scorching sparks that flew whenever they were in each other's company for more than two seconds.

"What you ask is impossible, William," Robin said slowly. "Kate and I don't suit. You know her feelings about convicts. Neither one of us would be happy. Is that what you want for your daughter?"

"I want what's best for her," William replied, "and I sincerely think you are what Kate needs, whether or not either of you know it." His words were spoken with such conviction, Robin was momentarily at a loss for words.

William jumped into the void. "Will you at least consider it?"

"Kate would be the first to admit that what you ask is utterly preposterous. She doesn't like me, William. Surely you've noticed how we constantly goad one another. You can't have missed the sparks we create."

"Aye," William acknowledged solemnly. He did his best to conceal the briefest of smiles that flitted over his gaunt face. "I've watched the two of you together, and what I've seen are two people strongly attracted to one another. Marriages have been based on less. Have you no feelings at all for Kate? Can you deny she's beautiful and desirable?"

Robin could not lie to William. "Aye, Kate is both beautiful and desirable. One has only to look at her to know that. As for admitting to strong feelings, that's something I haven't allowed myself to think about. Kate wouldn't permit it even if it were true. She's a strong-willed woman, William."

"Aye, my Kate is a woman to be reckoned with, but I think you're man enough to handle her. You haven't answered my question. Will you at least think about it?"

"Aye," Robin allowed grudgingly. "But once you mention the notion to Kate, I wager you'll change your mind."

"We'll see," William said sagely. He was tiring rapidly now and laid his head back on the pillow and closed his eyes.

Robin left a few moments later, shaking his head and chuckling to himself. He could well imagine Kate's reaction when William broached the subject to her. Robin wanted to be well out of range when that moment arrived.

The moment arrived later that night when Kate went in to kiss her father good night. He asked her to sit down and talk with him, and she complied.

"Is there anything special you wished to talk about, Father?"

"Aye, very special. Your future, Kate."

Kate frowned. "We've been over this before. I'm happy with my life the way it is."

"I've been doing a lot of thinking. You've been a good daughter, Kate, obeying me in things that counted yet still managing to retain your independence. I admire you for that, and I know it will help you once I'm gone."

"Father—"

"No, let me finish. We both know I won't be around much longer, and I've been thinking about what's best for you."

"I won't go back to England and Aunt Eudora," Kate returned stubbornly.

"I know that. That's why I think I've found a perfect solution to our dilemma." He inhaled slowly, looked at Kate squarely, and said, "I want you to marry Robin, Kate."

The chair toppled over as Kate leaped to her feet, her face incredulous. "Marry Robin! Are you mad? I can't believe you'd want me to marry a convict, a man capable of murder."

"I know all about Robin. Dare told me on one of his visits. Robin is neither a killer nor a vicious criminal. What he did was—"

"I don't care what he did, Father, I won't marry him. When did Robin put this crazy notion in your head? He wants McKenzie station. He owns nothing of value but thirty acres of land, none of it prime, and he's somehow wormed his way into your confidence. How long did it take him to convince you of this crazy scheme?"

"This isn't Robin's idea, Kate, it's mine. If you'd but give Robin a chance you'd find he's honest and trustworthy. And I think he'd make you a fine husband."

"I don't want a husband."

"Humor a sick man, Kate. Make my dying wish come true. I want to settle your future before I leave this earth. If I've done nothing else honorable in life, seeing to your welfare will make up for it. Trust me to decide what is best for you."

"You're too ill to think clearly, Father, else you wouldn't suggest such an outrageous thing," Kate said sourly. "Robin and I don't even like one another. Being married would create a living hell for both of us."

"Are you sure you don't like one another? The line between love and hate is so fine 'tis often misleading."

"Is that another one of Robin's notions? What kind of nonsense is he putting in your head? I should never have allowed him to see you so often. Love," Kate sneered derisively. "An ex-convict is hardly the kind of man I could love."

"Nevertheless, I'll see you married by Christmas."

"Never!"

"I didn't want to do this, daughter, but you force me to it. If you don't make up your mind by Christmas, I'll will McKenzie station to Robin and make him your guardian until you take a husband."

"You can't do that!"

"I can and I will. Just because you're twenty-six doesn't mean you don't need someone to look after you. Kate, Kate, don't fight me in this. Trust me, daughter."

"I'm sorry, Father, I don't wish to upset you, but I need time to think about this. Robin must want McKenzie station badly to present you with such a preposterous idea. I can't believe you'd let him talk you into such a thing."

William sighed wearily. He had argued so much today, his face was pale and his hands shaking. He only hoped his efforts weren't in vain. Both Robin and Kate had resisted his proposal vigorously— too vigorously, he reflected thoughtfully. Truth to tell, he'd like to be around five years from now to see what time had wrought. It certainly would be interesting to watch the fireworks explode between these two volatile people.

"I told you, it was my idea. Talk to Robin, find out his views on the marriage, then give me your answer. But remember, if you don't agree, McKenzie station goes to Robin. I've come to think of him as the son I never had."

Wild Land, Wild Love

Kate was in a fine rage when she left her father's room. Much too angry to confront Robin tonight without killing him. But when she tried to sleep, her mind refused rest, denying Kate the respite of healing slumber. After tossing one time too many, she rose from bed, threw a light robe over her high-necked nightgown, and lit a lamp. It was hot and stifling. Not even a breeze ruffled the curtains at the open window, and suddenly Kate felt the nearly desperate urge to go outside. Lamp in hand, she descended the stairs, leaving the lamp on a hall table before slipping out the front door.

Kate breathed in deeply, finding a certain comfort in the midnight blackness surrounding her. It matched her mood. She couldn't think beyond the fact that her father wanted her to marry a man who, of all the men she'd met, was the one who presented the most danger to her. To her soul, to her mind, to her very existence. She was too aware of Robin Fletcher as a man. If she were to marry him, nothing would ever be the same again.

"Couldn't you sleep either?"

Gasping in shock, Kate whirled. "You! What are you doing here at this time of night?"

Robin stood several steps behind her, having just risen from one of the porch chairs in the shadows. "The same thing you are, I would imagine. I couldn't sleep. Have you spoken with your father?"

"If you mean did he put that ridiculous proposal before me, the answer is yes. How long did it take you to convince him that we should be married?"

"It wasn't my idea. I think it as outrageous as you do, and I told William so."

"Lies, Robin, all lies! You want McKenzie station, and the only way it can be yours is if I marry you. It's yours even if I refuse to marry you. Either way you win and I lose."

"Bloody hell, I had no idea William would hatch up this scheme! Why should McKenzie station be mine if you refuse to marry me? I never considered any other option. We both know we don't belong together."

"Don't play games with me. You know well enough that Father is so set on our marriage that should I refuse he threatened to leave McKenzie station to you and name you my guardian until I marry. Which we both know is unlikely to happen at my age."

"Bloody hell!" Robin repeated. "I had no idea. I'm sorry, Kate, this is as much a surprise to me as it is to you. I don't want your land. I'm not looking for easy riches and I don't employ trickery. Nothing has ever come easily for me, but I've always managed to survive. I don't need you or your land. I'll build my own sheep station without outside interference and through my own efforts."

"I don't believe you, Robin. You talked Father into this, and now I want you to talk him out of it."

"Am I so repulsive that you can't stand the thought of me touching you?" The words hissed from his throat with a ferocity that frightened Kate. "I recall a few kisses we shared that you seemed to enjoy. Do you think me unworthy of your dainty hand?"

"I've never thought of you one way or another," Kate denied haughtily.

Wild Land, Wild Love

"Now you're the one who's lying." He stepped closer, so close her breath warmed his neck, closer, until her unbound breasts brushed his chest. She could feel his heat, smell his musky scent, almost taste his anger and arousal.

"Don't touch me," Kate whispered.

Her voice was shaky, her body trembling as she searched the hard planes of his face, finally settling on his lips. She recalled how they had tasted, remembered how soft and persuasive they'd become as they closed over hers. And his tongue. Dear God! His tongue was rough yet velvety soft, coaxing yet pervasive, demanding—wonderfully erotic.

"What are you thinking, Kate?" He didn't allow her time to answer. "Are you wondering how it would feel to have my lips on yours?"

"No!" Yes—yes—

"Are you dreaming about my hands on your body, touching you in places that give you pleasure, filling you with myself until you scream for mercy?"

"Stop! You're—you're—utterly devoid of decency," Kate cried, clapping her hands over her ears. His outrageous words made her think things no well-bred young lady had a right to think about. Especially a spinster lady.

"Kiss me, Kate."

He lowered his head, claiming her lips in a kiss she felt clear down to her toes. It went on and on, his hands sliding up and down her back, pulling her hips flush against the fullness of his loins. Violently she pulled away. Then she slapped him.

Robin merely smiled as if he found her antics amusing. "I've had my share of women, enough to know you're not completely immune to me."

"I'm going inside."

"Not yet. What did you tell William? Did you agree to our marriage?"

"Never!"

"He seems quite serious about this. What will you do?"

"You and I are going to change his mind. He's given me till Christmas to decide. That's nearly two weeks off."

"Being married to you wouldn't be all that bad," Robin said, watching Kate's face for her reaction. It came instantly.

"Perhaps not for you, with all you'd have to gain."

"Aye. You're a damn tempting woman, Kate. Bedding you will be a pleasure. You're soft and warm and make a man ache to possess you."

His words stunned Kate. Their marriage would bring him McKenzie station and make a wealthy man of him, and all he could think about was bedding her. A typical male response. She snorted.

"What's that for?"

"Because you'll never get the chance to bed me."

"Are you a virgin, Kate? Have you never experienced real passion?"

She raised her hand to slap him again, but he was too fast for her. She found her arm pinned behind her, her body molded to his, her breasts mashed against his chest. Then he was kissing her again, his tongue parting her lips, delving deep inside her mouth to taste of her sweetness. His other hand slowly worked its way beneath her nightgown, his fingers skimming the satin flesh of her thighs. Lord help him but he wanted this viper-tongued little hellion. Why? The question hung in the air like autumn smoke.

Outraged by his daring, Kate gasped as she felt his hand slip between her legs, higher, finally touching her where an ache had slowly begun to build. She struggled, but her movement only caused Robin's fingers to rub caressingly against a tender spot. She felt a moistness begin to gather, heard Robin groan, and flushed with the sure knowledge that she was responding in just the way he expected her to.

"You're so hot and wet, tell me now you're immune to me."

A strangled sound came from Kate's throat as Robin's finger slid inside her. She'd never felt anything quite so wonderful. She'd lie until she was blue in the face before she'd admit such a shameful thing. "I feel nothing at all, except for revulsion." *Lies, all lies.*

"You feel nothing?" Robin persisted, grinning down at her.

He reminded Kate of the devil, leading the innocent to hell as he increased the pressure of his finger, slipping another inside her beside the first, then starting a caressing motion that quickly brought her to a strange, shuddering ecstasy. It was reached so quickly, Kate didn't know what had happened, only that something inside her body was begging to be released.

"Robin!"

"Ah, so you do feel something."

"Please stop what you're doing! Please!"

Kate was draped against him now, held upright by the sheer strength of his big body. His answer was to bend and swoop her up in his arms, walking the few steps to the chair he had occupied earlier and settling her in his lap. Her legs shone like twin columns of alabaster beneath the pale moonlight as her nightgown settled around her waist.

"I don't think I can stop what I'm doing, Kate. It's something I've wanted to do since the day I met you. I'm going to give you your first woman's pleasure."

Slowly he began to unbutton the high neck of her nightgown, pulling the edges apart and gazing down in awe at the pale ivory mounds. "You're beautiful, Kate."

She wanted to protest, to stop the downward journey of his mouth, but then his lips settled over the peak of one breast and she was lost. When his hand found her moistness again, she couldn't have uttered a word.

At that moment Kate had never hated Robin more.

He made her feel deprived in a way she had never imagined possible. Never had she felt so dependent on a man. His fingers were doing wonderful things to her; his thumb had found a place so sensitive she nearly jumped out of his lap when he touched it. And his mouth! His mouth and tongue were making a delicious meal of her nipples.

Robin watched with restrained delight as Kate responded dramatically to his mouth and hands. He had no idea she'd be so wonderfully passionate. He wanted to release his straining manhood and plunge deep inside her. He ached from the need. His loins were on fire. Instead, he concentrated on bringing Kate pleasure, receiving joy from seeing her face contort and her eyes glaze over. He allowed her no respite as his hands and mouth worked diligently to bring her to climax. His fingers penetrated her so deeply he could feel her maidenhead stretched tautly in place, and was unaccountably delighted to discover she was still a virgin. It pleased him more than he cared to admit.

When Kate moaned and clutched at him, Robin's attention sharpened, increasing the pressure of his fingers and thumb until a muffled scream burst past her lips and a violent shudder drew her as taut as a bowstring. Still he did not desist, caressing her until her body grew quiet and her breath subsided to ragged gasps.

"You were wonderful, Kate," Robin praised in a strangled voice. He was hurting so badly he nearly doubled over with the pain. Why he didn't take her now while she was dazed and open from the violence of her climax was something he'd never understand.

Now it was too late, for her violet eyes snapped open, dark and stormy with rage, and something else that defied defining.

"You vile bastard! Why did you do that?"

"Didn't you enjoy it?"

"I hated it! I hate you!" She jumped off his lap, hastily twitching the skirt of her nightgown in place over her bare limbs and grasping the gaping upper edges to shield her breasts. "I want you off this place tomorrow."

To Kate's chagrin, Robin did not leave the next day. Nor the day after that. As far as he was concerned, William had asked him to stay, and as long as William lived, Robin intended to honor his request. He realized he had acted badly where Kate was concerned, but she did have a way of provoking him beyond reasonable control. Proving that she wasn't as immune to him as she would like to believe had seemed highly desirable at the time, but in retrospect it was a despicable trick to play on a virgin unaccustomed to passion. He was sorry, but nothing he could do or say seemed to appease Kate. In fact, Kate wouldn't even speak to him.

A week passed before William spoke to Robin again concerning marriage between him and Kate. This time Kate was present, sending him scathing looks whenever she deigned to look at him at all.

"Have you two reached a decision?" William asked anxiously. "Dr. Proctor will be here tomorrow, and I'm going to ask him to witness a new will if you don't make up your minds soon."

Kate sucked her breath in sharply. "Father, you wouldn't!"

"Aye, daughter, I mean it."

"Perhaps I'd be willing to marry someone else. Dr. Proctor, for instance. Or even Ronald Potter. Anyone is preferable to Robin."

"I don't like Potter," William said sourly. "And good man that he is, Dr. Proctor will never make a farmer. He's dedicated to doctoring. Robin is my choice, Kate, and Robin it will be."

"It's impossible, Father."

"Kate, darling girl, give over. Allow a dying man his last wish. If you have any love in your heart for me you'll grant me this."

"You know I love you, Father, but asking me to marry a man I don't love is unjust."

"Kate is right, William," Robin concurred.

"Are you saying you don't want McKenzie station?" William asked, his voice low and strident.

Glancing at Kate, Robin answered, "I'd be proud to own McKenzie station, but not at Kate's expense."

"Would you care for her and see that she never wants for anything?"

"Of course," Robin replied, puzzled by William's line of questioning.

"What more can you ask for, Kate?" William asked his daughter. "If you want me to die happy, marry Robin."

A look of incredible pain contorted Kate's face. She wanted to oblige her father, truly she did. But in her heart she felt Robin had put him up to it in order to gain McKenzie station for himself. He was probably laughing up his sleeve at her, at how easily he had brought her to shuddering passion and how easily he expected her to bend under his domination once she married him—if she married him. Why must a woman always bend to her man's will? Maybe other women were satisfied to be dominated, but she certainly wasn't. If she must marry Robin in order to please her father, then she fully intended to relinquish nothing of herself to him. She would remain her own woman even though technically McKenzie station would belong to her husband.

She looked at Robin squarely. "I'll marry Robin under one condition, Father."

"What condition is that, daughter?"

"That the marriage isn't consummated."

Robin looked startled for a moment, then chuckled, recalling Kate's wild abandon in his arms. If she married him he hadn't the least doubt that he'd win her to his bed. But truth to tell, he wasn't certain he wanted to marry Kate. She had none of the qualities most men desired in a wife.

"No, Kate," William replied sternly. "An unconsummated marriage is no marriage at all. The marriage will be consummated. What you do after that is your business—and your husband's."

Kate bit her lower lip until a drop of blood appeared at the corner of her mouth. God, this was difficult! "You and Robin win. I consent to the marriage."

For the first time in months William smiled in delight. "I knew you'd see it my way. Trust me, Kate, I'd never do anything to hurt you." Then turning to Robin, he asked, "Are you agreeable?"

"I—I—" Robin's mouth worked wordlessly. Becoming owner of McKenzie station was like a dream come true, but was it worth earning Kate's hate? But she already hates me, he answered himself. Would William defy Kate and change his will in my favor if Kate refuses to marry me? he asked himself. Yes, he decided. William was desperate to settle Kate's future before he died. In the end only one answer was possible. "Aye, William, I agree to the marriage."

The house was decorated with bouquets of flowers. It was Christmas Day. William had rallied and left his bedroom for the occasion of his daughter's wedding and was seated in the parlor in a huge chair that dwarfed his emaciated frame. Guests had already started to assemble in anticipation of the wedding, and Maude was turning out mounds of food in the kitchen. Kate was in her room dressing in her best dress with the help of Casey Penrod, her attendant. Dare was to be best man. Dr. Proctor was also present, looking decidedly downcast, and so was Ronald Potter, scowling furiously. For diverse reasons both men were disappointed to be losing a prize like Kate McKenzie.

Kate was strangely withdrawn as she dressed in her best gown, a pale ivory creation embellished with yards of lace on the wide skirt that made her waist look incredibly tiny. Her arms were bare to the elbows and she wore lace gloves. A wreath of flowers circled her head. She looked utterly gorgeous, and Casey told her so. The compliment did little to lighten Kate's dark mood, so Casey became quiet. Casey had so many questions to ask Kate about her relationship with Robin, she didn't know where to begin, but Kate seemed reluctant to speak. Casey thought it was shyness and fear of her wedding night.

"You have nothing to fear from Robin, Kate," Casey said, hoping to ease Kate's mind. "He is the gentlest of men and would never harm you. I hadn't realized you two were in love, but I'm glad he found you."

Wisely Kate refrained from answering. Evidently Robin hadn't mentioned to his best friends his reason for marrying Kate, and she didn't want to be the one to disillusion them about Robin's true motives. Then it was time for them to leave the room and walk down the stairs.

Casey looked nearly as beautiful as the bride in her gown of light green muslin, and as they walked down the stairs Dare wasn't the only one to think so. But Robin had eyes only for Kate. A preacher from Parramatta was on hand to perform the ceremony, and within minutes Robin was married to a woman who couldn't stand him. As Robin kissed Kate's cool lips he thought about the conversation he had had with Dare just before the ceremony.

"I had no idea you and Kate—that you were interested in her," Dare had said. "I haven't quite figured Kate out yet, but she's a vast improvement over Serena."

"Don't feel bad, Dare, I haven't figured Kate out myself," Robin had snorted.

"You must have fallen in love almost immediately, just like I did. Only I didn't realize it quite as soon as you did."

"This isn't a love match, Dare," Robin had admitted sheepishly.

Dare had frowned. "Don't tell me you're marrying Kate for the same reason you were going to wed Serena?" His voice was ripe with disapproval. "Is it McKenzie station you really want?"

"I wouldn't be marrying Kate at all if it wasn't for William," Robin had complained. He couldn't bear the thought of Dare thinking of him in such an unfavorable light. "William is dying. He is worried about Kate's future and asked me to wed her."

"And Kate agreed to that?"

"Lord, no. And neither did I, for that matter. But the man was adamant. I don't know how he did it, but he finally convinced Kate to marry me. The problem was, by then I didn't know if I wanted to marry her. She thinks I talked her father into the idea of our marriage and blames me for this whole mess."

"Bloody hell, sounds like you and Kate are starting off on the wrong foot. I wish you luck, mate."

Robin had been happy to let the subject drop when Dare leveled him an assessing look and asked, "What *are* your feelings for Kate?"

"I—I truly don't know. To be honest, I'll enjoy bedding her. But Kate is a sharp-tongued vixen who doesn't know how to be a real woman. She's argumentative, independent, stubborn, and so damn beautiful I can't keep my hands off her."

Dare had thrown back his head and laughed so loud and long, Robin wanted to strangle him. "What's so damned funny?"

"You, my fine friend. You sound just like me a few years back. And the woman you just described could be Casey. Don't try to deny you're smitten, mate, for I've been in your shoes. But a word of warning. If you try to dominate Kate, the marriage is doomed."

"I'm certainly not going to let Kate walk all over me," Robin had said huffily.

"Have a little compassion, Robin. Kate is marrying you to please her father, or so I assume, though she could harbor tender feelings for you." Robin snorted. "And McKenzie station is now yours by law, since a woman can hold no property in her own name. She is gaining little from this marriage."

Robin remembered Dare's words now as people crowded around them to offer congratulations. Kate looked so lovely, he wanted to whisk her away immediately and make her his in the most basic sense of the word. He'd thought of nothing else since she had given grudging consent to their marriage. He looked over at William, who seemed to have improved now that he no longer had to worry over Kate's future, and was suddenly glad he and Kate were man and wife, if only for William's sake.

Kate hadn't looked at Robin since they had been pronounced man and wife. She couldn't, not yet. The pain of being the wife of a man who had stolen everything from her was still too raw. Tonight the right to use her body in any way he saw fit was his alone. She stole a glance at her father, and suddenly the utterly peaceful look on his face made her sacrifice seem worthwhile. Squaring her shoulders, she accepted congratulations in good grace and finally dared a glance at her husband.

Chapter Seven

Kate's first thought was that Robin looked wonderfully masculine dressed in buff pants, black boots, white shirt, and dark jacket. The deep tan of his strong face was a stark contrast to the whiteness of his shirt, and the searing sun had streaked his sandy hair with pure gold. His blue eyes shone with intelligence and an emotion that defied description; his mouth was full and sensual and slightly pursed as he returned Kate's stare, his expression guarded. Then he smiled, a slow, knowing smile that caused little shivers to race down Kate's spine. She knew he was thinking outrageous thoughts, and her eyes blazed with contempt. Robin chuckled, then turned abruptly to talk to Dare. Kate chose that moment to go to her father.

"'Tis done, Kate," William said happily. "You'll not be sorry you married Robin, I swear it. But I want no foolishness tonight. This marriage will be a true marriage." His voice faltered and his eyes drooped with sudden weariness. Robin, attuned to every nuance of his father-in-law's illness, noticed and came to his aid.

"Would you like help getting to your bed, William?"

"Aye, you're a thoughtful man, Robin. Excuse me, daughter."

He grasped Robin's arm and started up the stairs. Halfway up he staggered, and Robin lifted the frail man in his arms and carried him the rest of the way to his room. Robin settled William on the bed and turned to leave. William stopped him with a touch on the arm.

"Heed my words, Robin. Kate will try her damnedest to wheedle her way out of doing her duty by you, but I'm putting my money on you."

Robin grinned. "I can handle Kate, William."

"Aye, that's what I was counting on."

The celebration was over. All the food had been consumed and the guests had all left. Maude and Lizzy were busy in the kitchen and William was sleeping.

"Time for bed, Kate," Robin said, holding out his hand.

"You go on, Robin, I'll come up later. I want to check on Father."

"He's fine, Kate, I just looked in on him."

"I—I need to instruct the servants."

Robin's jaw tightened, recalling William's words. "I told them to leave everything till tomorrow and seek their beds. Are you afraid of me, Kate? Are you afraid of the way I make you feel?"

"No man has ever frightened me," Kate declared, eyes blazing. "Let's get this over with if we must."

Robin chuckled, vastly amused. "You sound like a woman being led to torture instead of a new bride anticipating her wedding night."

"It's not something I look forward to."

"Oh, but it should be. I promise you'll find pleasure in my arms. Furthermore, I promise to give you pleasure each time we make love."

"If I have my way, this will be the only time," Kate declared staunchly. Lifting her chin at a defiant angle, she headed for the stairs, not stopping until she entered the room she and Robin would share.

Robin was mere steps behind her. He shut the door softly, but the sound brought Kate's heart leaping to her throat. They were alone. She was Mrs. Robin Fletcher and was expected to submit meekly to her husband.

Suddenly Robin was behind her, turning her to face him, her shoulders fragile beneath his big tan hands. "Kate, I don't intend to hurt you." He lowered his head and found her mouth.

For an instant Kate struggled, but he held her head forcibly with his hands, allowing her no escape as his mouth searched hers, gently at first, then fiercely, demanding. He teased the moist corners with his tongue, brushing the sweet fullness with slow enjoyment. Soft murmurings of protest gurgled in her throat, but he ignored her, deepening the kiss until he felt a barely perceptible softening, and his tenuous control began to erode. He nearly lost it completely when Kate swayed against him and opened her mouth to his tongue.

Breathing raggedly, Robin broke off the kiss, afraid if he didn't stop now he'd throw her on her back and ravish her immediately. That wasn't the kind of wedding night he wanted for his wife. He raised his head and stared at her, at her gleaming black hair still interwoven with flowers, at her violet eyes, so deep a purple they were almost black. Frozen, Kate watched him, her eyes in a turmoil, her mouth full and red from the pressure of his kiss. He allowed his eyes to stray to her breasts, now heaving beneath the ivory lace covering her bosom. With slow deliberation he unfastened the hooks and slid the garment from her shoulders.

Someone had lit the lamp in the bedroom before they arrived, and its meager glow turned Kate's breasts to gold. Robin stared, then slowly, oh, so slowly, removed his jacket and shirt. At the sight of his bare chest Kate blanched. With gut-wrenching realization she knew that after tonight her life would never be the same.

He closed his hand over the taut fullness of her breast, and saw her tremble. "God, you're lovely." He kissed her again, and as if by magic her dress slid from her hips and puddled at her feet. Her petticoats followed. Robin stepped back, a strange light in his eyes as he saw her fully unclothed but for shoes and stockings for the first time. After he looked his fill he scooped her up in his arms and laid her on the bed. Then he began removing his remaining clothing.

He straightened before her, magnificently naked, vibrantly male.

Kate looked at him, ashamed yet unable to turn her gaze away. So powerful, so beautiful, muscles rippling beneath bronzed skin. His manhood was thick, erect, eager. Frightening. He came down on her and she gasped.

"I can't ever recalling wanting a woman as badly as I want you right now," Robin said wonderingly. It was true! He'd always wanted Kate, but the fierce need he felt now was unexpected. His face was rigid with desire, his eyes glazed with lust. It was difficult to think, let alone pace himself until he had prepared Kate to accept him without unnecessary pain.

"Do you want me as bad as you want Casey?" The moment Kate said it she could have bit her tongue. It was a despicable thing to say at a moment like this.

A shadow seemed to pass over Robin's face, and suddenly he seemed angry. "Bloody hell, Kate, you sure know how to cool a man's ardor."

She started to rise, but he forced her back on the bed. He kissed her mouth, hard, then moved to her throat, her neck, the cleavage between her breasts.

With his tongue and teeth he teased the tips of her breasts, alternately sucking and biting until Kate cried out in protest. Ignoring her attempts to withhold herself from him, Robin moved with wild and hungry urgency down her stomach, nipping with his teeth, dipping his tongue into her navel until Kate was gripping the sheet and begging him to stop. Then his head was moving down again, and she felt his breath hot against the sensitive flesh between her thighs.

"Robin! For God's sake, no!" The words were no more than a ragged sob in her throat. With all her limited strength she pounded his head and shoulders, shocked by what he was attempting. And when his tongue slid experimentally over her swollen flesh she fell back on the bed and covered her face with the back of her hands, too ashamed to watch. Not in her wildest dreams did she imagine such things were possible. Even more incredible was how utterly wonderful he made her feel. God, she hated him!

Taking pity on her, Robin lifted his head, suddenly aware that Kate was far too innocent for this type of lovemaking. Sighing regretfully, he made a silent vow that one day he'd have her every way possible for a man to have a woman. His voice shook as he said, "Someday you'll beg me to do this to you, Kate."

"Never!" Kate denied hotly.

"We'll see. Spread your legs, love, we'll do it your way."

For a brief moment Kate considered resisting,

131

but quickly decided it would do little good. Spurred by her father, Robin was determined to consummate this marriage. Her legs parted.

"Wider, sweetheart. Ah, that's it," he said as he settled between her legs. "The first time will hurt, but I'll try to make it as painless as possible."

"Just get it over with, Robin," Kate replied from between clenched teeth.

He positioned the smooth tip of his shaft against her. Kate waited. But instead of shoving himself inside her, causing her considerable pain as she expected, he paused just beyond the opening, teasing her with soft, upward strokes. Then Kate realized just how consummate a lover Robin was when he slowly, methodically, continued to arouse her, drawing her nipples deep into his mouth and sucking gently, fondling her hips, stomach, and buttocks with long fingers. His ardent assault left her breathless and wanting, and Robin knew it. When his hand drifted between them and he found that same sensitive little bud he had discovered that night on the porch, Kate stiffened, her body as taut as a bowstring.

With wild abandon, she moved against his fingers. She was panting now, seeking to alleviate the terrible need building inside her. Her passion surprised and pleased him. With a start he realized she was ready to climax and reacted instinctively.

Kate felt him pressing inside her and gulped in fear. "Don't be afraid," he whispered as he felt her widen to accommodate him. Without realizing it, Kate shifted her hips, making herself more easily accessible, and Robin lunged forward, the thin membrane holding him back but briefly before ripping. Kate cried out. "Don't move!" It was an order he tried to obey himself as he drew in a deep, steadying breath.

"Please, you're hurting me."

"It won't hurt for long." He drew back, nearly withdrawing, then slowly thrust his full length into her.

Kate felt pain and rawness and wondered when it was going to stop hurting. He rocked gently, teaching her the rhythm as his hands grasped her buttocks to move her back and forth to meet his thrusts. Kate would have never believed her body could be so responsive as Robin led her by the pressure of his hands and gentle encouraging words.

"Lock your legs around my hips," he instructed. She obeyed, and he slid deeper still. "Oh, God!"

Then she felt his fingers coming between their bodies to find her and caress her. She pressed against him. He was filling her, thrusting, his fingers moving against her in rhythm, and then reality ceased. Release vibrated through Kate's body in wave after wave of incredible heat.

She screamed.

Then his hands were gripping her hips and his manhood was throbbing inside her, spilling hot liquid deep in her womb as he grew motionless and rigid for long, heart-stopping moments.

Gradually the world stopped spinning, and Kate glared up at Robin. He was smiling down at her and it made her angry. "What are you grinning at?"

"You, sweetheart. I never expected so much passion in that beautiful body. Being married to you isn't going to be such a chore after all."

"Being married to you is going to be pure hell," Kate shot back, shoving at his chest. "Get off me, you're heavy."

"A true romantic," Robin sighed, lifting himself off Kate and settling at her side. The moment he slid out of her he felt strangely bereft. "We may as well make the best of this marriage. I'm willing if you are. After what we just experienced there are bound to be certain benefits neither of us expected."

"Nothing will make up for what you've taken from me," Kate bit out through clenched teeth.

Robin's well-shaped eyebrows arched upward. "Are you referring to your virginity? It's past time you lost it. Besides, I'm your husband, remember?"

"How can I forget? I married you to please my father, but don't expect me to enjoy it. My virginity isn't important. I'm talking about McKenzie station. I suppose you'll rename it Fletcher station now."

Robin couldn't think past her remark about her virginity. "Your virginity was important to me," he said with quiet dignity. It was such an intimate remark and so solemnly spoken, the wind left Kate's sails. Deliberately she turned her back on him. "I'm not through with you, Kate."

"What else could you want? You've already taken your pleasure."

"I want to make love to you again."

That remark brought her up short. "Is that possible?"

Robin grinned with devilish delight. "Watch and see."

His hand went slowly to her thigh and slipped gently between her legs. He stroked her with his fingers, inside and out. "Are you sore?"

"What do you expect after putting that," she looked deliberately at his manhood, once again engorged and rigid, "in me. Leave me alone, Robin, I'm tired."

He felt sorry for her then and almost gave in to her request, until he recalled William's words. "I think not."

His fingers were working their way deeper, setting up a clamor inside her body, and she rotated her pelvis against his hand. It was meant to be a subtle movement, but Robin, attuned to her every need, perceived it and smiled. His thumb found the tiny button nestled between her legs and rotated gently as his fingers thrust and withdrew. Kate groaned, and Robin's answer was to take a nipple deep into his mouth and suck greedily.

"You—bastard!" Kate panted.

"Aye," Robin agreed amiably.

"Oh . . ."

"Ah, sweetheart."

His voice was strangled, his body aching as he saw Kate's face contort with the beginning of her climax. He thought her more beautiful at that moment than he'd ever seen her. Abruptly he removed his hand and rubbed the tip of his thick member against her swollen flesh. She exploded as he thrust inside her. He rode her fast, furious, his face twisted with the intensity of his own need. He arched upward, shooting his hot seed into her again and again. Then he dropped to lie drained and wet on top of her.

When he opened his eyes, Kate was watching him. The look was hostile yet curious at the same time. As if she couldn't quite understand what was happening between them. Lifting himself off her, he fell to her side, exhausted yet more exhilarated than he'd ever felt in his life. Not even gaining his freedom had made him feel this good.

Kate rolled away, presenting her back.

"Kate, I know this is all new to you, but you'll get use to it."

She turned to face him. "I doubt it, Robin, for this will never happen again. We're married and the marriage has been consummated. I've fulfilled my promise to Father. Tomorrow you can select another bedroom."

For the first time since he'd arrived in New South Wales, William felt well enough to join Robin and Kate for supper the next evening. Kate was ecstatic, thinking her father had finally shown some sign of improvement. Even his color looked better. Robin was not so certain. William's eyes appeared unnaturally bright, and though his cheeks were flushed, Robin thought the color artificial after weeks of waxy pallor. But he said nothing to Kate. In fact, Robin hadn't spoken to Kate since he left her bed early that morning.

Before daylight he had pulled her into his arms and made love to her again. Too sleepy to resist, Kate had once again fallen unwilling victim to his passion, answering with a reluctant passion of her own. When Kate awakened much later, Robin was already gone.

Later, when Robin sent his belongings over from the convict hut, Kate ordered them brought to a spare bedroom far down the hall from hers. When Robin arrived later in the day to bathe and dress for supper, he was no longer amused at Kate's antics. Kate, knowing he would be angry, had kept her distance until they met in the dining room for supper. Since William felt well enough to join them, Robin refrained from broaching the subject of his sleeping arrangements, though his resentment was apparent from the torrid looks he lavished on Kate during the meal.

Kate, aware that Robin would not upset her father by airing their problems at the table, thoroughly enjoyed her meal. She smiled smugly at Robin's piercing looks and devoted her conversation to her father. Later, when Robin thoughtfully helped William to his chamber, Kate escaped to her own room, securely locking the door behind her. Never again, she vowed with single-minded determination, would she allow Robin a glimpse of the woman she had become in his arms. Never would she forgive him for talking her father into pressing for their marriage. To be totally dependent on him for her support was more galling than if she had been forced to return to England and Aunt Eudora. She hated him for taking what was rightfully hers, no matter how legally it was accomplished, and for showing her a side of herself she didn't like. A side she didn't know existed until he took her in his arms and caressed her into shuddering ecstasy.

Smiling at how easily she had outwitted her husband, Kate prepared for bed. She would sleep well tonight, she decided, without Robin's intimidating presence beside her. Primly dressed in a high-necked nightgown, she climbed into bed and was about to douse the lamp when a loud knock at the door startled her. Without being told, she knew who it was, could even picture Robin's face, dark and glowering, storm clouds gathered in his blue eyes. She refused to answer, refused to be taken again to that place where nothing existed but what he did to her and how her body responded to him.

"Kate, I know you're awake. If you don't open the door I'm going to break it in."

Kate gasped. Surely he wouldn't do such a thing, would he? Of course he would, Kate thought, answering her own question. She would put nothing past Robin Fletcher. He was an ex-convict, for God's sake, and capable of anything.

"Don't you dare!"

"Open up, Kate! Do you want William to hear us?"

Wild Land, Wild Love

Robin had found the right words to move Kate. Reluctantly she slid out of bed and padded to the door. She turned the key in the lock, and the door swung open with a bang. Robin stood in the doorway, arms folded across his chest, legs planted wide apart and a scowl turning the corners of his mouth downward. He pushed inside and slammed the door behind him. A prickle of apprehension slid down Kate's spine as she backed away.

"Wha—what do you want?"

"Is it so unusual for a man to want to sleep with his new bride? Why did you lock me out?" His tone was cool and calm, but Kate was not fooled by it.

She faced him squarely. "I told you that what happened last night would never happen again. Your room is down the hall. Kindly leave me in peace. You got what you wanted, didn't you?"

"I want my wife, Kate." His voice became rough and strident, but he was not begging, merely stating a fact. "Do you realize how wild you were last night? I want to come inside you again, to feel you tighten around me, to thrust deep and move slowly, to—"

"Stop!" Kate cried, clapping her hands over her ears. "Why are you doing this to me?"

"Isn't it obvious? I want you."

"I don't want you. Do you think I enjoy being turned into something I don't recognize? It's bad enough I'm dependent on you for my very livelihood since our marriage. At least let me retain a part of myself that I can call my own."

"I want all of you, Kate."

"Go to hell!" Angrier than she had ever been in her life, she began pushing him toward the door.

With grim determination, Robin planted his feet firmly and became as immovable as an oak with mighty roots. He could only be pushed so far, and Kate had already shoved him beyond his limits. Reaching out, he grasped the edges of her prim white nightgown in both hands and ripped it apart. Without a moment's pause, he pulled it down her arms and tossed it aside. Vivid, cynical eyes that matched his dark mood stared down at Kate, raking her nude figure with scalding contempt. She forced herself to stand still as his gaze swept slowly, measuringly, over her. Devil eyes. Sharp and piercing, and so blue she was nearly blinded by then.

"You're beautiful, Kate, but I've seen better."

"You're despicable! You want me merely as a substitute for Casey Penrod."

Robin blanched, choking on Kate's words. Memory bathed the raw wound inside him as he thought of Casey and how much he had loved her. But he had always known it was an unrequited love, a love without reward or compensation. Casey had belonged to Dare from the moment of their first fateful meeting. Now, by a peculiar quirk of fate, he found himself married to another woman. A woman who hated him. A woman who accused him of manipulating her father in order to gain himself one of the best sheep farms in New South Wales.

The funny thing was that until a few weeks ago

Wild Land, Wild Love

Kate's bitter accusations would have been true. But with the passage of time his love for Casey had gradually turned to friendship and a deep, abiding respect. Exactly when or how it happened escaped Robin, but he no longer envied Dare and the love he and Casey shared. They had earned it. But that line of thought was far from solving his problems with Kate.

"I want you because you're desirable, Kate, and because you're my wife." He touched her breast, caressing the nipple with the tip of one finger. Kate cringed. A hint of something deep and painful contorted Robin's features when he saw her shy away from him. "Do you hate me so much, Kate?"

"I—yes." *But she didn't.* Even now she could feel her body responding to his touch, aching for more. But she'd die before she'd let that scoundrel know how profoundly he affected her. "I'd prefer we kept all our future dealings on an impersonal basis."

"What do you suggest I do when I want to make love to my wife?"

"Find another woman. I'm certain Lizzy will be happy to oblige. Or even Serena, if she has no qualms at bedding a married man." *Dear God, was she mad to even suggest such a thing?*

"Is that what you really want?"

What she wanted was for her body to remain her own, her heart to remain untouched, and she wanted to retain her sanity—be her own person. Robin Fletcher was too blatantly male to allow that.

"That's what I want," Kate replied, her eyes lowered to prevent Robin from seeing the sudden flash of denial.

"Then I bid you good night, love. Far be it from me to intrude where I'm not wanted. Obliging chap that I am, I'll not inflict myself on you nor insist on my marital rights. And since you've given me leave to take my pleasure elsewhere, I don't expect to hear you complain when I do so. On the other hand," he threatened ominously, "should you decide to take a lover, I will cheerfully strangle the man, and as for you, love, you can expect equal justice."

Kate was stunned. She had never expected him to acquiesce so easily. It was almost as if he were waiting for her to deny him so he could find his pleasure with another woman. But he didn't have to worry about her taking a lover. The thought was ludicrous. She was a married woman. Not once did she stop to examine that revealing statement.

Smiling thinly, Robin turned to leave, then changed his mind, spinning around and seizing Kate, the ruthless blue of his eyes boring into hers with a ferocity that left her breathless. His face was dark and foreboding as he swooped down on her mouth, plundering her lips with painful urgency. His hands were on the sweet mounds of her buttocks, pressing her so close that Kate could feel the rigid hardness of his member relentlessly prodding the naked softness of her belly.

A strangled moan escaped her throat when his tongue parted her lips and brutally plunged inside, where it did battle with hers. Now one of his hands left her tender backside and sought her breast. He didn't hurt her, but Kate could feel the pressure of his fingers as he deftly worked her nipples into swollen buds of pure sensation. My God, Kate thought raggedly, he's doing it again! Will he always affect me that way?

Then abruptly Robin released her, stepping back, a sardonic look on his face. Kate was breathing so rapidly her chest was heaving. Aroused and confused, she wondered what her husband was up to now. Was his word so lightly given that he was already prepared to break it?

"I just wanted to leave you with a little reminder of what you're missing by banishing me from your bed," Robin rasped, not as unaffected by Kate as he appeared to be. "Sleep well, love. You know where you can find me if you want me." Then he was out the door, slamming it behind him.

"Insufferable pig," Kate muttered to his departing back. Picking up her nightgown, she saw that it was beyond repair and flung it aside. Then, because she was so angry and upset, she climbed between the sheets nude, fuming and raging until she fell into an exhausted sleep.

It seemed like only minutes before a tap sounded on her door. Kate opened her eyes to full daylight, surprised that she had slept so soundly after Robin's late visit and their resulting argument. "Who is it?"

"'Tis Lizzy, I've brought you clean towels."

"Come in," Kate directed, relieved to learn it wasn't Robin demanding entrance.

Lizzy entered, set down the towels, and opened the curtains to let in the sunlight. She looked cautiously toward the bed, unaware that Robin hadn't shared Kate's bed the night before. She seemed somewhat surprised to find Kate alone, and disappointed. It was no secret that she was smitten with Robin and had been more than a little annoyed when he married Kate. Not that Lizzy could fault him for wanting to better his station in life. McKenzie station was worth any sacrifice, and Lizzy considered marrying a spinster like Kate a definite sacrifice on Robin's part. Of course everyone knew Robin didn't share Kate's bedroom, but they were newlyweds and Lizzy had at least expected to find Robin in Kate's room. Was something amiss? If so, she wondered how the situation could be worked to her own advantage.

Kate sat up and yawned, forgetting she was nude. When the sheet slipped down around her waist, baring her breasts, Lizzy smirked knowingly. Then she spied Kate's nightgown on the floor and picked it up.

"Would you like me to take this down to the laundry?"

Lizzy held it up and gasped. The garment was ripped from neck to hem. Kate flushed, suddenly realizing that she hadn't a stitch of clothes on. Quickly she pulled the sheet up around her neck. "Throw the damn thing away, Lizzy." Kate never

144

wanted to see that particular garment again. She needed no reminder of Robin and how thoroughly he had humiliated her. In fact, Robin Fletcher was a distraction she didn't need at all!

Chapter Eight

Two days after Kate's marriage to Robin, Roy Penrod came to visit. Kate thought him exceedingly handsome for a man in his late fifties. He was tall and still slim with black hair liberally dusted with silver, and one look at Roy told Kate where Dare had inherited his good looks.

After introductions were made, Roy said, "You're every bit as beautiful as Dare said you were. You couldn't have married a better man than Robin. I'm glad he found you."

Kate didn't want to disillusion Roy about Robin so she said nothing.

"I'm sorry to have missed your wedding, but since I've been appointed magistrate my presence is required often in Sydney. I miss my home, but my duties manage to keep loneliness at bay. Dare has his own farm and family to keep him occupied, and Ben is off seeking adventure and tempting fate. Ben is far too impetuous for his own good. But I have high hopes that one day he'll find a woman who will curb his wandering."

Though Roy made a joke of his solitary state, Kate could sense the longing he harbored in his heart for his family. That Roy Penrod was a lonely man was obvious.

"I've heard so much about you, I'm happy to finally meet you," Kate assured him.

"Is your father up to receiving visitors?" Roy asked. "I spoke with Robin outside a few moments ago and he told me he thought William would be happy to see me. I've been a poor neighbor. You've been here several weeks and I've yet to welcome you properly. I hope Dare has shown you the courtesy I've been unable to extend."

"Dare has been here on several occasions and has proved a wonderful friend. I'm sure Father will be pleased to see you, Mr. Penrod. He just finished a nap and should feel refreshed enough for company."

"The name is Roy." He smiled. "Thad McKenzie and I were friends for many years, and I hope the trend continues with you and your father."

Kate flashed a brilliant smile that quite dazzled Roy. He knew immediately why Robin had fallen in love with Kate and married her promptly before someone else stole her heart.

Kate took Roy to William's room, glad to note that her father seemed in good spirits today. She left them alone to become acquainted and bumped into Lizzy on her way down the stairs. The girl merely nodded, smiled a secret smile, and continued on her way. Kate thought Lizzy looked exceptionally smug these days and wondered if Robin had followed her ill-given advice and taken the girl to his bed. She certainly couldn't blame him, since she had given Robin leave to do whatever he pleased. The thought of Robin making love to Lizzy was strangely disturbing. Her heart thudded with pain as she pictured Lizzy in Robin's arms, writhing beneath his hard, muscular strength, the recipient of those tantalizing caresses that turned a woman into a wanton. Kate shook her head, trying without success to dislodge those arousing thoughts.

Since their turbulent wedding night, Kate and Robin had treated one another like polite strangers. Kate found she could barely look Robin in the eye after behaving in such an abandoned manner. Once he had taken her in his arms, her restraint had melted away like her clothes. She didn't like not being in control, especially when it concerned her emotions.

Each time Robin saw Kate he burned with remembrance. The memory of her climaxing wildly in his arms, of her utter abandon once he had aroused her and her passionate response to his lovemaking would remain with him always. She could lie until she was blue in the face, but Robin's instincts told him that somewhere in Kate's lovely body lurked a spark of feeling for him. She was just too damn stubborn to admit to feeling attraction for an ex-convict.

When Roy saw that William was tiring, he rose to leave, promising to return another day.

"Would you send up Kate before you leave?" William asked. Though confined to his bed, William knew Kate well enough to realize that already trouble brewed between the newlyweds, and he hoped to talk some sense into his daughter.

Kate was nowhere around when Roy arrived downstairs, so he went in search of her. Finding the parlor empty, he headed to the kitchen, stopping abruptly just inside the door. Maude was bending over a bubbling pot when she realized she wasn't alone. Swiveling her head, she stared into Roy Penrod's piercing gray eyes. Maude's cheeks were flushed a becoming pink from the heat and her hair clung damply to her rosy cheeks. Roy could do little more than stare at her.

Flustered by the handsome gentleman's attention, Maude asked, "Can I help you, sir?"

For a brief moment Roy forgot his errand. It had been a long time since he'd seen a woman as attractive as Maude. And longer still since a woman had captured his attention so completely. Though not young, Roy was still vigorous and healthy. But for years he had suppressed his natural urges, preferring instead to concentrate on his sons and making his farm one of the richest in New South Wales. His wife had perished on the ship after leaving England, and he had never forgiven himself for asking so frail a woman to come to Australia in the first place. Now, looking at Maude, Roy realized how desperately lonely he was.

"Who are you?" Roy asked abruptly.

Maude flushed, fearing she had somehow angered this handsome man. "Maude Lynch, the McKenzie's cook."

"Maude," Roy repeated slowly, savoring the name. "I'm Roy Penrod."

"Oh, I know your son. Pleased to meet you, sir."

Suddenly Roy remembered his errand. "I'm looking for Kate. Have you seen her?"

"She went outside to the herb garden a few minutes ago. Would you like me to get her?"

"No, Maude, I'll do it. Have you been in New South Wales long?"

"No, sir, I only arrived a few months ago. I—" she flushed, "I'm a convict."

"I know." Roy smiled gently. "Most servants are. My own daughter-in-law is an ex-convict, and I couldn't ask for a better woman for my son or mother for my grandchildren." He wasn't at all put off by Maude's timid confession, aware of the minor nature of the crimes that had earned transportation for some of the convicts in the colony. Instinctively he knew Maude couldn't have committed a vile crime but had been a victim of English justice, just like Casey. He also knew he'd be back, and soon, to see Maude Lynch.

Once Kate learned William wished to see her, she hurried to his room. "You wanted me, Father?"

"Aye, daughter. You've been married but a few days, yet I can sense you're not giving this marriage a chance to survive."

"Father!" Kate said, aghast. "Why are you plac-

150

ing the blame on me? I didn't want this marriage in the beginning."

"Aye, and that's exactly the reason I'm placing most of the blame on you. You're a stubborn woman, Kate, but I've always known you to be fair. Can't you look past the fact that Robin was a convict?"

William's barb stung. Kate had always considered herself a fair woman. Perhaps Father was right, she reflected sourly. She and Robin certainly had one thing in common, but whether or not getting along in bed was enough to build a marriage on was debatable. Especially in view of the way Robin had gone behind her back and used underhanded methods to gain McKenzie station for himself.

"I want your promise that you'll give Robin a chance, daughter. 'Tisn't too much to ask, is it? I feel certain he'll make you happy if you'd allow him to try."

Kate bit her lip to keep from screaming out the unfairness of it all, then slowly nodded her head. It was futile to argue with a sick man. "I'll try, Father, but I won't promise it will work."

"'Tis all I ask, daughter."

Kate mulled over William's words after she left his room. Her father was so set on her and Robin making their marriage work that she felt guilt over denying him his request. Perhaps—God, could she swallow her pride?—perhaps she should try to forget Robin's past and all he had done and try to concentrate on repairing the shambles of their marriage. After all, marriage was forever.

Robin received a similar lecture when he went in to bid William good night after supper that night. Kate had been unusually quiet, but Robin thought nothing of it. Their solitary meals were normally tense affairs with polite conversation limited to impersonal matters. Tonight's brief comments concerned Roy Penrod and his visit. When Kate headed up the stairs after supper, Robin went to look in on William.

William appeared to be breathing with some difficulty, and Robin adjusted the pillows behind his head. "Have you taken your medicine, William?"

"Aye," William gasped. "'Tis nothing but a little congestion." The sick man shrugged.

"Then I'll leave you to your rest."

"Robin, wait. I know you and Kate are having problems, and I feel responsible. I was the one who insisted on this marriage, and in my heart I still feel you and Kate were made for one another."

Robin wasn't quite so certain but declined comment. Instead, he said, "'Tis up to Kate, William. Whatever becomes of this marriage depends on your daughter and her stubborn pride. It was a mistake to agree to this crazy idea in the first place. I thought that I—" he paused, flushing. "Bloody hell, what difference does it make now? Good night, William, sleep well."

Robin had just peeled off his clothes and settled in bed when he heard the door open and shut. The meager light from the bedside lamp was too dim to reveal anything but the fact that his late night caller was a woman. Kate! The blood pounded in his head, and his heart thudded wildly. Had she finally swallowed her pride and come to him? It had been more difficult than he imagined to keep his promise to leave her alone, for he wanted her desperately. Not a moment went by that he didn't want to forget their angry words, take her in his arms, and make love to her. Now she was here, and suddenly all was right in the world.

The woman came closer, stepping within the circle of light. Stunned, Robin gasped. It was Lizzy, barefoot and wearing a sheer nightgown that billowed around her body like a wispy white cloud, revealing every luscious curve.

"Bloody hell! What are you doing here, Lizzy? Are you mad, coming to my room like this?"

"No, not mad, Robin, just eager to help you forget what that cold bitch is doing to you."

"That 'bitch' is my wife," Robin said coolly.

Lizzy shrugged. "She sure don't act like a wife. If I was your wife I'd be in that bed beside you right now instead of sleeping alone. Let me ease you, Robin, you won't regret it." She sidled further into the room, stopping when she reached the bed. Staring pointedly at Robin's bare chest and the place where the sheet came low on his hips, Lizzy licked her lips and sat down on the edge of the bed. "I know how to please a man, Robin."

She followed her words by boldly reaching out and touching him. "Bloody hell!" Robin burst out. He was hard. But he'd been hard and throbbing before Lizzy entered the room. Just thinking about Kate had done that to him.

Lizzy's eyes glowed as she ogled Robin's erection

making a tent of the sheet. Robin groaned. He started to rise to show Lizzy the door, then thought better of it. Dammit, he was naked, he was aroused, and there was a willing woman offering herself to him. What more could a man ask for? Kate. The answer was plain and simple. He wanted Kate. Yet his wife had given him permission to take another woman to his bed. If he was a man worth his salt he'd do exactly that. Lord knows he was randy enough right now to take Lizzy and several other women afterwards. Thoughts of Kate and how eagerly she had responded to him had driven him wild these past few days. Why wouldn't Lizzy do just as well?

Because she wasn't Kate.

"Get the hell out of here, Lizzy," Robin ground out, gritting his teeth in frustration as Lizzy continued to stare at that certain part of his body with unfeigned interest.

"I can see that you want me, Robin," Lizzy said delightedly. "I've had plenty of experience. I can do things to you your wife wouldn't dream of doing. I've wanted you since the moment I saw you."

"You're making this difficult," Robin panted, desperately searching for control. How much could a virile man take? "If and when the time arrives that I need a woman, I'd prefer to do my own asking. If you don't leave immediately, I'll see that you're transferred. The next people you work for might not be so kindly disposed."

Outside Robin's door, Kate paused. It had taken her a long time to reach the decision to go to Robin and try to iron out their differences. She wasn't certain she could survive long bleak years of an indifferent marriage. If she had to have a husband, Robin was no worse nor better than other men she had known. At least he seemed genuinely fond of her father and loved McKenzie station enough to make it prosper.

With her hand on the knob, Kate froze. The murmur of voices drifted to her through the closed door. One voice was soft and feminine, the other harsh and grating. Kate knew immediately whom she would find in the room with Robin. Hadn't she given him permission to take his pleasure elsewhere? But it still hurt to know he had waited but a short time before taking Lizzy to his bed. She turned to leave, then halted in her tracks as a sudden, unexplained rage seized her. If nothing else, she intended to let Robin and his—his doxy know she was aware of his infidelity. Squaring her slim shoulders, she whirled and flung open the door, marching into the room with all the bravado she could muster.

Robin seemed more startled at seeing Kate in his room than he was at being found with Lizzy draped over his bed. Why had Kate come? Did her visit mean that she wanted him as badly as he wanted her? Then he groaned aloud. If that was the case, finding him with Lizzy would serve only to reinforce her low opinion of him.

"I see you didn't waste time finding a replacement for me in your bed," she charged sarcastically.

"It's not what you think, Kate."

Lizzy smiled smugly but said nothing, aware of the conclusions Kate had drawn and not regretting them a bit. Any woman who would turn a man like Robin from her bed didn't deserve him.

"Isn't it? Do you expect me to believe Lizzy is merely paying you a friendly call in her nightgown at this time of night?"

Unwilling to make their argument public knowledge, Robin fixed Lizzy with a chilly glare and said, "Leave us, Lizzy. And don't come back unless you're invited."

"Robin—"

"Do as I say, Lizzy." Throwing Kate a murderous glance, Lizzy flounced from the room. Kate nearly screamed in frustration when she saw how blatantly the servant had exposed herself before Robin. The nightgown was so transparent, Kate could see Lizzy's breasts clearly. They were swollen, the nipples formed into large taut buds that pressed against the thin material in an obscene manner. The moment the door slammed behind Lizzy, Kate approached the bed, her face contorted in fury.

"How dare you!"

"I did nothing you didn't give me leave to do," he drawled with mocking humor. She's jealous—the thought slid into his mind with no accompanying warning. It pleased him.

"You could at least have taken her in the stable, or somewhere more appropriate than in my own home. Have you no shame?"

Robin chuckled. It was a curiously unsettling sound, and with a start Kate realized she was acting like a jealous fishwife. Actually, she didn't care whom Robin bedded as long as it wasn't her. Forgotten was the reason she had come to his room tonight and the talk she had had with her father earlier. Hell could freeze over before she'd be a wife to a lecher like Robin Fletcher.

"Believe what you want, Kate, but I didn't invite Lizzy here tonight. I was as surprised as you to find her here."

Kate eyed him with icy disdain, noting his near state of nudity. If not for the sheet he'd be fully exposed. "You were certainly prepared for her visit."

"I always sleep in the nude. If you'd been more of a wife to me you'd know that." No appropriate answer came to Kate's mind. "Why *are* you here, Kate?"

Kate scowled. Telling Robin that she had come to mend fences was the last thing she'd admit after finding him with another woman.

"Kate . . . Look at me. I know why you've come."

That statement caught Kate's attention quickly enough, and she turned her head to gaze at him. "If I did have a reason it's no longer valid. I wish you good night. Should I send Lizzy back up here?"

Robin caught her arm before she could flee. "I don't want Lizzy. If I did I would have taken her long ago. Can't you get it through your stubborn skull that 'tis you I want?"

"You don't need to lie to me, Robin. We both know why you married me. I'm certainly not beautiful and I'm much too old to be desirable."

"Nonsense. You have too low an opinion of yourself, love."

"Don't try to smooth-talk me, Robin," Kate argued, growing angry. "Nothing you say will alter the fact that you and Lizzy were—that you— dammit, let me go!"

"Did nothing I say get through to you? There are times I'd like to shake you until you gain the good sense God gave you, and this is one of those times."

"Don't you dare!" Kate threatened. With a strength she didn't know she possessed, she pulled herself free and lunged toward the door. She wasn't fast enough. Leaping from the bed, Robin grasped a handful of long black hair and spun her around to face him.

He was naked. And aroused. Kate gulped noiselessly as she eyed his magnificent proportions with misgiving. Had she done that to him or was it the result of Lizzy's visit? Robin seemed unconcerned over his naked state as he held Kate prisoner between his two powerful hands. But to Kate his blatantly masculine display was more disturbing than she cared to admit. She had to get away. Now!

"Let me go, Robin!"

"No. You came here for a purpose and I think I know what it is."

"You don't know a damn thing."

"I know you. I know how you feel beneath my hands. I know how you writhe and moan when my mouth and tongue bring you to climax. And I know how wonderful you feel when I'm inside you. You're slippery and wet and so hot I—"

"Stop it! Stop it!" She clapped her hands over

her ears to prevent his words from reaching her brain. They were erotic, outrageous, crude, and melted her insides to liquid fire.

"I'm going to give you what we both want, love." Then she was floating as Robin swept her into his arms and carried her to the bed. Before she could struggle free, he covered her with his body, pinning her to the mattress.

Then he was kissing her. Kissing her like a starving man, hard, hungry, his hands roaming desperately over her body, rediscovering all those places he'd known so briefly. With frantic haste he removed her gown and robe. A seam ripped, but neither seemed to notice. He held her head and devoured her mouth, probing her wildly with his tongue. She bit his mouth and tasted blood. It only made him more wild. Through a haze of hot, pulsing desire, Robin knew nothing but the terrible urgency with which he wanted the woman in his arms.

Kate felt a momentary thrill of elation at Robin's frantic need, aware that if he had already taken Lizzy he wouldn't be so frantic with need now. His face was rigid with desire, his eyes opaque with lust. He thrust into her. Kate screamed. Not from pain—oh, no—not from pain. She screamed from the magnificent sensation of his hard flesh slamming into her. She screamed because she couldn't help herself when he began thrusting, so hard and fast that just breathing was a luxury. She screamed because he had lowered his head and found her breast, suckling wildly.

"Put your legs around my waist," he panted,

raising his head. When Kate was slow to obey, he grasped her legs and raised them over his shoulders. He slid even deeper inside her. The feeling was fantastic and Kate quivered in response. Robin moaned, a choked sound that effectively conveyed his delight.

"Robin . . ."

"I know, love, I feel the same. Now, Kate, now!"

Their release came simultaneously, bodies arched, convulsed, exploded. Kate felt the hot spurt of Robin's seed deep inside her and spared a brief thought to the fact that Robin could have made her pregnant. Then thought became impossible as her soul left her body and floated slowly back to earth.

Kate lay still, one arm outflung, the other covering her eyes. Robin loomed above her, still deeply imbedded. With fierce possessiveness he stroked the length of her body, from her breasts to her knees. "You're mine, Kate McKenzie. Deny it all you want, but you'll always be mine."

Only after those ominous words did he pull out and lie down beside her. Still Kate said nothing, too afraid that he was right to contradict him.

"Kate, did you hear me?"

"I heard you," she said dully.

"Are you ready to admit to this attraction we have for one another and be a real wife to me?"

Actually, that was the reason Kate had sought out Robin tonight. But after finding Lizzy in his room she had changed her mind. "I need time to think."

"I want your answer now, Kate."

Wild Land, Wild Love

"I—" Suddenly Kate grew still. She thought she had heard something and paused to listen again. "Did you hear something?"

"You're stalling, Kate. I heard nothing. You know our marriage was what your father wanted. Why are you being so obstinate about this?"

"I swear I heard something. Perhaps I should check on Father."

"I saw him shortly before I came up to bed. He had just taken his medicine and was going to go to sleep."

"Still—"

Robin rolled her beneath him. "I'll make love to you all night if necessary, until you come to your senses and realize that our estrangement is only hurting ourselves." His callused hands were possessive, lingering, as he caressed her hip, then roamed over the curve of her buttock.

Suddenly all thought of William was forgotten as Robin rolled again and Kate found herself on top, straddling Robin's hips in a most unladylike fashion. He was fully erect again, his manhood rising thick and turgid between them, his lips feeding on her breasts as she bent over him. Then his hand was between them, his fingers playing on her, in her, until he made a mockery of her feeble resistance, and Kate was lost. She cried out. Again, then yet again when Robin shifted and slid into her. With effortless ease he brought them both to a shuddering climax.

When neither of them had anything else to give, Robin rolled over until they were both lying on their sides, facing one another. Gently he pulled her close, placing her head on his chest. "Go to sleep, love. Tomorrow I'll move back into your room." As far as Robin was concerned it was settled. He never wanted to fall asleep again without Kate in his arms.

The sun was shining when Robin awoke, but he reckoned it was still quite early. Kate was still sleeping, curled against him in a tight ball. It felt good, damn good. He touched her breast, delighting in the way her nipple puckered beneath his caress. She was so responsive, he felt blessed. Few men could boast a wife as wildly abandoned as Kate. He'd take her over Serena any day, despite the fact that Serena was younger and more experienced than Kate.

With slow, measured strokes he began caressing her, lavishing special attention on her beautiful breasts. Kate stirred but did not awaken. When he lowered his head and nibbled on her nipples, she opened her eyes and groaned. "Don't you ever sleep?"

"With you in my bed? Impossible! We've just time for . . ." The words died on his lips as Lizzy burst into the room. "What in the hell are you doing here? Can't you knock?" He scrambled for the sheet, pulling it up to shield Kate from Lizzy's probing gaze.

"It—'tis the master," Lizzy gasped, finally finding her tongue. Had things worked out differently, she would be the woman in Robin's bed this morning.

Kate lunged forward, oblivious of her nudity. "What about Father?"

"Maude couldn't rouse him when she brought in his breakfast. She thinks—that is—"

Lizzy stammered helplessly, but there was no need for her to continue. Kate was already on her feet, struggling into her robe. Robin was close on her heels. Lizzy stood there staring until Robin ordered her to leave. Kate was choking on her tears by the time she reached William's room. She didn't need a doctor to tell her William was dead. And from the looks of him, he'd been dead quite some time. Kate dropped to her knees, sobbing against his chest.

"We all knew it was bound to happen sooner or later," Robin soothed, genuinely distressed over William's death.

"I should have come to him last night," Kate insisted. "I heard something but I foolishly let myself be duped into thinking all was well. Because of you, Robin!" Her violet eyes were dark and accusing. Robin flinched but said nothing, astute enough to realize Kate needed to vent her spleen on someone. "I foolishly allowed my passion to get in the way of duty to my father. His death is my fault. Had I gone to him he might be alive now."

"You don't know that, Kate," Robin soothed. "You don't even know it was William you heard. It could have been a kookaburra, or a night bird, or anything, for God's sake."

"I'll never forgive you for this, Robin," Kate said unreasonably. "That is the last time I'll let my body rule my head. I was acting the wanton in your arms while my father lay dying."

"You were acting like a wife," Robin reminded her. "It's what your father wanted. He died happy, Kate. Wherever he is he knows I'll take good care of you."

Kate closed her mind to Robin's words. He stood for long minutes watching her sob out her heartache, then left her to her grief and went to make the necessary arrangements for the funeral.

The same preacher who had married Kate and Robin presided at William's funeral. He was buried beyond the billabong at the edge of the forest beyond the house. During the two days before the funeral, Kate seemed finally to have accepted William's death, though she remained strangely quiet and withdrawn, utterly rejecting Robin when he offered comfort.

The entire Penrod family was there but for Ben who had joined the Blaxland party in search of a route across the Blue Mountains. It was mid-January, 1813, and a blistering sun beat down on the group gathered around William's grave. One by one they all left but for Robin and Kate.

"Come along, love, it's too hot out here to linger. Your father was a brave man. He'd rest easier knowing you didn't grieve unnecessarily." He touched her arm.

Kate whirled, the blazing inferno of her violet eyes scorching Robin. "Don't touch me!" The words hissed through her teeth, their viciousness startling him. "I never want you to touch me again. Don't you understand? Father would be alive now

Wild Land, Wild Love

if you hadn't turned me into a woman I don't even recognize."

Robin's eyes narrowed thoughtfully. "You don't mean that, Kate. Soon your grief will pass. One day we'll have children, and life will take on a new meaning."

Kate looked at him as if he were some loathsome creature who had just uttered the vilest words possible. "I don't want your children."

Robin opened his mouth but nothing came out. He was too stunned to form a reply. He knew Kate was hurting, but to say something so despicable was unworthy of her. "You may already be carrying my child," he said quietly.

"I'd kill myself first."

Speechless, Robin merely stared at her. Then he slowly turned and walked away.

Chapter Nine

The heat was dry and blistering. Kate found it difficult to believe that it was February. In England it would be cold and dreary. In Australia the sheep in the pastures were woolly again and rams and ewes were mating with vigor. Soon it would be time to drive them down to the pens for shearing.

Robin found himself working longer and harder than he had ever worked in his life, except perhaps for the time spent toiling in the coal mines. When he came home at night he made certain it was too late for supper. It became increasingly difficult to face Kate's silent condemnation across the table. Words failed to move her. No matter how hard Robin pleaded, she remained polite but firm in her conviction that she was responsible for her father's death and that Robin was the cause of her inattentiveness. Her inflexible attitude had virtually destroyed all chances of their marriage succeeding. The more withdrawn Kate became, the more frantic Robin grew.

One bright note was Ben Penrod's return from the Blue Mountains. He came riding into the yard one day grinning from ear to ear. Robin happened to be in the yard, and they greeted each other exuberantly. Kate heard the commotion and drifted outside.

"Kate, come here," Robin called when he noticed her standing on the porch. "Dare's unpredictable brother has returned. I want you to hear his news."

Kate joined the two men, noting that Ben was as aggressively handsome as Dare and equally appealing. He was tall, raw-boned, and rugged, and his gray eyes seemed to miss nothing as they raked Kate from head to toe. She could tell immediately he was a rake, albeit a likable one. She'd heard that Ben Penrod was an adventurer whose daring was legend, and since meeting him in person she could well believe those tales. His wide smile was infectious, and she couldn't help smiling back.

"Pleased to meet you, Kate," Ben said once Robin made the introductions. "I'm sorry I missed the wedding, but from what Dare and Father tell me, old Robin here had eyes for no one but you. Now that I've met you I can see why. You're a lucky bloke, Robin," he said, slapping Robin on the back.

"Your time will come," Robin predicted, glancing at Kate.

"I understand you were with the Blaxland,

Wentworth, and Lawton expedition," Kate said, turning away from Robin's probing look.

"Aye." Ben grinned easily. "We've just returned and I'm bursting to tell Robin the good news. We've found it, mate! There were many days I seriously doubted we'd come back alive as we fought our way along the high ridges of the Blue Mountains. The silence of the place was awesome with its deep canyons, chasms, blue forests, and gray mists."

Kate listened, entranced, as Ben continued. "The air in those lofty reaches is cool and the breeze brisk. Far below we could see sunlit splashes of gold and yellow on dense forests. We lost several good men to those chasms and canyons, but we finally came to the western foothills. The view was spectacular. We could see plains and forests stretching out so far to the west it boggles the mind. There is already talk in Sydney of migration. There's no limit to how large a tract of land a man can own. Governor Macquarie sent Surveyor Evans to lay out a road and has promised convict labor to build a track across the mountains."

"That is exciting news," Robin agreed, his eyes shining. "I'd give anything to be one of the first men across the Blue Mountains. I recall how disappointed you were when Dare went on the last expedition and you were forced to remain behind."

"As it turned out, I was lucky," Ben said, growing sober. "If you remember, none of the party survived but for Dare and another man who stayed behind with Dare when he broke his leg. Dare was fortunate to make it back alive."

Kate's attention sharpened. She recalled Uncle Thad saying that Dare had been away when Mercy took ill. It had seemed rather strange at the time that Dare would leave his new bride for an expedition that might cost him his life.

Ben left soon afterwards, and Kate returned to the house. When she happened to glance back at Robin, Lizzy had materialized from nowhere and was talking earnestly with him. Much as she wished it were otherwise, Kate couldn't deny the pain she felt as she watched them together.

After several weeks Robin was at his wit's end. He couldn't live like this. If Kate wanted him out of her life, he was sorely tempted to leave her to her own devices. Since he had come to know his wife better he had realized that William was wrong; Kate could manage on her own quite well. She didn't need him, didn't want him, and he damn well didn't plan to hang around under those circumstances.

Hoping to dispel some of his gloomy feelings, Robin went off alone one day to visit Dare and Casey. Seeing how happy his friends were had always been uplifting in the past.

"Robin, I was just coming out to see you," Dare said. "You must be a mind reader." They sat on the porch, and Casey soon came out to join them.

"Is there anything special you wanted to see me about?" Robin asked.

Dare could barely contain his exuberance. "Aye,

good news, Robin. Father just returned from Sydney where the magistrates met to select another man to join their ranks. Governor Macquarie insisted he be an emancipist. There was much dissension at first, the argument being that another 'pure merino' should be appointed. But Macquarie won out."

"It's a big step for emancipists," Robin agreed solemnly, "and a long time in coming. Who is the lucky man?"

"Oh, Robin, can't you guess?" Casey asked excitedly.

Robin looked puzzled. "There are many worthy men. It would take me all day to pick one from among them."

"'Tis you, Robin! Governor Macquarie picked you to be our new magistrate."

"I—'tis unlikely the governor would pick me," Robin contended, stunned.

"'Tis neither unlikely nor unusual that Macquarie would want the best man for the job. You'll receive official notice soon and likely have to go to Sydney for confirmation, but I wanted to be the first to tell you," Dare said. He and Casey were both beaming from ear to ear, and when Robin merely scowled, they looked at one another in bewilderment.

"What is it, Robin? Aren't you happy about the appointment? It presents a wonderful opportunity for ex-convicts to gain status and become farmers and businessmen in their own right."

"It—it's a promising breakthrough for all emancipists," Robin said slowly, "and it's not that

I'm ungrateful for the honor. It's just that—well—the way Kate and I are these days, there are very few things that give me joy."

"I knew you and Kate were having problems," Casey said, "but I had no idea they had grown to such proportions. We're your friends, Robin. Sometimes it helps to talk about it."

Normally Robin wasn't one to take his problems to others, but he abruptly decided this was the one time it could do no harm. Besides, if anyone could make sense out of Kate, it was Casey.

"Aye, perhaps you can help," Robin acknowledged. "Kate hates me. Lord knows I've tried my best, but nothing works."

"Oh, surely you're wrong, Robin," Casey refuted. "She's still upset over her father's death."

"No, 'tis more than that. Kate never wanted to marry. She did so only to please William. I'm an ex-convict, and she treats me like I'm some loathsome creature undeserving of human kindness. She thinks I married her for McKenzie station. We nearly had that problem resolved when William died. Kate blames me for that, too."

"Surely not!" Dare said, stunned. "How could you be involved in William's death? The man had been near death for weeks."

"I kept her from going to her father the night he died," Robin explained tersely. "I know 'tis guilt she's feeling but I can't convince her of it."

"How in the world could you keep her from her father?" Casey exclaimed, puzzled.

"I—we—it was late at night—" Robin flushed, unable to continue.

"I think I understand," Dare said astutely. "You were making love, and now Kate blames you for keeping her from her duty."

"Exactly. I can't get through to her now. She's shut me out completely. We're like strangers when we chance to meet. Which isn't often," he said bitterly.

"You deserve better than that, Robin!" Casey cried, so angry at Kate she felt obligated to do something. "Would it help if I talked with her?"

At first Robin was skeptical, wanting to refuse the offer out of hand. But the longer he thought about it, the better it sounded. If Casey could talk some sense into Kate, he'd be eternally grateful.

"It couldn't hurt," Robin allowed hopefully. "Truth to tell, I'm at the end of my tether. I cannot live like this. If Kate insists on continuing like this, I have no choice but to leave. It's what she wants anyway."

"I'll call on Kate tomorrow," Casey promised.

Kate had taken over the bookkeeping, since Robin spent so much time with the convict laborers and rarely found a spare moment to give to the accounts. Robin had never asked, but she had been spending time in the office and took over the chore without being prompted. Normally she worked on the books daily until noon and sometimes after lunch. That was what she was doing when Casey Penrod came to call.

"Shall we sit in the parlor?" Kate asked when Lizzy showed Casey into the small office.

"No, this is just fine," Casey replied, seating herself in one of the comfortable chairs across the desk from Kate. The parlor wasn't private enough for what she wanted to say.

"This is a surprise, Casey. Wasn't Robin just out to see you and Dare yesterday?"

"I'm not here to see Robin," Casey said slowly. "Sometimes a woman needs another woman to talk to."

Kate looked perplexed. Were Casey and Dare having problems? Kate considered herself the last person in the world to give marital advice. "I'll be glad to help in any way I can."

Now it was Casey's turn to look perplexed. "I'm not talking about myself."

"Oh," Kate said dully. "You've been talking to Robin. What has he been telling you?"

"Only that you're both terribly unhappy and it's tearing him apart."

"Robin and I should never have married," Kate said grimly. "We have nothing in common and certainly don't love one another. He's an exconvict who took advantage of my father's kindness to gain a rich farm for himself. It mattered little who he had to hurt to get what he wanted."

"You're not talking about the Robin I know."

"Perhaps the Robin you know and the one I married are two different men," Kate said bitterly.

"I doubt that. Robin would never hurt the woman he loves."

Kate laughed harshly. "Love? Robin doesn't love me. You of all people should know that."

173

"Do you still believe that Robin loves me?"

"'Tis the truth. He knew he could never have you, so he settled for me and McKenzie station."

"I see a lot of myself in you, Kate. I was as stubborn as you are, but thank God Dare made me see that we belonged together. You have been married such a short time you don't even know what Robin is like. You're being unfair and unjust in your condemnation. I'm afraid you've pushed Robin too far, and one day soon you'll wake up and find him gone."

"You're a fine one to give advice, Casey," Kate charged. "You stole Dare from Cousin Mercy and were carrying on with him while he was still married. You can't deny that Brandon was conceived while Mercy and Dare were still husband and wife. And if that isn't enough, you murdered a man in England."

Casey was crushed. She had no idea Kate held such strong feelings against her. She had thought they had gotten past that stage in their friendship.

The moment Casey's face crumpled Kate was sorry for her harsh words. She would have snatched them back had it been possible. "I'm sorry, Casey, that was cruel of me."

"No, Kate, I'm the one who's sorry, sorry that you feel this way about me. One day I want you to know the whole truth about me, Dare, and Mercy. But not today. You're not ready to hear it yet, and speaking ill of the dead doesn't sit well with me. I hope when I do tell you you'll better understand about me and Dare and forgive us for any wrong,

174

imagined or otherwise, we committed against Mercy. Let's put that aside—'tis Robin I've come about. Are you willing to spend the rest of your life alone? Think about it. I suppose you don't even care that Robin was appointed magistrate by Governor Macquarie.''

Kate was stunned. "I—I had no idea."

A short time later Casey left, feeling that she had accomplished nothing.

Kate gave Casey's words considerable thought. She was still mulling them over when Robin returned to the house that evening in time for supper. He took his seat opposite her, looking extremely handsome in buff pants and a white shirt casually open at the neck. Kate felt a thrill of apprehension when his eyes sought hers across the table. She wasn't untruthful enough to deny the attraction that existed between them, nor was she oblivious to the fact that Robin Fletcher was more man than she'd ever known or was likely to know again.

It was for that very reason she feared him. He stole her reason, her wits, and everything that made her Kate McKenzie. He replaced it with the need to feel his arms around her, caressing her, possessing her with a hard, driving urgency that made her forget anything else existed but the pleasure she found with him. He was Satan, out to steal her soul, and she was determined to resist.

Kate didn't want a man who loved another woman.

"You look exceptionally lovely tonight," Robin

said when the silence grew oppressive.

"I—thank you. Are you home early for a special reason?"

"Aye, I go to Sydney tomorrow and I wanted to tell you good-bye."

"How long will you be gone?"

Robin shrugged. "A week or two." He looked at her sharply. "Was Casey here today?"

Kate nodded. "Why didn't you tell me you'd been appointed magistrate?"

"Would it have interested you?" His voice was laced with contempt, making Kate aware of just how badly she had hurt him.

"It's quite an honor," Kate hedged. "You should be pleased."

"Oh, I am. That's why I'm going to Sydney tomorrow. I received word that Governor Macquarie wants to confer the honor on me personally. Would you like to come along?"

"I—no, I don't think so. Someone should stay behind to carry on." She wanted to say yes so badly, the words nearly choked her.

A mocking smile curved Robin's lips. Evidently Casey's visit had done little to change Kate's attitude. She was still being stubborn and unbending. "As you wish. I might be gone longer than I expect if Macquarie requires my services immediately."

"I understand."

"Dare mentioned that hordes of settlers, their families, sheep, and household goods are already streaming over the Blue Mountains in high wagons. The road is still rough, hewn by hand from the sides of mountains by convict labor, but the settlers seem undaunted. 'Tis said the land is vast on the other side, and I've even heard tell gold has been found during the construction of the road. Of course it all belongs to the government. They are calling the settlement on the other side Bathurst."

Kate found this all interesting. It was difficult to imagine the vastness of Australia from the fifty-by-one-hundred-fifty-mile strip that now comprised New South Wales. "Sounds like a wonderful opportunity for those seeking a new life."

"Aye," Robin agreed wistfully. There seemed little more to say, so he fell silent. Suddenly he looked up. "Kate, what else did Casey say?"

Kate's face hardened. "Though it's none of her business, she said I was being foolish where you are concerned. That I was driving you away."

"She's right. I want a wife, Kate, a flesh and blood wife, not some statue who mouths polite nothings. You can be the wife I want you to be if you'd unbend a little and meet me halfway."

"You want to make me into a clinging vine, at your beck and call any hour of the night or day," she charged hotly.

"No, but I sure as hell would like to see a little warmth!"

He was growing angry now. Whenever they got within shouting distance the air exploded around them. Kate leaped to her feet, her violet eyes aflame, her body rigid with anger. God, she was magnificent! thought Robin.

"I can't be the woman you want me to be. I can't be like Casey. I don't even want to be like her."

"You couldn't be like Casey if you wanted to!"

Robin spat. "Casey is warm and loving and a wife in every sense of the word." His words only incensed Kate. "You're nothing but a spoiled child in a woman's body. The only time you've given an inch is when you're in my arms, and those times are few and far between."

"And not likely to happen again," Kate declared.

"I wouldn't count on that," Robin grated out. "I've acted the gentleman long enough. I want my wife and, dammit, I'm going to have her. Only a fool or an idiot would allow things to get out of hand the way they have. I'm not made of stone. I've suppressed my feelings long enough."

Kate froze. Never had she seen Robin this way. "What are you going to do?"

He was beside her before the words left her lips. "I'm going to make love to you. I'd hate for you to forget me while I'm gone."

"No!"

His mouth was grim, his expression bleak as he swept Kate into his arms and bounded up the stairs two at a time. "Yes!"

This wasn't the way he wanted to make love to his wife. It was meant to be beautiful, an experience to be shared and savored. The only excuse he had was that he wanted Kate desperately. Desperately enough to take her no matter how long and loud she protested. He knew that once he lavished her pouting mouth with kisses and caressed the silken length of her body she would turn wanton in his arms, enjoying their loving as much as he did. The guilt and recriminations would follow. But tonight was his, and he fully intended to love his wife until she was too exhausted to protest.

Once inside Kate's room he set her on her feet, his fingers working at the fastenings of her dress with grim determination.

"Robin, don't do this."

"I want to love you, Kate. I—I need you." It was an admission he didn't stop to analyze.

"If you need a woman, Lizzy is more than willing."

"I don't want Lizzy. I could have had Lizzy long ago. 'Tis you I want, Kate, only you. As long as I'm in this house, you'll be a wife to me."

His words stunned her. "You'd take me even if I'm unwilling?"

"You won't be unwilling long."

Rudely he shoved her gaping bodice over her arms, then yanked it, along with her skirt, past her hips. When it pooled around her feet, he lifted her out of the circle of material. Her petticoats were next to go, then her chemise, stockings, and shoes. When she was completely nude he grunted in approval, lifted her high in his arms, and tossed her onto the bed. She bounced once, then settled down. But not for long. She was on her knees and ready to flee in a moment. But Robin made short work of her escape as he flung himself atop her, pinning her to the bed. The wild inferno that raged inside of him seemed to sweep over her. She did not want him, she hated his touch . . . and still, it was as if he had set fire to her blood.

"Get off me, you're—"

The words died in her throat as Robin's mouth came down on hers. Kate cried out, lifting her hand against him in fury. She smacked his cheek, the mark of her fingers burning brightly on his skin. He caught her hand before it could do further damage and grasped the other, pinning them both above her head as he continued to plunder her mouth. He kissed her and kissed her, and the tempest thundered through her veins. His heat became a part of her. She could no longer fight. Then suddenly the savagery of his assault slackened, and Kate could feel the anger drain from him as he released her arms.

"Love me, Kate, for God's sake and mine, love me."

Kate could feel him against her, the hot, hard length of him. Their legs were entangled, his still clad, hers bare; his muscled chest teased her bare breasts, her mound was pressed against the rigid length of his powerful erection. His erotic words released some long-pent-up demon in Kate as she sobbed once, then began tearing frantically at his clothes.

"Damn you, Robin Fletcher!" she swore, then shuddered as his lips found her nipple and took the whole of it into his mouth. He filled her with fire and rage and a need so desperate it nearly consumed her.

He was naked now, his body pressing against hers, surrounding her, devouring her with his hunger. The bold proof of his desire was a live brand between them, hard and unyielding, eager to claim what was his. He caught her legs, spread them apart, then slid his mouth downward to nip lightly at her inner thighs, rising higher, higher, until he found the tender, succulent flesh at their apex. His mouth was hot, demanding, unrelenting. Her body trembled, she gasped and arched more fully into his intimate caress. The feeling was so good and so delicious that it was nearly unbearable. Instead of stopping him she twisted and turned to open herself more fully to him.

To her horror she barely considered the intimacy between them. Oh, no. She wanted his wet, encompassing hunger, yearned for the sensations building inside her—needed them! She convulsed and cried out, having reached the peak of ecstasy in mindless surrender. Again and again she exploded, and felt the molten liquid flowing inside her, and was bathed once again in little spasms of delight.

When she opened her eyes, she met Robin's triumphant gaze and realized how easily he had breached the barriers guarding her emotions. "Bastard!" she hissed.

"Wife!" he taunted as he slid up her body and thrust into her, bringing a gasp of dismay from Kate's kiss-swollen lips. Then it began all over again. The slow building of liquid heat as he moved in her, against her—thrusting, withdrawing, so deeply he touched her soul. "Wife," he repeated over and over. "You're mine, Kate, don't ever forget it. We may never be together like this again, but you'll always remember this night."

"Robin!"

"Aye, love," Robin panted in response. "Give to me, Kate, don't hold back. For this one time give yourself fully to me."

His impassioned words brought Kate to the edge, and when she toppled over into an abyss of lights and fire and profound splendor, Robin was beside her, cradling her in his arms until she floated back to earth. Stunned by the violence of his own climax, Robin spared a brief moment to analyze his emotions. What he discovered surprised him. He looked down at Kate, seeing that she had fallen almost immediately asleep, and an overwhelming tenderness welled up in him.

"I think I love you, Kate McKenzie," he whispered to the sleeping woman. "And if you would give us half a chance, you'd find that you could love me too. But I fear 'tis too late for us, love; much too late."

Once more before daylight Kate found herself the recipient of Robin's ardor. He loved her so thoroughly, with such utter tenderness and caring, Kate was moved as she had never been before. She held nothing back from him, and hated him for making her need him so desperately. When she awoke the next morning, he was gone. He had left for Sydney just as he promised, and Kate felt curiously bereft. No longer did she have the comfort of knowing he was here if she needed him, that she had only to ask and he'd come to her aid.

Two weeks passed with no sign of Robin returning any time soon. After another week he sent a note saying he'd be delayed several more weeks, that his duties prevented him from returning. By now Kate had a good grasp of what needed to be done on the farm and was supervising the shearing. Robin had left a "ticket of leave" man named Riley Kent in charge. Kent was a good worker whose intimidating size and strength kept the other convicts in line. He was a man Robin felt he could trust. According to Robin's instructions, Dare showed up often to make certain everything was running smoothly and that Kate wanted for nothing.

Though Kate gave the impression that she was doing well in Robin's prolonged absence, the truth was that she missed her husband dreadfully. Having to decide on every little issue was a chore that took every waking hour. She began to appreciate all that Robin had accomplished to keep the farm profitable. Though there were many things she couldn't forgive Robin for, his management of McKenzie station wasn't one of them.

At the end of six weeks Robin returned home. Kate watched from the parlor window as he rode into the yard. He looked tired, she thought, but so handsome it hurt to look at him. Lizzy must have thought so too, for she squealed delightedly when she caught sight of him. Kate frowned as Robin smiled at something Lizzy said and she beamed up at him in response. Kate was still frowning when Robin found her in the parlor a few minutes later.

She didn't even miss me, Robin thought as his eyes slid hungrily over Kate. He wanted to sweep her into his arms, tell her how much he'd missed her, and make love to her until she screamed for mercy. He did none of those things, merely waited silently for Kate to make the first move.

"Hello, Robin."

Robin's face fell. Is that all she could say after six weeks? "Hello, Kate. You look well."

Kate suppressed the sudden urge to fly into Robin's arms, to kiss the lines away around his eyes and melt against him in total surrender. Instead she said, "You look tired."

"Being a magistrate is more demanding than I would have imagined." His blue eyes turned smoky as he asked, "Did you miss me?"

Kate turned her head in brisk denial. "I managed quite well, thank you."

Robin's lips tightened. "That's not what I asked. I know you're a capable woman. Answer my question, dammit!"

"Don't swear at me, Robin," Kate said quietly. "If you want me to admit that I need you, I fear you'll have to wait a long time to hear that."

"I recall a night six weeks ago when you needed me."

Kate flushed. "Can't you forget that you forced a response from me? You're a virile, passionate man, Robin, and I learned that I have a weakness where you're concerned."

"A weakness? Is that what you call it?"

"Of course; what else could it be?"

"If you don't know, then far be it from me to force my opinion or my unwanted attentions on you. I want one honest answer from you before I tell you what I have decided. Had I received a warmer welcome, this wouldn't have been necessary."

"What are you talking about?"

Wild Land, Wild Love

"Are you pregnant, Kate? Has our loving resulted in a child?"

Kate was stunned. Truth to tell, she hadn't considered the possibility. She never was regular regarding her woman's time, and being late a few days had never worried her before. Her answer was as truthful as she could make it.

"To my knowledge I am not carrying your child."

A flash of something—disappointment?—contorted Robin's features but was quickly gone. "Then I see no reason to delay telling you of my decision. I'm certain it will come as a relief to you."

Kate stiffened. Hadn't Casey warned her what was coming?

"I'm leaving, Kate. Governor Macquarie needs a magistrate in the new city of Bathurst and he's asked me to fill the post."

Chapter Ten

Kate went still. "You're going to Bathurst?"

"It's what you wanted, isn't it? To be left alone to manage your own property without me around to remind you that we're married? Your wish is about to be granted, love. I wish you happiness in your cold bed."

Of course it was what she wanted, Kate tried to tell herself. She never wanted a husband.

"While in Sydney I signed papers making McKenzie station solely your own property. Governor Macquarie has granted me several thousand acres surrounding the town of Bathurst, and I'll soon own one of the richest sheep stations west of the Blue Mountains. If you want a divorce, you'll have to petition Governor Macquarie yourself."

Kate was stunned. She had never thought Robin would go so far as to leave her. And judging from his words, he never intended to return. "I—I wish you luck, Robin," she stammered. It was such a tense moment, she could think of nothing else to say. Pride would not allow her to beg him to stay.

Actually, Robin had been expecting more than that. He knew Kate would never beg him to remain—it wasn't in her nature. But the least she could do was show a little remorse. If not remorse, she could pretend a little and say she'd miss him. Robin grunted sourly, knowing how unlikely *that* was to happen.

"How soon are you leaving?"

"In a few days. I'll be driving a herd of sheep across the mountains and need to purchase them first. There's a party leaving next week, and I hope to be joining them."

Not once did he ask her to join him, Kate thought bitterly. Now where did that ridiculous thought come from?

"I hired a new station boss," Robin said. "He'll arrive before I leave. Jack Dent just recently arrived in New South Wales lacking the capital to buy land. He seems like a good man, though I can't vouch for his character. No matter," he said with mocking humor, "experience taught me you are perfectly capable of putting the man in his place should the need arise."

If that remark was meant to be an insult, Kate ignored the barb. "I'll get along just fine without you," she insisted stubbornly.

"Aye, I know that, else I'd not leave. If you would excuse me, I've business to attend to." He spun around and walked away.

"Robin!"

He paused but did not turn, his body expectant, his face hopeful. "Aye?"

"I—thank you—for everything."

"Does that include making a woman of you?"

"Think what you want, you will anyway."

His body held under rigid control, Robin continued on his way.

The following days were the most difficult of Kate's life. Robin came and went, saying little, asking for nothing as he prepared for his journey across the mountains. He bought sheep from Dare and several other people willing to sell and soon had assembled a sizable herd to take with him. He also outfitted several wagons with building supplies, staples, and everything else needed for a lengthy stay. He had no difficulty finding men to drive the wagons, for there were settlers aplenty going west to claim a portion of the vast lands beyond the Blue Mountains. Kate watched his preparations with considerable interest and a certain amount of trepidation.

Saying she wanted to be alone and actually being alone were two entirely different situations. Strangely enough, she had grown accustomed to having Robin around, though she'd not admit it to anyone, especially Robin. And when she thought of the way he made her feel when he made love to her, she nearly swallowed her pride and begged him to stay. Or to take her with him. Though Kate had known no other man's touch, she instinctively knew that Robin was a wonderful lover. When he caressed and kissed her, she felt loved and cherished even though it was all a lie. She reckoned Robin was the kind of man who made every woman he touched feel wanted and special. Fortunately, or unfortunately, however one wanted to look at it, she wasn't buying any of it. All he'd ever wanted was Casey Penrod and McKenzie station.

But Robin gave McKenzie station back to you, a little voice whispered. *Only when he had something better with which to replace it,* that same voice taunted.

The night before Robin was to leave, he went to Kate's room to bid her good-bye. He was polite, remote, and cool. Kate was stunned by the change in him. Had she done that to him?

"Good-bye, Kate. I wish you only the best. I never wanted to hurt you. I knew from the beginning our marriage would never work, but I wanted to please William."

"I—I want you to have half the flock," Kate offered lamely. She wanted to say more, much more, but the time for words was long past.

"No, Kate, they're yours, I have no need of them. I have my salary, the money I saved, and the profit from the thirty acres I sold. There is nothing more I need." His probing gaze disclaimed his words. His eyes told her he'd not leave if she'd ask him to stay. It was too late.

"How many settlers are in the party you're traveling with?" Kate asked. For some unexplained reason she didn't want him to leave just yet.

"There are forty families and a large number of convict laborers and "ticket of leave" men. Some of the families include emancipists."

"Do I know any of the families?"

Robin hesitated for several tense moments, shrugged, then said, "The Lynches are going. Fenton Lynch plans on opening a mercantile in Bathurst. Though his store in Parramatta is immensely profitable, there is a great need for a mercantile in Bathurst. He's a wise man to realize that greater wealth awaits in the vast lands west of the Blue Mountains. He's not the only businessman pulling up stakes to serve the needs of colonists and increase his own wealth."

Kate heard nothing past the family's name. "The Lynches? Serena's father? Is Serena joining them?"

"Aye to all those questions. I believe Serena is among the settlers going to Bathurst."

"I—see," Kate said slowly. So Serena was to have Robin after all. Kate had learned from Casey that Serena had been furious when she heard Robin and Kate had been married. According to Casey, Serena was planning on marrying Robin. "Do you plan on marrying Serena if I decide to divorce you?"

Robin's hands clenched at his sides. "I have no plans to that effect. If you decide to dissolve our marriage, that is your affair. I told you before it must come from you. Serena is—a friend. It shouldn't matter to you if we decide to renew our *friendship*. I already have one wife, I don't want another."

But that won't stop you from taking other women to your bed, Kate thought but did not say. Why should it matter to her? If she wanted Robin, she wouldn't let him leave like this. "I have no intention of obtaining a divorce," she finally said.

Robin shrugged expansively. "Then I'll expect you to conduct your life circumspectly. If you take a lover, I hope I never *ever* hear about it."

"What about you? Will you remain celibate? Somehow I doubt it."

"It will take one helluva woman to replace you," Robin said earnestly.

Kate didn't know what to make of Robin's answer, so she said nothing.

"If you have problems you can't solve, Dare has promised to help," Robin explained. "If"—he paused, sending her a searching look—"I need to return for any reason, send word to me. May I kiss you good-bye?"

They were standing several feet apart, facing one another. When Robin reached for her, she went willingly into his arms. This kiss, she thought grimly, might have to last her a lifetime, so she put heart and soul into it. The moment their lips met, Robin knew it had been a mistake to press for this final offering. He tasted her lips, the sweetness of her response, the soft giving of her body, and knew if he didn't break it off immediately he'd never leave. He pulled away, only to have Kate drag his lips back to hers. He groaned, a sound more despair than pleasure. Was she doing this merely to torment him, or was her body actually conveying her innermost feelings? Too late—too late—

"Good-bye, Kate. I—I'll keep in touch."

"Robin . . ."

"If I don't leave now, love, I'll not be responsible for my actions. I'd like nothing better than to give you a proper good-bye, but I don't think you'd want that."

"Don't tell me what I want or don't want, Robin Fletcher!" Kate exploded. The air around them crackled and the inevitable current that flowed between suddenly churned into violent motion.

"Why is it I'm good enough to make love with but not good enough to be your husband?"

"Can't we forget questions tonight and just concentrate on saying good-bye?"

"Then a proper good-bye it is," Robin said grimly as he rent her nightgown from neck to hem and tossed it aside. "You might hate me afterward but you certainly won't forget me."

Stripping off his clothes, he carried her to the bed and made love to her violently, tenderly, erotically, using hands, lips, and mouth to bring her to climax again and again. Not one tiny inch of skin was neglected as he plied himself diligently and without restraint, containing his own eruption until he had brought her to the peak and pushed her over time after time. Kate was wildly responsive, panting, clawing, using her mouth to bring

Robin the ultimate pleasure. When it was finally over they both lay exhausted and spent.

Kate's eyes were closed, basking in the rosy aftermath of total satiation. Robin crouched over her, waiting—waiting expectantly for words he knew would never come. He rose slowly, sadly, glancing down at Kate one last time before flinging on his clothes. Her eyes still closed, too spent to speak and nearly half asleep, Kate didn't hear Robin leave and close the door behind him. When she finally found the energy to speak, it was to an empty room.

"Don't leave, Robin. Don't ever leave me. I need you."

When no answer was forthcoming she slowly opened her eyes. Robin was gone. Leaping from the bed, she ran to his room, unconcerned that she was as nude as the day she was born. The room was empty. Running through the house calling his name, Kate began to suspect he had decided not to wait till morning but had already left. Suddenly the sound of pounding hooves caught her attention and she ran to the window. But it was too late. Robin was already too far away to hear her voice when she called out to him. She was alone now, and it was her own fault for sending Robin away.

Kate faced the following days and weeks with appalling apathy. McKenzie station ran smoothly, Dent was working out well, and Dare was doing his part by stopping by weekly to check on her. Sometimes he came alone, and sometimes Casey and the children accompanied him. Dare was unfailingly polite, but Casey's open condemnation was more than Kate could bear. Kate finally realized she didn't want Casey for an enemy. Whatever had happened between Casey, Dare, and Mercy was no concern of Kate's. Kate realized she should have been mature enough to judge Casey on her own merits and not from heresy or Ronald Potter's biased opinion. When she attempted to mend fences with the beautiful redhead, Casey was decidedly cool. It saddened Kate, but she could not blame Casey for being leery of a woman who had avoided her friendship.

Though the trip across the Blue Mountains should have taken no longer than ten days, Kate had heard nothing from Robin. One day Ronald Potter showed up at her door, and since she was lonely, Kate invited him in for a glass of lemonade.

"I thought you could use some company, Kate," Potter said. His knowing smile caused Kate a moment's apprehension, but then she chided herself for being foolish. "If I were your husband I'd never leave you alone. You're far too fetching to ignore. But then I'd not have another woman waiting to take your place."

"What! What do you mean?"

"Why, 'tis common knowledge, my dear, that your husband and Serena Lynch have renewed their friendship and are traveling together to Bathurst."

"That's not true!" Kate refuted hotly. "Serena is traveling with her family."

"Is that what Robin told you? 'Tis true the Lynches are among the settlers crossing the mountains, but I doubt not they've heard of your—er—estrangement, and are encouraging Serena to renew Robin's acquaintance. Divorce is not impossible here in New South Wales, and now that Robin is magistrate he's considered a good catch by more than one eager parent."

"What are you talking about?" Kate cried, distraught. "There's been no talk of divorce. Robin is still my husband."

"You forget, Kate, servants talk and news travels, even out here on the Hawkesbury. 'Tis common knowledge that you and your husband have separated."

"Lizzy," Kate said tightly, determined to have a talk with the girl. She was far too free with her tongue.

"No, matter," Potter said smugly. "I'm here to lend a hand with whatever you need done. If it's a divorce you seek, then I certainly know the right people to grant you one without fuss or bother. Just say the word and 'tis done. You never gave me a chance to court you properly before you married that convict."

Abruptly, Kate stood up. "Perhaps you should go, Ronald. I'm not very good company today."

"Will you consider my offer? I do want to help in any way I can. Ridding you of Robin Fletcher will be a pleasure."

"You're a master of deceit, aren't you, Lieutenant?"

Kate whirled, surprised to see Casey standing in the doorway. Evidently she had heard Potter's last sentence.

Potter smiled coldly. "I'm no longer a lieutenant, Mrs. Penrod, as you well know. You never did get to know me well enough to judge me."

"I know you only too well, Lieutenant Potter, much to my sorrow."

Kate listened to the exchange with growing curiosity. "I think you should leave, Ronald," Kate repeated.

"If you insist," Potter said as he sent Casey a hostile glare. "Don't listen to anything Casey Penrod tells you, she's always been a liar and a wh—"

"That's enough, Ronald!" Kate warned sternly. "Please remember that you're a guest in my house, just like Casey."

"That man appalls me," Casey shuddered after he'd gone. "I can't stand the sight of him."

"He seems pleasant enough," Kate remarked.

"You don't know him, Kate. He took me from the Penrods and made me a servant in his house, then tried to rape me. He held me prisoner for weeks until Dare arranged for my freedom."

"Dare arranged for your freedom? How did he do that?"

"It's a long story, one I don't have time for right now. I came to see if you've heard from Robin."

"No, I've heard nothing," Kate admitted. "I—I really don't expect to."

"Are you sorry he left, Kate?"

"Perhaps," Kate hedged. "I miss him more than I imagined."

"I could say I told you so, Kate, but I won't. Why don't you go to him?" Casey suggested. "It's not too late."

"Is Serena in Bathurst?"

"I—yes, she and her parents crossed the mountains with the same group Robin is traveling with."

"I doubt that Robin wants me now that he has Serena," Kate said, her lower lip trembling. "I may have been a fool, but I'll not sacrifice my pride and beg him to take me back when he no longer wants me."

"You don't know that," Casey charged. "It's clear to me that Robin loves you."

"If he loved me he wouldn't have left me."

"Did you offer to go along?"

"I—no, but that's no excuse."

"I thought I was stubborn, but you're much worse. Both of you are obstinate, and neither of you realize that you love one another. What will it take to convince you that you and Robin belong together?"

"I don't know," Kate mused slowly. "It would help if I knew Robin no longer loved you, or that he wasn't taking advantage of Serena's presence in Bathurst."

"Robin may have loved me once, or thought he did, but that's no longer true. You won't know for sure unless you go to Bathurst."

"Never!"

Exasperated, Casey sighed and changed the subject. "I strongly suspect this is a decision you'll have to come to on your own. I do want to leave you with a piece of advice, though. Don't let Lieutenant Potter near you. The man is dangerous. I wouldn't lie to you about something so serious."

Casey departed soon afterward, leaving Kate with much to consider.

Robin stood at the crest of the mountain and gazed down at the lovely bowl-shaped plain below. Until the party had reached this point, it had been a steady uphill climb over difficult terrain—and some of the most spectacular scenery Robin had ever seen. Driving sheep over the rough-hewn track was an enormous task, but the pioneers who followed the surveyors over the Blue Mountains were a hardy lot. All along the track, convict laborers still worked on the roadbed, and some of the territory Robin traveled over had yet to be carved out of the mountain.

They had forded streams, breached chasms, and avoided canyons, but danger still lurked in the rough terrain leading down to the new settlement of Bathurst. Robin had lost several sheep during the first five days of the crossing, but he wasn't the only one. Almost all the settlers had lost something of value, many their household belongings that plunged down deep ravines. But fortunately, no life had yet been sacrificed.

Blue mist shrouded the bush and lush forest surrounding him, and Robin glanced back at the lumbering wagons following in his wake. The forest was dense with mountain ash, eucalyptus, snow gum, black wattle, grass trees, gray mangrove, and others he couldn't identify. In addition, the profuse array of flowers nearly dazzled the eye. Orchids abounded everywhere, in a variety of colors and species, and the wild call of birds provided a constant serenade. Brilliant parrots, cockatoos, and birds of paradise flew from tree to tree, and every so often a kangaroo with a joey in its pouch, wallaby, or kiwi burst forth from the bush. It was a world Robin had never seen before, and he looked his fill. The only thing missing was having Kate here to enjoy it with him.

"Have you ever seen anything like it, Robin?"

Startled from his reverie, Robin whirled to find Serena standing at his elbow. "It is rather awesome, isn't it?"

"We'll be starting down soon. In a day or two we'll be in Bathurst. I don't mind telling you," Serena admitted coyly, "that when Papa announced we were moving to Bathurst I was terribly upset. Until I learned you were going along. The rumor is that you've left your wife. Is that true?"

"I've been appointed magistrate of Bathurst, Serena, you know that," Robin said patiently. "Kate can't just up and leave McKenzie station at a moment's notice."

"Then she'll be following later?" Serena probed.

"I—didn't say that," Robin said evasively.

Serena smirked. "Rumor further has it that you're contemplating divorce, that you only married that spinster because her father wished it and promised you McKenzie station as a reward."

"Dammit, Serena, stop listening to gossip mongers!" When he found out who started that rumor he'd wring the man's neck—or woman's.

"Are you denying it?"

"Perhaps you'd best leave," Robin said tightly. "The wagons are already starting down the mountainside. Shouldn't you be with your parents?"

"They're not worried; they know I'm with you. Besides, it's such a lovely day I think I'll walk along with you."

"Suit yourself." Robin shrugged, turning his attention back to the pioneers.

Two of the huge wagons had already begun the arduous trip down the track with several more in line to follow. Robin's wagons, driven by the men he hired, were ready to roll. The Lynch wagon was near the rear. Robin had decided to remain behind to help with the sheep, for they were the most important commodity next to human lives.

One by one the wagons negotiated the winding trail, avoiding a deep chasm that loomed to the right of the track. At times it seemed that the wagons clung perilously to the side of the mountain, so steep and dangerous was the trail, and Robin held his breath each time a wagon veered close to the edge of the chasm. Ten wagons had made it safely, including his own, when the Lynch wagon began its descent. All seemed well until one of the bullocks hitched to the team misstepped and went down. Robin held his breath as the clumsy bullock struggled to right itself. He seemed to be gaining solid ground when his rear hoof loosened a clod of dirt at the edge of the ravine and sent an avalanche of dirt and debris sliding down the mountainside.

Robin watched in horror as the remaining bullocks were pulled into the chasm, dragging the Lynch wagon with it. Serena screamed. The sound released his frozen limbs, and he dashed down the track, ignoring tree limbs that slapped against his face and tore at his clothing. By the time he reached the spot where the Lynches had plunged down the ravine, Robin's chest was on fire, his legs trembling. Peering over the edge, he saw the smashed wagon lying on its side, furniture and goods littering the entire distance down the hill.

By now several other men joined Robin. They peered over the edge, shaking their heads.

"Bring me a rope!" Robin bellowed. "Quickly."

"You're not going down there, are you?" one of the men asked. His name was Fred Deal and he was bringing his family to settle in Bathurst.

"They might still be alive," Robin said when someone handed him a rope. He tied it around his waist while another of the men secured the other end to a stout tree.

"'Tis unlikely anyone lived through that," scoffed Deal.

Serena arrived, her eyes fearful, her face white. She appeared to be in shock, and one of the women took her in hand, offering words of comfort. Serena shrugged off the woman's attempts to comfort her and rushed to Robin, pleading, "Help them, Robin, please help them."

If Robin had any doubt before about descending into the dangerous ravine, Serena's pleas galvanized him into action. Inch by painful inch he lowered himself into the chasm. Footholds were precious rarities, and his hands were raw and bleeding as he sought and found the strength to continue. At times the incline was so steep he dangled helplessly from the rope. He looked up once and saw Serena's white face peering down at him, anxious and frightened. It lent him the courage necessary to complete the task he set for himself. Words of encouragement drifted down from above, but Robin was too involved in staying alive to acknowledge them.

Then suddenly his feet touched solid ground. His legs nearly gave way beneath him as he stood and removed the rope from his waist so he could move around freely. He approached the wrecked wagon with trepidation, common sense telling him no one could live through such devastation. He was right. He found Dora Lynch's body almost immediately, lying beneath the wreck. It took a little longer to find Fenton Lynch's body. He had been thrown clear of the wagon and was lying some distance away, his neck broken. None of the animals had survived. Robin signaled to the men above, and Serena's high-pitched scream told him she understood. Someone lowered a shovel, and Robin set to work burying the bodies. As for the goods in the wagon, most had been smashed to smithereens. He managed to salvage a trunk of clothing belonging to Serena, money, and a few personal items, which he sent up attached to the rope. It seemed like hours before Robin had completed his grisly task and was pulled out of the ravine.

He ascended to an eerie silence. It was the first loss of life during their crossing, and the Lynches had been well-liked. Their loss would be felt by many of the settlers. Serena was left virtually alone in a strange place with no one to protect or shelter her. Of course there were offers aplenty to provide shelter for the lovely young woman, most of them from men, but Serena turned them all down. Besides, most of the wives weren't too happy about having so beautiful and tempting a young woman in their household. It was from Robin that Serena sought succor and comfort, and Robin didn't think twice about offering it.

He had known Serena a long time, had respected her parents, and if he hadn't met Kate he would have married Serena. He felt obligated as magistrate and friend to take Serena under his wing, never considering the gossip that was bound to follow. Even if he did realize the scandal, he still would have accepted responsibility for Serena.

Two days later the pioneers rumbled into Bathurst, a settlement with scattered buildings surrounded by sheep and cattle stations of pioneers who followed the surveyors and claimed the land. Already a market, dry goods store, and cattle auction were doing business, and a government house and police station were being constructed by convict labor.

By the time they reached Bathurst, Serena had finally emerged from shock over her parents' sudden and violent death. She was wan and pale and clung to Robin as if her very life depended on him. He was her lifeline in this strange new settlement. When Robin suggested she return to Parramatta, she adamantly refused.

"There is nothing in Parramatta for me, Robin. What few relatives I have are in England, and I have no desire to return. I left when I was a small child and remember little of my land of birth."

"What will you do, Serena?" Robin asked gently.

"There is money in the bank in Parramatta. I'm not penniless, you know. But I need time to think."

"What about marriage? Surely there is someone . . ."

"Someone . . ." Serena repeated wistfully. "No, no one I'd want to spend the rest of my life with. Perhaps one day—" She looked at Robin hopefully. "Can't I just stay with you until I decide?"

"There's bound to be talk," Robin reminded her, unhappy over the developing situation but unable to change it.

"I don't care," Serena said stubbornly. "I don't trust anyone but you. You saw how those men looked at me." Unfortunately, Robin knew exactly what most men were thinking when they looked at Serena. "Besides, their wives don't want me." Robin had to agree. "Please let me stay with you. I won't be any trouble, I promise. I can cook and clean and—"

"Serena, that won't be necessary. Of course you can stay with me. Do you think I'd turn you out? Perhaps you'll find a man you could love and marry. It's the best thing you could do."

Wild Land, Wild Love

"I've already found that man, Robin, and he's already married," Serena said earnestly.

Robin flushed. "There will be no more talk like that, Serena. I *am* married, and that's all I'm going to say on the subject."

The subject is not closed, Robin Fletcher, Serena thought to herself. *You may be married, but your wife is too far away to claim your love. If I have my way, I'll be more a wife to you than she ever was.*

Chapter Eleven

Kate bitterly resisted the idea of seeking a divorce. Somehow the thought of cutting herself off completely and irrevocably from Robin was repugnant to her. To make matters worse, Ronald Potter did not give up, urging her on each of his frequent visits to seek a divorce. He was very vocal in denouncing Robin's desertion and vowed that Kate was too good for an ex-convict. Even Dr. Proctor was openly condemning of Robin's defection and expressed doubt about Kate's marriage. Though everyone, except perhaps for "pure merinos," applauded Robin's rise to magistrate, most felt he should have taken his new bride with him to Bathurst. When news filtered back to Parramatta that the Lynches had been killed in an accident and Serena was openly living with Robin, Kate became an object of pity.

Kate first heard of the arrangement from Potter, who had hurried out to convey the news the moment he heard it. It was delivered with so much malice, the blow was devastating to Kate.

"I—I don't believe it," she said, thoroughly shaken. But wasn't it exactly what she had feared and expected all along?

"I have it on good authority, Kate, that several families offered Serena shelter. She turned them all down in favor of Robin's more—er—titillating offer. They are living together now in the cabin Robin built. They say he is building a grand house on his land, and the cabin is only a temporary shelter."

"You're very knowledgeable on what transpires in Bathurst," Kate contended.

"Since the road has been completed, 'tis only four days from Parramatta to Bathurst. People come and go freely and news travels fast."

Robin had been gone two months, and already Bathurst had the makings of a thriving city. It was becoming obvious that the richest sheep and cattle stations in New South Wales would lie over the mountains. A constant stream of people were arriving in Bathurst, and Robin found himself busy dispensing justice and making decisions that affected the lives of all who now lived in the city and those that would follow. With the completion of police headquarters, Governor Macquarie dispatched policemen to keep order.

Kate didn't want to think that Robin and Serena were living openly together, but she had no reason to doubt Ronald. Casey and Dare scoffed at the gossip, insisting that Robin had more sense than to do something so outrageous. Even Roy Penrod, who had been a frequent visitor of late, expressed outrage over the gossip mongers and advised Kate to ignore them until she learned first-hand what was going on in Bathurst concerning her husband.

A budding romance was blossoming between Roy and Maude, and Kate couldn't have been happier about it. The older man had seemed so lonely, and Maude was an unfortunate woman who had been transported for a minor crime. When Roy confided that he was trying to get Maude's sentence remitted, Kate was genuinely pleased. Of course she'd lose a wonderful cook, but it was of little importance compared to the happiness of two people she was fond of.

Kate was astounded and angered the day Ronald Potter showed up with a petition of divorce. He had taken the liberty of having the papers prepared in Sydney and presented them with a flourish for her signature.

Kate's mouth worked wordlessly. When she finally found her voice it was loud and condemning. "How dare you! You had no right to go behind my back like this."

"Kate, forgive me," Potter said obsequiously. "I truly thought this was what you wanted. You're still young and beautiful. Why should you be denied the comfort of a man's arms while your husband chooses to dishonor his marriage vows? I want to marry you. Have I ever done anything to cause you a moment's grief? I know Casey Penrod constantly belittles me, but she is hardly the kind of woman one should trust."

"No, you have been nothing but helpful," Kate admitted. "I—know all about Casey and I don't want to hear any more from you about her character. I'll make my own decisions. But I can't possibly divorce Robin until I speak with him, or at least judge for myself whether or not he is—is involved with Serena."

"But gossip—"

"—is often false."

"If I didn't know better I'd swear you love that scoundrel," Potter said shrewdly.

Kate flushed. "How I feel about Robin is no concern of yours, Ronald."

"I think it is, Kate. I've never asked another woman to be my wife."

"I'm already married."

"I'm aware of that. You won't be married for long if you'll sign these divorce papers."

"I'm sorry, Ronald, I'm not ready for that yet."

"Take your time, Kate, I'll just leave them here with you. Let me know when you're ready and I'll take them to Sydney for you. Or," he said, his eyes narrowing slyly, "I'll take you to Bathurst myself. Once you learn the truth, you'll sign the papers readily enough."

After Potter left, Kate spent hours just staring at the divorce petition. Vaguely she wondered if it was what Robin wanted. What he'd expected of her after he left. But, dammit, why should she do what

Robin wanted? Why should she give him free rein to marry Serena? It stung to know that once he no longer needed McKenzie station he had left her without a backward glance or thought. True, the farm now belonged to her, but somehow ownership of McKenzie station brought her little comfort. No matter that it was what she had wanted all along. No matter that she was dependent on no one but herself. Her life was her own to do with as she pleased, and despite her father's misgivings, she was managing quite well.

But Robin is gone, a little voice nagged.

Robin had another woman on whom to lavish his love.

Robin neither needed nor wanted her. Why couldn't she forget him? Why couldn't she seem to get her life in order and go on without him?

Because somehow he's made his way into your heart and refuses to be dislodged. The voice inside her head was becoming quite loud and persistent.

Kate stared so long at the divorce papers, they became blurred and unreal. She blinked, but when she opened her eyes they were still there, reminding her of Robin's sins. Not that she was entirely guiltless. She had sent him away, and when she'd tried to call him back it was too late.

I'll take you to Bathurst myself. Suddenly Ronald Potter's words were like a lamp illuminating her brain. OF COURSE! Once she saw Robin in person she could come to grips with her feelings and lay to rest nasty gossip. Kate didn't know whether or not to believe that Robin was living with Serena, but if she didn't go to Bathurst she'd never forgive herself.

Vividly she recalled their last night together, the tender way in which he'd made love to her. He was bold, passionate, wild, a consummate lover; he brought a splendor to her life she'd never imagined. Since Robin had put McKenzie station in her name, she'd begun to doubt her own conviction that Robin had talked her father into demanding their marriage. Had she wronged him all along? Had her guilt over being in Robin's bed when William died caused her to deny the love she was beginning to feel for him? It was a thought that needed exploring.

Kate did a lot of thinking in the following days. The decision she arrived at wasn't an easy one. It demanded she try to save her marriage, if it wasn't already too late. To do that she had to go to Bathurst and confront Robin in person.

Once her mind was made up, Kate wasted little time. When Ronald Potter came to visit a few days later, she took him up on his offer to take her to Bathurst. Potter, more than a little startled, readily agreed.

"I'll provide the wagon and supplies," he said. "We'll leave in three days; does that suit you?"

"Perfectly," Kate replied eagerly.

"Dress warm, Kate. It may be only fall down here, but the mountains can be bitter this time of year. Winter is just around the corner. I only hope we can still get through."

"We have to," Kate said, lifting her chin in grim

determination. "Just promise me one thing."

"Anything, Kate."

"Don't tell anyone I'm going with you to Bathurst. Especially not the Penrods. They'll want to send someone along to protect me, and I see no need to trouble them."

"What will they think when they find you gone?"

"I'll tell Dent, the station boss, that I'm going to Sydney for a few days."

Potter swallowed a secret smile. Kate's request played right into his hands. He didn't want any of her friends to talk her out of traveling with him, for he had nefarious plans in mind for Kate. He intended to seduce her on the trail and make sure her husband knew about it. Once Kate's divorce was granted, he would marry her and beat her into submission. She was too damn independent and willful for his liking. A beating or two would make her meek and pliable. That's where Fletcher had made his mistake, Potter reflected. He should have pounded some sense into Kate. But, more important, Potter would own McKenzie station. Potter had heard through the grapevine that Fletcher had placed McKenzie station solely in Kate's name, and once Potter married her, he'd have a sheep station he could be proud of, possibly one of the richest this side of the Blue Mountains.

Kate hummed happily as she rode beside Ronald Potter. They had started out at first light and were well into the foothills below the Blue Mountains. The high wagon was bulky and awkward, but the bullocks pulled steadily, with seemingly little effort. The fall colors were spectacular, and Kate was entranced with the ever-changing panorama. As they climbed higher it grew colder, but not uncomfortably cold. Thus far they had encountered no snow. And since little rain had fallen during the summer and fall, the track was dry, though impossibly rutted.

They stopped for lunch beneath a huge eucalyptus, and Kate munched on the cold fare provided by Potter as she laughed at the antics of a koala in a nearby tree. When Potter told her to watch for snakes, she nearly jumped into his lap.

"Snakes?" she squeaked.

"There are many poisonous varieties in Australia, including cobra, krait, adder, and rattler. Then there are the python and mamba. Though chances are they are hibernating now and will cause us little distress."

Kate drew in a ragged breath. "Thank God for that."

They continued on till dark descended on the land and Potter pulled the wagon a short distance into the forest where they could not be seen from the track.

"Must we stray so far from the road?" Kate asked uneasily.

"I'd prefer we not be seen," Potter said smoothly. "Bushrangers are everywhere."

"Even in the mountains?"

"Especially in the mountains. There is no longer danger of becoming lost if one follows the track, and since gold has been found by convict laborers building the road, bushrangers have swarmed into the area."

"I didn't realize crossing was so dangerous." Kate shuddered.

"Don't worry, my dear, I'll protect you," Potter boasted, making a great show of drawing his pistol. "But for safety's sake we should sleep close together."

Kate was decidedly uneasy but didn't object when Potter placed their bedrolls side by side. She was grateful to him for deserting his farm and taking her to Bathurst. Surely Casey was wrong about him, she decided, for Ronald Potter was a wonderful friend.

Potter didn't press Kate that night. He wanted her to become accustomed to his presence before seducing her. Tomorrow, he thought gleefully. Tomorrow night he'd take the arrogant little bitch and show her how a real man treated his woman.

Robin had found little time to call his own since arriving at Bathurst, but whatever moments he could spare were devoted to thoughts of Kate. How she'd looked when he left her, all rosy and spent from his loving. Her lips swollen from his kisses and her eyes glazed with passion. Then he recalled how he had waited in vain for her to ask him to remain with her and how bitter he had felt when she'd allowed him to leave without a word, not even a good-bye. He had no clear notion why he spent so many fruitless hours tormenting himself by thinking about her and wondering how she fared. He had received messages from Dare saying all was well at McKenzie station, but he'd heard nothing directly from Kate.

It stung to think Kate was managing so well without him.

Bloody hell, he missed her!

When had he realized he loved the stubborn minx? he wondered bleakly.

Almost immediately. He wouldn't have married her otherwise. And in his heart he felt Kate cared for him. Never had he been more wrong, he thought glumly. Kate enjoyed his lovemaking, but that was as far as it went. Any man would do.

Robin's land grant was so vast, it boggled the mind. Already his sheep were grazing on the hillsides, and he had hopes of increasing the flock. He had forty convict laborers working for him and had built a two-room cabin for himself until he could construct a larger, permanent home. Robin found it difficult to believe how his fortunes had improved since he'd been pardoned. He owed most of his good luck to Governor Macquarie, who was a firm believer in equality for emancipists and "pure merinos" alike. The free and rich often called Macquarie a despot, and Robin supposed he was, for slowly but surely Macquarie was doing away with inequalities. Under his rule the convicts and poor of Australia were being given the opportunity to increase their fortunes and rise in importance in the colony.

Robin appreciated his good fortune and all he had accomplished, but it would have held more meaning if Kate were here to share it. He often thought he should have been more forceful and insisted she accompany him, but living with a woman and wanting her so desperately when she hated the sight of him gave him little pleasure.

It was irksome to Robin that Serena was still with him, still clinging to him as if he were her lifeline. Her parents' deaths had affected her greatly, but after two months she ought to have been ready to resume her life. The problem was that Serena wanted Robin and would settle for no one else. She shared the small cabin with Robin, cooking and cleaning, but mostly presenting a temptation that daily became more difficult to resist. She flaunted her body shamelessly before him, batted her long lashes, and blatantly offered to replace his wife who was in truth no wife at all. Until now Robin had politely refused her advances, even going so far as to try to interest her in other men. He didn't have the heart to turn Serena out—where would she go?—but neither did he want her dependent on him forever.

Robin was exhausted and irritable when he returned that night to his cabin: exhausted from his heavy work load and irritable because he needed his wife. After more than two months, Serena was becoming more and more appealing to him. She was beautiful, he had enjoyed her love-making often enough in the past, and after two months any woman would look good to him.

Serena's eyes lit up when Robin entered the cabin. She had gone to great pains tonight to have a good supper on the table and a cozy fire in the fireplace. It annoyed her greatly that Robin had resisted her seduction this long, and she was determined that tonight was going to be different. She had even managed to find a bottle of French brandy that had been brought across the mountains.

"You look weary," Serena commiserated. "Sit down, supper will be ready directly. I—I even baked a pie," she said, looking up at him coyly through feathery lashes.

"I'm not very hungry," Robin said sourly. "You shouldn't have gone to so much trouble."

"Nothing I do for you is trouble. Would you like a glass of brandy?"

"Brandy? How did you work that miracle?"

"I flirted with the man who owns the market and he sold me a bottle he'd been saving for himself."

"You're incorrigible, Serena," Robin replied, managing a tepid smile.

She poured two glasses of brandy and handed him one. She sipped delicately, but Robin tossed his down in one gulp. She refilled it instantly. Robin stared morosely into the amber liquid, swirling it around his glass and frowning.

"Why so glum?" Serena asked, moving to sit at his feet.

"'Tis nothing for you to be concerned over."

"Everything having to do with you concerns me. I think I know what's bothering you, Robin, and I want to help. Make love to me. I want you, Robin. Everyone thinks we're lovers anyway, so why are you resisting?"

"We've been over this before, Serena," Robin said patiently. "Lord knows I'm no saint, but

you're wasting your time. I'm married. Find someone who can return your love. You're a beautiful,
passionate woman, Serena. Any man would be
glad to have you for his wife."

"Perhaps you'll change your mind when you
read the message that came for you today."

"Message?" Robin perked up immediately. Had
Kate finally decided to communicate with him?
"Where is it? Who brought it?"

"It's from Dare Penrod." Robin's face fell as he
reached for the folded sheet of paper. "It was
delivered by a man who just arrived from Parramatta."

"Did you read it?" Robin asked sharply.

"No, of course not," Serena lied blandly. "What
does it say?"

Hastily Robin read the message, cursed roundly,
then read it again. When he finished he flung it
across the room. "Bloody hell!"

Serena leaped up to retrieve it, briefly scanned
the contents, and sent Robin a searching look.
"What does this mean?"

"It means, Serena, that my wife has petitioned
the governor for a divorce. Dare learned of it from
a friend who keeps records at Government House.
Not only that but she has been keeping company
with Ronald Potter. We all know the man is the
worst kind of bastard."

"I think he's rather charming," Serena said,
adding fuel to the fire. "Evidently Kate thinks so
too. I can't imagine what Ronald wants with a
dried-up old spinster like Kate McKenzie."

Wild Land, Wild Love

"Kate is not dried up," Robin said indignantly, "and she certainly is not old."

"What does it matter, Robin? You're going to be a free man soon. That means you can marry again, and you know how much I want you." Deliberately she poured another glass of brandy. "Have another drink, love, forget about Kate. She's not worth the anguish she's put you through."

"You're right, Serena, the hell with Kate! What do I want with that cold bitch when I have a warm, loving woman right here in my house?"

God, it hurt, Robin thought as the scalding brandy slid down his throat. The bottle was nearly empty now, but still Robin was sober enough to think, to feel the terrible pain of betrayal, of knowing that the woman he loved cared so little for him. Yes, dammit, he *did* love Kate. Argumentative, exasperating, bitter woman that she was, he loved her. LOVED HER!

"Robin, are you all right?"

"I'm fine, Serena, just fine. For the first time in weeks I know exactly where I stand with Kate."

Serena's face grew radiant. Dare's letter had accomplished in minutes what she'd been trying to do for the past two months. "You still have me, Robin," she said, planting herself in his lap. "I still want you. I've never stopped wanting you. Kiss me, Robin, please kiss me."

Robin searched Serena's face for the space of a heartbeat, then slowly lowered his head. Her lips were soft and moist and opened eagerly beneath his, her hot little tongue searching the inner

219

reaches of his mouth. He tasted deliciously of brandy, and Serena squirmed excitedly in his lap. Her little hands found their way inside his shirt and her fingers squeezed his flat male nipples. Mindlessly she kneaded and caressed the taut muscles of his chest. Her hands moved downward across his stomach, slipping inside his pants to massage the stiff length of his erection.

"You want me, Robin," Serena crowed delightedly.

Robin stared down at her, at her profusion of blond hair falling over his arm, almost to the floor. He gazed into the hot centers of her blue eyes, at the rise and fall of her round breasts as her excitement grew, and couldn't deny her words. The mood he was in, any woman would do.

Holding her close, Robin rose unsteadily from the chair, supper all but forgotten, and staggered the short distance to the bed. He was drunker than he'd thought. He sprawled ungracefully on the bed, nearly dropping Serena in the process, but she ended up on top of him, exactly where she wanted to be. She tore at his clothes, receiving little help from Robin yet managing to remove his shirt and boots, then reaching up to pull down his pants.

"Dammit, Robin, help me!"

He lifted his hips but offered no other encouragement. "I need a drink."

"You've had enough," Serena panted, finally working his pants over his hips.

"Bloody hell, Serena, give me a drink!"

Muttering crossly, Serena flung herself off the

bed and poured the last of the brandy from the bottle into Robin's glass. "Here," she said sourly. "I just hope you're sober enough to know what you're doing." He swallowed the contents in one gulp.

"Get those damn clothes off and I'll demonstrate that I can please you whether drunk or sober. You've had no cause for complaints in the past."

He watched through glazed, narrowed eyes as Serena stripped, thinking that her ample curves would one day turn to fat while Kate's slim figure would remain lithe and supple forever. Once she was nude, Serena posed before Robin with an expectant look on her face, waiting for his expansive words of praise for her lush body. When none were forthcoming, she sighed in exasperation and lowered herself atop him, every luscious curve molded to his hard length.

The brandy hit Robin's empty stomach like a jolt of lightning. Normally he drank little, but after downing the first glass the others had come easily. Especially after reading Dare's letter. All he wanted to do now was forget, forget he loved an exasperating woman named Kate. Forget he had married the little termagant and allowed her to work her way under his skin. Forget that she was so eager to rid herself of him that she'd applied for a divorce. He had no idea how drunk or how utterly exhausted he was until he tried to carry Serena to bed.

Robin knew he was being undressed, but offered little help, merely lying there as if he were a spectator to his own seduction. Not even Serena's nude loveliness seemed to affect his brain, though it sure as hell affected his body. What man could look on a sensual woman like Serena and not rise to the occasion? Robin groaned when Serena lay atop him, but his mind was so fuzzy, he could barely concentrate on what was happening. When Serena began kissing and caressing him, he tried to respond with kisses and caresses of his own, but his drink-drugged brain had suddenly shut down. He was tired—so tired. . . . His eyes closed, and when Serena straddled him she was astounded and angered to find he had fallen asleep.

"No! Not now! Damn you, Robin, wake up! I've waited a long time for this. How dare you fall asleep on me?"

Lost in the void of profound slumber, Robin heard neither her pleas nor the curses that followed.

Finally, in a fit of rage Serena flounced down beside Robin on the bed and snuggled as close to him as she could get. Normally she slept on a cot across the room, but tonight she'd be damned if she'd give up the pleasure of sleeping beside Robin. Besides, if he woke up she wanted to be where he could easily find her.

Chapter Twelve

Kate awakened early the next morning. Despite her misgivings about Ronald Potter, he had behaved like a perfect gentleman. She found it difficult to believe he was the same man Casey had warned her about. Even Robin had portrayed Ronald as a villain. Except for taking it upon himself to obtain a petition of divorce in her name, he had done nothing to earn her distrust.

Potter cast a sly glance at Kate, admiring the enticing sweep of her breasts as she smoothed out her wrinkled skirt. Tonight, he thought with keen anticipation. Tonight he'd show the haughty Kate McKenzie that he was a man capable of taming a woman like her.

Since it was so late in the fall, they were virtually

alone on the road. A sudden snowstorm at this time of year could prove fatal, but Kate's luck held. The day was cold but clear and the track not too difficult to negotiate. They stopped at dark, and Potter couldn't wait to place their bedrolls side by side and begin the seduction he had planned so carefully. When he leaped down from the wagon, his foot landed in a wombat hole and the ground came up to meet him. Kate was immediately at his side, helping him to rise.

"Are you hurt?"

"I don't—oh, dammit—my ankle. I twisted my bloody ankle." The pain was so intense, Potter's plans for Kate went flying out the window. They ate cold fare that night and were soon abed, Potter's moans as much from thwarted frustration as they were from pain. He wanted Kate so damn bad he wasn't certain which hurt worse, his loins or his ankle.

The next day Potter awoke feeling much better. The swelling in his ankle was nearly gone, and he knew this was his last chance to seduce Kate before reaching Bathurst the next day. He vowed that nothing, absolutely nothing, would stop him tonight.

As the day progressed, anticipation and confidence made Potter exceptionally boastful as he regaled Kate with stories of the Rum Corps and the nefarious deeds of their members. When they stopped for the night, he pulled so deep into the forest that Kate feared they might become lost.

"Is it necessary to pull so far off the track?" she asked nervously. "We've met only one or two other wagons since we left Parramatta. And for some reason you've allowed them to pass us while you hung back to take the rear."

"No sense hurrying, Kate. The weather is good and I enjoy your company. I wanted us to get to know one another better during this trip. We'll be in Bathurst tomorrow, and I pray you'll not be hurt by what you learn there. I tried to warn you about what to expect in regard to your husband and Serena Lynch, but you were quite adamant about making this journey. The least you can do is enjoy it."

"It has been pleasant, Ronald," Kate admitted grudgingly, "but going to Bathurst is something I had to do. I know you understand or you wouldn't have offered to take me."

"Of course, Kate, I understand perfectly. And I applaud your desire to confront your husband openly. After you see for yourself what Robin Fletcher is capable of, you'll no longer have any doubt about marrying me."

Kate sighed but said nothing. The closer she got to Bathurst, the more nervous she became. What if the gossip were true? What would she do if she found Serena happily ensconced in Robin's house and in his heart? Why had it taken her so long to discover that she felt more than physical attraction for Robin? He had told her that he cared for her; why couldn't she accept that? Marriages were built on less, and Robin was more man than most she had met. It wasn't until after he had left that Kate realized how much she really cared for Robin. Enough to go to him now and tell him she had made a mistake, that she was willing to try again if he was agreeable. Please, Lord, let him be agreeable, she silently prayed.

Potter shot a wallaby that strayed into their camp that evening and they feasted royally. When it came time to retire, Kate lay down on her bedroll fully clothed, as was her habit since they left Parramatta. She fell asleep almost immediately. The dreams that followed were vividly realistic and so erotic that her body ached and throbbed with a hunger only Robin could appease. And in Kate's dreams Robin was there, beside her, loving her, while she begged him to come inside her, to fill her with himself, to bring her to shuddering completion.

His hands undressed her; he was so excited he ripped her bodice in the process. He caressed her breasts, sucking on her nipples so vigorously Kate cried out in pain. Why was he hurting her? His nails dug into her thighs as his caresses grew violent. When he began biting her breasts, Kate was jolted out of her sleep into cold, cruel reality. It wasn't Robin straining over her, it was Ronald Potter! Her bodice was open, her skirt and petticoat shoved up around her waist. Potter was staring down at her, his face contorted with cruel pleasure as he fumbled with the front of his pants.

Kate surged against him, trying to escape what she perceived as a vicious intent to rape her. "What are you doing?"

"Ah, Kate," Potter panted, "don't deny you like what I'm doing, I know better. Your face is glazed with passion. Nothing Fletcher did to you will compare with what I'm going to do. Once we marry I'll do it to you every night. Perhaps I'll beat you first. The pain is so exquisite you'll come to enjoy it as a prelude to lovemaking."

"You call this lovemaking?" Kate screamed, pounding him on the back, shoulders, wherever she could reach. "I call it an abomination! Why? Why did you have to do this? I had come to trust you. I know now that Casey was right about you. I should have heeded her warning."

"You little bitch, hold still," Potter gasped, attempting but failing to pry her legs apart. "If you're thinking your husband will mind me sampling your wares, you're mistaken. Everyone knows he's getting all the loving he needs from that bold little piece in Bathurst."

Kate was at the end of her endurance. Potter's superior strength was taking its toll, pounding her into unwilling submission. As a last resort, she opened her mouth and screamed, a long, loud wail that would have roused the dead as well as the living had anyone been within hearing distance.

Potter finally succeeded in freeing himself from his pants and was prodding ruthlessly between Kate's legs. Kate's resistance was heroic, her strength born of rage and disbelief. How naïve she must have seemed to Potter when she'd innocently asked him to take her to Bathurst. Had he planned to ravish her from the beginning?

"Why don't you relax and enjoy it?" Potter advised between ragged breaths. "If you quit struggling I'll make it good for you. So good you won't care if Fletcher beds every woman in Australia."

"Conceited pig!" Kate bit out grimly as she renewed her efforts to dislodge Potter. But it was useless. The man was simply too strong and had caught her unawares while she slept. Nothing seemed to deter him, not her struggles, her curses, or her screams.

Kate knew that all was lost when he finally succeeded in wrenching her legs apart. She gritted her teeth, closed her eyes, and waited for his violent entrance into her resisting body.

"That's better," Potter grunted as he slid between her legs and felt her resistance ebb. Though she still fought a losing battle, he knew he had subdued her into compliance and crowed jubilantly. "You're wise to submit. If I wanted, I could kill you and leave you in the forest where no one would ever find your body. But I want you for my wife. Combined, Potter station and McKenzie station will be the richest and largest monopoly in New South Wales."

Potter flexed his hips, ready to ram himself forward, and Kate's mind went blank, divorcing herself from what was happening to her.

It took several minutes for Kate to come out of the trance in which she had voluntarily transported herself and realize that Potter's weight was no longer pressing down on her. She opened her eyes and blinked. The moon was a round bright ball in the sky, but its brilliance was blotted out by a huge figure standing above her. His muscled legs were planted far apart, almost as if they had taken root. His bulging arms were akimbo, his massive chest heaving as if he'd run a great distance. In one gigantic hand he held a thick tree branch.

Kate paled. If she had been frightened before, she was terrified now. Who was this giant? Had she traded one rapist for another? Only one thought came to mind. Bushrangers! Potter had mentioned that bushrangers roamed the forest freely since the settlement of Bathurst had been founded. Suddenly the man squatted down beside her, looking at her strangely. But because of the position of the moon behind the man's shoulder, Kate couldn't make out his features. Just as well, she thought grimly as her heart beat a wild tattoo in her chest.

Suddenly she recalled her state of undress and pulled the gaping edges of her bodice together. She shuddered in fear and held her breath as the man reached out toward her bare legs. She dared breathe again when the giant merely flipped her skirts down over her legs.

"Wh—who are you?" Kate asked shakily.

"Did he hurt you?"

That deep booming voice—where had she heard it before? "N . . . no, but he would have if you . . . What did you do to him?" Kate glanced around and saw Potter lying at her feet. "Is he dead?"

"Nay, lass, I just bashed him good. I'll kill him if you want me to."

"Kill him?" Kate echoed dully. Potter certainly deserved death, but killing a man in cold blood didn't appeal to her. "Why would you want to kill him for me? Aren't you a bushranger?" After voicing those words she clamped her mouth tightly shut, fearing she had said too much.

"Don't you recognize me, lass? 'Tis Big John."

Comprehension dawned as Kate recalled the huge man who had saved her once before.

"Big John," Kate repeated slowly. "Yes, I remember. What are you doing here?"

"Same as you, I reckon. I'm goin' to Bathurst. Rumor has it that many opportunities exist in the new settlement, and I'm countin' on no one rememberin' that I'm an escaped convict. Years have passed since I escaped, and the town is so far removed from Sydney that mayhap I can make a new life for myself there."

He held out his hand to her, and Kate grasped it and pulled herself to her feet. "What about—him?" she asked, motioning toward Potter sprawled on the ground.

"I reckon he's out till mornin'. Hop in the wagon and I'll drive us to Bathurst."

"How did you know I was in trouble?" Kate asked. "Did you recognize me right away?"

Big John grinned. "I heard you scream, lass. You got a mighty fine pair of lungs. I didn't recognize you till I squatted down beside you and saw your face. Where's your man?"

"Robin is in Bathurst. Haven't you heard? He was appointed magistrate by Governor Macquarie. I—I was going to join him."

"With a man like Lieutenant Potter? Are you daft, lass? As far as the Rum Corps was concerned, he was one of the worst in the regiment. Just ask Casey, she'll tell you."

"She did tell me." Kate flushed guiltily. "But I chose to ignore her. I thought Ronald Potter was my friend. Thank you, Big John, you probably saved my life."

"Let me help you into the wagon," Big John said, embarrassed by Kate's gratitude.

"Can you drive the wagon in the dark?"

"I know this track by heart," Big John boasted. "Followed the surveyors, I did, and watched the settlers swarm over the mountains. Besides, 'tisn't too far to Bathurst now."

"Should we leave Potter lying there?"

"Aye, he'll come 'round soon enough. My guess is that he'll head back to Parramatta. He'll assume you were taken by bushrangers. Coward that he is, he'll hightail it back and tell everyone you were abducted."

"No one knows that I am with him," Kate admitted sheepishly.

"Then I reckon he'll just keep his mouth shut and see what happens."

Kate dozed off now and then during the rest of the night, trusting Big John to see her safely to Bathurst. When it grew light, they stopped and ate the last of the food Potter had packed for the trip. When they plodded on again, Kate grew thoughtful. "I can't imagine you doing anything serious enough to merit transportation."

A tense pause lengthened into long minutes before Big John replied, "I killed a man, Missus Fletcher."

"You—killed a man?"

"Aye. And I don't regret sendin' the bastard to his reward. He was a lord who lived in a fine, big house. The woman I loved worked as a maid in his home. We were goin' to be married when I had enough money saved to support her. She was a pretty little thing with blond hair and big blue eyes. The lord took a shine to her and raped her. She couldn't live with the shame and confessed to me before she threw herself off London Bridge.''

"I'm sorry, Big John," Kate said sincerely.

They both fell silent, intent upon their own thoughts of what might have been had things worked out differently for each of them.

At mid-morning they drove out of the foothills into the settlement of Bathurst. Kate was awed by the vast loveliness of rolling plains that seemed to go on forever against the dramatic backdrop of the lofty Blue Mountains.

"I'll ask around and find out where Robin lives," Big John said as he reined the bullocks to a halt before one of the stores lining the rutted street. "I'll take you there myself, seein' as how you're not too good at pickin' people to trust." Though gently spoken, his words held a hint of censure.

Serena stretched languorously, smiling when she felt Robin's solid warmth beside her. How she loved waking up curled next to him. Raising to her elbow, she looked her fill at his strong, virile body. His manhood was not as glorious in repose as it had been last night before the brandy put him to sleep. Too late she realized the brandy had been a mistake, but it had succeeded in destroying the barriers that had shut her out of Robin's heart. If Serena didn't know better, she'd swear Robin loved Kate, old maid that she was. The letter from Dare had been the most effective weapon to breach Robin's defenses. Now that his marriage was all but a memory, no obstacle remained to keep Serena from winning the man she wanted.

Rubbing herself against Robin like a satisfied cat, Serena admired the long, muscular length of his legs, the way his taut muscles molded his arms and shoulders, and the promise of his manhood magnificent even as it lay like a sleeping giant between his legs. It wasn't the first time she had viewed Robin like this, but it was the first time since he'd met Kate that she'd been afforded the opportunity. It rankled that she'd been unable to coax Robin into making love to her before he passed out last night. He had left her wanting and unsatisfied, yearning to feel his strength inside her, bringing her to climax in all the wonderful ways she had known in the past.

Unaware that Serena was watching him like a greedy kitten, Robin moaned and flung out an arm. His hand filled with soft, warm woman's flesh and his eyes flew open. He lifted his head and groaned, the pain shooting into his brain like hundreds of stabbing knives. "Bloody hell, what happened?"

"What's wrong?" Serena asked sympathetically.

Despite the knives cutting his brain into little hunks, Robin turned his head, astounded to find Serena lying next to him without a stitch of clothes on. "Serena, what in the hell are you doing in my bed?"

Serena's eyes narrowed slyly as wheels began turning in her head. "Don't you remember?"

"I—bloody hell! I recall nothing beyond that blasted letter from Dare. And the brandy, of course." He moaned again, closing his eyes as if he wanted to find Serena gone when he opened them again. "Why are you in my bed? Where are your clothes?"

Serena rewarded Robin with a blinding smile. "You were wonderful, Robin. You were right when you said you're as good in bed drunk as you are sober."

"I said that?" Robin asked, confused. Surely he'd remember if he'd made love, wouldn't he?

"Your loving left me breathless, just like it always did."

"I—bloody hell! I'm sorry, Serena, this never should have happened. In fact, I'm still not sure it did. Are you certain that we . . ."

"Oh, yes, Robin," Serena said breathlessly. "More than once. Before you fell asleep you promised we would do it again this morning."

Robin groaned and flung his arm over his eyes. "Forget what I said. I was foxed. Leave me alone, Serena, I've got too much to think about. What happened between us last night only complicates matters. I had hopes that Kate and I . . ."

"Forget Kate," Serena urged, caressing the hard length of Robin's broad chest. When she reached his stomach and would have continued downward, he grasped her wrist and flung it aside.

"Christ, Serena, why do you insist on making

this so damn difficult? What time is it?"

"Mid-morning, I imagine," Serena pouted, using her tongue to lick along his neck when Robin kept pushing her hands off various parts of his anatomy.

Somehow Robin had to find the energy to lift himself off the bed, keep his head from splitting open, and discourage Serena, all at the same time.

Kate was quiet when Big John halted the wagon outside the snug little cabin. Beyond the cabin she could see the shell of the fine new house Robin was building. Sheep grazed on nearby hills and plains, and convict laborers were clearing land for planting next spring. All was quiet inside the cabin, and Kate leaped down from the wagon without waiting for Big John to come around and help her. Her heart was beating furiously and her knees shook so badly she wasn't certain she could walk the short distance to the door.

What if Serena were inside? What if Robin didn't want to see her? What if—Lord, there were too many "what ifs" to enumerate. The only way to find out what was going on in Robin's life was by boldly bursting inside the cabin before she lost her nerve.

"Should I wait, Missus Fletcher?" Big John asked, looking somewhat skeptically toward the door. He had a bad feeling about this.

"No," Kate replied confidently. "I'm certain my husband will be glad to see me." Her words sounded hollow to her ears, but bravely she cast aside her trepidation.

"Well, if you're sure," Big John said doubtfully. "I'll just leave the wagon here and walk back to town. It's not far."

"Wait, where will you go?"

"I think I'll just hang around town first to get the lay of the land. If no one recognizes me, I'll ask around for work."

"Come back, Big John, I'm certain Robin can find something for you."

"Aye," Big John answered as he picked up his swag from the wagon bed and walked away.

Kate watched him leave, then turned slowly and approached the door, trying to decide whether or not to knock. She finally decided to try the knob. If the door was unlocked, she'd simply enter without being announced. When the knob turned beneath her hand, Kate drew in a ragged breath and pushed the door open. It was the second worst mistake she'd ever made in her life. The first was coming to Bathurst hoping to find—what? That her husband was living the life of a monk while waiting for her to come to her senses? That he missed her as much as she missed him? How utterly foolish she had been to hope Robin was different from other men. What she found inside that cabin was her worst nightmare come true.

Robin and Serena were still abed, legs and arms entwined, as naked as God made them. But not as innocent. Obviously they had been engaged in more than just idle chatter. Serena was nibbling Robin's neck while Robin held both Serena's hands, guiding them to various parts of his body.

Wild Land, Wild Love

Robin had just about had it with Serena and her persistence. She always was a greedy little baggage, but he had neither the will nor inclination to satisfy her needs. His head hurt like hell, his body was sluggish from overindulgence, and he had no desire to make love to Serena. If indeed he had made love to her last night it was because he was out of his head from drink and crushed by the news in Dare's letter.

Robin wasn't aware that someone was standing in the door until an errant patch of sunlight fell on him. The cabin was small, consisting only of a kitchen and a large room that served as bedroom and sitting room. Focusing his bloodshot eyes on the slim wraith standing in the sunlit opening, Robin attempted to rise from bed, realized he was naked, and grabbed for the sheet.

"Kate!" It was Serena who finally recognized their intruder as the name tumbled unbidden from her lips.

"Bloody hell!" Robin sputtered, shoving Serena rudely from the bed. "What in all that's holy are you doing here, Kate?"

Serena shrieked angrily, snatched a blanket from the bed, and retreated sulkily to her own cot.

Kate gulped back the bile rising in her throat before finding her voice. "Obviously I made a mistake." Her voice quivered shakily, and she would have turned and fled if her pride hadn't demanded she stand her ground.

Wrapping himself in the sheet, Robin rose unsteadily to his feet, shaking his head to clear out the cobwebs. "Kate, it's not what you think. I didn't—" He couldn't continue. Of course he did. Even though he didn't remember it, he had made love to Serena last night. There was nothing he could say to Kate that would explain away the truth. And there was no name Kate could call him that he hadn't already called himself. Damn Serena! Then and there he vowed never to take another drink.

"I'm no fool, Robin. I have two good eyes. My mistake was thinking you'd be glad to see me. I heard the rumors but refused to believe them."

"What rumors, Kate?"

Kate slanted an accusing glare at Serena, who was looking decidedly pleased with herself. "I don't think you need me telling you what everyone in Parramatta is gossiping about. I hope you and Serena will be very happy together." She turned to leave.

"Kate, dammit, don't go. Give me a chance to explain."

Kate paused, chewing on Robin's words. With all her heart she wished Robin could explain away everything she had seen this morning. "It's too late, Robin."

"No, Kate." With surprising speed considering his bursting head, Robin was beside her, his hand staying her. "We need to talk." He whirled toward Serena, who was still sitting on her cot. "Leave us, Serena. Kate and I need to be alone."

"What! Where will I go?"

"How in the hell do I know? Just go! And don't come back any time soon."

"Can I get dressed first?" Serena asked with snide innuendo.

"Get dressed," Robin snarled, sick over the thought of what had happened between them last night and uncaring whether or not he ever saw Serena again. He should have found a home for her weeks ago but he'd been so busy he hadn't given a thought to Serena's future.

Kate and Robin remained as motionless as statues while Serena dressed. They could hear her muttering and cursing beneath her breath, but neither so much as glanced in her direction. It was like a tableau frozen in time. When Serena finally flounced out the door, Robin slammed and locked it behind her. If he had remembered to lock the door last night, Kate might not have found them in bed.

"Sit down, Kate," Robin invited as his hungry eyes devoured her face and figure. She was just as lovely as he remembered.

As Robin's gaze slid over her, Kate felt a languor stealing over her. She felt herself drowning in the pools of his magnetic blue eyes and knew she had to do something fast or she'd be lost forever. Self-preservation forced her into a protective show of anger. "Shouldn't you get dressed?" she asked with a brittle snap in her voice.

"Aye," Robin agreed, "but only if you promise not to leave before we've had a chance to talk."

"You can talk all you want, Robin, but it will do little good," Kate sniffed haughtily. She sat poised on the edge of a chair while Robin retreated to the rear of the room and hastily donned pants and shirt. His sexual magnetism was galvanizing, and it took all Kate's willpower to keep her eyes averted. She could well understand Serena's obsession with Robin, for Kate had experienced the power of his attraction many times in the past. In fact, she still wasn't immune to it.

"I have no idea why I allowed you to talk me into listening to your lame excuses. I expected to find Serena ensconced in your house, but I didn't expect to find you two lounging in bed in the middle of the day. Is she so tempting that you can't keep your hands off her long enough to tend to business?"

"Kate, I don't find Serena tempting at all."

"Do you often take women to bed you don't find tempting?" Kate prompted after an impatient moment.

"I was drunk last night," Robin explained. "If I took Serena to bed, it was the first time."

"What do you mean 'if'?"

"I mean I don't remember what happened last night," Robin said so seriously that Kate almost believed him. "You have some explaining to do yourself."

"What are you talking about?"

"Dare wrote me that you've petitioned the governor for a divorce. I know it's what you wanted, but it still came as a shock."

"How would Dare know that?" Kate asked, suddenly angry at herself for not confiding in Dare and Casey. If she had told them about Ronald acting without her consent in the matter, Dare might never have sent the damaging letter to Robin.

"Dare's friend who works in the records office at Government House told him. I also heard you're seeing a lot of Potter. You have lousy taste if you'd turn to a bastard like Potter in my absence. Has he bedded you yet?"

Red clouds of rage smothered her brain as Kate leaped to her feet and flew at Robin. "How dare you judge me after the way I found you and Serena!"

Robin moved fast despite his pounding head. Grasping her hands, he pulled her close until every inch of their bodies touched. "I don't want Serena, dammit. I haven't wanted her since the first day I set eyes on you."

"You have a strange way of showing it," Kate charged derisively.

"Let me show you in another way," Robin said, his voice low and hoarse.

Slowly his head lowered and his mouth closed over hers. He kissed her thoroughly, ravenously, his lips speaking to her of his need to fully possess her, to enter her and slide deeper and deeper behind the curls of ebony until his body filled her and she cried out with the sheer ecstasy of their wild mating.

He kissed her and kissed her, thrusting his tongue into her mouth, tasting her sweetness, moaning as he grew excited. "Kate—oh, God, Kate, it's been so long."

Kate's face grew red, certain she would suffocate before Robin allowed her to breathe again. Struggling frantically, she finally broke off the kiss. Emotion weakened her voice until it was a mere whisper.

"How dare you touch me after bedding that—that woman!"

Chapter Thirteen

Kate spun around, facing the door. She couldn't bear for Robin to see how deeply his kiss had affected her.

"Dammit, Kate, haven't you heard a word I've said? Is it so difficult to believe I want only you? I can't even recall bedding Serena, for God's sake!"

"I think the little scene I interrupted this morning speaks for itself." Why did it hurt so badly?

"Turn around and face me! I dislike intensely talking to your back."

Kate turned slowly, her violet eyes misty with accusation.

"Why did you come here, Kate?"

"I—I wanted to see for myself if the gossip was true."

"How did you get here? Who brought you?"

"I—" She worried her lower lip, choosing her words carefully. It would do no good to lie; she never had learned the art of telling falsehoods. Besides, sooner or later Robin was bound to learn the truth. "Ronald offered to escort me to Bathurst."

"Before or after you obtained a petition for divorce?"

"I didn't petition for a divorce!" Kate exclaimed hotly. "It—it was all a mistake. Ronald assumed that's what I wanted and took it upon himself to file the petition in my name. It's what you wanted, isn't it?"

"What I wanted! I wanted my wife. I left McKenzie station because I could no longer bear being treated like an outcast by my own wife. I gave you sufficient time to recover from your father's death and come to your senses regarding our marriage. How soon after I left did you take up with Potter?"

"I never 'took up' with Ronald," Kate refuted heatedly. "He was a visitor in my house, nothing more. I—thought he was my friend."

"Thought?" Robin asked sharply. "Has that bloody bastard done anything to hurt you?"

Kate's eyes became hooded. Would Big John tell Robin about Potter's attack on her? Dare she refuse to reveal the extent of Potter's vicious attempt to rape her? The choice was taken from her when Robin grasped her shoulders, demanding roughly, "Tell me what he did to you!"

"Nothing! He did nothing." A strangled sob

burst past her lips. Now that it was out in the open she wanted to break down and cry against Robin's broad shoulder, to be comforted and protected from vile men like Potter. "He—he tried but—but didn't succeed. How could I have trusted someone like him?"

"I'll kill him," Robin said quietly. "Dare should have killed him long ago. He'll not find me so merciful."

"No, Robin, I won't have you jeopardizing your freedom again. He's probably on his way back to Parramatta. Big John said he doubted if Potter would come here after what he tried to do to me."

"Big John? What's he got to do with this? Perhaps you should tell me what happened."

"Ronald offered to bring me to Bathurst and I foolishly accepted his offer. He's always been so friendly and helpful I thought I could trust him. He—wanted me to get a divorce so we could marry. I was angry when he brought the papers for my signature. They're still in the house; I never signed them. Not even when I learned you were living openly with Serena."

Robin let that remark pass. "Go on, what happened next?"

"I left with Ronald, deliberately lying about my destination so Dare and Casey wouldn't become worried. All went well until the third night. I awoke with Ronald trying to—to—oh, God . . . I don't want to talk about it."

"He tried to rape you," Robin said quietly. "What about Big John?"

"Big John was on his way to Bathurst when he heard me scream and came to my defense. He bashed Ronald on the head and brought me to Bathurst himself. Thank God he was camped nearby that night."

"What? Big John is in Bathurst? Doesn't he know how dangerous it is in town for him?"

"He's hoping no one will remember him."

Robin uttered a sharp oath. "How could anyone forget him? I don't want to talk about Big John right now, I want to discuss you. Are you certain Potter didn't . . ."

"He touched me but that's all," Kate assured him. "He said you wouldn't care what he did to me since you had Serena."

"The lying bastard." The words hissed out from between clenched teeth. "Look at me, Kate." With thumb and forefinger he gently lifted her face until their eyes met. "I think there is another reason for your coming to Bathurst. A reason you don't even want to admit to yourself."

"Perhaps," Kate admitted slowly. "But if there was another reason, it disappeared the moment I laid eyes on you and Serena cavorting in bed."

"Can't you forget what you saw? I told you I was too foxed to know what I was doing."

Kate hesitated, unable to forget or forgive those two naked bodies intimately entwined on the bed. "I'm sorry, Robin, the picture of you and Serena is etched on my brain forever. I'll make arrangements immediately for my return to McKenzie station. If you like, I'll sign the divorce petition and send it to Governor Macquarie so you and Serena can marry."

Robin groaned. Was there no way of convincing this obstinate woman that he wanted no one but her? Then suddenly he thought of something that might sway her. If it didn't change her mind it certainly would give her pause. Of course he'd have to swallow his pride and lay bare his soul, leaving himself open for ridicule. But pride no longer mattered when he was on the brink of losing the woman he loved.

"Kate, I don't want a damn divorce. I want my wife. I've always wanted you, only you. I—love you, Kate." There, it was out. Let her laugh if she wanted, but he felt better for saying it.

Kate was stunned. Love her? How could Robin love her when it was Casey he loved? What about Serena? Why was he playing with her heart like this?

"What about Casey?"

"What about her? Casey is Dare's wife. I realized long ago that my infatuation with Casey was hopeless. We're the best of friends, nothing more. Serena was just someone available until I met you. I was friends with her parents. When they were killed in an accident during the crossing to Bathurst, I felt responsible for Serena. She had no one to turn to, no one to look to for protection. Would you have had me abandon her?"

"Serena's parents were killed? I—didn't know," Kate said. "How terrible for her."

"Is that all you can say?" Robin asked, disgruntled. "Does it mean nothing that I love you?"

"I—don't know, Robin. I'm confused. So much has happened the last few days, I don't know what to think. You could be lying."

"I have no reason to lie to you, love." His voice was a seductive purr, his eyes a provocative shade of smoky blue as his arms went around her. "I meant every word. I want you with me always. I want to cherish and protect you. I want to love you—now. I want to be inside you so damn bad I'm nearly bursting with the need."

Those were exactly the same things Kate wanted, but she was afraid, so afraid to open her heart after what she had just witnessed between Robin and Serena. How did she know it wouldn't happen again? If not with Serena, then with another woman? Robin might have good intentions now, but from what she knew of men they were faithless creatures who uttered promises they intended to break at the first opportunity. Besides, how could Robin truly love her after loving a woman like Casey Penrod? "I dislike being judged by the standard set by another woman."

Robin spat out a bitter oath. "You're not going to walk out of my life, Kate, not again, not ever. You're the only woman in my life."

"You're the one who walked away," she reminded him.

"Only after I became desperate. Couldn't you tell I needed you, that I couldn't bear the thought of living in the same house without making love to you?"

The quiet conviction of his words shook the firm ground of her anger. He sounded so sincere, and she wanted to believe him, but—

His arms tightened around her almost painfully as his body reacted violently to her nearness. "Can't you feel how much I want you?" Instinctively Kate looked down to where his swollen manhood pressed against her abdomen. "Not just there, but here." He took her hand and dragged it to his chest. She felt muscle and heat beneath the material of his shirt, firm, strong, and the rapid beating of his heart. Her fingers tried to clench and draw away, but he held them steady. His eyes glowed with a deep and steady fire, and their gaze was so intimate they seemed to sear her skin.

"Can you deny your heart is beating just as rapidly?" His other hand pressed against her left breast, embracing the frantic, erratic thunder of her own heart.

"Stop." What was meant to be a shout was a choked-off whisper. She tried to twist away, to deny she felt the same cravings he did, but her feeble efforts were wasted.

His face filled her vision now, intense with emotion and fierce with demand. His breath heated her face. And his mouth covered hers. His masculine scent filled her nostrils. Never was she more aware of the attraction between them. She closed her eyes and succumbed to the magic he was spinning inside her; an intoxicating swirl of dizzying sensations swept away all thoughts of denial. Then she was floating as he carried her to his bed, the pain of his infidelity already thrust aside as stronger emotions arose inside her to take its place.

"I'll never stop, love. You don't want me to."

She felt her clothes being stripped from her body, roughly, and hastily thrown aside. She felt his hands warming her bare skin, felt his fingers sliding between her legs, forcing them apart until she was open and vulnerable to him.

"Do you know how often I've dreamed of seeing you like this? You're so beautiful, every part of you. I want to see all of you, love, every perfect inch."

Kate's face burned, but she couldn't seem to pull her eyes away from his expressive features as he looked his fill. He remained absolutely motionless so long that Kate thought he had turned to stone. Part of him did. That male part of him that gave her so much pleasure thrust boldly out before him like a granite pillar, hard and thick and throbbing. Kate drew in a ragged breath when she became aware of his expression. He was grinning at her so wickedly, her hands flew down to cover herself.

"Don't," he commanded her. "Don't ever hide yourself from me. I'm your husband; nothing we do in the privacy of our bed is wrong."

Suddenly he was pressing the full weight of his body against her. "I'm sorry, Kate, I can't wait. I promise next time we'll go slow." Then he was thrusting inside her, filling her until she was mindless with pleasure. She groaned his name over and over in incoherent, ragged rasps of sound that had no meaning.

Their mating was fast, furious, their climax bursting upon them with explosive fury. It was several minutes before either of them could speak.

Kate stirred. Robin turned to her and said, "Lie still, love." Then suddenly he was gone, returning a few moments later with a small basin filled with water and a cloth. Ignoring her murmurs of protest, he gently spread her thighs and proceeded to bathe all traces of him from between her legs. Then he quickly cleansed himself and lay back down beside her. "I meant what I said, next time will be better. I apologize for my haste, but it's been so damn long."

Since this morning, Kate thought but did not say. Her scalding thoughts skidded to a halt when Robin slowly lowered his head and kissed her. This time the kiss was slow and lazy and sweet. He spent considerable time exploring the rich contour of her lips with his tongue before sliding inside to continue his examination with maddening thoroughness.

The sweet torture went on endlessly when his lips left hers and found the stiff peaks of her breasts. Then his fingers were sliding between her legs, seeking the moist flesh of her most intimate being. His hands were wonderfully arousing, caressing her, slipping rhythmically inside, tantalizingly, until the pressure built and became a frantic heat that thrummed in her veins like quicksilver. He sucked gently on one sweetly aroused nipple, laving the tight crest with his tongue while his hands stroked the inner lips of her swollen flesh, finding the tiny bud that brought her so much

251

pleasure. Threads of blistering heat shot through her, radiating from where his fingers thrust.

"Robin!"

"Aye, love, you're almost there. Don't hold back, I want to watch your face when it bursts upon you."

The ache of need knotted in her womb. His heat, his scent, his presence engulfed her as she moved restlessly against his questing fingers. Sliding his mouth downward, he sought her moist inner folds, his tongue stroking where his fingers had been just moments ago. It was more than Kate could bear. She stiffened, cried out, and arched again and again into his mouth as wave after wave of incredible heat seared her body. When she opened her eyes, Robin was watching her.

"You're more beautiful now than I've ever seen you." His face was moist with sweat, his eyes glazed from his own need and the restraint he had exerted for her sake.

With a low growl, he raised himself and sank onto her, into her, pressing deep, deeper. Kissing her tenderly, he slowly withdrew his body almost but not quite out of her. Then he eased into her again and again, each impalement deeper, more profoundly moving, until he created a need in Kate she hadn't known existed, especially after her violent climax only moments ago. Then, with cries of joy, each found the splendor they had sought.

Minutes later Robin was jolted rudely from his state of euphoria by the sound of Kate sobbing. Rolling over, he took her in his arms. "I didn't mean to hurt you, love. Was I too rough?"

"You weren't rough at all," Kate hiccupped. "It's just that you've done it again."

"Done what?" What could he have possibly done to bring on such a flood of tears?

"You rob me of my very soul!" The accusation was wrenched from her throat and flung at him like a stinging barrage of pebbles. "When you make love to me I forget everything but how you taste and feel and how wonderful you make *me* feel."

Robin chuckled. "Is that bad?"

"Yes—no—I don't know. I don't like being robbed of my reason. What I dislike even more is being used."

"Used! What the hell are you talking about?"

"You used me to get McKenzie station. And when you no longer needed it you walked out on me. You used me again just now to make me forget what I interrupted today between you and Serena. And worst of all, Robin Fletcher, you tried to make me believe you loved me."

"Women," Robin spat disgustedly. "I'll never understand them. I do love you, Kate. Do you think I could make love to another woman in the same way I make love to you? I've never experienced anything that powerful with another woman." He leaped from bed, dragging on his clothes.

"Where are you going?"

"I should have been about my business hours ago. We'll talk tonight. Somehow I'll make you understand there is no other woman in my life. Get some sleep. I'll find Big John and offer him work if he's still around.''

Kate watched him storm around the small cabin, gathering his clothes and making himself presentable. He didn't bother scraping the blond stubble off his face, but slammed out the door the moment he was dressed.

Sighing wistfully, Kate sank gratefully into the soft mattress. She'd had blessed little sleep the night before, and Robin had exhausted her quite thoroughly. Time enough for decisions when he returned.

When Serena stormed out of the cabin at Robin's request, she had no idea where she would go. She walked into town and wandered aimlessly down the street, oblivious to the hungry stares following her slim figure. Serena was a beautiful, sensual woman; there wasn't a man, married or single, who could look at her without wanting her in his bed. Silas Dodd, the man who owned the market, was one of those men. He knew little about the relationship between Serena and Robin Fletcher other than what he'd heard, but he envied the man. He'd waited all his adult life for a woman such as Serena and lamented the fact that she belonged to another man. He knew that she was still unmarried, and it heartened him somewhat, though it did nothing to stem the tide of desire that swept over him each time Serena came into his store.

Just yesterday Silas let her talk him out of a

bottle of fine brandy, then cursed himself afterward, well aware that it would go down the gullet of her lover. Of average height with a shock of reddish-brown hair that seemed to have a life of its own, Silas Dodd was a likable enough man who had been transported for the crime of insurrection in his native Ireland and recently emancipated. When Bathurst was established as a settlement, he sold his thirty acres, used the money to stock his market, loaded it all on a wagon, and crossed the Blue Mountains, hoping for a better life and equality.

Not only did Silas run the store but he homesteaded a large tract of land several miles to the west and planned on raising cattle as soon as he earned enough money to buy stock. Until funds were available, he lived in the back of his store and served the citizens of Bathurst with his usual good humor and resourcefulness.

When Silas saw Serena wander into his store, his lively brown eyes lit up with pleasure. "Hello, Miss Lynch. How may I help you today?"

Serena looked up at Silas with blank eyes, as if unaware of what she was doing here or why she had come. She only knew that he had always been unfailingly kind to her and was a pleasant man. Handsome, even, in his own rough way. His body was muscular and well-formed, his eyes quickly intelligent, and his features pleasantly aligned.

Silas took note of Serena's vacant stare and became alarmed. "What is it, Miss Lynch? Are you ill?"

"Ill?" Serena repeated dully. "No, not ill, just—just—" Words failed as big round tears slid from the corners of her huge blue eyes. It seemed she had wanted Robin half her life, and just when it looked as if she'd finally won him, his wife arrived to stake her claim. She was sad, angry, and so damn frustrated with thwarted passion that Silas's tender concern set off another paroxysm of tears.

"What is it, Miss Lynch—Serena, you can tell me. Has someone hurt you?" The thought of some lout laying hands on his idol brought out all his protective instincts. "Perhaps you ought to sit down a few moments and compose yourself, away from prying eyes. Come, my back room is just steps away."

In a trance, Serena made no objection when Silas led her behind the curtain to his cramped but neat quarters furnished simply with cot, dresser, table, chair, and hearth where he cooked his plain but nourishing meals. He poured a glass of water from a pitcher and handed it to Serena. While she drank, he hurried back into the store, placed a closed sign in the window, and locked the door. He was back at Serena's side before she finished the water.

"Are you feeling better?" he asked, his brown eyes devouring every aspect of her spectacular figure and face. She looked deliciously tousled, as if she had just recently awakened and thrown her clothes on hurriedly. Her bodice was buttoned unevenly, and Silas gawked at the tempting white mounds pushing above the uneven edges.

Serena sighed. She wouldn't feel better until she found out why Kate had come to Bathurst and what Robin had told her about their relationship. She hoped Kate would think the obvious, that Serena and Robin were lovers, and go back to McKenzie station where she belonged.

"Can I help you in some way?" Silas asked when Serena remained silent and pensive.

Serena studied Silas from between thick lashes the color of ripe gold. He was an attractive man, she mused, though not nearly as handsome as Robin, and seemed very concerned about her. It felt good to have someone fuss over her as if she were someone special. For the past several weeks Robin had all but ignored her.

Silas tried again. "How was the brandy? Did Mr. Fletcher enjoy it?"

Brandy! That damn brandy had destroyed her plans for Robin last night. Just when she'd finally had him ready to make love to her he'd passed out. She sighed again, wondering why Silas was being so kind to her. Did he find her attractive? Did he want her? It was gratifying to know that *someone* wanted her.

"Do you find me attractive, Mr. Dodd?" Serena blurted out. Her strange mood forbade caution and restraint. All her life she'd thrived on adulation. First from her parents and then from her admirers. Her life would be sadly lacking if she suddenly found herself without anyone to admire or praise her.

"Attractive!" Silas sputtered, stunned. "Why,

you're the most beautiful woman I've ever seen! You're a goddess. I envy any man who has the good fortune to claim you."

Suddenly Serena perked up as her agile mind seized upon an audacious idea. Her eyes narrowed slyly and she leaned toward Silas in a provocative manner. She arched her back, batted her long lashes, and smiled beguilingly into his eyes. "Tell me about yourself, Silas."

An hour later Serena sailed from Silas's store. Her step was buoyant, her spirit gay and light-hearted. Her mood had improved dramatically, and she no longer had any doubts about winning Robin. One day soon he would forget Kate forever and make Serena his wife. Silas watched Serena prance down the street, a stunned look on his face. Never in his wildest dreams could he have imagined what had just transpired in his room behind the store. If it was a dream, he hoped he'd never awaken.

The door to the cabin crashed open with a bang, jolting Kate awake. She rubbed her eyes, disoriented and confused. Only when she saw Serena glaring hatefully down at her did she remember where she was and all that had happened since she'd arrived in Bathurst. Frantically she searched the room for Robin, but he was nowhere in sight. She struggled to sit up, feeling strangely lethargic. Serena's eyes settled on Kate's breasts, and with a start Kate realized she was still naked and belatedly pulled the sheet up to her neck.

"Are you still here?" Serena taunted maliciously. "I thought by now Robin would have gotten rid of you. What kind of lies did he tell you about us?"

"As you can see, I'm still here," Kate replied with icy disdain. "What lies are you referring to?"

"Did he try to deny we are lovers?" Serena charged. "You must have believed him, the room reeks of sex. Robin is an insatiable devil. I would have thought he'd be sated after loving me last night and again this morning, but I see I was mistaken. It surprises me that he still had the energy to satisfy you. He did satisfy you, didn't he?" she asked boldly.

"You're lying," Kate hissed. "You'd say anything to take Robin from me. Well, it won't work. I simply don't believe you."

"Don't you? Deep in your heart you know that Robin and I weren't living here like brother and sister all these weeks. Robin loves me, Kate, he always has. He only married you for McKenzie station. He told me so himself. Now he doesn't need you or McKenzie station. And I have enough money of my own to enable Robin to build the richest sheep station this side of the Blue Mountains. Robin feels pity for you but little else."

"Pity! Why would he pity me?"

"You were a lonely spinster when he married you, but at least you had your virginity to commend you. Since you no longer have that, he feels no man will want you once you are divorced. He's too kindhearted to say that to your face, but it's what he is thinking. We've had many a good laugh over you and how you fought the marriage, when all along you both knew he was marrying you only for what you owned.''

Serena was only guessing that Kate had fought the marriage, but the well-aimed barb seemed to hit home. Kate turned white, realizing that Serena would have no way of knowing such things unless Robin had told her. Which meant that everything else Serena had said was true. Too hurt and angry to care, Kate disregarded her nudity and flung herself out of bed. With hurried, jerky motions she gathered up her clothes and began to dress.

"What are you going to do?" Serena asked slyly.

"Get out of here, for one thing."

"What will I tell Robin when he returns?"

"Tell him—tell him—it doesn't matter. I'm going home."

"What about the divorce?"

"Do you know about that, too?"

"Of course," Serena smirked. "Robin tells me everything. We laughed about that also. It's what he wanted all along."

A noise that sounded suspiciously like a sob slipped past Kate's lips. "If Robin wants a divorce he can damn well get it himself, I'll not stop him."

Serena frowned. It wasn't exactly the reaction she'd expected but it would have to do. She hadn't counted on Kate being so obstinate. "I'm sure he will," she said somewhat uncertainly. "Robin wants children of his own one day, and I'm still young enough to give them to him. I may already be increasing. Lord knows, if I'm not it isn't from lack of trying. You know Robin," she snickered, rolling her eyes in a suggestive manner. "He's quite insatiable."

"You're a little bitch, Serena, and I wish Robin joy of you. You deserve one another." Tossing her mane of black hair, Kate stomped from the cabin, slamming the door behind her. She could hear Serena's tinkling laughter echoing behind the closed door.

The wagon still sat in the yard, the bullock still hitched to the leading lines. Kate didn't think twice about hoisting herself up on the seat and setting the bullock into motion. The wagon didn't belong to Robin anyway, so it shouldn't matter to him if she took it. She made but two stops before she started back up into the mountains. One was at the market, where she bought enough food for several days, and the other was at the mercantile, where she purchased a pistol. It was a cumbersome affair with three revolving chambers, but once the storekeeper demonstrated how to load and fire, Kate felt fairly certain she could shoot it. Without a backward glance she guided the bullock onto the track leading to Parramatta.

Darkness was just minutes away when Robin strode briskly from the partially constructed Government House, mounted his horse, and took off at a gallop. There was still much he had to discuss with Kate. Lord, that woman was obstinate, he thought glumly. Not that Robin could blame her after the way she had found him and Serena in bed. He still couldn't believe he'd made love to Serena. The whole thing just didn't seem right to him. He'd been drunk before, but never drunk enough to forget making love. If Kate would forgive him his indiscretion, he vowed to find a home for Serena— even a husband, if need be.

Serena was bent over the fireplace, her face flushed becomingly, humming a merry tune as she cooked supper. "You're home!" she cried, rushing to greet him. She would have kissed him, but Robin brushed her aside.

"Where is Kate?"

"Why should you care?" Serena pouted. "Obviously the woman cares little for you."

"Dammit, Serena, stop playing games! Where is Kate?"

"I don't know," Serena said sullenly. "She left."

"Left? When? Where did she go? What did you say to her?"

"I didn't say a thing!" Serena lied. "She left hours ago. She didn't tell me where she was going."

Storm clouds gathered in Robin's eyes and his face turned to granite. For the first time since knowing Robin, Serena felt real fear. She'd seen his anger directed at others but never at her. "Are you sure Kate said nothing? You'd better not be lying to me, Serena, or I swear I'll beat you to within an inch of your life."

"I'm not lying, I swear! Kate just up and left. I saw her drive the wagon out of the yard. Beyond that I know nothing. What does it matter? You have me. I'll never leave you, Robin."

"That's what I'm afraid of," Robin muttered darkly as he slammed out of the cabin.

Chapter Fourteen

Robin turned the settlement upside down before he accepted the fact that Kate had returned to Parramatta. From what he'd been able to learn, Kate had left alone, driving the wagon herself. Thank God she had had the good sense to purchase food supplies for the trip as well as a handgun with which to protect herself. This he learned from the shopkeepers who had sold her the food and weapon.

Crossing the mountains was treacherous in itself, but what truly terrified Robin was the fact that at this time of year the most vile weather could swoop down from the skies without warning. One consolation was the fact that on horseback he could easily overtake the clumsy wagon pulled by the sluggish bullocks. As much as he wanted to dash off into the mountains immediately, Robin employed his usual good judgment and decided to wait until morning.

Meanwhile, he had encountered Big John, but it was too late. Because of the seriousness of the crime Big John had committed in England, the price on his head had risen to five hundred pounds. Unfortunately, one of the men sent to police the settlement had recognized him. Few men possessed the awesome stature of Big John, and he was quickly surrounded by a dozen men, subdued, and placed in jail until he could be transported back to Sydney to be either sent back to the coal mines or hanged. Since he was one of the most notorious bushrangers, the most Robin could do was promise to use his influence as magistrate and try to get his sentence commuted.

Before he left the bereft man, Robin questioned him closely about Kate and Potter. When Big John revealed to Robin exactly how he had found Kate and Potter, Robin vowed to kill the treacherous viper on sight.

"Don't do nothin' you'll be sorry for, mate," Big John warned. "Freedom is too precious to waste. The only freedom I'll ever see is death. You've earned your appointment as magistrate. Your appointment by Governor Macquarie to a position of responsibility has struck a blow against inequality between the rich and the poor. No one but the 'pure merinos' will win if you kill one of their own. Heed my words, mate, there are other ways to punish a man like Potter."

"Your words make sense, Big John, but I don't

know if I'm strong enough to keep from killing a man who tried to violate my wife in such a violent manner. Nor will I ever forget what he did to Casey."

"If I was free I'd help you look for your missus," Big John offered. "Perhaps—well, who knows, no jail has been able to contain me so far." His huge face suddenly lifted into a grin as big as Australia.

A short time later Robin returned to the cabin, the picture of utter dejection. His shoulders were slumped as if he carried the weight of the world on them, and his eyes were bleak with despair. He fervently prayed he'd be able to convince Kate to return to Bathurst with him once he found her. He'd make other arrangements for Serena despite her protests, for Kate was more important to him than commitment to any other cause. If necessary, he'd spend the rest of his life earning her trust. Kate could deny it all she wanted, but Robin knew she could love him if she gave herself half a chance.

Serena took careful note of Robin's moody silence and wisely held her tongue. She could wait, she decided, gloating over her good fortune in ridding herself of Kate so easily. Now that Kate was gone for good, Serena had all the time in the world to win Robin. She wasn't prepared for his announcement shortly before he retired for the night.

"I'm leaving in the morning. When I return, Kate will be with me. I suggest you make other living arrangements. If not, I'll make them for you when I return."

"Where are you going?" Serena asked, stunned.

Wild Land, Wild Love

"After my wife."

Serena's face grew mottled. "Kate doesn't want you, Robin. Let her go. I'll make you happier than she'll ever make you."

"I don't love you, Serena. I felt a certain responsibility for your safety but I never intended to bed you. You'll have to believe me when I say that it was a terrible mistake and I won't allow it to happen again. You're much too beautiful to waste your time on a married man. Good night, Serena."

"Robin, you don't mean that! You're too proud to want someone who doesn't want you."

"I have good reason to believe Kate loves me."

"Then you're a fool," Serena spat, flouncing off to her own corner of the room. She had said all she was going to say on the subject, but she wasn't going to give up on Robin. She'd bide her time, continue with the plan she had devised to keep Robin from leaving her, and wait and see what happened when he returned.

Time and again Kate cursed the clumsy slow-footed animals pulling the wagon. Why hadn't she taken one of Robin's horses? she asked herself, disgusted with her lack of foresight. If Robin had any thoughts about coming after her, he'd catch up with her easily in one day. That thought brought a harsh laugh from her throat. Why would Robin come after her? He had Serena, he no longer needed McKenzie station, and obviously had made a whole new life for himself in Bathurst, a life separate from her.

Kate camped early that night, having covered

little ground since she had gotten a late start that day. Fortunately, she chose a spot where another wagon carrying a family of emigrants had camped for the night, and they invited her to share their meal. Just knowing she wasn't alone in the vast emptiness of the rugged mountains dispelled some of her fear. Paul and Vera Crocker were appalled to learn Kate was alone, but since they were traveling in the opposite direction, to Bathurst, they could offer only advice about the pitfalls of traveling. Kate thanked them for their concern but assured the kind folks she'd do just fine on her own. The next morning they parted company, and Kate continued east across the mountains while the Crockers descended into the foothills above Bathurst.

At mid-morning the unexpected happened. The wind howled through the towering eucalyptus with bone-chilling ferocity, ushering in the first snowstorm of the season. At first the snow was merely a nuisance, pelting her face and exposed skin with fine grains of wind-driven snow. But within an hour the snow abruptly changed in character, becoming heavy wet flakes that obscured Kate's vision and chilled her to the bone.

She stopped and dug through the bundle of clothes she had brought along to Bathurst and found a pair of warm gloves, which she pulled on immediately. Then she spied the bedroll Big John had thoughtfully thrown in the wagonbed when he rescued her from Potter. Pulling out a blanket, she wrapped it around her shoulders and climbed back onto the driver's seat. Somewhat more comfortable, Kate slapped the reins against the bullocks' broad backs and plodded forward.

Shortly after noon it had grown so dark and the snow so thick that Kate seriously considered stopping. She knew from the previous trip that the track was treacherous in places, literally carved out of the steep mountainside, and one misstep could send her plummeting to her death. She was shivering now; her teeth chattered and her face felt as if it were frozen solid. The bullocks were straining against the traces, slipping and sliding in an effort to gain solid footing.

The thought crossed Kate's mind that she wished Robin *would* come after her. How long did storms last in the mountains? Was this the worst of it or was there more to come? Almost as if in answer to her silent questions, the wind increased in intensity and the snow became a blinding white inferno, nearly suffocating her as it blew into her nose and mouth and stung her eyes. Panic seized her when she realized she could not go on. She could very well die up here in the mountains without anyone ever finding her body. She wouldn't be the first person to perish in the Blue Mountains.

Suddenly the right wheel struck a rut and became mired in a growing mound of drifting snow. The wagon lurched, then shuddered to a halt. Caught unawares, Kate was hurled from the seat like so much baggage, fortunately landing in a clump of bushes instead of being thrown from the opposite side of the wagon, which seemed to hang precariously on the edge of the incline. Several minutes passed while Kate fought to catch her breath and cautiously moved her limbs to check for breaks or sprains. When all her parts seemed in working order, she slowly extracted herself from the bushes in which she had landed. That was when she discovered her toes were so cold she could barely stand.

Tottering back to the wagon, she assessed her chances of setting it back into motion and came to the sad conclusion they were practically nil. Suddenly the wagon lunged to the right as one wheel slid over the edge of the incline. The bullocks bellowed helplessly as they strained against the drag of the heavy wagon. Kate saw in an instant that if she didn't unhitch the bullocks they were in danger of being dragged down into the ravine along with the wagon. Manipulating her frozen fingers around the ropes and harnesses, she managed to free one animal before the wagon slid a few more inches toward oblivion. Suddenly Kate realized that her food, gun, and clothing were still in the wagon bed.

Cautiously approaching the slanting vehicle, she climbed back into the driver's seat, reached behind her, and began tossing to the ground whatever her hands could reach. A small pile of food and belongings landed in the snow before the wagon lurched crazily and began slipping inexorably down the steep snow-shrouded incline. Kate jumped clear just as the wagon toppled over the edge. She stared in horror as the poor bullock was dragged to its death. The animal she had managed to free ambled off into the forest, where it undoubtedly would end up in the bellies of bushrangers. Within a short time fresh snow would leave no trace of the wagon and erase all signs suggesting that humans had recently traveled this road.

Painfully picking herself up from the ground, Kate piled the food she had managed to rescue in one of the blankets, flung it over her shoulder, and trudged down the road. Within minutes her feet were like solid chunks of ice and her fingers numb from cold. It soon became evident that unless she found shelter she'd likely perish. While still able to think rationally, Kate reviewed the types of shelter she was likely to find in the uncharted wilderness of the Blue Mountains.

She could crouch under a tree, but she'd probably fall asleep and freeze to death. Seeking refuge beneath an outcropping of rock offered a slightly better choice, but careful scrutiny revealed nothing in the immediate area that would suffice. Her next option was finding a cave which would offer adequate shelter from the harsh elements. From the looks of the storm it could go on for days.

Ahead of her the track seemed to rise at a steady angle as it climbed toward the crest of the mountains. On the left lay thickly forested hills, and on the right was a drop of several hundred feet. It occurred to Kate that if she stuck to the road she'd never find a cave. Taking off into the forest was much more dangerous but afforded a greater opportunity of finding shelter. Yet if she left the road she'd probably miss fellow travelers who might help her. Ha! she silently scoffed, who but fools would cross the Blue Mountains at this time of year? Kate had no choice. To survive she must find shelter. Taking a deep breath, she plunged off into the forest.

It was as still as death beneath the towering trees. Deep snow cushioned Kate's footsteps. It gave her the eerie feeling that nothing existed but her, the snow, and the wind whistling through the trees.

Kate trudged on.

Endlessly through the forest.

Until her legs grew weak and she wanted to lie down and sleep so desperately it was a constant pain inside her. Only one thought kept her on her feet.

Robin.

If she surrendered to exhaustion and despair she'd never see Robin again. Never feel his arms around her. She could deny it till hell froze over, but she did love him. There was no other explanation for the feelings he aroused in her and the gamut of emotions she experienced when they made love. She might not like him at times, but she loved him with all her heart. Until the thought of dying became a reality, Kate had felt certain she never wanted to see Robin again. But she knew different now. Without Robin, life would indeed be dull. Just as it had been before they met and he had turned her life into a tumultuous world of ecstasy and pain, of wild rapture and betrayal.

Kate's thoughts had plunged her to the depths of

hell and lifted her to the heights of heaven before she realized she had fallen to her knees, unable to continue. Her legs were like lead, her body too heavy to drag another step.

"Well, well, the old adage that good things come to those who wait is true."

Barely conscious, Kate thought death had come in person to take her. The apparition who stood above her might well have been the specter of death. His face was pale; blood trickled from his head down over his forehead into his eyes, which were slightly dilated and wild. His breath was harsh and labored, as if he had run many miles. His eyelashes were covered with snow and so was his clothing. A spark of recognition flared in Kate, but before the name took form in her mind she passed out.

Kate groaned and stretched out her legs. The heat against the soles of her feet was intense and she jerked them back. How could she feel so hot when only moments ago she was freezing? Had she finally found her reward in Hell? She had expected much better. Turning on her back, she cranked her eyes open. A gasp came to her lips when she saw a low ceiling of earth and rock rising a few feet above her. A small fire burned close to her feet. On either side of her rose a wall of solid granite.

"It's about time you woke up."

The moment she recognized the voice, Kate realized she had truly found hell. Ronald Potter was smiling down at her with a smile so sinister it made her cringe in fear. "Ronald!"

"Aye. Did you think that giant bastard killed me? I wasn't out all the time. I came to just as you were driving off in my wagon. I lay there the rest of the night and far into the next day too injured and groggy to move."

Too stunned to reply, Kate merely stared at Potter as he continued. "You left me nothing. No food, no blankets, no transportation. How did you expect me to survive?"

Finally finding her tongue, Kate lit into him. Never would she allow him to know how frightened she was. "You vile animal! You tried to rape me. How do I know you wouldn't have killed me as you threatened and left my body to rot in the forest?"

"You don't." Potter smiled nastily. "But I never dreamed I would be given a second chance."

"What are you doing here? Where are we?"

"When I finally came to my senses I realized a storm was brewing. My chances of being found were nil. Few settlers make the crossing this time of year. I knew I'd never make it out on foot in foul weather, so I immediately looked for a place to take shelter until the storm passed. Fortunately, I found this cave, and it was damn cold in here until I stumbled on you with your swag of food, matches, and supplies. Now you and I will stay nice and cozy while the storm rages outside. I've gathered firewood while you were sleeping, and when that runs low we can create our own heat." He leered wolfishly at her, raking the length of her body with salacious intent. "Oh, and if you're thinking of using that gun for protection, forget it. It's now safely in my pocket."

"Bastard!" Kate hissed. "I'll see you rot in jail if you harm me."

"Do you really expect to see civilization again? The only way you'll leave here alive is by agreeing to go through with your divorce and marrying me."

"Like hell!"

"We'll see. But tell me, did you get to Bathurst? Or did Big John decide to put that lovely body of yours to good use and then turn you loose in the forest to become fodder for wild animals?"

"Contrary to your beliefs, Big John isn't like that. He's a gentle man. I reached Bathurst quite safely, no thanks to you."

"If you had succumbed to my seduction there would have been no need for violence. I never meant to hurt you. I intended to make you my wife. But your callous disregard for my feelings angered me. No man I know of likes being ridiculed or spurned by a woman. Now you'll pay, perhaps with your life if you continue to disregard my wishes. But as long as we're sharing confidences, I'm curious to know why you left Bathurst so soon? You could have no more than arrived before turning around and starting back. Did Fletcher throw you out? I didn't lie to you about Serena, did I?"

"That's the only thing you were truthful about," Kate said sourly. "But Robin didn't throw me out. He begged me to stay. I chose to leave of my own accord."

"On foot? Did you intend to walk all the way to

Parramatta carrying your swag over your shoulder?" He laughed uproariously. "You do have guts."

"No, I didn't walk! I drove the wagon, but it slid into a ravine when the road became slick."

"Was it my wagon, perchance? And my bullocks that went into the ravine?"

"It was."

"Ah, well, once your fortune and land are mine I can buy many, many wagons and bullocks."

"My fortune isn't nearly as large as yours."

"It's not your money I'm after, 'tis your land. It's prime land and I've coveted it for a long time. Land grows scarce this side of the Blue Mountains, and I've no inclination to settle west in that wild country beyond the mountains. 'Tis too raw and unsettled for my liking. I prefer to remain close to Sydney and the harbor where ships arrive daily with luxuries I crave. Go to sleep now, I'm too tired to do you justice. Tomorrow and the next day and the next, as long as the storm holds us prisoner, we can get to know one another. By the time we leave this cave I'll know your body as intimately as it is possible for a man to know a woman."

Kate compressed her lips into a thin line, cursing fate for bringing her back into the clutches of Ronald Potter. This time there was no Big John standing in the wings to rescue her. This time she must survive on her wits alone.

"Oh, and if you're thinking of leaving while I'm sleeping, I'd strongly advise you to reconsider, unless you are ready to die. You wouldn't last an hour in that snowstorm. But just to make certain you don't get any crazy ideas about bashing me on the head or some such foolish thing, I'm going to tie you up."

"What! No!"

Potter crawled to an obscure corner of the cave and returned with a length of rope. "Did you know someone has used this cave before? I found an old rusted coffee pot, rope, and several other implements. Someone from one of the earlier expeditions must have found the cave and used it as shelter at one time. Aborigines have definitely been here sometime in the ancient past, judging from the drawings on the wall."

Kate looked around curiously, noting for the first time the markings on the wall of the shallow cave. Firelight illuminated the beautiful and mysterious ocher and crimson figures. One picture looked suspiciously like an owl, crudely yet beautifully drawn with simple lines indicating plumage. Just above it was a handprint outlined in deep red ocher. Further along the wall were drawings of hunters with drawn spears and female figures, outrageously defined with large pendulous breasts and fuzzy hair. Every one of them carried swags slung over their backs. The opposite wall held a drawing of a huge man holding a bolt of lightning. Kate was enthralled with the sight, and Potter took advantage of her distraction to quickly seize and bind her arms and legs.

"That should hold you until I'm ready for you," he said, taking one of the blankets from her swag and throwing it over her. He used the other to roll up in as he lay down beside her. In minutes she heard the even cadence of his breathing and knew he had fallen asleep.

Robin left Bathurst early the next morning after Kate's hasty departure. He rode his sturdiest horse and carried food, warm clothes, and blankets in a swag attached to his saddle. Having lived in New South Wales many years, he had often seen from afar storm clouds gathering over the mountains, but none had looked more ominous than those that now darkened the horizon. He fervently prayed the weather would hold until he caught up with Kate, but in his heart he knew a vicious storm was brewing and likely to unleash its fury at any time. He recalled clearly what had happened to the Lynch wagon and to the Lynches themselves, and he shuddered to think of Kate negotiating the treacherous trail alone.

It began as a whirlwind of stinging, pelting snow, dressing the trees and bush in silent white shrouds, and Robin groaned in despair. Tracks became impossible to follow as the snow drifted to obscure all signs of human passage. Early that morning he had passed the Crocker family who told of seeing Kate, and Robin had been jubilant, thinking he couldn't be too many hours behind her. Now this. It was almost as if fate were conspiring against Kate and Robin to keep them apart.

Despite his growing panic over failing to overtake Kate, Robin plugged on, driving his poor horse through the swirling white mist until he was ready to drop. But somehow he continued. He stopped briefly for the night, sheltering beneath an overhanging cliff, then set off again at daylight. When he began the downhill descent into the foothills above Parramatta, Robin began to hope Kate had reached home safely, that he was worrying needlessly. On the fourth day he came out of the foothills, blurry-eyed and exhausted. His face was shadowed with blond stubble and his eyes circled with purple shadows. Once he left the high elevations, the snow had all but stopped, making the going easier. The temperature had risen too. In the lower elevations it was above freezing. By the time he reached McKenzie station, his horse was more dead than alive.

Maude was stunned when Robin staggered into the kitchen. She stood with her mouth open as he collapsed onto a chair.

"Is Kate here?" His voice was harsh and grating, his manner abrupt.

"No—no, sir, she's not here, and frankly I'm worried. 'Tis not like her to be gone so long. Days ago she said she was going to Sydney, but I expected her back long before now."

Robin groaned as if in pain. "She was in Bathurst, not Sydney."

"Bathurst! Why—why—I don't understand."

"It's a long story, Maude. Suffice it to say she left Bathurst days ago and I followed, but a cursed storm prevented me from finding her. She may be lost somewhere in the mountains."

"Lord preserve us," Maude exclaimed. "The poor dear thing. Why would she lie about her destination?"

"I've no time for lengthy explanations, Maude.

Fix me something to eat while I bathe and change and prepare a fresh horse. After I talk with Dare I'm going back into the mountains. Never fear, I'll find Kate if it's the last thing I do." *It very well may be the last thing I do*, he thought but did not say.

An hour later, looking more presentable but still exhausted to the point of collapse, Robin, riding a fresh horse from Kate's meager stable, rode to Penrod station.

"My God, Robin, I thought you were in Bathurst. You look like hell. Don't tell me you made the crossing in that raging storm. Casey and I were remarking just this morning on the ominous clouds hovering over the mountain. What brings you home?"

"I'll bet it was Kate," Casey said with a secret smile. Ever astute, she was convinced real love existed between Robin and Kate.

"Aye, I'm here because of Kate. She's missing, Dare."

"Missing! How could that possibly be? I admit duties have kept me from visiting McKenzie station as often as I would have liked, but everything was fine the last time I talked with Kate and her station boss."

"Kate came to Bathurst. I still don't know why. She arrived the day after I received your message informing me about that bloody petition of divorce. The news distressed me so much I—I drank too much that night and somehow ended up in bed with Serena. Kate burst in on the scene the next morning."

Wild Land, Wild Love

Casey groaned. "Men!" she spat in disgust.

"I swear I don't remember it, nor was it intended. It—just somehow happened. Don't you think I've chastised myself a thousand times for the way Kate found us?"

"Then the gossip is true," Dare said slowly. "You are living with Serena."

"Not in the way you think. She had no place to go, and I merely offered her a place to stay until other arrangements could be made. She was alone and I felt responsible for her."

"Of course," Casey said, rolling her eyes heavenward.

"Needless to say, Kate left before I had a chance to explain fully, not that I didn't try. She just wasn't listening. But that's not the worst of it. She accepted Potter's offer to take her to Bathurst, and the animal attacked her. If not for Big John, Lord knows what would have happened to her."

"Big John?" Casey asked, wide-eyed with disbelief. "That wonderful man has a tendency of being around just when you need him."

"Unfortunately, he's now in jail waiting to be transported to Sydney to stand trial. It doesn't look good."

"Why did he go to Bathurst in the first place?"

"From what I've been able to gather, he thought he wouldn't be recognized so far from Sydney, making it possible for him to obtain work. The man is anxious to lead a normal life, but fate has conspired against him. Let's forget Big John for a moment. I'm going after Kate. She could be lost in

281

the mountains. She may even be dead. She could have run into bushrangers or—or—even Potter. Or frozen to death by now."

"Get some rest first, Robin, you look ready to drop," advised Casey, her voice full of concern.

"I can't spare the time. I'm going to see Potter first, then head back into the mountains."

"I'll go with you," Dare offered.

"No, stay here with your wife and children. I won't have you jeopardizing your life on my account."

"If you won't accept my help, may I make a suggestion?"

"Of course. I value your opinion."

"Take Culong. He's the best aborigine tracker in New South Wales. He can track a shadow."

"I don't have time to look for him," Robin protested.

"No need, he's here. He's been working for me for some weeks. Whenever he returns from one of his walkabouts he turns up here for work. You'll find him in the bunkhouse."

"Robin, good luck," Casey called after him. "I know you'll find Kate."

Chapter Fifteen

With Culong keeping pace beside him—aborigines didn't like to ride horses—Robin rode into the foothills of the Blue Mountains. Warmly clad in kangaroo-skin clothing, the native tracker ran effortlessly alongside Robin. The storm had abated, shrouding the land in pristine white and turning the majestic trees into fairy creatures sporting lacy gowns.

Robin's face was grim, his eyes bleak. He had learned from Potter's station boss that Potter had left several days ago and hadn't returned. Which indicated he could still be somewhere in the mountains, possibly with Kate. The thought slammed into Robin's gut like a well-aimed sledgehammer. The resulting pain was a constant reminder of how close he was to losing Kate. Not only did she have the elements to battle, but Potter, too, should their paths cross.

Too uncomfortable to sleep, Kate moved restlessly beneath the light blanket, listening to the howling wind outside the cave and waiting for Potter to awaken and untie her. Sharp pains shot up her arms and legs, and she cursed Potter for binding her.

Kate glanced at her captor for the thousandth time. He appeared to be deep in sleep, his breath rasping through his mouth and nostrils as if breathing were a terrible effort. Illuminated in the light provided by the dying embers of the fire, Potter's face appeared flushed. His forehead was beaded with perspiration and his body twitched beneath the blanket. Kate frowned thoughtfully, wondering what it all meant. Even though Potter didn't look well, Kate couldn't find the compassion to worry about him.

Light filtered in through the opening of the cave and Kate realized it was daylight. She knew it was still snowing outside, for a small drift of snow piled up where it blew in at the cave's mouth. Finally Potter stirred. His movements were slow and deliberate, as if his bones pained him. He sat up, a confused look on his face. When he saw Kate lying beside him, his frown deepened.

"What are you doing here?"

"Don't you remember?" Kate asked, growing alarmed. "Are you ill?"

"I—don't know. It hurts like hell to breathe and

I'm hot all over. My head feels like it's been bashed in."

"Untie me," Kate said, holding out her arms.

"Did I do that?" Potter asked. Kate nodded. "Why?"

"You didn't want me to escape."

"God, I'm confused. Be quiet while I think." Slowly he made his way to the fire and piled on more wood.

"You're sick, untie me so I can help you."

Suddenly Potter looked up, his face mottled and ugly. "I remember now. That bushranger bashed me in the head. Then I found you lying in the snow. You're the cause of all my misery." He had grown so angry he looked ready to explode. "I tied you so you wouldn't escape the punishment I have planned for you. But—I—don't feel well enough for what I had in mind. You'll keep."

After uttering those words he lay back down and closed his eyes.

"Ronald, wait! Don't go to sleep. Untie me first. What if you get sicker? Who will take care of you? I'll need to go for help when it stops snowing."

"Later," Potter muttered. "Too bloody tired."

"No! Please!"

Her words fell on deaf ears. Potter was sleeping again, his labored breathing reverberating loudly in the shallow cave.

Miserable beyond description, Kate struggled mightily to free her hands and legs, but it was useless. Potter's knots held. Growing desperate now, Kate screamed his name, over and over, until her throat hurt and her voice grew hoarse and grating. Then she tried crying, but that only made matters worse. The rest of the day passed with Kate alternately screaming at Potter and sobbing her heart out. Finally she fell asleep.

She jolted awake the next morning to find Potter bending over her with a knife clutched in his hand.

Kate screamed. But by now her voice was reduced to a painful squeak. She could see at a glance that Potter was still ill, barely able to stand on his feet. Did he plan to kill her? Had fever driven him mad? The knife was lowered, and Kate closed her eyes. Then she felt the knife slice into the rope binding her wrists. The moment her bonds fell away, the pain was excruciating as blood rushed into her arms and hands. She rubbed them vigorously until circulation was restored. When Potter made no move to free her legs, she grabbed the knife and cut through the ropes herself. Potter made no protest as he sank weakly to his knees, then fell flat on his back.

Once she was able to move without pain, Kate knelt beside him, noting with alarm his mottled color and ragged breathing. "Water," he gasped, looking at her through pain-glazed eyes.

Though Kate felt nothing but contempt and animosity for Ronald Potter, she wasn't the type of person who could stand idly by and watch a man die. Kate was no expert, but it appeared to her that Potter was in imminent danger of dying. Rising quickly, she found the coffeepot Ronald had spoken about and walked to the entrance of the cave. She filled it with snow that had gathered just inside the opening and carried it back to the fire.

Nothing but embers remained of the fire, and Kate fed it small kindling until it flared up and burned brightly once again. The snow in the coffeepot melted in minutes, and Kate carried it back to Potter. But he had either fallen asleep or lost consciousness and lay unmoving on the hard ground. Kate hunkered down on her haunches, watching his chest heave and listening to his breath rattle in his throat. She felt helpless, realizing that she didn't have the medical knowledge required to help him. All she could do was cover him with both blankets and try dribbling some of the water down his throat. After a while she realized she was hungry and rummaged around in her meager supplies for the tea and dried meat she had purchased in Bathurst. She ate and drank hungrily, aware that she needed her strength if she expected to hike out of the mountains once the snow abated. When Potter remained comatose, she lay down and slept.

Late in the night Kate awoke abruptly, feeling oddly unsettled. Utter silence vibrated around her. Glancing at Potter, she saw that he still lay in the same position. His chest was flat and motionless. A terrible fear gripped her as she crawled shakily to Potter's side. Gingerly she touched his face. He was cold, cold as death. Leaping backwards, her hand flew to her mouth, stifling her scream. Potter was dead! She was so certain, she needed no doctor to confirm her suspicion.

Scooting away from Potter's corpse, Kate turned ashen as shock seized her. When her back came in contact with the wall, she hugged her knees and rested her head on her raised limbs. She sat like that for hours, unable to move, unable to think, her eyes closed, her mind blank.

If Kate had left any tracks, they had long ago been obliterated by the heavy snowfall. Robin stood at the crest of the mountain, looking down. How far had Kate come before snow forced her to stop? he wondered dismally. Was she even now lying dead beneath a snowbank? Had he passed her and not even known it? Culong didn't seem to think so. He sat on his haunches, studying the ground with such intensity Robin began to think the aborigine could actually read the signs beneath the snow.

"What do you think, Culong?"

"No wagons come through here in many days," he said with unshakable confidence.

"Perhaps Kate was on foot," Robin suggested, hoping he was wrong.

"Perhaps," Culong grunted thoughtfully. "Culong think she not come this far. Culong think we find your woman closer to Bathurst. Let us continue." He moved down the mountainside, Robin close on his heels.

They spent a cold night huddled beneath a rocky ledge, then started off again early the next morning. About midday Culong, who had ranged ahead, suddenly stopped, an odd look settling over his bold features. He had reached the spot where the Lynch wagon had plummeted over the incline. Robin watched the aborigine walk to the edge of the ravine and look down. When he looked his fill, Culong made a slow perusal of the immediate area, dropping to his knees in several places and rooting around beneath the snow.

"What is it, Culong?" Robin asked, his breath slamming in his chest. "Do you think Kate—that she—" Words failed him as his eyes remained fixed on the deep chasm into which Kate might have plunged. The fall would have ended her life instantly.

Suddenly Culong stood and turned toward the forest. Slowly he raised his arm and pointed into the pristine wonderland of white-cloaked trees and lace-frosted scrub.

"Surely Kate wouldn't go off into the forest!" Robin said fearfully. "Once she left the track she would become hopelessly lost."

"If your woman is alive, we will find her in the forest," Culong said with quiet conviction. He plunged off into the woods, forcing Robin to dismount and lead his horse by the reins through the thick, snow-shrouded bush.

The going was rough, but they continued doggedly until Culong came to an abrupt halt. His eyes narrowed in deep concentration, as if something had just occurred to him. Then once again he dropped to his knees, pushed aside fresh snow, and studied the results of his mysterious digging. Grunting in satisfaction, he lifted an object from the snow and handed it to Robin. It was a piece of woman's clothing. Robin recognized it immediately as Kate's. He had seen her wear that particular skirt often in the past; it was one of her favorites.

" 'Tis Kate's," he said, shaking out the delicate folds.

"Your woman stop here," Culong stated, still reading the signs. "She not alone."

Robin froze. "Not alone? What do you mean?"

"Signs say man come, drag her away."

Robin's face turned ashen. "Potter!" Culong merely grunted, his face contorted in deep concentration. "How long ago?" Robin asked. His voice was shaking as a terrible dread seized him.

"Three, four days." Culong paused, made careful note of his surroundings, then fixed Robin with dark, piercing eyes. "Culong find your woman."

"You know where she is?" Robin's yelp rattled the snow-mantled trees and shook the profound silence surrounding him. "Bloody hell, man, where is she?"

"Not far from here is an ancient cave inhabited by my people in 'dreamtime.' Culong find it on one of his walkabouts." "Dreamtime" was what the aborigines referred to as the beginning of life.

"You think Kate could have found the cave?" Robin asked. He was breathless with excitement and hope.

"Signs tell me someone come from direction of cave," Culong replied cryptically.

"Can you find it?"

Culong nodded and moved quickly off. Robin was hard put to keep up with him but so elated he no longer felt the bone-weary exhaustion of the past several days. He smelled the smoke long before they reached the cave. Smoke meant fire, which was followed by the thrilling realization that a live person had to start the fire. Robin lost sight of Culong for a moment but came upon him suddenly, standing before an opening in the hillside from which wisps of pungent smoke issued forth.

Robin rushed forward to crawl through the opening, but Culong deliberately held him back. "Culong go first." The aborigine wasn't certain what he would find and didn't want Robin to blunder into a grisly scene involving his wife.

"No, Culong, it's all right," Robin said tightly. "If Kate is dead, I want to be the first to know." Crouching low, he stepped through the opening.

It took several seconds for his eyes to adjust to the dimness. The fire had burned low; elongated shadows danced on the nearby walls, and Robin's eyes were drawn to the crude but strangely moving drawings illuminated by the flames. Tearing his eyes away from the ancient signs depicting the beginning of mankind, Robin shifted his eyes toward the dwindling fire.

"Sweet Jesus!"

Seeing the blanket-shrouded form lying on the ground hit him like a physical blow, and he immediately thought the worst. His feet were incapable of moving him toward that still body. Fortunately Culong saved him from the anguish of looking into what he suspected was the still face of his dead wife. Dropping to his knees, Culong shoved aside the blanket and stared for what seemed to Robin like hours. When he raised his head he was grinning, and Robin dared to breathe again.

"It is not your woman. It is *him*—Potter." There were few men in New South Wales, black or white, who did not know Ronald Potter, his arrogance, and his cruelty. Few, if anyone, would miss him.

A string of curses grated past Robin's lips. "The bastard died before he could tell us what he did with Kate."

He was interrupted by a noise that sounded suspiciously like a sob. Whirling, Robin peered through the shadowy darkness to the rear of the cave. There, her head resting on her drawn knees, he saw Kate, and his heart leaped in joy. For some strange reason she seemed oblivious to the fact that she wasn't alone. Softly, Robin called her name. When he received no response he dropped to his knees beside her.

"'Tis Robin, love, you're safe now. I've come to take you home."

Silence.

"Kate, do you hear me? Did that bastard hurt you?"

Lifting her head as if the effort were nearly too great, Kate stared dumbly at Robin, her eyes blank and unfocused.

"She's in shock," Robin said as Culong came to crouch at his side.

Settling down beside her, Robin took her in his arms, rocking and cooing as if she were a child in desperate need of comfort. Initially Kate didn't respond. Then she moaned loudly and began sobbing as if her heart were breaking. Enormous relief surged through Robin. He knew now that she was going to be all right. Kate was a survivor, tough when it counted, yet all woman at those times that demanded she be soft and yielding. Falling hopelessly in love with her had been the easiest thing he had ever done in his life. He let her cry until the last tear had been wrung from her eyes and she relaxed in his arms.

"You came," she said quietly. Her voice was hoarse, her throat raw as her words rasped through her lips.

"Did you think I wouldn't?" he asked with lazy humor.

"I—didn't know, but I hoped . . ."

Suddenly she spied Culong squatting beside Robin, studying her silently through intelligent black eyes. Fear seized her, and she drew more deeply into Robin's embrace. "Who is he?"

"Don't be frightened. If not for Culong I might never have found you. He's the best aborigine tracker in New South Wales. Thank God Dare talked me into bringing him along. Culong, this is my wife Kate."

Culong nodded at Kate, his strong features wreathed in a tentative smile. Though his body was squat and sturdy, his facial features were bold and proud, his lips thick, his nose and cheekbones prominent.

"Thank you, Culong," Kate croaked, her voice still scratchy. "I don't know how you managed to find this cave, but I'm grateful."

"What we do with *him?*" Culong asked, pointing at Potter's body.

"Oh, God," Kate groaned, reliving the horror of the past few days.

"How did Potter die, Kate?" Robin asked gently.
Silence.

"Kate, don't shut me out now. Talk to me, tell me what happened."

More silence.

"Have you looked closely at the body?" Robin asked Culong.

"Culong look. No wounds, no broken bones."

"He was sick," Kate said slowly. The words were forced from her with tremendous effort. "He had difficulty breathing and—and was feverish. Toward the end he was unconscious and his breath rattled in his chest."

Robin grew thoughtful. "Could have been pneumonia, but we'll never know for certain." Kate grew so still, Robin feared she was slipping away from reality again. Staring at Potter's body couldn't be doing her any good. "Get him out of here, Culong," he said, exchanging knowing looks with the aborigine.

Robin turned Kate's head aside, into the hard surface of his shoulder while Culong dragged Potter's blanket-shrouded body out of the cave. It mattered little what the aborigine did with the body as long as it wasn't around as a constant reminder to Kate of what she had endured at his hands. Robin had long thought the man was demented and cursed the fact that Potter had died before he could kill him.

Culong was gone a long time, during which Kate fell into an uneasy sleep in Robin's arms. Her dreams must have been fraught with demons, for she stirred and cried out often. Robin coaxed her back to sleep with soothing words and gentle caresses. She was awakened later by the drone of voices as Culong and Robin spoke in low tones.

"It is done," Culong said cryptically.

Robin merely nodded, too concerned about Kate to care what Culong had done with Potter.

"Is your woman well?"

"Kate will be fine once the initial shock wears off. She hasn't spoken much about what happened, but once she realizes she is no longer in danger, I'm certain she'll confide in me."

Culong's dark gaze was filled with compassion as he looked at Kate. Intelligent as well as astute, he knew she needed time now, time to be alone with her husband, time to heal from her ordeal. Shouldering his swag, he said to Robin, "Culong go now."

"Go? 'Tis dark and bitter cold outside. Stay the night with us."

"Culong go," the aborigine insisted stubbornly. "Cold and darkness mean nothing to me."

Robin saw there was no forestalling Culong. "Tell Dare what happened. Tell him to report Potter's death to the authorities and let them know what you did with the body."

A man of few words, Culong acknowledged Robin's instructions with a grunt, then turned and disappeared through the cave entrance.

"Where is he going?" Kate asked.

"Back to Parramatta."

"Can you find your way out of the forest?" she asked fearfully.

"Aye, 'tisn't too far off the track. We'll wait until you're strong enough to travel. There are plenty of supplies in my swag and a strong horse that can carry both of us. Will you be all right if I leave for a few minutes to unsaddle the poor animal and bring him inside along with the supplies?''

"I—of course," Kate said somewhat dubiously. She hated the thought of Robin leaving her even for a minute. The solid strength of his big body was the only comfort she had known in days.

"I won't be long," Robin promised. "When I return I'll fix us something to eat."

When Robin returned fifteen minutes later leading his horse inside the cave, Kate was still sitting against the wall, strangely lethargic and unable to move. Robin recognized the lingering signs of shock and sought to snap her out of her apathy. "Feed the fire, love, while I unsaddle the horse and fix our meal."

Kate looked at him stupidly. She had already tried her legs and they didn't work. "I—I'm so tired, Robin."

"No, love, you just slept. Come, let me help you." Recognizing her lack of energy for what it was, he strode swiftly to her side, grasped her wrists, and pulled her to her feet.

Kate cried out when he exerted pressure on her wrists, and for a moment Robin was puzzled. Then he looked down and saw the raw abrasions where the rope had cut into her tender flesh. He cursed so vehemently, Kate cringed. "Did Potter do this to you?''

Kate looked down at her wrists curiously, saw the blood-encrusted bruises, and recalled the long hours she had been trussed up like a Christmas turkey. "He tied me up so I wouldn't escape while he slept. Then he got sick and couldn't untie me until much, much later, even though I begged and screamed not to be left like that."

"Sit down, love. I'll melt some snow and bathe them for you. What else did the bastard do to you?" he asked tightly.

"He tied my ankles, too," Kate said, misunderstanding his question.

"Kate, don't you understand what I'm asking you? Did he rape you?"

Kate's face contorted in pain, and Robin assumed the worst, until she spoke and put all his fears to rest. "No, he didn't rape me. He was too sick."

Tears of relief sprang to Robin's eyes. Nothing Potter could have done would have changed his love for Kate, but he knew rape was the most heinous crime a man could commit against a woman and some victims never recovered from the shock. Dashing away the moisture with the back of his hand, he busied himself by building the fire, melting snow and tenderly bathing Kate's wrists and ankles and binding them with pieces of her petticoat.

When the fire was blazing brightly, he filled the coffeepot with snow to be boiled for tea and made "damper." Damper was a mainstay of hunters and explorers, consisting of dough made of flour, salt, and water, placed in hot ashes and baked. Most washed it down with hot billy tea, rounding out the meal with boiled salted beef. Using supplies from his swag, Robin prepared the simple fare and served it to Kate with a flourish.

"Eat, love, you need your strength."

Dutifully, Kate picked at the food, and after a few mouthfuls decided it tasted wonderful and gobbled her entire portion and drank down the scalding tea. When she had finished she offered Robin a tentative smile. Robin grinned back, heartened by her rapid recovery. He felt confident that Kate, blessed by a hearty constitution and amazing recuperative powers, would suffer no lingering aftereffects from her ordeal.

"Do you want to tell me why you left Bathurst so abruptly?"

"If you don't know by now, my explanation doesn't matter."

"Tell me, Kate. I want to hear it from your lips. Did Serena say something to upset you?"

"Upset me?" Kate cried, anger dispelling her earlier shock. "Why should it upset me that Serena could be carrying your child? She's younger than I am, after all, and far more likely to conceive."

"What in bloody hell are you talking about?"

"What if Serena conceives your child?"

"From one encounter?" Robin scoffed. "That's highly unlikely."

"Not according to Serena."

"Dammit, Kate, this is all conjecture. *If* I slept with Serena, and I'm still not certain I did, and *if* she conceives, we'll cross that bridge when we come to it. I tried to explain that I got drunk and remember nothing of that night except what Serena told me. Is there anything you want to tell me about Potter and those damn divorce papers you filed in Sydney?"

Wild Land, Wild Love

"There is really nothing to tell." Kate shrugged. "Ronald kept urging me to divorce you and marry him. I know now he wanted McKenzie station, but at the time I thought he cared for me. When I refused to consider a divorce, he took it upon himself to obtain the papers in my name and bring them to McKenzie station for my signature. As far as I know, they are still lying on the table in the parlor where I left them. I refused to sign them until I saw for myself that you and Serena were— were living openly together. I was a fool to think you would remain celibate all that time we were apart. Why should you? I gave you permission to do as you pleased."

"No, love, you're certainly no fool. I felt sorry for Serena and offered her shelter, but I never bedded her. Lord knows she was tempting enough, but I couldn't forget the violet-eyed vixen I left in Parramatta. Dare's letter telling me about the divorce knocked the wind out of my sails, and when Serena produced the brandy I saw no reason not to indulge. I'm asking you to forgive me that one time, Kate. You're the only woman I'll ever love."

Kate bit her lower lip until she tasted blood. It was the only way she could prevent herself from confessing her own love for Robin. She wanted to, but a little voice in her brain warned her to wait. Serena's words kept coming back to haunt her. What if Serena was indeed carrying Robin's child?

"Kate, did you hear me?"

"I'm confused, Robin," she replied evasively. "I—I've been through so much that I need time to put my thoughts in order."

Connie Mason

"I'm sorry, love, I didn't mean to hound you, especially not now. I'll spread my blankets so you can lie down and sleep."

Kate watched while he made up a pallet next to the fire. When he finished he pulled her to her feet and led her to the crude bed. "Aren't you going to sleep?"

"Aye, I'll join you when I've fed the horse and cleared away our meal."

Kate lay down but could not sleep. She was too aware of Robin moving noiselessly around the small enclosure. His vital presence evoked too many memories. With her memories came poignant yearning. For a big man he moved with the grace and stealth of a panther, his body sleekly muscled and magnificently virile. She could picture him nude, poised above her, his member fully extended and eager to impart pleasure. Turning her head, she closed her eyes and cursed herself for the wild longing that had taken over her senses. How could she want a man who had taken another woman to his bed? she asked herself. Her eyes flew open when Robin eased down beside her.

"I thought you were asleep," he said when he felt her stiffen and draw away. He had no idea she was withdrawing because his nearness created a need in her that she feared, a need she craved. Her body ached with an extravagant anguish the likes of which she'd never known before.

"It's not easy to sleep after . . ."

"Kate, don't think about Potter, think of something pleasant."

"I was," Kate admitted with slow reluctance. "I

was remembering how wonderfully you make love."

Air hissed through Robin's lips in a loud exhalation of breath. "Do you realize what you just said? Are you asking me to make love to you? Bloody hell, Kate, don't torment me like this if you don't mean it!"

Kate grew still. What if this was the last time she'd be alone with Robin? What if this was the last time she could experience the magic of his lovemaking? Once he returned to Bathurst and Serena, Kate feared she might never see him again. Was it such a dreadful sin to want to feel the full glory of physical love with the only man who could transport her to paradise?

"Make love to me, Robin. Make love to me as if I were the only woman in the world."

Chapter Sixteen

Blood pumped furiously through Robin's veins. Kate's request stunned him. She had just been through a ghastly ordeal, and he'd assumed she wouldn't want him or any other man touching her after her terrifying experience at the hands of Potter.

"Are you sure, love?" Robin asked, his voice low.

Her reply was to reach up and pull Robin's face down to hers, offering her lips. Robin groaned, seizing her lips in a violent frenzy. Kate welcomed his passion, responding eagerly with an ardor that nearly matched his. She needed his strength, yearned for the rapture only Robin could give her. It didn't matter what happened tomorrow or the next day, this night was theirs; tomorrow was another day.

"I've never been more sure of anything in my life."

They undressed each other slowly, savoring every precious moment, haunted by the memory of how close Kate had came to losing her life. When they were both naked, Robin's gaze wandered over her body like an invisible caress. His slow perusal was so thorough and so devastating that Kate felt heat sizzle through her. When he moved above her, Kate stiffened and pushed him aside. Robin's brow furrowed in disappointment, thinking she had changed her mind.

"Lie back, Robin, I want to love you tonight. I want to do some of those wonderful things you do to me."

Her words were so arousing, so sexually stimulating, Robin nearly embarrassed himself by prematurely ending Kate's plans. Only his enormous strength of will kept him from exploding immediately. His eyes were wary as he lay down to await Kate's pleasure. During the following hours Robin learned that pleasure could hardly describe what Kate had in mind for him. Torture was a more appropriate word.

With slow deliberation she mapped an erotic course over Robin's hard body. His muscles became putty beneath her exploring fingertips, his flesh a mass of quivering jelly. When her hands tired of their sport, her mouth and lips quickly took their place, trailing moist kisses over his sensitive skin and finding the places that gave him the most pleasure with the hot tip of her tongue.

"Bloody hell, Kate, you're driving me mad!"

Kate grinned impishly. "Now you know how I feel."

Then her mouth was on him again, causing him untold anguish with her searing foray into forbidden territory. Robin moaned, lost in a torment of ecstasy and hell. He felt himself growing harder than he had ever been before and knew he had to put a stop to Kate's erotic journey or—

"Bloody hell!"

Her lips found him. He arched upward in an agony of need so excruciating he felt his soul leave his body. Kate barely heard Robin's sharp intake of breath as she continued to lavish him with the most tender loving care she had ever bestowed upon another human being. Unable to bear another moment of such sweet torture, Robin reared up, seizing Kate and thrusting her beneath him.

"Turnabout is fair play, little vixen," he growled as his lips came down on hers. His kiss was rough and demanding, demonstrating to Kate the terrible need she had created in him. He kissed her and kissed her, until she grew dizzy and her head spun.

Then his fingers were thrusting inside her, stroking, caressing, until her lower body began to throb and swell. He covered one sweetly erect nipple with his mouth, nipping it gently, then licking it with his tongue. A delicious tension was building inside her, and when Robin found the sensitive bud of femininity nestled in the folds of flesh at the apex of her thighs, Kate screamed out his name.

"Robin! Please!"

He held himself above her, his face strained with

the frantic fever of desire. Then he came into her, her name upon his lips. His hands moved beneath her, lifting her into his thrusts as she moved with him rhythmically, feeling the sensations rise in splendid fury. With every thrust she sought the cascading climax, yearned for appeasement of the deep, desperate ache building inside her. The answer to her ferocious hunger came as Robin penetrated again and again her wet, sleek moistness. He cast his head back and groaned from sheer joy.

The explosion burst upon her in unending waves of undulating sensations that seemed to wrench her body apart as Robin pushed deep—deeper into her. Her breath came in quick, frantic pants as she felt him swell and vibrate inside her. Then his seed left his body in hot spurts of raw fire. Kate felt it, and something deep inside her whispered that something extraordinary was in the making. The feeling was so wonderful it was nearly unbearable.

Exerting the last of his energy, Robin rolled to his side, pulled Kate into his arms, and drew the blanket up over them.

"It gets better every time," Kate murmured wonderingly. "If only . . ."

"I intend to keep it that way," Robin vowed solemnly. "I don't ever want to do anything to hurt you again, Kate. I love you too much. I—know how badly I hurt you when I—what Serena and I—bloody hell, I don't even want to talk about it. All I want is for you to love me. Not just my lovemaking, but *me*."

Silence.

"Kate, I've not heard you say it. You do love me, don't you?"

Silence.

"Kate? Don't shut me out now. Not after what we just experienced together."

Not one to mince words, Kate looked at him squarely and said, "I've been confused ever since I found you and Serena together. Did you know I was coming to Bathurst hoping to give our marriage another chance?"

Robin's heart leaped with joy, then plummeted at her next words. "Now I'm not entirely certain that's wise."

"Nothing has changed, love. I still believe we can have a good marriage. It doesn't matter if you don't love me in the same way I love you. Your response to my lovemaking proves that you care for me."

"It's true, Robin, I do care for you. When I'm in your arms I forget my own identity. In the past I've always resented that feeling, but I've come to accept it, welcome it even. I accept it because I recognize the fact that I couldn't respond to you as I do if I didn't care for you deeply. But after finding you with Serena I don't know what to believe. How do I know that what happened with Serena won't happen again with another woman?"

"You have my word, love."

Kate sighed, turning thoughtful. Could she trust Robin? Did Serena really mean nothing to him? What about Casey? Did all men need more than one woman to keep them satisfied?

Taking her silence for acceptance of his solemn

vow, Robin continued blithely, "We'll leave here as soon as you feel able. I suggest we don't wait too long. Another storm could come hard on the heels of the last."

"I agree. I know firsthand how dangerous the mountains are and how easily one can become lost. I'll be ready to travel in the morning."

"Good, I was hoping you'd say that. I won't rest easy until you are back in Bathurst with me where I can keep you safe."

"Bathurst?" Kate said in a thin voice. "I—I'm not going back to Bathurst. I'm going to McKenzie station."

Robin's mouth flew open. "Whatever gave you the idea I was taking you to McKenzie station? I'm needed in Bathurst. In the spring I'll take you back to Parramatta and you can make arrangements to sell McKenzie station. I'm sure Dare will be interested."

"I'm not going to Bathurst, Robin, and I have no intention of selling McKenzie station," Kate said with quiet determination.

A sinking anguish brought Robin's lips together in a thin line. Never had he experienced such suffocating frustration. "I'm getting rather tired of pouring my heart out to you only to have you stomp on it. Have you heard nothing I've said?"

"I've heard everything," Kate whispered shakily. "What about Serena?"

Robin groaned. "Must we go through that again? I care nothing for Serena. If it will make you feel better, I'll find her a good husband."

"Robin, what if Serena—what if she—"

"That won't happen. She isn't carrying my child. Don't ask me how I know, but I know. My home— our home—will be completed soon, and I want you with me. I'm building it for you, even though I wasn't certain you'd ever occupy it."

"As long as a doubt remains in my mind about Serena I won't live with you in Bathurst," Kate stated firmly.

"How long will it take for your doubt to be resolved?" Robin asked bitterly.

"When you come and tell me Serena isn't carrying your child. I couldn't bear it, Robin, if she were to have your baby while I am still your wife. I couldn't survive that kind of pain. Perhaps it's because I *do* love you that I refuse to be humiliated like that. Take me home, to McKenzie station. Come back in the spring, and if—if all is well and you still want me, I'll gladly return with you to Bathurst."

"Want you! Bloody hell, Kate, I'll always want you. Nothing will ever change that."

"Then you'll give us both till spring to resolve this dilemma."

"The dilemma is in your mind, love. There is no problem that I can see."

"Please, Robin, indulge me. I promise to be a wonderful wife if everything works out to our benefit. I'll happily sell McKenzie station to live with you in Bathurst. I want nothing hanging over our heads when—if—we resume our marriage."

"There is no 'if' about it, love. I see no need for this separation, no need at all."

"I won't go to Bathurst," Kate repeated obstinately.

"Why do I have to love such a bullheaded woman?" Robin bit out angrily. "If you loved me with only half the zeal that you waste in stubborn refusal, we'd be the happiest couple alive."

"I'm sorry, Robin, that's just the way I feel. I don't want to share you. I'd rather lose you than have Serena and—and a child claim part of you."

Her logic defeated Robin. "Very well, Kate, I'll take you back home. But I'll return for you in the spring, and you'll see how foolish you've been to waste all that precious time we could have been together."

"I'd rather be foolish than sorry."

"If we're going to be apart for another two months, let's not waste another moment of our time together," Robin said, reaching out to tenderly stroke her cheek. "I want to love you again. This night will have to last until I come to you in the spring."

Two days later Robin and Kate started the descent into the foothills above Parramatta. The going was extremely difficult, and often they had to lead the horse through snowdrifts. When they finally reached the lower elevations, conditions moderated dramatically. By the time they reached Parramatta, the normal winter temperature of fifty degrees prevailed and little or no snow covered the ground. From there, McKenzie station was an easy journey. When Kate finally walked into the house,

Maude nearly fell all over her with joy.

"Thank God," she breathed shakily. "We were so worried about you. One or other of the Penrods have been here every day to see if you had arrived yet. Roy came yesterday and said Culong had returned with the welcome news that both of you were safe and would be returning soon. I knew you'd find her, Robin."

"Culong deserves all the credit, Maude," Robin said. "Kate's trail was so elusive at times, it appeared as if Culong were tracking a ghost."

"You must be freezing and hungry. I'll have something hot for you to eat before you know it."

"A bath first, Maude," Kate requested, "then food."

"Aye," Robin agreed wholeheartedly. "Go on up to your room, love, I'll heat the water and carry it up to you."

A short time later Kate relaxed in a big wooden tub before a blazing fire. She had scrubbed her skin until it was nearly raw and washed her hair several times with a bar of fragrant soap. She felt so good and so relaxed, the effort of leaving the comfort of the warm water was nearly beyond her. She closed her eyes, her mind slipping back to recall those wonderful moments she'd spent with Robin in the cave. If she hadn't seen him with Serena she'd be content to spend the rest of her life with him, loving him and being loved in return. He was so strong, so virile, so magnificly male. And he made love with splendid abandon, as if he were created for no other purpose.

"Aren't you finished yet, lazy?"

Wild Land, Wild Love

Robin stood just inside the door, leaning against the wall, an indolent grin on his lips. "I've already had my bath." His face and chin were scraped bare of stubble and he was dressed in spotlessly clean clothes. Kate sucked her breath in sharply. No man had a right to look so superbly fit and wonderfully handsome.

"It feels so good to just sit here and soak, I couldn't bring myself to leave the tub."

"Do you need help?" His grin was outrageous.

"We don't have time for what you have in mind," Kate replied with an answering smile.

"Do you know me so well?"

"I'm beginning to know that look."

"As a matter of fact, we've plenty of time. I told Maude it would be at least another hour before you were ready."

"You what! I can be out of here and into my clothes in ten minutes."

"No you can't," Robin stated calmly as he began peeling off his shirt. "It will take me much longer to examine you properly. I want to make certain you didn't sustain hidden injuries during your ordeal." He stepped out of his pants.

Kate squealed when he bent and lifted her out of the water, carrying her dripping to the bed. It was over an hour before they appeared for supper, flushed and exhausted from the splendor of their lovemaking.

When Robin came to her bed that night, Kate didn't protest. If these next few days were to be all she would ever have of Robin, she intended to make them the best of their lives. Though Kate deliberately refrained from mentioning it, she had a terrible premonition that once Robin returned to Bathurst things would never again be the same between them.

Dare Penrod arrived at McKenzie station bright and early the next morning. Robin had sent word to him the day before, and he came in all haste. Kate and Casey talked in the parlor while Dare and Robin closeted themselves in the study.

"You can't believe how worried we were about you and Kate," Dare said with heartfelt relief. "When Culong showed up alone, we naturally assumed the worst."

"Did Culong tell you what happened?"

"Aye, we got the whole sordid story from him. 'Tis no more than the bastard deserved. I should have killed Potter years ago for what he did to Casey. But in the end he got his just desserts."

"Did you report his death to the authorities?" Robin asked.

"Aye, I went to Parramatta immediately and talked with the magistrate. I took Culong along so he could tell him where Potter was buried. A short inquest will be held as soon as you're able to attend. I foresee no problems. There are enough witnesses to verify that Potter died from illness."

"That's the truth of it, Dare. Potter did die from illness. Perhaps it's best that way, otherwise I would have killed him when I saw what he did to Kate."

Dare's eyes narrowed. "He—he didn't . . ."

"No, he didn't rape her, but he abused her, and for that alone I would have killed him."

"Thank God it all ended well. What now? Will you wait till spring to return to Bathurst? Will Kate go with you?"

"I'm going back to Bathurst as soon as the inquest is over," Robin explained. "There are—loose ends I must take care of before Kate joins me. For one thing I want to make certain my house is completed and ready when Kate arrives."

"Then you two have settled your differences."

Robin's expression turned grim. "Not entirely. There's still Serena to contend with."

There were few times in their long friendship that Dare had been openly critical of Robin. This was one of them. "I had expected better from you."

"It's not what you think, Dare. Serena shared my house but not my bed. I love only Kate in that way." Suddenly Robin flushed, recalling the one supposed time he had made love to Serena. Not that he remembered the act itself, but he had waked up in bed with her draped around him like a second skin. "Except for that one time."

Dare groaned. "Bloody hell, Robin, once is all it takes. Is Kate determined not to forgive you?"

"Not exactly, but suffice it to say that she refused to come to Bathurst with me immediately. She pleaded with me to return her to McKenzie station. She promised to leave here if I decided to come back for her in the spring."

"And you agreed to that?"

"What in the hell could I do? I hurt her terribly by bedding Serena. But I love Kate enough to wait two months for her. Are you interested in buying

313

McKenzie station when I return in the spring? I've decided to make my home in Bathurst, and Kate agreed to the arrangement—if—if things work out, and I'm certain they will."

"What about Serena?"

"Once she realizes there is no hope for her, she'll accept one of the many offers she's received. She's a beautiful woman, any man would be glad to have for his wife."

Robin sounded so absolutely confident that things would turn out right that Dare didn't doubt him for a moment.

Meanwhile, Kate and Casey were having an intense conversation of their own.

"I know what you went through," Casey said, commiserating with Kate over the dangerous situation she had survived. She could recall her own ordeal at the hands of bushrangers. "Thank God you're a survivor like I am and have a man who loves you enough to surmount any obstacle in order to save your life."

Kate merely nodded, unwilling to expose the problems that still faced her and Robin.

"Have you and Robin reconciled?"

"There are still problems, but by spring I hope they will be resolved."

"Is Serena one of your problems?"

"Serena is a big part of them."

"Robin never loved Serena."

"Perhaps not," Kate allowed. *But he does love you*, she wanted to add but wisely refrained. "This is something we'll just have to work out for ourselves."

Casey sighed, disappointed that Kate still did not feel comfortable with her or trust her enough to discuss her problems or seek advice. A short time later the Penrods left.

Two days later Robin and Kate attended the inquest for Ronald Potter. It was brief and concise. Ronald Potter's death was declared an act of God due to illness. The entire Penrod family attended. Roy Penrod lingered behind to talk with Robin and Kate after the rest of his family departed.

"I suppose you know I've been a frequent visitor in your home during your absence," he remarked.

"Aye." Robin grinned knowingly. "It couldn't be Maude that draws you to our home, could it?"

"Aye, she's a fine woman, Robin. I'm working to have her sentence remitted. Governor Macquarie has promised to give my petition his full attention as soon as he can. He's a busy man these days with all the projects he's undertaken. No other governor has done so much for convicts and emancipists."

"Do you plan on marrying Maude?" Kate dared to ask.

Roy frowned. "Aye, what else? My wife has been dead many years, and Dare and Ben have lives apart from mine. Until now I haven't found a woman I could love. I want to spend what years I have left with someone to care for, someone who cares for me in return."

"And Maude is that woman," Robin stated. "Feel free to visit anytime you desire, Roy."

"By all means," Kate added once she was certain of Roy's intentions.

They rode back to McKenzie station in silence. Robin knew it was time to return to Bathurst and his job and dreaded being parted again from Kate. Kate realized that Robin would be leaving soon and despised the thought of him returning to Serena.

Later that night, after they had made love and lay quietly in each other's arms, Robin expressed his need to leave for Bathurst immediately.

"I wish you were returning with me, Kate," he pleaded softly.

"We've already been through this, Robin. Two months isn't so long to wait, is it? Please understand that I have to be certain about Serena. When you return to McKenzie station and tell me Serena's future is settled with another man, then and only then will I feel free to love you."

"Are you still consumed with the notion that Serena is carrying my child?"

"I can't help but think about it."

"Did you stop to consider the fact that you might be carrying my child? Lord knows we've tempted fate often enough."

"No, I don't believe I am," Kate replied with a certainty that confounded Robin.

"Are you saying you can't have children?"

"I'm nearly twenty-seven."

"So great an age," Robin chuckled with wry amusement. "But I will bedevil you no longer, love. Expect me in the spring. Meanwhile, speak to Dare about buying McKenzie station. I'm building a magnificent house for you and our children, whether or not you believe we will have any. You see, I'm not nearly the skeptic you are."

Kate was indeed a skeptic when it came to children she and Robin might have together. In all the times they had been together she had not conceived. At first it pleased her, but when she came to the realization that she loved Robin, she longed to have his children. Naturally they would all be boys and all look like him. But after each time they had made love and she failed to conceive, she began to think that she was flawed in some way, or that she was simply too old to conceive and bear children. Whenever she thought about asking Dr. Proctor to explain the intricacies of conceiving and child bearing, she became too embarrassed to pursue the subject.

"Would you be too disappointed if we don't have children?" Kate asked with her usual honesty.

Robin thought a long time before answering. "Naturally a man wants children, but if God decides they're not for us, then I can be perfectly satisfied with just you. But I see no need to worry over something that's not yet happened. You'll see, there will be plenty of children to satisfy both of us. But not unless you shut up and let me love you again. Two months is a long time."

The next day was exceptionally warm as Robin prepared for the crossing to Bathurst. He carried sufficient supplies to last several days, for one never knew when another storm would blast down into the mountains. Kate prayed that wouldn't happen, carefully scrutinizing the horizon over the Blue Mountains and deciding that nothing threatening was brewing. If the weather held and barring all accidents, Robin would arrive in Bathurst in three to four days. The fact that Robin wasn't traveling alone eased her mind somewhat.

Since the settlement had grown considerably, Governor Macquarie was sending two more police officers to Bathurst. They had learned in Parramatta that Robin was returning to the settlement and expressed the desire to travel with him since it was their first crossing and a winter endeavor at that. Robin accepted with alacrity, not only glad for the company but eager to have two more officers available to keep peace in Bathurst. The two men were waiting a short distance away for Robin to join them.

"Good-bye, love," Robin said, bending down to kiss her. "Wait for me, I'll be back."

Kate returned the kiss with all the fervor in her body and soul. *Please come back*, she silently begged. But the premonition that had plagued her since returning from Bathurst was relentless. Some dark force functioning against them was already at work. She felt it in her bones and feared it with every fiber of her being.

She watched him ride off until he was a tiny speck in the distance, then returned to the house where she was confronted by an irate Lizzy.

"You sent him away again!" she accused hotly. "I hope you're satisfied. What kind of woman are you? If you were any kind of wife to Robin, he would never have left McKenzie station." With an angry twitch of her skirt she flounced off.

Kate had plenty of time to reflect on Lizzy's

words in the lonely days that followed. True, she might have driven Robin away in the beginning, but certainly not this time. He had made a new life for himself in Bathurst, had accepted a position of responsibility from the governor and no longer needed McKenzie station. Yet Kate couldn't purge the thought from her mind that a wife follows her husband wherever he decides to settle. Nothing about her marriage to Robin was normal. It defied every definition of what a normal marriage consisted of. How many well-bred women married ex-convicts? None that she knew of.

How many spinsters found such profound passion in the arms of a man? The answer was probably the same as for the previous question. Yet she *had* married an ex-convict, a man whose crime she had yet to learn. And she *had* found undeniable ecstasy in the act of lovemaking with Robin. Few women could boast of finding joy performing their marital duty, and Kate felt no guilt in doing so. But did she have to think about how wonderful Robin made her feel every waking hour as well as most of those she spent sleeping?

She remembered his outrageous smile, his wry humor, the way his mouth curled upward when he teased her and curved downward when he was angry. He had taught her the meaning of passion. He had watched her come alive in his arms. He had demonstrated that not all men were alike, that some could be depended upon to do what was right. He had made her see that she was vulnerable to danger despite the fact that she was smart enough and strong enough to survive on her own.

And he made her understand that being alone, totally dependent on no one but herself, wasn't the most important thing in her life.

Loving and being loved in return were ever so much more rewarding.

Serena . . .

Whenever Kate's thoughts painted glorious pictures of the future, Serena intruded to bring her back to reality.

Chapter Seventeen

Robin preceded the new snowstorm that swept over the mountains by mere hours. There were moments when he doubted he'd make it to Bathurst before the full brunt trapped him and his companions in the snow-covered passes. But his luck held and they reached the lower elevations ahead of the squall. It was then, when the most pressing danger was past, that Robin's luck deserted him. His horse's rear hoof slid on a patch of ice and was unable to regain its balance. Both horse and rider went tumbling head over heels down an incline.

Robin fought desperately to put an end to his headlong flight, but there was nothing to hinder his fall but brittle scrub and withered bushes that broke off in his hands. He hit the bottom with a painful jolt that jarred his insides and knocked the wind out of him. The hill that he had rolled down wasn't excessively steep, and his companions quickly scrambled down to help him. When he tried to move it felt as if a hundred knives were attacking his chest. Robin groaned, certain that he had broken one or more ribs and eternally grateful he hadn't sustained more serious injuries.

The poor horse had to be destroyed, and Robin was forced to share one of his companion's mounts. Since they were so close to Bathurst and the temperatures more moderate in the lower levels, this didn't create too great a burden. It was the excruciating pain that was unbearable. Robin's chest was on fire; each breath was a new torment, more agonizing than the one that preceded it. When Robin reached his cabin, he was nearly mindless with pain. Once the two police officers delivered him into Serena's hands and saw that he was made comfortable on the bed, they left.

"What happened, Robin?" Serena asked, alarmed by his pale complexion and shallow breathing.

"Broken ribs," Robin gasped. Speech was difficult, lengthy explanations nearly impossible.

"Tell me what to do."

"Bind them, as tightly as you can." Since no physician had come to settle in Bathurst, those with minor illnesses and injuries were forced to doctor themselves, often with disastrous results.

"I don't think I can," Serena said, gulping back the bile that rose in her throat.

Wild Land, Wild Love

Robin spat out a curse, then groaned when it served only to intensify the pain.

"Tear up one of your petticoats, then help me remove my coat and shirt. I'll tell you what to do next."

Reluctantly Serena did as she was bid. By the time his torso was bared, Robin was sweating profusely and gritting his teeth against waves of excruciating pain. His terse instructions were precise, and somehow Serena managed to wind the strips of cloth around his chest and fasten them so they did not slip. Once that was done, Robin lay back dazedly, falling asleep almost instantly. Serena pulled off his pants and threw a blanket over him. Later, she stripped and crawled in beside him.

Robin slept the night through, feeling much better when he awoke. The warm body beside him stirred and cuddled closer. Bemused, Robin reached over to caress a pert breast that had been pressing against his back all night. God, he loved waking up with Kate next to him, he thought foggily.

Serena drew her breath in sharply. "Oh, Robin, I've missed you so desperately. I was afraid you had come back with Kate, but thank God you were too smart to want someone who doesn't want you. Or did you fail to find her?" she asked hopefully.

Robin drew back as if he had been struck. "Bloody hell, Serena, you've gone too far this time. I found Kate alive and well and took her back to McKenzie station for the time being. What are you doing in my bed? Don't try to tell me we made love,

323

for I was in no condition last night to make love to anyone."

Serena flushed, too canny to try that tactic again. Besides, once was all that was needed for what she had in mind. "No, of course not, I wouldn't lie to you about something so intimate and wonderful between us. I—I just wanted to be close to you. I've missed you. I really am glad Kate is all right."

"Get dressed! And don't ever try anything this outrageous again. I haven't changed my mind about you. In fact, just the opposite. In the spring I'm going to bring Kate to Bathurst to live."

With an angry toss of her head, Serena flounced from the bed, shamelessly flaunting her nakedness before Robin. When she had struggled into her clothes, Robin attempted to rise. Though his ribs didn't hurt nearly so much as they had the day before, he realized it would be weeks before the bones knit together and he would be able to move about unhindered. When he tried to dress, throbbing pain speared through his chest, forcing him to stop and take short, halting breaths. To his chagrin he was reduced to asking Serena's help in dressing.

Too weak yet to sit a horse or attend to duties, Robin lay back down on the bed while Serena prepared their meal. When she brought him a tray and sat down beside him on the bed, Robin began a rather lengthy explanation of what had happened in the mountains. Wide-eyed with curiosity, Serena listened with rapt attention. When Robin repeated his intention of bringing Kate to Bathurst in the spring, Serena grew silent and sullen.

Wild Land, Wild Love

"I wouldn't think you'd want Kate after Potter raped her."

"Haven't you been listening? Potter didn't rape Kate. Besides, it wouldn't have mattered if he did. I told you before, Kate is my wife and I love her."

"Does she love you? It seems to me that she'd be here with you now if she loved you."

"Kate suffered a terrible shock when she found us in bed. I want her forgiveness and am willing to allow her time to overcome the distress we caused her."

"Are you certain that's all there is to it?" Serena asked astutely.

"Positive," Robin replied, his eyes refusing to meet hers. "Which brings us to another subject. We cannot continue to live together like this. My house will be completed shortly and I intend to occupy those rooms that are finished immediately. Or as soon as I'm able to move around freely with these blasted broken ribs."

"What! What about me?" Serena demanded to know. "Are you throwing me out to defend myself against that pack of wolves out there who would take advantage of me?"

"I wouldn't be so cruel, Serena, though Lord knows you've given me nothing but problems. You may live here in this cabin for as long as you like. It's on my land and will be yours for as long as you need it. But I strongly urge you to marry soon. Haven't you met anyone who strikes your fancy?"

"No one!" Serena said with a vehemence that startled Robin.

It sounded almost as if he were an obsession

with her. Did she cling to him with such tenacity because he had taken the place of her dead parents? he wondered. Or was she merely obsessed with wanting him because he was no longer available? Whatever her problem, Robin reasoned, Serena had to find another man on whom to focus her obsessive affection, for he was simply not interested.

"Nevertheless, Serena, I suggest you decide what you want to do with your life and where you want to live it. I know for a fact there are men in Parramatta who would welcome you back in their midst. But whatever you decide, I'll be gone from this cabin in a matter of days. I'll help you all I can to adjust, but don't expect me to be at your beck and call every minute of the day."

Considering the subject closed, Robin finished his meal while Serena sulked. Afterwards he napped fitfully. Serena took the opportunity to hurry off to the market, ostensibly to buy groceries for the next day. She arrived just as Silas Dodd was filling the order of his last customer of the morning. It was his usual custom to close the store between twelve and one o'clock while he fixed his lunch. His eyes lit with unbridled joy when Serena entered, and shortly after the customer left, the closed sign was hung in the window. An hour later Serena left by way of the back exit, and Silas walked on clouds the rest of the day.

Two weeks passed before Robin was able to move into the finished portion of his house. He was back to performing the duties of magistrate and had little time to waste on Serena's comings and goings. Government House was now completed, and his office was constantly filled with people seeking his services. Since his office empowered him to act as justice of the peace, he was beseeched with men and women wanting to be married. He was so swamped with duties, time flew by at an alarming rate. Spring burst upon the land before he was ready for it.

In Parramatta spring rains came in torrential downpours. There seemed to be no end to the dark, gloomy days when Kate could hardly see past the gray curtain outside her window. The land was blanketed in downpours that persisted both day and night. Kate knew from talk that the Hawkesbury was often known to flood its banks, stripping away crops and topsoil and leaving the land barren. She prayed that would not happen again but held out little hope as the Hawkesbury neared flood stage.

She had no idea what to do to prevent the house and animals from being swept away should the Hawkesbury go on a rampage, and the station boss seemed more frightened than knowledgeable. Dare had come by two weeks ago and warned of imminent danger, but either had been too busy or too hampered by rain to return and give further instructions. Meanwhile the rains continued unabated and the Hawkesbury rose ominously.

If the dismal rain and worry over floods weren't enough, Kate fretted constantly over the fact that

Robin still hadn't returned to McKenzie station and spring was well upon them. Had his promise meant nothing, or had Serena finally succeeded in capturing Robin's affection? Or—and the thought was too painful to dwell on—had the unthinkable happened? Had Robin discovered that one time was enough to conceive a child? Kate could think of no other explanation for Robin's continued absence, though she hoped fervently that her fears were groundless.

Another nagging worry was Kate's state of health. Normally of robust constitution, she had felt absolutely terrible these past two weeks— queasy all the time and dizzy at certain other times. At first she thought she had influenza, but she wasn't feverish, nor was she coughing or sneezing. It was downright puzzling. If it weren't raining every day she would have consulted Dr. Proctor. Just today she noticed that certain parts of her body, like her breasts, were tender and swollen. She didn't want to mention it to Maude for fear of being embarrassed. It could be just a figment of her imagination. Loneliness could have driven her to invent nonexistent illnesses.

The rains continued another week, and Kate grew frantic with worry. Then, shortly after lunch Ben Penrod arrived, drenched to the skin despite the slicker he wore. Kate was so happy to see him, she nearly threw herself into his arms.

Shaking the rain from his midnight black hair, Ben grinned with rakish delight at Kate's exuberant welcome. "Had I known I'd be given such a warm welcome I'd have come sooner."

Kate's face turned a bright pink. "You're always welcome, Ben."

Ben and Dare looked so much alike it was uncanny. Both had silver-gray eyes, both were tall, outrageously handsome, and charming. But after knowing both brothers, Kate found the resemblance ended there. Ben was far more outgoing, more outrageous, less serious, his personality more magnetic and his restless spirit more adventurous. Of course Dare had Casey and his children and had good reason to settle down, whereas Ben had stated time and again that he never intended to marry.

"Thanks, Kate, but my visit isn't for pleasure. I've come to lend a hand. Dare said the Hawkesbury has reached flood stage and is due to crest tomorrow. There are preparations to make, and since Dare has all he can handle with his own farm, I've come to offer my help."

Waves of gratitude and relief washed over Kate. "What about Penrod station? Aren't you needed there?"

"Father can handle things without my help, he's an old hand at it. But you're just a woman and unprepared to deal with harsh realities and destruction wrought by the elements."

Kate bristled at being called a "mere woman" but needed Ben's help so desperately she swallowed her hot rebuttal. One day, she predicted, he'd find a woman who would make him eat his disparaging words. Handsome devil that he was, arrogant as well, he was the type of man who would fall and fall hard.

"I appreciate your coming. Tell me what must be done."

"First we must organize the convict laborers into groups. Some will make sandbags while others will place them along the bank of the river to stem the flow. I'm not certain it will work but it's worth a try. Both Father and Dare have already begun their preparations. What about the sheep?"

"Fortunately they're already on high ground. They were driven into the foothills when the rains persisted and are grazing contentedly."

Ben grinned with devastating effect. Kate thought him the most appealing man she'd ever met, not counting Robin whom she loved. "Good girl. And the cattle?"

"The station boss had them taken to high ground also. There is nothing in danger but the crops and buildings."

"Perhaps you'd best have the servants carry food and other necessities up to the second floor in case we can't contain the floodwaters. I'll report back when I'm able. In the meantime, try not to worry. I won't let Robin down."

Kate set Maude and Lizzy to carrying food and supplies to the upper floors immediately. She prayed they wouldn't be needed but wanted to be prepared in case they were. She forced herself to continue when a strange weakness made her body heavy and lethargic. She disregarded the dizziness and nausea and all the other ominous signs that plagued her, but when Ben returned to the house for something hot to drink and eat later that night, Kate was near exhaustion.

"How does it look, Ben?" she asked anxiously.

"Not good," Ben answered tiredly. Deep lines of weariness etched his brow. He had toiled beside the convicts until placing one foot before the other became an effort.

"Rest awhile," Kate advised, forgetting her own weariness. "Let Dent handle things for a few hours."

"I can't, Kate, it looks like the next few hours will tell the tale. If water starts seeping under the doors, go upstairs immediately."

Kate nodded. "Perhaps we could help . . ."

"No, three more hands will make little difference. It's too dangerous out there for you and the women. Thanks for the food, it tasted wonderful. Perhaps you should get some rest yourself, you look worn out."

Though the light cast by the lamp was dim, Ben thought Kate looked unwell. Her wonderful violet eyes were deeply circled and her face was pale and drawn. "I'm all right."

"When do you expect Robin? Dare said he would be returning in the spring."

Kate worried her bottom lip. "I—I'm not sure. He must be very busy and—well, I'm just not certain."

Ben thought it sounded suspiciously as if Kate were making excuses, but he couldn't spare the time to delve more deeply into the subject. He stood to leave. Kate, who had been sitting at the kitchen table across from him, also rose. But as she did, the world began spinning around her. Rich velvet blackness surrounded her, enveloped her, and the floor came up to meet her. The chair crashed behind Ben as he raced to her side, scooping her into his arms just before she hit the ground.

Kate awoke moments later to find Ben gently bathing her forehead and face with a wet cloth. "What happened?"

"You fainted," Ben said, looking at her curiously.

"Impossible, I've never fainted in my life."

"Never?" Ben repeated skeptically. "Have you been unwell?"

Kate hesitated. She wasn't accustomed to discussing her state of health with men, but Ben's concern was so real she found herself confiding in him. "I have felt rather queasy and upset recently. I thought I might have caught influenza and intended to see Dr. Proctor, but the rain has kept me from visiting his office."

"I doubt you have influenza, Kate," Ben said, his eyes twinkling with mysterious humor. "How long has Robin been gone?"

Kate frowned, perplexed by his line of questioning. "Two months. Why?"

"Have you no inkling what might be ailing you?"

"No, do you?" It seemed highly unlikely that Ben knew anything about medicine.

"Perhaps I'm being presumptuous, but I do have a niece and nephew and saw much of Casey during her last pregnancy. It's entirely likely that you're increasing."

Kate was stunned. A baby? "That's impossible!" she blurted out.

Ben's dark brows arched upward and he grinned cheekily. "Somehow I doubt that, knowing Robin as I do."

Bright red stained Kate's cheeks when she grasped Ben's meaning. "Oh—I didn't mean—of course it could be true but I just didn't think—" She lapsed into silence, still trying to digest the notion that she might be expecting Robin's baby. She had been so consumed with Serena she never considered she would be the one to become pregnant. Lord knows she and Robin had done nothing to prevent it. She had just assumed that since she hadn't gotten pregnant before it wouldn't happen.

"Shouldn't Robin be told?" Ben asked gently.

"If it is true, and I'm still not convinced, I'll tell him when he returns—if he returns," she added cryptically.

Ben sighed, more convinced than ever not to take the plunge into the state of matrimony. He hoped never to experience the difficulties both Dare and Robin encountered with their wives. Women were God's greatest masterpiece, and Ben fully intended to avail himself of their many charms, but marriage just wasn't for him.

"Are you feeling better now?"

"Much." Kate smiled. "Thank you—for everything.

Suddenly Ben assumed a thoughtful expression. "Listen!"

"I don't hear anything."

"That's just it. The rain has stopped." He ran to

the door, flinging it open and stepping outside. As if by magic the sky had cleared and stars were shining brightly.

"Do you think the rain has stopped for good?" Kate asked hopefully as she peered over his shoulder.

"Looks like it," Ben mused, "though I'm no expert. Let's hope the dike holds when the river crests tomorrow. Go to bed, Kate, I think the danger is over for the night. I'll bunk with the men in the convict quarters."

The Hawkesbury crested at ten o'clock the next morning. Some muddy water rushed over the makeshift dike, flooding the low-lying fields, but the damage was not as severe as it might have been had Ben not arrived to direct the sandbagging operation. He shrugged aside Kate's profuse thanks, stating that Robin would have done the same for him. Before he left he advised Kate to see Doc Proctor if her illness persisted.

A week later Kate followed Ben's well-meant advice. Dan Proctor confirmed her pregnancy. She would bear Robin's child in seven months. Unable to contain her happiness, Kate had to tell someone and confided in Casey the following day when Kate called on her.

"Robin will make a wonderful father," Casey enthused. "He's so fond of Brandon and Lucy. Shouldn't he be returning soon to McKenzie station?"

"He should have already arrived," Kate admitted. Her voice hinted of fear and hopelessness. What if Robin decided he no longer wanted her?

What if Serena was—No, she wouldn't think those depressing thoughts, it wasn't good for the baby.

Casey frowned, aware of what Kate was feeling. Damn men for their thoughtlessness and careless ways. "He loves you, Kate, he'll be back."

"I believe Robin loves me, but I doubt he'll ever love me the way he loved you."

"That's ridiculous!" Casey refuted hotly.

"If you were his wife, Serena would never have been able to tempt him," Kate said resentfully. "I dislike living in the shadow of another woman, but I can put up with that as long as I know you don't return Robin's feelings."

"I love Dare, Kate. I've always loved Dare. Nothing will ever change that."

"I know," Kate admitted. "It's obvious you two belong together. That's the only reason I'm willing to take second place in Robin's heart. But I won't stand for Serena interfering in our lives. I want my children to be Robin's only children."

"Kate . . ." Casey's words fell to an abrupt halt. She knew what Kate was referring to and could offer no words of comfort. But there was something she could do to bring Robin back to McKenzie station, and she fully intended to do it, even at the cost of interfering where she wasn't invited.

Pressing duty had kept Robin in Bathurst past the time when he should have returned to McKenzie station. Spring had brought an influx of settlers to Bathurst and many problems arose from minor confrontations. It was Robin's job as magistrate to see these problems settled. He finally came to the conclusion that Bathurst needed another magistrate and intended to talk to Governor Macquarie concerning the matter as soon as possible. When his workload slackened, Robin made plans to return to Bathurst for Kate. Three days before he was to leave, Serena arrived at his door, throwing his life and his world into turmoil.

"What is it, Serena?" Robin asked crossly as Serena sailed past him into the house.

She spent several minutes taking in every detail of the comfortable home Robin had built on his land. One day he would be immensely wealthy, and she fully expected to share that prosperity with him. "I love your home, Robin. Once it's furnished properly it will be quite imposing."

"I'm certain Kate will do an admirable job with furnishings," Robin replied. "Did you wish to discuss something with me? I'm quite busy. I'm returning to Parramatta for Kate in a few days."

Deliberately Serena turned to face Robin. "I'd do a much better job than Kate with the house."

"We've been over this before, Serena," Robin sighed wearily.

"No, Robin," Serena refuted, her eyes shining with strange highlights. "What I've come about hasn't been discussed before."

Robin frowned, struck by the suspicion that he definitely wasn't going to like what Serena had to say. "Then tell me what's on your mind so I can get on with my preparations."

Serena dragged in a steadying breath. She knew Robin was going to hit the ceiling and mentally prepared herself for it. Not that it would change anything. The die was cast, the deed done. "I'm pregnant, Robin. I'm going to have your baby."

"Bloody hell, Serena, you've picked the wrong man to jest with. Your joke is sick."

"It's no joke, Robin, I *am* going to have your baby. In seven months, to be exact. We both know when it happened, we both knew it was a possibility."

Robin's face turned ashen as his hands swept angrily through his thick blond hair. "You're lying! 'Tis highly unlikely that you became pregnant from our one—time together. Furthermore, I have no recollection of our mating."

"Are you accusing me of taking other men to my bed?" Serena asked, her chin raised to a stubborn angle.

Robin heartily wished he could accuse Serena of whoring, but he knew for a fact she had seen no other men since her arrival in Bathurst. Gossip in the settlement would have quickly spread had Serena found solace in the arms of another man. In fact, Robin often wished Serena would find someone other than him to lavish her affection on.

"I'm accusing you of nothing, Serena, except perhaps for lying. I simply don't believe you."

"I wouldn't lie about something like that," Serena pouted sullenly. "Aren't you happy?"

"Happy! Jesus, if you're telling the truth you've just ruined my life. Kate will never understand, nor will she forgive me. She's expecting me to return to McKenzie station with the news that you will never interfere in our lives again. Let me find you a husband, Serena," Robin said, growing desperate.

"I promise you'll be happy with my choice."

"Do you want another man to raise your child?" Serena challenged. "I expected better from you, Robin. What man wants a wife who is carrying another man's child?"

Robin began pacing angrily, unwilling to accept what Serena had just told him. But what if it was true? he asked himself. Could he let another man accept responsibility for his child? He didn't love Serena, didn't even want her, but an innocent child was another matter entirely. How would a child by Serena affect his life with Kate? The answer came with stunning anguish. There would be no life with Kate if Serena was carrying his child. Kate was too proud to put up with such humiliation. She would file those accursed divorce papers so fast it would make his head spin.

Suddenly the sight of Serena sickened him. He didn't want to make any decisions until he had come to some kind of conclusion concerning the future of Serena and his child. Since there was still no doctor in Bathurst, there was no one to confirm Serena's condition. Time would tell, of course, but he was already overdue to leave for Parramatta. He had promised Kate. If he failed to arrive, she would know immediately that what they both feared had come to pass. Perhaps it was better that way, he reflected glumly. He couldn't face Kate's hurt nor bear the pain of her terrible anguish when she learned the reason for his delay.

"Get out of my sight, Serena," he spat bitterly. "When I'm ready to deal with this I'll let you know.

I'm in shock right now. You've ended all my dreams for a future with Kate."

"What about my future and the future of our child? Don't we deserve your consideration?"

"You deserve nothing but my contempt, but I can't bring myself to despise an innocent child. If you hadn't climbed into bed with me when I was too foxed to know what I was doing, this would have never happened."

"We can be happy together, Robin," Serena pleaded desperately. "We would have married if Kate hadn't come along. Once she divorces you, things will be as they should have been. There will be other children and—"

"Bloody hell! I want no children by you, can't you understand that? If this child does materialize, it will be the only one. I intend to spend the rest of my life persuading Kate to forgive me."

"What about me and our child?"

"You'll want for nothing, but I'll never be a husband to you. I can't predict how I'll feel about the child. Right now I feel profound resentment for what I'm being deprived of. I suggest you leave, Serena. I've some soul-searching to do and right now I can't stand the sight of you."

"Will—will I see you later?"

"I don't know how long it will take to resolve the dilemma I find myself in, but when I do you can be damn certain you'll be the first to hear. Just leave now, before I forget you're a pregnant woman and wring your neck—*if* you are indeed increasing."

Serena knew when to retreat, and left Robin to

fume and rant in private. She expected him to be upset but had no idea he would be so unreasonable. Still, she had accomplished what she set out to do, despite the fact that she had shattered two lives to do it, and possibly a third. Silas's hurt and disillusionment when Serena abruptly discontinued their furtive meetings didn't count. He had merely been a means to an end. Robin was the man she wanted, and she'd have him even if she had to use deceitful methods to snare him. All was fair in love and war.

Chapter Eighteen

Robin existed as if stunned during the following days. His plans irrevocably altered, he did not leave for Parramatta as planned. Instead he fretted and stewed, and for the first time in his life seemed unable to make a decision or even think clearly. He performed his duties with mechanical efficiency, but his mind was focused elsewhere. Deliberately he refrained from seeing Serena, afraid of what he might do if he confronted the woman who had ruined his chance at happiness with Kate.

Serena, meanwhile, was astute enough to realize that she was walking a thin line where Robin was concerned. She could wait, she reasoned, for in the end Robin would be hers. Biding her time wasn't easy, especially when Silas Dodd followed her with adoring eyes whenever she walked through town. A part of her regretted the shameless way she had used him, but the wonderful thought of her and Robin together forever made it all worthwhile.

Robin was sitting in his office in Government House one day in early October when he had an unexpected visitor. It was a beautiful spring day, and settlers were streaming in droves across the Blue Mountains with their sheep, families, and belongings. Robin was so engrossed in his morose thoughts that he failed to hear the door opening and closing. The first inkling he had that he wasn't alone came when a deep male voice barged into his thoughts.

"Bloody hell, Robin, why aren't you in Parramatta with your wife?"

Startled, Robin looked into the cool gray depths of Ben Penrod's eyes and saw accusation and bewilderment. "Ben, what are you doing in Bathurst? Off adventuring again?"

"Just visiting this time, mate. When I helped forge a route across the Blue Mountains, I never suspected a town like Bathurst would emerge so quickly. I wanted to see for myself what had been accomplished in so short a time. I'm leaving for England after the new year to see more of the world and thought I might want to settle here when I return, so I've come to look the town over."

"Have you seen Kate?" Robin asked anxiously.

"Aye, I've seen her," Ben allowed. His voice held a note of censure Robin found puzzling. "The Hawkesbury flooded its banks a few weeks ago. I went immediately to McKenzie station and offered my services to Kate."

"Jesus! What happened? Is there something you're not telling me?"

"Relax, Robin, everything is fine," Ben assured him. "The rains stopped just in time and the damage was minor. Have you heard nothing from Kate?"

"Not recently," Robin admitted. "It was good of you to help her in my absence."

"We're friends, for God's sake, you'd do the same for me."

"Aye," Robin agreed distractedly. Suddenly he looked at Ben through new eyes, realizing he was extremely handsome and very near Kate's age. "Are you sure that's the only reason you offered to help Kate?" He knew he was being unreasonable, but being in love was so new to him he couldn't contain his jealousy.

"Bloody hell, Robin, I could bash you for saying something so utterly ridiculous. Do you think so little of me that you believe I would attempt to seduce my best friend's wife?"

"I'm sorry, Ben, it's just that—you can't begin to understand the kind of hell I'm going through."

Deliberately Ben settled himself in a chair across from Robin. "No, but I'm willing to listen. Then I have something to tell you. Something Casey thought you should know. You might first explain why you're not at McKenzie station like you promised."

Robin looked so miserable, Ben felt sorry for him. His friend's pain only served to reinforce

Ben's views on marriage, and he silently renewed his vows never to fall in love and wed.

"I'm certain you know the story of how Kate found me and Serena when she arrived in Bathurst a few months ago. I had the devil's own time convincing Kate that Serena meant nothing to me, that it was all a terrible mistake. But it seems as if Serena put ideas in Kate's head, ideas that Kate couldn't put aside easily. She agreed to come with me to Bathurst when time proved Serena had no hold on me, if you get my meaning."

"Aye," Ben said warily, suddenly realizing what had happened to keep Robin from returning to Kate as he'd promised.

"Is that all you can say, Ben?" Robin raged helplessly. "Several days ago Serena informed me she was pregnant."

"And you believe the child is yours?"

"Aye, or so she tells me. I have no reason to doubt her. She's been with no man that I know of since she arrived in Bathurst. What else can I believe? One time, Ben, one lousy time I can't even remember. It's not fair! I love Kate, but she's too proud to have me now. My life has been cursed since the day I was born."

"You don't know for certain Kate won't have you," Ben suggested.

"I know," Robin said with grim conviction. "She told me as much when I left her at McKenzie station two months ago."

"But that was before—" His words trailed off, suddenly aware of what he was saying.

"That was before what? What in bloody hell were you going to say?"

Ben stared at his feet for several minutes before glancing back at Robin. Robin felt impaled by the relentless gray of Ben's eyes and felt doom closing in on him. He had no idea what Ben was about to divulge, but it must have been of monumental importance for Casey to have sent him with a message. Ben might have come to Bathurst merely to look around, but somehow Robin doubted it. Ben was here at Casey's request, and it concerned Kate.

"Casey thought you should know," Ben said cryptically.

"Know what? Are you going to tell me or am I going to drag it out of you?"

"Kate is pregnant. Doc Proctor has confirmed it."

Astonishment touched Robin's ashen face. Any other time those words would have sent him leaping for joy. But now they cast him into the deepest despair. He took deep breaths until he was strong enough to raise his head and face Ben.

"Are you all right, Robin?"

"Aye." But he wasn't all right. He was sick and miserable and so damned angry with himself and Serena that he wasn't certain he could ever look at her without wanting to wring her blasted neck.

"What are you going to do? Kate's expecting you at McKenzie station."

"I don't know," Robin said, still numb with shock. He had joked with Kate about her becoming pregnant, but she had been so adamantly certain she could not be that he had promptly banished it from his mind.

"Kate needs you, Robin, go to her. She'll understand."

"I doubt it," Robin returned, highly skeptical. "What I did is so despicable no decent woman could ever forget it."

"You're not being fair to Kate. Give her the chance to tell you herself that she wants nothing more to do with you. Has Serena's condition been confirmed by a physician?"

"No, there are none in Bathurst. Time will tell."

"There is no time to waste," Ben reminded him. "From what I know of Serena, she isn't above lying to get what she wants. Hell, I've had her myself a few times. She isn't to be trusted. Take her to Doc Proctor. Let him examine Serena and give you the verdict."

"You've bedded Serena? No wonder Dare didn't want me to marry her. I knew she wasn't a virgin but I never suspected—Hell, it doesn't matter now, does it?"

"It matters greatly to you and Kate."

Suddenly Ben's words began to make sense. The lad was more astute than Robin gave him credit for. While Dare and Robin had been involved in their own adventures, Ben had grown into manhood. And what a man he was! He pitied the woman who fell in love with the irresistible devil.

"Dammit, Ben, you're right! Kate deserves better than to be abandoned in favor of a schemer like

Serena. Wallowing in self-pity serves no one. I'll learn the truth even if it kills me, but one way or another I'll convince Kate that she and our child mean more to me than my own life. Oh, I'll take care of Serena's child, if it comes to that, but I'll never hurt Kate by turning away from her merely because I'm too shamed to admit to fathering another child."

"Now that's the Robin I've known and respected all these years." Ben grinned delightedly.

"Aye," Robin said thoughtfully. "I'll take Serena to Parramatta and get to the truth of the matter."

"When will you leave?"

"As soon as Serena can be ready. Certainly within a day or two. What are your plans?"

"I plan on remaining in Bathurst for several weeks. I may even do a little exploring to the south. When the land around Bathurst is settled, men will look elsewhere for expansion. My ship doesn't leave until January, and there is nothing to keep me home till then."

"Please feel free to use my house while you're in Bathurst, Ben," Robin offered. "I can't predict when I will return, but Fletcher station needs someone to keep an eye on things in my absence. My station boss is dependable, but I'd prefer to have someone I know in charge."

"I'll be glad to help out," Ben returned. "Don't worry about Fletcher station while you're away. Just concentrate on putting your life in order."

Once Robin made up his mind he moved swiftly. That very day he stopped by to see Serena on his way home. Her welcome was enthusiastic and warm, but Robin's dour mood and curt words soon dimmed her sparkle.

"Start packing, Serena."

"Packing? Where are we going?"

"To Parramatta."

"Oh, Robin," Serena gushed, "I knew you'd see reason. Are you taking me home with you? Are you finally prepared to tell Kate that we're expecting a child and there is no room in your life for her?"

"I have no intention of telling Kate any such thing. I'm taking you to Doc Proctor. If he confirms your condition, I'll make arrangements for you and the child. Those arrangements won't include me."

Serena was stunned and disappointed but recovered admirably. "I look forward to being examined by the doctor, if that's what it takes for you to believe me." Her words were delivered with such confidence that Robin's heart shriveled and died.

"How soon can you be ready?"

"Tomorrow. Is that all right?"

"That's fine. I'll come by for you in the morning. Dress warmly, 'tis still cold in the mountains. I'll make arrangements immediately." Then he spun on his heel and was gone.

Serena smiled happily. Being alone with Robin for four days suited her just fine. She eagerly anticipated their crossing, imagining all kinds of intimate situations she could take advantage of. If Robin expected the doctor to refute her pregnancy, he was going to be badly disappointed, she smirked knowingly. She was pregnant, all right. There were too many signs for it not to be true.

When Serena learned that several other people would accompany them to Parramatta she sulked the entire four days. She was unceremoniously dumped in a wagon with another family while Robin rode ahead on his horse. At night she was forced to endure the company of the female members of the Krentz family while Robin placed his bedroll elsewhere. In fact, she saw little of Robin until they left the foothills and rode into Parramatta. Once they bade good-bye to the Krentz family, Serena assumed she would be going to McKenzie station. She learned just how mistaken she had been when Robin hustled her immediately to Doc Proctor's office. Fortunately, he was in, and when Robin stated the reason for his visit, the good doctor merely looked at Robin strangely and nodded.

Robin paced nervously while Serena was being examined. He felt certain the examination would disprove Serena's claim, but he couldn't help fidgeting. The way his luck was running lately, he wouldn't put it past fate to throw his life askew. Mrs. Krentz had informed Robin that Serena had been unwell during the crossing—that she had vomited several times and appeared to be in discomfort at other times. Robin had listened to all this with ominous portent, but still held a slim hope that Serena could merely be shamming.

Doc Proctor emerged from the examination

room wearing a frown that sent Robin's world spinning. "Well, mate, what's the verdict? Is Serena pregnant or isn't she?"

"Serena is increasing, right enough. Some man will be the father of a baby in seven months." He looked at Robin sharply. "Have you any idea who the father is?"

"Aye," Robin allowed grudgingly.

Not one to pry, Doc Proctor did not pursue the subject. He had his suspicions, though, and prayed he was mistaken. He'd known Robin a long time and didn't believe him capable of acting in so despicable a manner, especially where Kate was concerned. He knew they had their problems, but what married couple didn't?

"I imagine you're thrilled about being a father," Proctor said, assuming Robin had already seen Kate. "Kate is a healthy woman; she should come through it beautifully."

"I haven't seen Kate yet," Robin said distractedly. "As soon as I find a place for Serena I'm going home."

Serena entered the outer office in time to hear Robin's last sentence. "I have a place, Robin; it's with you," she stated vehemently. "Now that you know I wasn't lying, there is no need for you to deny that we were intimate."

"That's enough, Serena," Robin warned sternly. He certainly didn't want to air his faults and weaknesses before his friends. "We'll discuss this later. I would appreciate your discretion in this matter, Dan."

"I never discuss my patients, Robin," Proctor

assured him. His eyes held a note of censure while his voice remained professionally correct. He felt pity for Kate and worried over what would become of her when she learned about Serena. He had always admired Robin, but now he was having second thoughts.

Proctor wasn't the only one who was worried. Robin was devastated. He couldn't wait to find somewhere to park Serena and go home to Kate. He had no idea what Kate would do or say when she learned about Serena, but he damn sure wasn't going to lie to her.

Kate had just gone upstairs to bed when she heard someone pounding on the front door. Hastily donning a robe, she hurried downstairs before the racket awoke the servants asleep at the rear of the house. "Just a moment," she called through the door as she shoved back the latch. Too late she remembered that there was no man in the house should she need protection. Dare and Robin had both warned her not to open her door at night unless she knew who was on the other side. The door flew open with a bang, and she stepped back in sudden fright.

Her name was a whisper on his lips as he stepped through the door, closing it softly behind him. She recognized him immediately and was in his arms before she knew how she got there.

"Robin, you're really home."

"Aye," he conceded with a dazzling smile. "I'm home, love."

Scooping her high into his arms, he raced up the

stairs two at a time. His hair was dripping, as if he had bathed first in the stream behind the house, and he smelled fresh and clean. She hugged him tightly, thanking God for making everything right in her world again. She silently vowed to put that little episode with Serena behind her and concentrate on Robin and the birth of their first child. He carried her into their room, slammed the door shut with his heel, then set her on her feet. Lamplight bathed the room in golden shadows as Robin quickly stripped the robe and gown from Kate. He stepped back, his blue eyes alight with pleasure as he looked his fill.

"You're so beautiful it hurts my eyes. Jesus, I've missed you!"

Suddenly Kate was swamped by the need to touch him, to feel his hard flesh against hers, and she reached out to him in mute appeal.

"Aye, love, I know what you're trying to say, and I feel the same way."

"I've missed you, too, Robin. I never thought it possible to be so lonely. I never want to be parted from you again."

"Never," Robin vowed emphatically.

Then he was kissing her, his mouth hot and hungry, his arms crushing her against the hard wall of his chest. His arousal was swift and violent as Kate felt him surge against her. Eagerly she returned his kisses, parting her lips for his tongue when he demanded entrance. Robin deepened the kiss and Kate responded with an ardor that thrilled him. His hands found the twin mounds of her buttocks, pulling her tightly against him. Then his mouth left hers and was sliding down her body, between the sweet flesh of her breasts, finding a nipple and suckling with gentle insistence.

He dropped to his knees, planting soft, hot kisses along the upward curve of her thighs, higher toward the curly thatch of hair and throbbing moistness it shielded. Then his fingers were parting the dark forest, revealing the tiny center of her pleasure. Rapture seized Kate as the hot roughness of his tongue caressed and stroked her molten center. She stiffened and cried out, clutching at Robin's broad shoulders to keep from spinning into space. His mouth tormented her ruthlessly while his hands slid over her smooth buttocks, holding her in place against his ravaging lips.

"Robin, please, I can stand no more!"

Taking pity on her, Robin rose shakily to his feet, by now so aroused his face was contorted in sweet anguish. But he was not finished with her, as she soon learned. Lifting her off her feet, he carried her to the bed. He meant to follow her to the soft surface, but Kate placed a staying hand on his chest.

"Take off your clothes, Robin. I want to see all of you." She was as hungry for him as he was for her. She was aroused and restless, surrendering to the urge to touch and taste.

He complied eagerly, ripping out buttons when they refused to yield swiftly enough to suit him. He stood poised at the edge of the bed while Kate's violet gaze roamed appreciatively over his hard masculine flesh, lingering on the bold proof of his desire. Her eyes on him made him grow harder than he had ever been before. Then he was pressing down on top of her, fully engorged and ready to burst. He pulled her tightly against him and she ground her hips against him. She lifted her hands to cup his face, and moving her fingers to the back of his neck, pulled him to her. Her mouth crushed against his and when she felt his lips open to her, she pushed her tongue inside him.

Suddenly Robin shifted and Kate found herself on top, straddling his slim hips, her legs doubled beneath her. Robin broke off the kiss, his eyes alight with mischief and humor. "Ride me, Kate. Take me into your body and ride me like a wild stallion."

Kate's brow furrowed, for a moment unaware of what he was asking of her. But as his staff prodded between her thighs his meaning became clear. Rising slightly, she shifted her buttocks and slid down on his distended member. An agonized groan burst past his lips. "Ah, Kate, you're so hot and tight. So good—so damn good." He flexed his tight-muscled buttocks to thrust into her again and again, holding her hips to guide her into his thrusts.

At first Kate set the pace, but as their rapture grew in leaps and bounds, Robin took over, meshing their hips in wild, frantic abandon. Throwing her head back, Kate rode him fiercely, demanding his heart, his body, his very soul. She received all of those and more. Answering the thundering need in Kate, Robin reversed their positions, raising her legs over his shoulders and sliding in deeper still.

Gritting his teeth, he thrust relentlessly, keeping tight rein on his own passion until Kate's had been satisfied.

It started with a tiny spark deep inside her body, spreading, spreading, becoming a smoldering flame, bursting into a blazing inferno when the powerful contractions of climax overtook her. Her body stiffened, her head thrashed from side to side, her hands balled into fists at her side. She screamed, a sharp staccato burst of blissful ecstasy that seemed to go on forever. Watching Kate's face as she climaxed brought on Robin's own reward, and he soon joined her in their journey to the stars.

Words were unnecessary as they drifted back to reality. They were both content to hold one another, gently stroking and caressing, murmuring words that held no meaning. Kate's breathless words broke the spell.

"I expected you much sooner."

"I was unavoidably detained," Robin replied evasively. "I wasn't too rough on you, was I?" Belatedly he remembered that Kate was expecting his child, and he didn't want to hurt either of them.

"You were exactly the way I wanted you."

He waited for her to tell him about the baby. When she didn't, he sighed and decided not to reveal just yet that he had learned her secret. He wasn't ready to tell Kate about Serena. Not tonight. Tonight was theirs alone.

"Is everything settled in Bathurst?" Kate probed, waiting for Robin to tell her whether Serena had found a husband.

"Everything is—fine," Robin said, refusing to look Kate in the eye.

"Dammit, Robin, you know what I'm talking about!" Why was Robin being so evasive? she wondered distractedly. He was dancing all around the issue.

"Kate, let's not spoil our night together with talk about Serena. I want to love you again."

Before she could protest he was kissing her, leaving her breathless and mindless with wanting. Serena was quickly forgotten as his hands and mouth drove her once again to the edge. Kate reciprocated, tasting, touching, memorizing the hard contours of his male flesh with her hands and lips. He showed her another way to love when he gently rolled her onto her side, snuggling up behind her. Then he lifted her leg and pressed boldly inside her. His thrusts were relentless, demanding, as the fingers of one hand fondled her erect nipples and caressed her breasts. His other hand plunged between her legs, rotating and massaging the swollen bud of her desire between finger and thumb.

Suddenly Kate erupted as wave after wave of unbearable pleasure coursed through her. Only when she lay quiescent beneath his stroking fingers did Robin succumb to his own climax.

"Robin."

"Ummm."

"I want to talk."

"Later," Robin said. "You've worn me out." Weariness was a large part of his reluctance to talk, but it was mostly because he knew where Kate's questions would lead. He fully intended to tell her about Serena, but not tonight.

Kate's persistence would not be quelled.

"I want to know about Serena. Is she still in Bathurst. Where is she living?"

Realizing he could not postpone Kate's request for information, Robin sat up in bed, pulling the sheet up over both of them as their bodies began to cool after their long bout of lovemaking. "What do you want to know, love?"

"Where is Serena living?"

"I moved into our new home nearly two months ago and allowed Serena to stay in the cabin since I had no other use for it." Kate frowned but accepted the explanation without complaint.

"Is she still in Bathurst?"

"No, she is in Parramatta."

"You brought her back with you?" Her frown deepened.

"Aye, but we weren't alone. We traveled with another family. I rarely saw Serena during the crossing."

"I assume, since you are here, that—that Serena has no hold on you."

"Serena never had a hold on me," Robin said.

Though Robin seemed to be answering truthfully, an unexplained wariness seized Kate. Something was amiss, something that filled her with panic. "Robin, I sense your reluctance to speak about Serena. I'm afraid, but if there is something I should know, please tell me."

"Jesus, Kate, I'd rather cut off my right arm than tell you this. I never wanted to hurt you. I love you."

Kate's heart leaped into her throat, nearly choking her. All the color drained from her face, and her mouth worked noiselessly. Words tumbled from her brain but her lips refused to release them. She merely looked at Robin, her eyes so huge they nearly swallowed her face. Robin was struck anew by their incredible violet depths as she stared at him in mute appeal.

"I'm sorry, Kate. When Serena told me, I refused to believe her. That's why I brought her to Parramatta. I knew Dan Proctor would tell me the truth. God help me, God help us all, but Serena is expecting my child."

Robin would have given anything to prevent the stricken look on Kate's face. "Are—are you sure the child is yours?"

"Aye," Robin said grimly. "As certain as I could be. Serena has seen no other man since arriving in Bathurst. I would have known if she had. Bathurst is still a small settlement with few single men outside of convicts."

Kate digested the news slowly and painfully. She gulped convulsively as it settled like a lump of raw fire in her gut. Slowly she rose from bed and walked woodenly to the window, oblivious to her nakedness. She stared into the midnight blackness, unable to think beyond the fact that Serena was expecting Robin's child and she had yet to tell Robin about the child she was carrying.

Robin joined her at the window, embracing her from behind and pulling her against the hard wall of his chest. "It isn't the end of the world, love. It doesn't change how I feel about you. I'll take care of Serena and the child, but you're the only woman I want. Our children are the only children I desire."

Kate shrugged out of his arms, whirling to face him. "You owe Serena more than that," she said caustically.

"I told you I'd see that she and the child want for nothing. I'll find her a good husband."

"I'm going through with the divorce, Robin. It may be a long time in coming, but Serena will wait."

Robin groaned. "Bloody hell! I don't want Serena."

"It's a little late for those sentiments."

"Don't you think I hate myself for something I can't even recall? Not a day goes by without me cursing my weakness."

"Where is Serena now?"

"I left her with Dare and Casey. They weren't too happy about the arrangement, but I sure as hell wasn't going to bring her here. I want you to forget about that blasted divorce and concentrate on our marriage and raising our child."

Kate froze. Did Robin know about the baby she carried? "What makes you think we have a child on the way?"

"Dan Proctor told me."

"I can raise my child without you. I got along

Connie Mason

just fine without you in the past and can do so again. McKenzie station is all I need, that and my baby."

"Our baby."

"My baby!" Kate spat from between clenched teeth. "Take Serena and go back to Bathurst. I'll send word when the divorce has been granted. In fact, I want you out of my house now."

Chapter Nineteen

Robin's nails bit into the palms of his tightly clenched fists. He'd had about all a man could take from this contrary, obstinate woman he had married. She refused to listen to reason, was unable to cope with the fact that he loved her and only her, and wanted to end their marriage at a time when she needed him most. Time and again he had yielded to her flawed thinking and obliged her when it was what neither of them wanted. No more. No longer would he let Kathryn Molly McKenzie have her way. His pride had suffered irreparable damage because of her stubbornness, and she now mistakenly assumed she could lead him around like a tame dingo.

"I'm not leaving, Kate," Robin said with quiet determination. "And furthermore, when I return to Bathurst you're going with me. You're my wife and you'll stay my wife until one of us leaves this earth." His pointed blue gaze nailed her to the wall and his words pierced her like daggers.

"You can't dictate to me!" Kate sputtered indignantly. "McKenzie station is mine and I'll stay if I want to. Once I get the divorce . . ."

Robin flung her a condescending glare. "There will be no divorce. Potter misled you if he told you it could be easily had. A word from me, and Governor Macquarie will relegate the petition to an obscure place in his desk where it will never see the light of day. Besides, you're going to have my child, and that alone will influence his judgment."

"I'm not the only one having a baby of yours," Kate grumbled resentfully.

Robin ignored her spiteful remark. "I don't care what you do with McKenzie station. Sell it or rent it or give it away, it makes little difference to me, but when I leave here you will be with me. Now go back to bed. We'll discuss this tomorrow."

"You can't—"

"Dammit, Kate, not tonight! I said we'll discuss it tomorrow."

Stunned, Kate stared at Robin. He'd always been so gentle with her she couldn't believe he was speaking to her in such a disparaging manner. He was a complicated creature who infuriated and intrigued her; a man she loved and detested at the same time. But when he made love to her, the emotions that raged through her had little to do with hate. He possessed an inner strength and confidence she had come to depend on, and she disliked that even more.

Turning on her heel, Kate marched back to bed, cowed for the moment but not defeated. If she had seen the devilish grin that settled on Robin's roguish features she would have stood her ground and argued until doomsday.

Climbing into bed and pulling the covers over her, Kate was startled when Robin followed, lowering himself beside her. "Move over, you're hogging the bed."

"What! You're not sleeping in my bed," Kate complained with offended dignity.

"I'll sleep wherever I please and it pleases me to sleep with my wife," he replied flippantly.

Kate slanted him a quelling glare, scooted to the edge of the bed, and held herself stiffly as Robin settled comfortably at her side. When he reached for her and pulled her into the curve of his body, she grumbled obscenities beneath her breath and tried to go to sleep. Never had her pride and dignity suffered so severely, and she didn't like the feeling.

Robin surrendered to sleep first, and when Kate realized he didn't intend to make love to her again she relaxed and allowed sleep to claim her. She had already decided to fight him with her last breath if he attempted to seduce her again.

It seemed she had been asleep mere minutes when Kate awoke feeling a delicious languor creep through her limbs. At first she didn't recognize the source of her body's delightful response, until the pressure of Robin's hands on her body brought her abruptly to her senses. No! She wouldn't let this happen again, she scolded herself. Why was it that the moment he touched her her body remembered what her mind refused to accept—the wild, unquenchable hunger, the terrible need to be loved by this particular man?

This time Robin wasn't going to have his way, she silently vowed, squirming to escape his stroking fingers. Let him go to Serena if he wanted loving. Flinging herself from the bed, her breasts heaving, her breath coming in angry pants, she stood over him, hands on hips, her violet eyes challenging.

"You will *not* make love to me again!"

Robin smiled indulgently. "I love the way you hate me."

Grappling with those curious words, Kate whirled and struggled into her robe, so angry her fingers fumbled clumsily with the buttons and ties. Rising languidly from the bed, Robin shoved her fingers aside and fastened the robe properly while Kate fumed in impotent rage.

"Take care of your needs, Kate. I'll meet you downstairs for breakfast. There is much we need to discuss." He was gone from the room before Kate had time to formulate a nasty reply.

I love the way you hate me.

Robin's cryptic words blew through her mind like a ravaging wind. It was true that Robin's touch catapulted her into a world of sensuality, a world she had never known until that rogue convict had come into her life. She had even begun to believe she loved him, until that day she found him in bed with Serena. And even after that she couldn't deny the fact that what she felt for him was more than mere lust. It wasn't until she learned that Serena was expecting his child that those feelings died. He still had the ability to arouse her, to make her body crave fulfillment, but she was certain she no longer loved him. She heaved a dispirited sigh. If Robin thought she was going to Bathurst with him, he was sadly mistaken.

I love the way you hate me.

Did she hate Robin? He certainly had given her sufficient reason to hate him. But she was justified—wasn't she?

Robin was waiting in the dining room when Kate finally arrived downstairs. She merely nodded and helped herself from the sideboard where Maude had laid out an array of tempting food. Kate was ravenous, helping herself to a generous serving of everything. Robin must have been hungry too, for he heaped his plate full and dug in immediately. Kate lifted the first mouthful, chewed thoughtfully, then frowned as her stomach revolted. She dropped the fork, gulping convulsively in an effort to keep down what she had swallowed.

"Oh!" she said, and realized she had to leave the room immediately or embarrass herself. She whirled and fled back up the stairs. She was just sliding the chamberpot under the bed when Robin entered the room.

"Can I help?"

"You've already done enough, thank you," she said icily.

Robin grinned cheekily. "It will pass. Do you feel well enough to talk?"

"I'd just as soon get this over with." She sat on the edge of the bed, motioning Robin toward a chair some distance away.

"Don't you trust yourself with me?" Robin asked. His voice was laced with an arrogance Kate found disgusting.

"It's you I don't trust. What is it we need to talk about?"

"I'm leaving for Sydney tomorrow. I'll only be gone a day or two, and when I return I'll expect you to be ready to accompany me to Bathurst."

"I'm not going," Kate returned tightly. "What about McKenzie station?"

"Sell it to Dare. The deed is in your name, but according to law everything you own is mine. I like Bathurst. I intend to settle there permanently and raise our family on my own land."

"Does that include Serena and her child?"

Robin flushed guiltily but did not waver before Kate's taunts. "No, Serena and the child will be taken care of. If she doesn't want the child, I'll raise it myself. Just as I will our child if you decide to leave me once it's born."

"What? You can't do that!" Kate had indeed been thinking along those lines. While still pregnant she was vulnerable to his decisions, but once the baby was born she could take her child and leave Robin, maybe even go back to England.

"I have every right. The law is on my side. I'd

prefer to have both of you, but if you insist on leaving, the baby stays with me.''

Robin realized he was being deliberately cruel but he couldn't continue to indulge Kate and end up without either her or the baby. He knew she'd never leave her child behind and felt confident she would come to realize they belonged together. Her body knew it; he just had to convince her mind.

Kate sulked in impotent rage. He didn't own her, did he? The reason she'd never considered marriage before was the fact that she'd have to belong to the man who became her husband. Belonging body and soul to a man angered and terrified her. What kind of law made women mere chattel? A law devised by men, she sneered derisively. McKenzie station was hers, yet it wasn't hers.

''Are you asking me to raise Serena's child if she doesn't want it?'' Kate asked quietly.

''It will be my child too,'' Robin reminded her. ''But I don't think we have to worry about that.''

''Why not?''

''Serena wouldn't give up her child to me. I know her too well. She'll hang on to it as a means of insinuating herself into my life. But it won't work. I hope to find her a husband. One who can keep her in line.''

A scowl drew Kate's brows together. ''You're a fool, Robin Fletcher, if you think Serena will give you up so easily.''

''We'll see,'' Robin said cryptically. He rose to leave. ''There is much to be done before I leave for Sydney tomorrow. Rest this morning; you look peaked.''

"Are you planning on seeing Governor Macquarie?" Kate couldn't help but ask.

"Aye, there are several things I want to discuss with him. For one thing, Bathurst needs another magistrate. I'm hoping he'll appoint another ex-convict. While I have his ear I'll plead with him to reconsider Big John's sentence and issue him a 'ticket of leave.' The man deserves another chance."

"I'd forgotten about Big John," Kate cried. "What happened to him? Was he taken back to Sydney for trial?"

"Aye, but he never reached Sydney. He overpowered his four guards and escaped into the forest. For all I know, he's still hiding in the mountains."

"Do you think the governor will take your request into consideration?"

"He's a fair man, and Big John isn't a vicious criminal. He's proved that many times over. When I explain to Macquarie the reason Big John committed murder, he may be more kindly disposed toward giving him a 'ticket of leave' until his sentence is expired."

Suddenly Kate thought it would be a good time to ask Robin about his own crime. Had he been transported to New South Wales for a vile crime such as murder or rape? Or had his sentence been cruelly unjust? Her father had tried to tell her once, and she had stubbornly refused to listen. But when she opened her mouth to pose the question, Robin was already on his way out of the room.

"Don't forget, Kate," he flung over his shoulder, "be ready to leave when I return from Sydney. I'm going to Dare's house now to ask him if he'd like to purchase McKenzie station.''

"And to see Serena," Kate flung after his departing back. If he heard, he gave no indication.

Kate made a point to stay out of Robin's way the rest of the day. When she retired that night she was outraged when Robin insisted on sharing her bed.

"This is where I belong, Kate," he said, calmly taking off his clothes and climbing nude between the sheets.

"I'm going to one of the spare bedrooms," Kate insisted, gathering up her night clothes.

"I think not," Robin refuted. "I'll just carry you back here if you insist on leaving."

"Why do you continue to force yourself on me when it's obvious I don't want you?" Kate flared angrily.

"The only thing that's obvious to me is that you are fighting what you really want, what we both want. Come to bed."

"Only if you promise not to touch me. I can't stand the thought of you seeing Serena today and—and—whatever you did with her."

"I did nothing. In fact, I didn't even see Serena. She was still abed when I arrived, and I was closeted in the study with Dare most of the time. Dare was delighted with the prospect of buying McKenzie station, by the way."

"I hate you."

Robin's reply was to leap from bed, scoop Kate up in his arms, and carry her to the bed. Amidst her shrieks of protest, he quickly rid her of her clothes, then kissed her soundly. He kissed her until she was dizzy, until her lips softened and opened to his probing tongue, until her arms circled his neck and pulled him closer. What happened next was pure magic as his sweet, wild kisses left hot imprints on her flesh, traveling the length of her body, worshiping every inch of sensitive skin. He paused at her stomach, fondling the slightly rounded mound with loving care, then continued down to the moist flesh of her womanhood. With slow deliberation he lowered his head and his teeth nibbled gently, his hot tongue sucked and stabbed—deep—deeper.

"No!" Kate cried raggedly. "Why do you do this to me?"

"Can't you guess, love?" Then his mouth was doing things to her that made her writhe and cry out and beg for him to come into her.

Robin obliged, sliding up her body to thrust into her. "Ah, love, I truly do love the way you hate me."

But Kate was beyond thinking, beyond hearing as the thunder in her ears obliterated all but the insatiable need pounding through her veins.

Robin was already gone when Kate awoke the next morning. She was sick again and cursed him soundly for placing her in this position. She tried to tell herself that she didn't want his baby, but the lie stuck in her craw. She'd die if anything happened to her baby. She wanted it, wanted it fiercely. She just didn't want its father. Kate seriously thought about refusing to be uprooted and taken to Bathurst, but knowing Robin, she realized he would pick her up bodily and put her in the dray if she wasn't prepared to leave with him.

Sighing dispiritedly, she began packing her personal items, wondering exactly how Robin intended to resolve the problem with Serena. One thing for certain, the problem would not go away. After several hours of sorting through clothing, hunger gnawed at Kate and she went downstairs for lunch. She had just reached the bottom of the stairs when she heard a terrible racket at the door.

"I'm coming," she called, then flung open the door. She was stunned to find the aborigine tracker, Culong, standing on the doorstep.

"Robin Fletcher," Culong said. He was breathless, as if he had been running a great distance. "Culong must see Robin Fletcher."

"He's not here," Kate said, alarmed by his urgency. "Robin left for Sydney early this morning."

Culong's dark brow wrinkled in a frown and Kate quickly added, "Can I help you?"

"Robin's woman go with Culong."

"Go with you? Go where?"

"To my village. Hurry!"

"Wait, can't you tell me what's wrong?"

"Giant man sick, maybe dying. Mantua say he calls for Robin Fletcher."

"Giant man? Are you referring to Big John? Who is Mantua?"

"Mantua is medicine woman of tribe and sister to Culong. Culong hear Robin call giant 'Big John.'"

371

"What is wrong with Big John?"

"Snake bite," Culong said dourly. "Culong find him in forest. You come."

"Yes, I'll come," Kate said, disregarding the danger she might face traveling to Culong's village. Big John had saved her life once, and she could not refuse to go to him in his need. Perhaps he would tell her what he wanted of Robin. "Is it far?"

"Not so far," Culong said, gesturing vaguely toward the forest visible in the distance.

"Should I bring the dray?" Kate asked.

"No dray. Forest too thick." He turned to leave, expecting Kate to follow.

"Wait, I must tell someone where I am going."

Culong waited patiently while Kate hurried off to find Maude. Maude was aghast when Kate told her she was going with the aborigine. "Oh, no, Kate—" Kate had insisted Maude call her by her first name. "You can't go alone with that aborigine. What will Robin say?"

"Robin trusts Culong," Kate assured her. "He's the one who tracked me in the mountains. If not for him I'd be dead now. I must go, Maude. Tell Robin where to find me."

"Aye," Maude agreed reluctantly. "Be careful."

They left immediately. Kate was hard pressed to keep up with Culong, but the native, realizing her disadvantage, stopped often to wait for her to catch up. They walked for what seemed hours through wild bush ablaze with a splendorous array of wildflowers and forest so dense with tall eucalyptus and gum trees they blotted out the sky. When they interrupted a spiny anteater gorging itself on ants from a huge anthill, Kate carefully skirted the strange-looking animal. She did the same with a huge lizard sunning itself on a rock, though she enjoyed immensely the pink and gray cockatoos perched in the trees, the small brightly colored parrots called lorikeets, and the lyrebird and emu that scurried before them in fright. She kept a sharp eye out for snakes and dingos, the wild dogs that terrorized man and beast in the outback of Australia. Not to mention bushrangers who could be camped in the forest. Suddenly Kate began to realize how foolish she was to accompany Culong into the bush where danger lurked behind every tree.

"Stop, I have to rest," Kate cried out when she lagged too far behind Culong to catch up. She dropped down at the base of a gigantic eucalyptus and rested her back against the rough trunk while Culong trotted back to join her. "How much farther?"

"Not far now."

Kate was sweating profusely, wishing she had brought a bottle of water. "I'm thirsty," she complained.

Culong looked at her curiously, shrugged, and said, "Wait here, Culong bring water." Then he turned and walked off before Kate could question him. Actually, she was grateful for the opportunity to rest and hoped he wouldn't return too soon.

She was starting to doze when a gunshot brought her abruptly alert. It sounded fairly close by, and Kate looked around frantically for the source of the sound. She heard and saw nothing.

Panic seized her, and she wanted to run but had no idea where she would go or which direction to take. Culong said his village wasn't far, but from past experience Kate knew how deceptive and dangerous the forest could be. She'd be hopelessly lost in a matter of minutes. Determined not to yield to panic, she decided to wait for Culong to return.

"Well, now, look what I found."

Kate nearly fainted when a man appeared out of nowhere carrying a musket under his arm. The remarkable part was that Kate recognized the man. It was Gil Bennett, the man she and Robin had interviewed as a possible station boss for McKenzie station. He was leaner than she recalled, his eyes more wild, but he was the same oily creature she had loathed on sight. He was grinning evilly as his lewd gaze raked Kate from head to toe.

"Are you lost, lady?"

"Yes, I am. Can you take me back to McKenzie station?" Kate asked hopefully. She realized she was being an optimist to think Bennett meant her anything but harm, but it was worth a try.

"Well, now, that depends. Are you with that black devil I found down by the waterhole?"

"What did you do to Culong?"

"Fond of dark meat, are you?"

"You're despicable," Kate rasped hatefully. "I'll find my own way back. But first tell me if you've harmed Culong."

"Australia would be a better place if they did away with all those black-skinned devils."

"You bastard!" Kate hissed from between clenched teeth. "I refuse to stand here and listen to you. I'm leaving."

When she started forward, Bennett pointed his gun at her. "I don't think so. I heard you married Fletcher. You both turned me down when I needed a job. You were an uppity bitch then and you still are. It's about time someone took you down a notch or two. Besides, I haven't had a woman since the Parton—" His words ground to an abrupt halt as he was aware of what he was about to admit.

"It *was* you!" Kate accused. "You *are* the one responsible for the death of an innocent girl."

Bennett scowled, then grinned slyly. "Aye, she was a gullible wench who actually believed I considered her attractive. The only thing I wanted of her was betwixt her legs. Then the dumb bitch had to go and get herself in the family way and spoil my fun. Serves her right," he complained bitterly. "No one could actually prove it was me who knocked the bitch up, but when she begged me to help her get rid of the bastard, I obliged. Who knew the bitch would die? Talk spread, and I found it impossible to find work, so I took to the bush. 'Tis easier to steal what I need than work for a livin' anyway."

"What—what do you intend to do with me?" Kate stammered, considering several methods of escape but finding them all lacking. At least while that gun was pointed at her.

"I'm gonna use you like God intended," Bennett guffawed crudely. "Like I said before, I ain't had a woman in so long the first time won't last more than a few minutes. But after that expect to be used long and hard and often. Lay down."

"Robin will kill you."

"He'll never find me. I'm headin' across the mountains. Hear tell there's plenty of gold layin' around just for the pickin'."

"The gold belongs to the government."

"Gold belongs to them that finds it. Quit stallin'. Are you gonna lay down or do I have to knock you down?"

"I'm—pregnant," Kate revealed, hoping it would influence the bushranger. It didn't.

"Your belly's not too big so it won't bother me none. I did it to Annie Parton when she was increasing, and it didn't feel no different."

Kate realized that nothing she said seemed to faze the man. He was determined to defile her in the most vile manner, and she was just as determined that he wouldn't touch her. She did the only thing that offered her a slim hope. She turned and ran, hoping Bennett wouldn't shoot her. If he wanted her alive—which his words indicated—he'd not use his gun. If he merely gave chase, she'd stand a good chance of losing herself in the dense forest.

Bennett was right behind her, crashing through the bush and laughing wildly at her feeble efforts to escape. He knew he could catch up with her at any time, but it piqued his perverse sense of humor to let Kate think she was getting away. Finally he tired of the chase, and several long strides brought him even with her. He grasped her long, trailing hair, bringing her to an abrupt halt.

"This game bores me, lady," he growled, throwing her to the hard ground.

He stood over her, grinning with malicious enjoyment as a look of utter horror passed over Kate's face. Kate squeezed her eyes shut, expecting Bennett to fall on her like a ravening beast. All her senses leaped with awareness when a strange buzzing sound filled the air around her. Cranking one eye open, she saw that Bennett was slowly sinking to his knees, his face growing slack, a look of disbelief glazing his eyes before they fell shut. Then she saw it, lying on the ground at Bennett's feet. A boomerang. One of those odd weapons used by aborigines for protection and to kill game. It was effective as well as deadly accurate.

Shifting her gaze, Kate was stunned to see a dozen aborigines stepping from behind the concealment of surrounding trees and bushes. They gazed at her in silent awe, and Kate wondered if any of them spoke English and if they intended to harm her. She had heard that most aborigines were friendly though wary of whites, whom they called "white ghosts." She also wondered if they were from Culong's tribe. Picking herself up from the ground, she boldly faced the intimidating natives.

"I am a friend of Culong," she said loudly.

Silence.

"I am a friend—"

"They will not harm you."

Kate swiveled her head to see Culong limping from the forest, leaning heavily on the shoulders of one of his tribesmen.

"Culong! Thank heaven you're not dead. I was afraid—"

"White ghost not kill Culong. Culong's friends hear gun noise and come to help. Come, Robin's woman, we are nearly to village."

Kate needed no urging as she quickly fell in step with the aborigines. Nearly an hour later they stumbled into the village of a dozen grass huts. Aborigines lived in small villages, sometimes never meeting another aborigine from a different tribe. They were nomads and hunters, never having learned to cultivate or conserve. They were intelligent, with unbelievable skills in tracking and hunting, and used the most ingenious, primitive weapons known to man. Their knowledge of the earth and its creatures was remarkable.

Kate was taken immediately to one of the grass huts. She had to stoop to enter, and it was so dark inside she had to adjust her eyes to the dim lighting. Once she became accustomed to the darkness, she saw a woman bending over a figure lying on a pallet near the rear of the hut. Gingerly she approached, noting as she did that Culong was now being carried inside by his companions. The wound in his side was bleeding profusely, and he seemed to be growing weak. The woman tending Big John turned, saw Culong, and gave a cry of distress. She was beside Culong instantly, paying little heed to Kate, who sidled past in an effort to approach the pallet where Big John lay.

Instinctively Kate realized the woman must be Culong's sister, Mantua. They conversed in quiet tones while Mantua inspected her brother's wound. She set to work almost immediately, gathering supplies necessary for removing the bullet. All the while Mantua tended her brother, no sound of pain escaped from the lips of the stoic aborigine. His face was utterly devoid of emotion as Mantua dug for the bullet. Kate looked away, concentrating on Big John.

"Big John, 'tis Kate."

Big John opened his eyes. They were hollow and bloodshot and filled with anguish. Beneath the light kangaroo skin his body appeared gaunt and shrunken, though his size was still huge compared to the short, stocky aborigines.

"Where is Robin, lass?" Big John asked.

"He's in Sydney. Can you tell me what it is you wanted from Robin?"

"You've come all this way to ask me that, lass?" Big John asked, amazed.

"Aye," Kate said. "'Tis no more than fitting after what you did for me. How do you feel?"

"I hope Robin realizes what a brave lass he's found in you. As for how I feel, let's just say I've seen better days."

"You'll survive, Big John," Kate predicted. "You're too tough to die from a snake bite. What is it you wanted to tell Robin?"

"'Tis—'tis about Serena. 'Tis somethin' I saw from the jail in Bathurst where I was held. I heard the guards talkin' about Serena. One of them said she's expectin' Robin's babe—you know how gossip is in a small settlement like Bathurst—and I didn't believe it. I thought he should know what I saw. I was makin' my way to Parramatta when I was snakebit.''

Chapter Twenty

About the same time as Kate was on her way to Culong's village, Robin was conferring with Governor Macquarie. Robin's expression was intense, his words impassioned.

"I urge you to reconsider Big John's sentence, Governor. I firmly believe the man is no longer a menace to society. He needs the chance to prove himself. I know he escaped from the coal mines at Newcastle, but what man wouldn't, given the opportunity? He's lived in the bush stealing what he needed to keep himself alive, but his actions on several occasions proved he's no ordinary bushranger."

Governor Macquarie stroked his chin thoughtfully. "What you say may be true, but the man did commit murder."

"I told you the circumstances," Robin argued with relentless determination.

"He also overpowered his four guards and escaped into the forest," contended Macquarie.

"Aye," admitted Robin, "but none of them were hurt. Had he been a vicious killer he would have made no effort to spare their lives."

"If I do grant Big John a 'ticket of leave,' how will you find him? The man is a master at surviving in the bush and avoiding contact with other humans."

"I'll find him," Robin vowed. "He also seems to know what is going on in surrounding towns. Somehow he'll know that he's been granted a 'ticket of leave.'"

"You're absolutely certain he won't turn vicious once he's given a 'ticket of leave'?" Macquarie wanted to know.

"I'd stake my life on it."

Macquarie was known to be liberal in regards to convicts and emancipists; that was why the exclusionists fought bitterly to have him recalled. Macquarie believed that once a convict had become a free man he should be considered on the same footing as every other man in the colony. All former bad conduct should be forgiven and forgotten. Consequently, he leaned toward leniency regarding convicts who were truly repentant.

"Because you have personally vouched for Big John, I will issue him a 'ticket of leave,' but on one condition," Macquarie stipulated. "You must keep him in Bathurst and employ him yourself. 'Tis the only way I can be assured he will have proper supervision. Under no circumstances will he be allowed to return to the more populated towns of Parramatta and Sydney."

Elated, Robin nodded slowly. "Aye, I agree."

"There is one other thing. Another seven years will be added to his sentence until he proves trustworthy enough to either reduce his sentence or remit it."

"I'm certain Big John will agree to those terms."

"Then 'tis settled. Your other request for another magistrate to serve Bathurst is a reasonable one. There are several good men qualified to serve. I shall appoint one from among them soon and send him to Bathurst."

"I strongly urge you to consider another ex-convict," Robin suggested. "Surely there are many candidates available for consideration as well as those who would welcome the appointment."

"There are also some who would violently protest placing another ex-convict in a position of importance. But as long as I am Governor of New South Wales I will continue to seek equality for all men."

"Thank you, Governor," Robin said warmly as he rose to leave.

"Spend the night at Government House, Robin," Macquarie invited. "Later you can apprise me of what is taking place in Bathurst."

"I'd be honored, Governor, but I must leave at first light tomorrow. My wife is—expecting our first child and I don't like leaving her alone."

"Congratulations," Macquarie said with genuine pleasure. "I understand completely your unwillingness to linger in Sydney longer than necessary."

Robin left shortly afterwards. That evening he had a long chat with Macquarie and went to bed early. Bright and early the next morning he was on the road to Parramatta.

Kate was stunned when she heard Big John whisper Serena's name and hint at information he had about her. She bent closer as his words trailed off and his voice grew weak.

"What is it, Big John? What do you know about Serena? I'll see that Robin gets your message."

"Robin is an honorable man; he'd never——" Suddenly Big John gasped, his face grew red, his eyes rolled in his head, and his breath came in short, labored pants.

Kate cried out in alarm, bringing Mantua to her side. "What is wrong with him? Don't let him die, oh, please don't let him die." A profound feeling told her that Big John had something vitally important to tell her. Something that could change the course of her life.

Mantua worked frantically over Big John. Since she spoke no English she did not answer Kate's plea. When she finally lifted her head she spoke in quiet tones to Culong, who hovered nearby. When she finished speaking, Culong turned to Kate and said, "Big man unconscious, not dead. Big man very sick, maybe die, but Mantua's medicine is good. Mantua's medicine will take poison from big man's body. It will take much time."

"How long will Big John remain unconscious?"

Culong conferred again with Mantua.

"Two, three days."

"Two or three days?" Kate cried, genuinely distressed. "Are you certain he will be all right?"

"Not certain. Only the gods know if a man's life is worth saving."

"I'll not leave him," Kate said, kneeling beside Big John's pallet. "Tell Mantua I will help nurse him."

Kate spent the night sleeping on a makeshift bed in a corner of the grass hut. When she awoke the next morning she immediately rushed out to vomit the meager contents of her stomach. Mantua slanted her a knowing glance and offered a concoction for her to drink. Kate did not hesitate, trusting the medicine woman implicitly. Once she downed the mixture, which tasted pleasantly of herbs, she felt much better and took up her vigil again at Big John's side.

The fifteen-mile trip from Sydney to Parramatta on horseback took Robin several hours, and he arrived at McKenzie station in time for lunch. Though he had left Kate the day before, he was anxious to see her again. He hoped she had accepted his decision to leave McKenzie station, for he was adamant that she accompany him to Bathurst. As for Serena, he was still in somewhat of a quandary. He knew of several men in Parramatta who would gladly marry her were it not for the child she carried. One or two, he was certain, would wed her despite the child. Yet the thought of another man raising his child nagged at him. Even if the child was unwanted, it was still an innocent human being who deserved every chance in life.

Robin seriously considered approaching Dan Proctor. Dan needed a wife, and Robin knew him to be a good man who would raise Serena's child as his own. Bloody hell, Robin grumbled beneath his breath, how in the hell had he made such a muddle of his life? How could he have made love to a woman and not even remember it? He'd been drunk before, but in the past had recalled everything he did or said.

The moment Robin entered the house he sensed something was amiss. Kate! His first thought was that something was wrong with Kate. She had been sick the morning he left; had she lost their child?

"Kate!" His cry echoed hollowly through the empty house. "Kate! Where are you?"

Maude came running from the kitchen, her eyes wild, her face awash with relief. "Thank God you've come."

"What is it, Maude? Where is Kate? Has something happened to her?"

"Kate is fine, or she was the last time I saw her. She's not here, Robin. She left yesterday with that black man."

"What black man?" Panic-stricken, Robin's voice rose so high it cracked.

"Kate called him Culong."

"Bloody hell! What did Culong want with Kate?"

Wild Land, Wild Love

"He didn't want Kate. He wanted you. Kate went with him when you weren't available. Seems like Culong found Big John near death in the forest and brought him to his village. Big John was asking for you, and Culong came to get you."

"Kate had no business going with Culong in her condition," Robin raged.

"In her condition?" Maude asked. "Is—is Kate increasing?" Robin nodded grimly. "Oh, Lord, had I known I'd have tried harder to stop her."

"'Tis not your fault, Maude. I'll find her. Fix me a swag, I'll leave as soon as I change. I'll go afoot; 'tis easier than trying to ride a horse through the bush."

"Do you know where to find Culong's village?"

"I know where it is. I've been there many times in the past."

An hour later Robin left McKenzie station, walking briskly toward the forest. He arrived at the village without mishap shortly before dark and was taken immediately to the grass hut where Kate sat hovering over Big John, who still hadn't regained consciousness. He burst through the door in a fine rage.

"Bloody hell, Kate, are you mad to travel through the bush in your condition? I don't know what I would have done if you or our child had been harmed."

Kate's heart leaped in sheer joy when she saw Robin standing in the narrow doorway. "Robin! I didn't expect you so soon. I thought you'd be in Sydney for days."

"I returned this morning after speaking with Governor Macquarie yesterday," Robin informed her, still angry at Kate for her reckless behavior. "What's wrong with Big John?"

"He was bitten by a poisonous snake," Kate revealed. "He was lucid when I arrived but fell unconscious while I was speaking with him and hasn't roused since."

"I still haven't heard your excuse for coming here when you knew it might be dangerous for our child."

"Culong said Big John might die and was asking for you. Since you weren't available, I decided to come myself. As you can see, I am fine." She didn't dare tell him about Gil Bennett, not yet, not until his temper cooled.

"Did Big John tell you what he wanted?"

"No, not exactly. He said it had something to do with Serena."

"Serena? What could Big John know about Serena?"

"I—I don't know. He fell unconscious before he was able to divulge what it was he wanted to tell you. I haven't left his side since, and he hasn't uttered a word. He hinted that it was important. Evidently he heard gossip concerning Serena's pregnancy, and I got the feeling he discovered something you should know."

Robin's long fingers tunneled through his thick thatch of blond hair. "I wonder," he mused thoughtfully.

"Wonder what?"

"Nothing. Until Big John regains his wits 'tis

senseless to speculate. One thing is certain, though. I'm taking you home."

"What? And leave Big John before you know what he wanted to tell you?"

"Big John could remain unconscious for days. You don't belong here in a grass hut. Once you're safely at McKenzie station I'll come back and wait until Big John is well enough to communicate."

"I don't—"

"Argument will do you no good, Kate," Robin said sternly. "I'm taking you home and that's the end of it. I'm going to talk to Culong now. We'll spend the night and leave in the morning."

He left the hut before Kate had time to protest his overbearing, arrogant manner. Of late all he seemed to be doing was dictate to her, expecting her to acquiesce meekly. She wondered if this was a portent of the future. If so, she intended to set him straight at the earliest opportunity.

Later that evening Mantua provided a meal of roasted meat and vegetables, which Kate devoured greedily. When Robin failed to return to the hut, she lay down on the makeshift bed she'd occupied the night before and drifted off to sleep. Sometime later Robin entered the hut. He went first to Big John, saw he was still unconscious, then found Kate stretched out on a pallet nearby. He lay down beside her, pulling her into his arms and holding her close. It had nearly torn him apart when Culong related what had happened out in the bush. Bushrangers were a constant menace, and Kate should have known better than to traipse off without considering the consequences.

What if he had lost her? What if the bushranger had raped Kate and as a result she had lost their child? Robin's body convulsed in a shudder, and he hugged Kate closer. He didn't even want to think about living without Kate.

Instinctively Kate responded to the pressure of Robin's arms by snuggling closer. Though she was still drugged by sleep, the feel of his big body next to hers lent her a measure of comfort she had missed all those weeks they were apart. Her spontaneous response brought a smile to Robin's lips.

"Ah, Kate," he crooned softly in her ear, "you try so hard to hate me. When are you going to realize that what you feel for me is a much deeper and stronger emotion than hate?"

Kate murmured something not quite intelligible but did not awaken. Robin silently thanked God she was safe in his arms and fell asleep immediately. It had been a long, exhausting day since he left Sydney that morning.

Ignoring Kate's vigorous protests, Robin insisted they return to McKenzie station the next morning. They left after eating breakfast. Robin looked one last time at the unconscious form of Big John and promised Culong he would return the following day. The going wasn't so difficult this time, Kate thought as she plodded beside Robin, who had kept the pace deliberately slow and easy to accommodate his pregnant wife. They stopped often to rest, once beside a bubbling billabong to drink their fill and another time beneath the spreading branches of a giant gum tree. It was during one of these stops that Robin questioned Kate about the bushranger.

"Culong told me he was shot by a bushranger when he was bringing you to his village. Do you want to tell me about it?"

"I wish Culong hadn't mentioned it," Kate said sourly. "It—it was nothing."

"Nothing! Do you call almost being raped by a bushranger nothing? If you care nothing for your own safety, you should have thought about our baby."

An angry flush spread over Kate's cheeks. Did Robin think she had deliberately set out to harm their child? She might not like Robin, but she certainly held no such feelings about her baby. "I didn't think anything could happen as long as I was with Culong."

"Now you know that nothing or no one is safe in the forest as long as bushrangers roam free."

"I—knew the man," Kate ventured.

"You knew the bushranger? Who was he?"

"It was Gil Bennett. He admitted he was the man responsible for Annie Parton's death. He—he even joked about it." A shudder traveled the length of her spine. "Did Culong tell you his friends arrived in time?"

"Aye, he told me, but that doesn't make what happened any easier to bear. Bloody hell, Kate, Bennett could have killed you! Or hurt you and left you for wild animals to devour. I thought you learned your lesson with Potter. Do I have to chain you to our bed to keep you safe?"

"You wouldn't dare!" The challenge hissed through her teeth in an explosion of angry indignation.

"I'd dare anything where you are concerned. Are you rested enough to move on now?"

"I can keep up," Kate declared, lifting her chin at a stubborn angle as she surged to her feet.

They reached McKenzie station by late afternoon. Robin thought about returning to the aborigine village immediately but decided against it. He wanted to make sure Kate was suffering no ill effects from her long trek before taking off again. Maude was exuberant upon their return, whisking Kate off to the bedroom with the promise of a hot bath. Lizzy seemed less than enthusiastic over Kate's return, merely staring at her with something akin to jealousy and hatred.

When Maude and Kate were out of sight, Lizzy turned to Robin and said, "Maude tells me your wife is increasing."

"Aye," Robin said absently, having more on his mind than Lizzy's inane chatter.

"Are you sure 'tis your child? Mr. Potter was a constant visitor after you left for Bathurst."

It was all Robin could do to keep from backhanding the little witch. "You've a vicious tongue, Lizzy. If you can't curb it, I'll find another place for you. One where you'll not have it so easy. I love my wife and trust her implicitly. Set your sights elsewhere, I'm already in enough trouble for trying to help someone."

Properly chastised, Lizzy said, "Are you referring to Serena Lynch?"

Wild Land, Wild Love

"How do you know about Serena?"

"Gossip travels. Serena has been to Parramatta and told anyone who would listen that she's expecting your child. Is it true?"

"'Tis none of your concern. You shouldn't listen to idle chatter. Your duty is to serve Kate and keep your mouth shut. Unless you wish to find work elsewhere."

"N—no, I like working here," Lizzy insisted, recognizing the need to withdraw before she landed in more trouble. Time after time she had tried to lure Robin away from Kate with no visible results except for earning Robin's contempt. She was smart enough to know when to desist and aim her sights elsewhere.

"If you enjoy working for me, I suggest you start packing. Kate and I are leaving for Bathurst soon and we'll need reliable house servants. Since your work is satisfactory, you can come along if you wish. Otherwise I'll find you another position."

"Bathurst?" Lizzy squeaked.

"Aye, and I'll take Maude, too, if she wants to go."

"Go where?" Maude asked, having just entered the room.

"Kate and I are settling in Bathurst. I've built a grand home there and want to raise our children on my own land. We'll need a cook and would like you to accompany us."

Maude shuffled her feet, looking decidedly uncomfortable. Leaving Parramatta would mean leaving Roy Penrod. "I—I—'tis not that I'm not grateful, Robin, 'tis just that—well, I've become

393

fond of a gentleman and I have reason to believe he feels the same about me. If I leave here I might never see him again."

"Are you referring to Roy Penrod?" Robin asked, aware of the attraction between the two and the many visits Roy had made to McKenzie station for no apparent reason.

"Aye, he's a fine gentleman. I realize he's too good for me but I—"

"No, Maude, don't hold yourself cheap. You made a mistake once and are paying for it. You deserve whatever happiness comes to you."

"Then you won't mind if I don't go with you to Bathurst?"

"No, I understand. In fact, I'll speak to Roy about you before I leave."

"Thank you, Robin," Maude smiled happily. She turned to leave.

"One more thing, Maude. I'm going back to the aborigine village tomorrow. I want you to look after Kate while I'm gone. Don't let her move out of the house without you in attendance."

"You can depend on me, Robin."

Kate was still in the tub when Robin entered the room a short time later. He stood just inside the door for a long time admiring the seductive sweep of her shoulders, the shiny length of ebony hair hanging over the side of the tub, and the sweet upward curve of her breasts visible above the water line.

"Must you stand there and stare at me?" Kate complained.

"What would you have me do, Kate?" Robin taunted. "I could lift you out of the tub and make love to you. Lord knows that's what I want to do. But I know you're tired and need your rest, so I'm merely admiring what I'll be missing tonight."

Why did his words make her yearn to leap out of the tub and into his arms? Kate wondered, puzzled by her constant need for the handsome ex-convict she had been forced to marry. Right now making love with Robin sounded heavenly.

"Hand me the towel," Kate said in a slightly belligerent tone. She didn't want him to know how profoundly he affected her.

He ambled over to the bed, picked up the towel left there for Kate's use, and offered it to her, dangling it several feet from the tub. "Is this what you wanted?"

"You know it is. Give it to me."

He didn't move. "Here it is."

"Dammit, Robin, why do you delight in tormenting me?"

"Am I? Am I tormenting you? If I am, 'tis only because you torment me merely by being in the same room with me. I crave you as I've craved nothing else in life."

Kate's breath slammed in her chest. She stood slowly, her eyes locked with his as she stepped from the tub and reached for the towel. Robin's eyes widened, drinking in every tantalizing inch of Kate's dripping flesh. Her breasts were fuller than normal but her waist was still slim. The gentle rise of her hips narrowed into long, molded thighs, and her belly held only a sweet hint of her pregnancy. Between her thighs glistening pearls of water clung damply to her maidenhair, and her buttocks were perfect mounds of soft white flesh.

Robin's reaction was everything Kate had expected—and more. Her eyes fell to the bulge in his trousers, and a secret smile curved her lips. He didn't yet know what torment was, she thought in silent glee. She'd have him begging in no time, then leave him wanting. It was no more than he deserved for trying to dictate to her.

Robin finally found the will to move his frozen limbs as he wrapped Kate in the towel. "What in the hell do you think you're doing?" he rasped hoarsely.

Kate turned, throwing the towel aside and stepping into his arms. "What do you think?"

"I—I thought you'd be tired."

"You thought wrong."

"You want me to love you?"

"Don't you want to?"

"More than I want anything in my life."

Her fingers moved to his chest, unfastening the buttons of his shirt with maddening slowness. When she moved too slowly, Robin threw her hands aside and finished the job, tossing the shirt to the floor. His pants followed. When he bent to scoop her in his arms, she stopped him.

"The water is still warm. Why don't you bathe? I'll scrub your back."

Robin looked at Kate oddly, wondering what in the hell she was up to. He didn't trust her, not one damn bit. Yet he couldn't resist the seductive spell she was weaving around him. He climbed into the tub, offering his back for Kate to scrub while trying to subdue the passion raging through him long enough to bathe. When he turned to see why Kate had not taken up the soap and cloth he offered, he was stunned to see she had quietly left the room.

"Kate! Come back here, you little vixen!"

He heard a door slam down the hall and leaped from the tub, unmindful of the water dripping off him onto the floor. He didn't bother finding a towel but ran from the room as naked as God made him. Fortunately the hallway was empty. Trying each door, he came to one that was locked, and halted, glaring ferociously at the closed panel.

"Open up, Kate!"

"You were right, Robin, I am tired," Kate called back. "I need a nap."

"Open up or I'll break down the damn door!"

"You wouldn't!"

"Try me! What in bloody hell were you trying to prove back there?"

Slowly the door opened. Kate was still clad in the towel, having had no time to retrieve her clothes before she left so abruptly. "I just wanted to pay you back for dictating to me and for all those outrageous things you say to me."

Robin pushed the door all the way open, stepped inside, and closed it firmly behind him. Kate gasped. "Where are your clothes?"

"I imagine they're in the same place yours are.

Now, where were we?" He reached out and snatched the towel from her body. "Ah, that's more like it, now we're on even footing."

"I was just about ready to take a nap."

"Good idea, I'll join you."

Before Kate knew what was happening, she found herself lying on the bed with Robin draped over her. What transpired next was a wild coming together as Robin's lips and hands touched and stroked her everywhere, lingering in places that made Kate cry out and writhe and curse. Though careful not to hurt her, Robin used every trick he had learned to bring Kate pleasure, piling one sensation upon another until she begged for release. When she tried to wriggle from beneath him, he reversed their positions, placing her on top. When his staff prodded insistently against her belly, she waited for him to enter her, but he deliberately held off, wanting her to make the first move. Nearly mindless with wanting, Kate raised her hips and took him inside her. Then she was aware of nothing but sublime rapture as she rode him furiously.

The pleasure was so intense, Robin knew he would burst. Kate's alluring fragrance became a part of him. Then suddenly he reversed their positions again and her body became his as they moved together in a rhythm and melody that sang through his veins. Never would he outlive his wild hunger for this vixen he had married. Drenched with ecstasy, Robin feared he couldn't wait for Kate to reach fulfillment before he exploded. But he needn't have worried. Kate was with him all the way, riding out her own storm as her body convulsed and contracted around him. Numb and dazed, Robin allowed his own passion free reign as he hung suspended in the eye of the storm Kate had created. Then he was spinning, whirling, seeking the highest reward known to man. When he floated back to earth he was filled with the most incredible sense of peace and satisfaction.

"Did I hurt you, Kate?"

Silence.

"Kate? Are you all right?"

"I didn't mean for this to happen."

"No? I could have sworn this is what you had in mind when you teased me so outrageously."

"You're wrong. I merely wanted to pay you back for—for—"

"For loving you?"

"How can you love me after being with Serena?"

"I might be able to answer your question if I remembered what happened with Serena. Isn't it time we came to terms with what happened?"

"It's difficult to forget that another woman will bear your child, perhaps on the same day I have mine."

"I'm promising nothing, but perhaps Big John can shed some light on the subject."

"Do you think he knows something about Serena that could make a difference?"

"God, I hope so," Robin said. "Go to sleep, love. I'm leaving for the aborigine village tomorrow and don't plan on returning until I hear what Big John has to say. Do you still hate me?"

"I—yes," she lied, crossing her fingers behind her back.

Robin flashed a roguish grin. "I don't know if I could survive our lovemaking if you ever decided you loved me."

Chapter Twenty-One

When Kate awoke the next morning, Robin was preparing to leave for the aborigine village. "I don't know when I'll be back. With any luck, Big John will regain consciousness before long and I can return quickly."

"What if the authorities find him? Won't they take him to jail?"

"I didn't get around to telling you last night, Governor Macquarie agreed to issue Big John a 'ticket of leave.' He'll be on probation until he proves himself. Macquarie's only stipulation was that I take Big John to Bathurst and employ him on Fletcher station."

"How wonderful," Kate exclaimed.

Robin dressed quickly, then bent to kiss Kate

before leaving. "Be good and take care of yourself while I'm gone."

His kiss was sweet and tender and left Kate yearning for more.

Inhaling deeply, she hugged the pillow where his head had rested, his alluring masculine scent still clinging to the linen. Why did Robin have such a devastating effect on her? she asked herself as she stretched languorously. With tantalizing clarity she recalled their passionate coming together last night. Kate couldn't deny that she had initiated their lovemaking after Robin announced his intent to let her rest in peace following her ordeal. Oh, yes. She admitted it readily enough, she just couldn't understand it.

She craved Robin with an intensity that defied explanation. No matter how many times she proclaimed her hatred for Robin, he laughed in that special way of his and treated it as a huge jest. It rankled to think that Robin didn't take her words seriously, but what could she expect when she didn't believe them herself? How could she hate Robin, yet respond to him in such a wanton manner? Kate knew herself better than to believe she would give herself so completely to just anyone. She wanted to love Robin—Lord, yes, were it not for Serena and the child Serena carried—Robin's child.

Kate sighed dispiritedly and arose from bed to begin her day. At mid-morning an uninvited and unwelcome visitor arrived. Red-faced from the relentless sun and out of breath from her long walk, Serena stood on the doorstep, demanding entrance. Cognizant of Serena's delicate condition, Kate could not deny her request, though Serena was the last person she wanted to see right now.

"What is it you want, Serena?" Kate asked. She couldn't help showing her distaste for Serena's unwelcome appearance.

"First a drink of water," Serena snapped waspishly as she shoved past Kate and stomped into the parlor. She plopped down into a chair and began fanning herself vigorously with the brim of her bonnet. "'Tis a hellish long walk from Penrod station and hot enough to sizzle the brain."

"Lizzy!" Kate called, knowing the girl hovered nearby. "Bring our guest a glass of water."

The silence grew oppressive while both women waited for Serena's drink. Lizzy appeared with it shortly and stared goggle-eyed at Serena, her curiosity running rampant.

"You may go, Lizzy," Kate said tightly when Lizzy made no effort to leave.

Disappointment passed briefly over Lizzy's expressive features before she turned and flounced out the door.

"Are you recovered enough to tell me what you want?" Kate asked once Serena set the empty glass down on a table.

"I don't feel so well," Serena complained. "If I had known how hot it was outside I never would have attempted to walk so far."

"Why did you walk all this way? It must have been important."

"I want to see Robin," Serena insisted with a

pout. "I haven't seen him since he dumped me off at the Penrods'. I have no idea what his plans are for me and his child, and I'm angered over his failure to keep me informed. Are you going to divorce him? It would be best for everyone if you did. I'm the one who's having his baby."

Kate grew still. Evidently Serena did not know that Kate was pregnant. "You're wrong, Serena. Robin surely is a potent devil, for we both are having his babies."

Serena turned red, then white, then colorless as she swayed in the chair. "You—you're pregnant? That's impossible. Who is the father?"

"If you weren't such a little ninny I'd smack you," Kate said, her voice tinged with disgust. "Robin and I are married. I'm the only one who can bear him a legitimate child."

Serena was stunned. Was all her scheming and conniving for nothing? She had been so certain— so utterly certain—that Kate would divorce Robin so he could marry Serena and give their child a name. She had thought Kate too old to bear a child, while she, Serena, was in her prime and able to bear Robin many children. Oh, God, what was going to happen to her now? Robin would never leave Kate while she carried his legitimate heir.

"I—I don't feel at all well," Serena whined.

Indeed, she didn't look well, Kate thought, suddenly feeling pity for this child/woman who fought so desperately for a man who didn't love her. Serena's face had turned a sickly shade of green and her eyes had the stricken look of a lost puppy.

"Perhaps you should lie down for a while," Kate suggested.

"Yes, yes, I'll lie down and wait for Robin. Since my parents died he's always been there to look after me. I—I have no one, no one but Robin."

Serena was so close to tears that Kate felt an unwelcome surge of compassion as she helped the girl from her chair and led her up the stairs to one of the spare bedrooms. Serena clung to her as if she were drowning and Kate was her lifeline, seeking solace from the very woman she had wronged. Suddenly Kate was infuriated with Robin for creating such an impossible situation.

Kate paced restlessly once she had settled Serena in bed and returned to the parlor. She racked her brain for an answer to the dilemma she and Robin faced regarding Serena and could find no solution. Their one hope was that Big John had something to tell Robin that would make a difference, though Lord only knew what it could be. It wasn't yet lunchtime when Kate's second visitors of the day arrived. Casey and Dare had come to discuss the sale of McKenzie station.

"Robin isn't here," Kate said, ushering them into the parlor. "He left this morning for the aborigine village."

"Why would he go there," Dare asked, "when there is so much here that needs his attention?"

"He received word that Big John was desperately ill and had been taken in by Culong and his sister. For some unknown reason Big John was asking for Robin, and Robin went to the village as soon as he arrived from Sydney." Kate deliberately withheld the information concerning her own sojourn in the aborigine village. She had already been chastised by Robin and didn't want to go through it again with the Penrods.

"If Robin had let me know, I'd have gone with him," Dare said.

"Are you so anxious to leave me, Dare?" Casey teased.

"You know better than that, love, but the forest can be a dangerous place for a man alone."

"Perhaps you ought to follow?" Casey suggested, barely able to contain her mirth. Since Dare had married and become a staid family man he'd had little adventure, and Casey knew he longed to follow Robin to the aborigine village, though he'd never admit it.

"Do you really think I ought to?" Dare asked, slanting Casey a quizzical look. They were so in tune with one another that Casey possessed the uncanny power to read his mind. It never failed to amaze him.

"Go on, Dare, I can get myself home. Just be careful, love."

Dare flashed a devastating smile that rivaled the sun. "What would I ever do without you?" he said, pulling her to her feet and kissing her so passionately, Kate felt obliged to look away.

"Men!" Casey laughed once Dare was gone. "I knew Dare was itching to join Robin. Do you mind if I stay and chat awhile, Kate?"

"No, not at all, though I think you should know

your house guest is upstairs in one of my spare bedrooms.''

"Serena? I hadn't seen her all morning and assumed she was still abed. How did she get here?"

"She walked; that's why she's resting now. Truth to tell, she wasn't looking at all well.''

"You're a good woman, Kate,'' Casey said admiringly. "I'm not sure I would have done the same in your place. Serena can be a little bitch when she wants to, which is most of the time.''

"I'm sorry Robin dumped her on your doorstep,'' Kate replied.

"I'll admit it is a chore being pleasant to her, but Robin is our friend and Dare wouldn't dream of denying him when he asked us to shelter Serena while she remained in Parramatta. What did she want?''

"She wanted me to divorce Robin so he could marry her and give their child a name. When I told her I was expecting a child myself, the shock was nearly too much for her. Truthfully, Casey, I don't know what is going to become of us or how Robin intends to work this all out.''

"You intend to stay with Robin, don't you?'' Casey asked anxiously.

"Robin refuses to let me leave. He—he was very emphatic about it.''

"He loves you, Kate. I hope by now you've come to realize that you're the only woman in Robin's life.''

"I want to believe it, Casey.''

"I know you've never considered me a friend,

Kate, and I'm sorry for it, but I do have your best interests at heart. You no longer believe that Robin still loves me, do you? It might have been true a long time ago, but what Robin and I share is friendship and a kind of love that has nothing to do with passion or romantic attachment. All the Penrods share that same love with Robin. Ben, Dare, and Robin are like brothers. Robin thinks of Roy as a father."

"It's taken me a while," said Kate, "but I know now that what you, the Penrods, and Robin have is something special. I'm sorry for spurning your friendship and sorrier still for mistaking the closeness you share with Robin for—for romantic love . . ."

". . . but?" said Casey. "I sense there is something else you want to say. Something that has been bothering you for a long time."

"I can't help it, Casey. There are just too many unanswered questions concerning you, Dare, and Cousin Mercy."

"Then 'tis time I eased your mind," Casey said. "You never really knew Mercy, she was so young when she left England. She was spoiled and vain and quite determined. She wanted Dare, and might have had him if I hadn't come along when I did."

"But Mercy did have Dare! He married her first!" There was accusation in Kate's words that spoke eloquently of her inherent sense of family and the outrage she felt when an injustice against a relative was involved.

"I'm not going to go into the details for they

don't bear repeating, but I will tell you that Dare only married Mercy because she promised that her father, who had influential friends in the Rum Corps, would obtain a pardon for me. He never loved Mercy. I was already carrying Dare's child before their marriage, but no one knew it. Dare and I were to be married, until I was arrested, convicted, and sentenced to another seven years for aiding an escaped convict."

"The same convict Robin helped?" Kate asked.

"Aye. Robin made it possible for a fine young man named Tim O'Mally to escape the country."

Kate was quiet a long time. "Did you and Dare marry after Mercy died?"

"No. Mercy told Dare I was dead before she succumbed to pneumonia, but in truth I had gone to England, thinking Dare no longer wanted me. Several months later Dare had reason to go to England, and we met there by accident. One day I will tell you the entire story, but I think I've given you enough to digest for one day."

"Aye," Kate said slowly. "I'm sorry for all the pain Mercy caused you and Dare. I only hope you don't hold it against me for being a McKenzie."

"Nothing could be further from the truth. I liked and respected you the moment I met you. I could tell immediately you were nothing like your cousin Mercy. Now enough about Mercy. What are we going to do about Serena?"

"I wish I knew." Kate sighed despondently. "I wish I knew."

"Are you talking about me?" Serena, looking much rested, stood in the doorway.

Two heads, one black as a moonless midnight, the other the color of flame, swiveled to regard the blond who had intruded into their conversation.

"Why did you leave without telling me?" Casey asked.

"You're not my keeper," Serena huffed as she dropped into a nearby chair. "I want to see Robin and I'm not leaving until he arrives."

"You may have a long wait," Kate warned.

"I've nothing to do and nowhere to go. I'll wait."

Casey and Kate exchanged speaking looks. One needed the patience of a saint to deal with Serena and her petulant complaints.

No matter how much cajoling Casey and Kate employed, Serena refused to leave McKenzie station until she saw Robin. Unwilling to use force, Kate accepted the situation with as much grace as she could muster and invited Serena to remain. A short time later Casey left McKenzie station alone.

The one thing that astonished Kate was Lizzy's outrage when she learned Serena would be a guest at McKenzie station. The girl suddenly became very protective of Kate. It was as if learning that Kate was expecting Robin's child had brought a complete turnabout in Lizzy's character.

"How can you allow that woman to stay in your home?" Lizzy stormed at Kate when Kate went to the kitchen to check on supper. "She's a schemer who would dare anything to get Robin. Don't you care that she slept with your husband?"

"Lizzy!" Maude said, aghast at the girl's outburst. "Watch your tongue."

"If you must know, Lizzy," Kate said thoughtfully, "I pity the girl. She's young, has lost both her parents in a tragic accident, and latched on to Robin when she had no one else to rely on. I can sympathize with her, though I can't find it in my heart to forgive her."

"Surely you don't intend for her to live with you and Robin!"

"No, certainly not. But I think Robin intends to find Serena a good husband, which will be the best solution to a difficult problem. Let's hear no more about it. It's bad enough having to look at Serena and see her—never mind—I don't care to discuss Serena. I will take supper in my room tonight; see that Serena is served in hers."

Sleep did not come easily for Kate that night. With Serena in the house all those terrible memories of finding her in bed with Robin came back to haunt Kate. Even though Robin had no recollection of making love to Serena, the proof was in the pudding, so to speak. Kate's life would be considerably less complicated if she could forget the lusty devil and leave him to Serena. How strange, Kate thought as her eyes closed drowsily, that love was the only emotion without limits or boundaries.

Dare reached the aborigine village several hours after leaving McKenzie station. Surprised to see Dare, Robin greeted him warmly, glad for a friend to share his vigil. Dare spoke with Robin in quiet tones while they shared an evening meal. Big John showed definite signs of regaining his wits but had yet to recognize Robin.

"Kate is fine," Dare said, forestalling Robin's

question. "Casey is with her. When I heard you were here I decided to join you. What happened to Big John?"

Robin related the events leading to Big John's illness and then told Dare about Governor Macquarie's decision to issue Big John a "ticket of leave."

"What do you suppose Big John was so desperate to see you about?"

"Something to do with Serena, but I can't imagine what. Mantua says he's going to get well and predicts he'll be able to communicate tomorrow. I pray he'll be able to shed some light on our dilemma. Truth to tell, I'm at my wit's end. I don't know where to turn to seek a solution. There is only one thing I'm absolutely certain about. I will not lose Kate. I love her too much."

They bedded down in the grass hut that night and in the morning awoke to the sound of disjointed words and phrases coming from Big John's lips. Robin was instantly alert, kneeling over Big John, trying to make sense out of his babbling.

"Big John, 'tis Robin. I'm here, mate, what is it you wanted to tell me?"

Big John cranked his lids open. His eyes glazed as they tried to focus on Robin. Several agonizing minutes elapsed before recognition dawned. "Robin? Is it you, mate?"

"Aye, Big John, 'tis me. Dare is here too."

"I—I dreamed your woman was here."

"She was here, mate, but I took her home. You've been unconscious for several days."

"Am I gonna die?"

Robin grinned. "You're too tough and too ugly to die. Mantua cleansed your body of poison and assured me that you'd live. The venom would have killed a lesser man, but your size saved you. I have more wonderful news for you. I've convinced Governor Macquarie to issue you a 'ticket of leave.' You're to accompany me to Bathurst and work on my sheep station. You'll be station boss. Does that please you?"

At first Big John merely looked confused, until everything that Robin had told him had time to register in his fuzzy brain. When he finally understood, a wide grin split his face. He couldn't be called handsome but neither was he ugly. His features were pleasant enough; it was his size that was intimidating.

"Do you mean it, mate? I've been hidin' in the bush so long I feared I'd die there with no one to care or mourn my passin'. I'll work hard, mate, you'll see. You won't be sorry for standin' up for me. If there is any way I can pay you back—" His words ground to a halt and an arrested look came over his face.

"What is it, Big John?" Robin asked.

"I just remembered what it was I wanted to tell you. 'Tis about Serena. I heard one of the police officers talkin' and he said Serena was expectin' your babe. Is it true, mate?"

"'Tis what Serena told me, and I have no reason to doubt her," Robin admitted slowly. "I don't remember bedding the little witch, but I must have since she turned up pregnant a short time later. Is that all you wanted to tell me? That you heard

413

someone discussing Serena's pregnancy?"

"No, there is somethin' else. Damn, if my head wasn't so fuzzy.'"

"Rest, mate, you can tell me later," Robin advised, realizing the man was recovering from a serious illness and needed time to recuperate.

"No, 'tis important. I wanted you to know—to know—"

"Know what?" Dare prompted, growing impatient. Robin was a much more patient man than he had ever been.

"Ah, yes, I remember now. The jailhouse where I was held is situated across the road from the market in Bathurst."

"Aye," Robin nodded, wondering where all this was leading. Was Big John still addled from his illness?

"After your wife left Bathurst, I saw Serena enter the market nearly every day. At first I thought nothin' of it."

"Most women go to the market daily," Robin said, his hopes sinking. Somehow he'd expected more.

"Aye, 'tis true, but whenever Serena arrived at the market Silas Dodd placed a closed sign in the window and left it there for an hour, sometimes more. What's more, I never saw Serena leave. The only thing I could figure out was that she left by a back entrance."

"I don't—"

"Bloody hell, Robin, are you dense!" Dare cried jubilantly. "What the man is trying to tell you is that Serena took a lover. She deliberately led you to believe you were the only man she bedded, when all along she was having an affair with Silas Dodd! More than likely the child she carries belongs to Dodd. All you have to do is get the man to admit he bedded Serena."

"Are you certain, Big John, absolutely certain?" Robin questioned, unable to believe the reprieve he'd just been handed.

"Aye," Big John said with such utter confidence that Robin could no longer doubt him. "I was comin' to tell you when I was snakebit. I wanted to tell you that you weren't the only man beddin' Serena."

"I'm fairly certain now I never bedded her," Robin said thoughtfully. "I doubted it from the beginning, but when Serena turned up pregnant and I could lay the blame with no one else, I assumed I had done the deed while drunk and not remembered it. I could strangle the little witch for lying to me. Hell, I felt sorry for her. She was alone and I felt responsible for her. I treated her like a sister while she was living in my house."

"What are you going to do about it?" Dare asked, recalling how Mercy had nearly succeeded in separating him and Casey forever. He didn't want the same thing to happen to Robin.

"I'm going to Bathurst to learn the truth," Robin said with grim determination.

"I'll go with you," Dare offered.

"I'd rather you go to McKenzie station and tell Kate where I've gone. I don't want her to worry."

"Should I tell her what Big John told you?"

Robin considered Dare's question carefully.

"No, I don't want to give her false hopes if things don't work out as I think they will. I'll explain everything to her when I return. Just say that I'm going to Bathurst for a few days on Big John's behalf. Tell her—tell her I love her."

"Do you intend to walk?"

"I—I hadn't thought about that. No, it would take too long."

"Go to Father's house, 'tis closer. He'll lend you a mount. Are you sure you don't want to see Kate first?"

"I want to but don't dare. I couldn't bear to see her disappointment should I return without good news. No, I'll borrow a mount from Penrod station and leave immediately for Bathurst."

"What about Big John?"

"I'll go with Robin," Big John offered.

"You're still too weak to travel," Robin replied. "Rest and get well, and I'll come by here to pick you up on my way back from Bathurst."

Big John nodded reluctant agreement. As sick as he'd been, it would still be several days before he regained his strength.

Dare and Robin parted outside the aborigine village. Dare went to McKenzie station to inform Kate of Robin's plans before going home to Casey, and Robin hurried off in the direction of Penrod station, where he borrowed a horse and supplies from Roy. He camped in the foothills of the Blue Mountains that night and four days later rode into Bathurst.

Ben Penrod, who was still staying at Robin's house, greeted him warmly when he rode into the yard. "You're back earlier than I expected," Ben said, looking about for either Kate or Serena. When he saw neither woman he slanted Robin a quizzing glance.

"I'm alone," Robin said.

"Did you find out if Serena was lying about the baby?"

"Aye. She's increasing, all right. Dan Proctor confirmed it."

"Bloody hell!" Ben spat. "Of all the rotten luck. What are you going to do?"

"First of all I'm going to find out who the father is."

"What? I thought . . ."

"So did I." Then Robin proceeded to tell Ben the surprising development he had learned from Big John.

"Silas Dodd. That explains many things."

"What in the hell are you talking about?"

"Not a day goes by that Silas doesn't ask me when you're returning and if Serena will accompany you. I thought it a case of unrequited love, for I couldn't imagine Serena attracted to a man like Silas, though he isn't a bad sort. He's just an unobtrusive man who minds his own business and has little to say. He strikes me as a hard worker who is determined to make a place for himself here in Bathurst. His business is thriving, which says a lot for the man's ability."

"You seem to know all about him," Robin said curiously.

"Aye," Ben grinned. "I've been in Bathurst long enough to figure things out. Not much gets past me. Dare says I'm naturally inquisitive and accuses me of being too domineering for my own good."

"If Dare says that, it must be true," Robin laughed. "I think he recognizes himself in you, and that's his way of warning you to change your arrogant ways. Seriously, though, if what you say is true, I feel like I'm finally coming out of a tunnel and into the light. I just want to clear up this mess so Kate and I can get on with our lives. I want no other children except those that Kate gives me."

"What do you intend to do?"

"I'm going to talk to Dodd as soon as I freshen up and have something to eat. He's the only one who can shed light on this whole mess with Serena."

Two hours later Robin entered Dodd's market. Silas was waiting on a customer, and Robin chafed impatiently as he waited for Dodd to finish up and the customer to leave. When Silas saw Robin standing in his store, his eyes lit with a joy Robin found difficult to interpret.

"Welcome back, Mr. Fletcher," Silas greeted. "Is your business all taken care of in Sydney and Parramatta? I hope all went well."

"Aye. Bathurst will have another magistrate soon and I'll be moving my wife here permanently," Robin replied, watching closely for Dodd's reaction.

The storekeeper's response was all Robin hoped for. "How wonderful! That your wife will join you, I mean. Did Serena Lynch return with you?" he blurted out, unable to contain his happiness over Robin's news. With Robin devoted to his wife, Silas hoped Serena would look more favorably on him and renew their—friendship.

"No, she remained in Parramatta with friends for the time being."

Dodd's face fell. He looked so forlorn, Robin actually felt pity for him. Not a doubt remained in his mind that Serena had been intimate with the storekeeper. As soon as he got Dodd to admit it, his problems would disappear and he could get back to Kate.

"If I didn't know better I'd say you held a certain fondness for Serena," Robin prodded.

Dodd flushed nervously and shuffled his feet. He had promised Serena he'd tell no one their secret. "She—she's a real beauty, Mr. Fletcher. I consider myself lucky just knowing her."

"You know Serena quite well, don't you, Dodd?" Robin probed relentlessly.

Dodd's head flew up and his eyes grew wide with terror. Had Robin found out about him and Serena? Had he come to punish him? Was he jealous? All these things ran through Dodd's mind as Robin confronted him with his suspicions.

"I—I don't know what you mean! Serena came in here often and I—I admired her."

"You may as well tell the truth, Dodd, for I don't intend to leave here until you do. I don't care how many times you slept with Serena as long as you admit to the deed. I won't have Serena naming me the father of her child when another man is responsible."

Dodd was stunned. Being a quiet man who kept mostly to himself, he had heard none of the gossip circulating about Serena. "Baby? Serena is increasing?"

"Aye. Are you going to admit to being the father?"

Dodd's face was lit by a thousand candles and he grinned stupidly, so dazed that all he could do was nod. His delight was so obvious, so downright pathetic, Robin could not find it in his heart to be angry at the man.

"Tell me. I want to hear you say you bedded Serena and fathered her child."

"Aye," Dodd shouted loud enough for all the world to hear. "I love Serena. She let me make love to her, and if she's increasing, the child is undoubtedly mine." Suddenly he looked stricken. "Unless you . . ."

"No, I never bedded Serena," Robin said quietly. "The honor was all yours. Now, what are you going to do about claiming your child?"

Chapter Twenty-Two

Kate stared out the window at the shimmering dappled patterns created by the sun shining through the branches of the giant gum growing in the yard. The scorching heat of summer beat down relentlessly as dust devils whirled in the searing breeze. Kate thought the heat oppressive. Being pregnant at this time of the year was no picnic, she decided. Robin's absence only added to her distress. When Dare had stopped by several days ago to tell her Robin was in Bathurst, the news had stunned Kate. Since Dare had been deliberately vague concerning Robin's reason for leaving, Kate felt hurt and abandoned. Did Robin intend to leave her saddled with Serena?

Of course not, she told herself, scoffing at the ridiculous notion that Robin would abandon her to handle the volatile Serena as best she could. Whatever had taken Robin to Bathurst was important enough to demand his immediate attention, Kate told herself. Drawing a frustrated breath, she turned from the window and wandered aimlessly from the parlor to the kitchen. Sheer frustration over having Serena underfoot made her irritable. Added to her woes was the fact that she was still sick in the mornings and unable to sleep at night.

Dare had hinted that Robin's urgent trip to Bathurst had something to do with Serena but admitted nothing, except to say it concerned Big John. At least Big John was well on the way to recovery, Kate thought. And once he was well he'd be free to work for Robin in Bathurst.

Entering the kitchen, Kate smiled when she saw Roy Penrod and Maude standing with their heads together, engaged in intimate conversation. "Roy, I didn't know you were here."

"I was just on my way to find you," Roy said, reluctantly turning his attention from Maude. "I hope you don't mind me saying hello to Maude first."

"Of course not," Kate said, swallowing a grin as Maude blushed furiously.

"Has Robin returned yet?" Roy asked.

"No, and frankly I'm puzzled. He's been gone nearly two weeks."

"I know it must be difficult for you with Serena underfoot. Is there anything I can do for you? Robin is like one of my own sons. If you need help you have only to ask. Perhaps I could persuade

Serena to go back to Dare's house."

"I appreciate your offer," Kate said sincerely, "but I'm afraid it will take more than persuasion to move Serena. In a way I pity the girl. She has no one, and clings to Robin with a tenacity that's frightening. I fear her parents' violent death affected her in ways that none of us realize."

"I admire you for defending the girl, considering how she tried to destroy your marriage," Roy said.

"I—I'm not really defending her," Kate said thoughtfully, "'tis just that I understand some of the feelings she's experiencing. Father's death devastated me, and for a long time I held myself responsible. I was incapable of making rational judgments, and I believe Serena is even more unstable. I don't know how this will all end, but I'm counting on Robin to find a solution."

"Robin is a good man, Kate," Roy said. "He needs your love and understanding. I don't know how this situation with Serena happened, but I'm willing to bet Serena caught him in an unguarded moment. Robin loves you deeply, he told me so, and from what I've observed it appears that you were made for one another. 'Tis a rare marriage that isn't beset with some kind of turmoil. If love is present, the marriage will surmount all obstacles and be stronger for it."

"Casey has made me understand many things," Kate said cryptically. "I won't give Robin up so easily, no matter what mischief Serena has contrived to prevent our happiness."

Roy's lined face broke out in a broad grin. "I

always knew you were a fighter, Kate. The years have taught me many truths. One of them is that life is fragile and fleeting. Don't reject what happiness it offers, for you may never have a second chance. That's why I'm not going to let Maude get away from me."

"Roy!" Maude admonished, vivid color staining her cheeks.

"'Tis true, Maude, I don't care who knows it. One day you'll be my wife."

Kate hoped with all her heart that things worked out for Roy and Maude. Still vigorous and handsome, Roy had lost his wife many years ago, and Maude wasn't a vicious criminal who deserved to live on the outskirts of society. That these two people should meet and develop a mutual attraction in the autumn of their lives was a living tribute to the power of love. Love was ageless, timeless, and limited only by the imagination.

After Roy left, Kate wandered outside, watching the station boss and convict laborers drive the sheep down from the hills for shearing. With the help of yapping dogs, they drove them through the billabong so the water could cleanse their thick wool, then out the other side to dry in preparation for shearing. The whole process was fascinating, and Kate watched until the sun, heat, and dust drove her to the shaded porch, where she settled into one of the rockers. She was glad that Serena had yet to make an appearance that morning, for no matter how hard she tried, resentment and anger at the beautiful girl made life difficult. She was only human; swallowing her pride for Robin's sake was a bitter pill indeed.

Kate had nearly decided to go inside for lunch when she noticed several riders approaching the house. Her heart leaped with joy when she recognized Robin mounted on one of the horses. Ben Penrod rode beside him and two men rode double on another mount. By virtue of his enormous size, Kate realized one of the men riding double was Big John. The other man she did not recognize immediately, probably because he was partially hidden behind Big John's bulk.

When Robin saw Kate on the porch he spurred his horse and rode ahead. For days he'd thought of nothing but Kate and how she would react when he told her Serena was carrying another man's child. His feet were on the ground before he had completely reined to a halt. In the next instant he was running toward Kate with his arms stretched wide.

Like a puppet pulled by a string, Kate left the shelter of the porch and stepped into Robin's arms, feeling his love surround and protect her. The sensation was wild and wonderful—as wild as this land she had come to love. She and Robin had been married for a year, but until this moment she had fought love with every fiber of her body. First, because she thought Robin was trying to steal McKenzie station from her, then because she was convinced he would never love anyone but Casey Penrod, and lastly because Serena had come between them. But suddenly everything that had happened before this moment didn't matter. She loved Robin, she was going to have his baby, and no one was going to part them.

"Kate, my wild and passionate Kate," Robin murmured in her ear. "I love you so very much and I have so much to tell you. I've missed you, love. I promise we'll never be parted again."

It didn't matter that Robin's companions were looking at them bemusedly, or that workers nearby gaped at them. Nothing mattered except that Robin had returned to her and she loved him. Winding her arms around his neck, she pulled his head down and kissed him with all the pent-up emotion and longing in her body. He pressed her close—closer, as if he never intended to let her go.

"Ahem—" Ben cleared his throat as he gulped back a bubble of laughter.

Big John, uncomfortable on horseback, dismounted. So did the man riding pillion behind him. Ben remained mounted, intending to leave for Penrod station immediately.

Reluctantly Robin broke off the kiss, turning to face the men who had accompanied him. Only then did Kate recognize the fourth man. She had seen him only once, when she had gone to the market in Bathurst to purchase food for her crossing to Parramatta. She didn't know his name, but his face was definitely familiar. What was he doing here? she wondered.

Robin sensed her confusion and answered her unspoken question. "This is Silas Dodd, Kate."

Serena stepped out on the porch. She had heard the commotion from her bedroom and wondered what it was all about. She picked Silas Dodd out of the group of men immediately and nearly fainted. "Oh, no! No! What are you doing here?" Seeing Silas Dodd with Robin was her worst nightmare come true.

"Serena!" In his haste to get to Serena, Silas stumbled, righted himself with Big John's help, then rushed pell mell to embrace Serena. "Why didn't you tell me you were expecting my baby before you left Bathurst?"

Serena groaned and swayed, fainting dead away in Silas's arms.

"Take her inside," Robin barked crisply as the stricken man lifted Serena in his arms. Robin's own arm tightened around Kate, aware of the shock she had just been dealt.

Silas's words may have been a shock to Kate but they were a welcome one. She felt only joy, and the sensation of having a great burden removed from her. She squeezed Robin's hand and followed the others inside, all except for Ben who took his leave. He had no intention of interfering in family business. Because he didn't know what else to do, Big John followed them inside.

Lizzy was standing at the door, wide-eyed with curiosity as the group swept into the house. When her eyes fell on Big John, an arrested look came over her face. Never had she seen such a big man! She thought him handsome and rugged and vital. He certainly looked big and strong enough to make a woman faint from pleasure, she thought, repressing a giggle. Not even Robin could compare with the impressive giant. Robin noted Lizzy's preoccupation with Big John but was too involved with his own problems to wonder about it.

"Lizzy, take Big John in the kitchen and see that he has something to eat. Then ask Dent to find him a bed in the convict quarters."

Lizzy batted her long lashes at Big John as she led the way into the kitchen. Big John. She had heard of him. Who hadn't? He was one of the most famous bushrangers in New South Wales. Legends had been built around the man, and here he was bigger than life at McKenzie station. She wondered if the authorities knew he was here and vowed to learn the reason for his visit—if it was a visit. Perhaps she could even entice him to divulge all the details of his life in the bush. Suddenly Lizzy was happier than she had been in years.

Meanwhile, Silas had placed Serena on the sofa, hovering over her like a mother hen. "Will she be all right?" he asked anxiously. "I knew seeing me here would be a shock, but I never expected her to faint. She'll hate me for coming after her like this."

"I wouldn't worry about what Serena thinks, Silas," Robin said tightly. "You have a right to claim your child. I believe Serena will have a good life with you. You should marry her and give your heir a name."

"I—I don't understand," Kate said, bewildered. "How did you know about Silas Dodd? Is that why you went to Bathurst so abruptly?"

"Aye. It was something Big John told me." Robin related all that Big John had revealed, and reaffirmed his conviction that he had never bedded

Serena. "From the beginning I found it difficult to believe I had bedded her. I knew she was determined but didn't know she was conniving as well."

"She's coming 'round," Silas said, concern coloring his words.

Serena opened her eyes, blinked rapidly to make certain she wasn't dreaming, then quickly squeezed them shut when Silas's face loomed before her. "Why did you have to come?" she asked in a voice so low Silas barely understood. "You promised you'd tell no one."

"I didn't tell," Silas quickly explained. "Robin came to Bathurst and told me you were expecting a child. When he said it couldn't possibly be his, I knew it was mine."

Serena's eyes swung around to settle on Robin. "How did you know?"

"It doesn't matter," Robin said. "Suffice it to say I am now aware of the truth and Silas was good enough to fill me in on your—affair. Bloody hell, Serena, you nearly ruined my life!"

"Don't yell at her," Silas demanded, swinging around to face Robin. "It's not good for her in her condition."

"Jesus, Dodd, Serena is a scheming bitch who lied about the baby. She was prepared to ruin my future with Kate for her own selfish reasons. I don't love her, I never did."

Silas winced. It hurt to hear truths about Serena that he wasn't prepared for. But none of it mattered. He loved Serena. She carried his child. What she'd done in the past was none of his concern. All that mattered now was providing a home for Serena and his child.

Serena was sobbing quietly, an inkling of the havoc she had created finally getting through to her. But she was justified, wasn't she? Robin was the only person who cared about her. The only man she could trust and depend upon. Her parents had always taken care of her, and their deaths left a terrible void in her life, one that could only be filled by Robin.

"Don't cry, Serena," Silas crooned softly. "I'll take care of you and our child. No one will harm you while I am around. You've made me very happy."

Serena looked at him stupidly. "Happy?"

"Aye. We'll be married and I'll build you a fine house. A house big enough for all the children we'll have. My store has done very well in Bathurst, and I intend to expand soon. You'll see, things will work out well for us. I've always loved you, you know."

"But I don't love you!" Serena wailed dispiritedly. "Don't you understand, I was only using you."

A sad look contorted Silas's face, but he remained calm. "You're distraught, sweetheart. You don't know what you're saying. Just relax while I go to Parramatta for the preacher. We'll be married this evening, if it's all right with Robin."

"You certainly have my blessing," Robin returned quickly.

"And mine," Kate added with a silent "amen."

"Nooooo!" Serena protested violently. "Don't I

have anything to say about this?"

"I'm afraid not. You're going to marry me and that's final!"

Stunned by Silas's authoritative manner, Serena stared at him, mouth agape. It was so unlike mild-mannered Silas to act assertive, it rendered Serena speechless. Previously he'd behaved like an adoring puppy, earning nothing but her contempt. It wasn't that Silas wasn't a good lover. She had been shocked by his passion and pleased by his inventiveness in bed. But that didn't mean she felt anything for him. It was Robin she loved—wasn't it?

"It appears that Silas has finally found his courage," Robin laughed as he listened to the exchange between the two. "By the way," he asked Kate, "what is Serena doing here?"

Kate drew Robin aside, leaving Serena and Silas alone to hash out their problems. "She showed up here demanding to see you after you left for the aborigine village. When she learned you were gone she planted herself in the spare bedroom and refused to leave until you arrived. I—I couldn't throw her out, not in her condition, so I let her have her way. I trusted you to somehow make things right."

"You did? Do you realize that is the first time you admitted to feeling anything but hate for me? You've come a long way, love, if you can truthfully admit to trusting me. 'Tis not exactly what I've longed to hear but—"

"I love you, Robin."

"What! Am I hearing right, Kate? I thought you hated me. You've told me often enough, right after you loved me with more passion than most women display in a lifetime. I've always loved the way you hated me, so I suppose I'll adore the way you love me—if I survive."

Kate grinned impishly. "You always say the most outrageous things."

Robin grinned with slow relish, all the pain and bitterness of those previous years of hardship and heartache dissolving in the promise of Kate's smile. His appointment to a prominent position in local government, becoming a respected owner of a rich sheep station, having a wife he loved to distraction and a child on the way, all combined to bring him more happiness than he'd ever expected to find in his bleak life. Marrying Kate was the single best thing he had ever done.

"Shall we leave the lovebirds alone to solve their problems?" Robin asked, his voice taut with promise.

Kate glanced at Serena and Silas, sitting side by side on the sofa. They were talking softly, or rather Silas was talking. Serena merely stared at him mutely, shaking her head at nearly everything he said. Kate felt sorry for Silas. Serena would certainly make his life miserable if he didn't assert himself right from the beginning. Realizing that Robin was waiting for her answer, Kate smiled and, taking his hand, led him up the stairs to their room and blessed privacy.

"I want to make love to you, Kate."

She stepped into his arms, joining their mouths, trembling when his kiss sent shivers of desire dancing down her spine. "I want you to love me. And I don't hate you, I never did."

He undressed her quickly, too eager to waste precious minutes in slow disrobing when he was so hungry for her. His own clothes were dispatched with shocking haste and then he was lifting her against him, luxuriating in the warm responsiveness of her body. Kate's hands drifted lazily across the rippling fan of muscles that spread over his back. Her eyes slid down his narrow waist to the contrasting paleness of his pelvis and buttocks. His staff rose like an ivory pillar from the tangled blond nest at the juncture of his thighs.

Robin stared at the intoxicating beauty in his arms. Her long hair cascaded down her back like an exotic waterfall, so black and shiny it rivaled the darkest midnight. He sank onto the bed with her still in his arms, covering her breasts with the dark blanket of his own desire. He played with her lips, licking, nibbling, outlining their full contours with his tongue, then dipped into the wet heat of her mouth. His chest expanded with the fullness of his need, and his lungs felt ready to burst.

Caresses followed kisses, drifting past her shoulders to settle disconcertingly on her breasts. The friction of his fingers playing over one nipple matched the moist, lush lapping of his rough tongue at her other nipple. Intense pleasure sent a coil of splendid rapture spiraling through her, flooding her womanflesh with liquid anticipation.

433

She moved against his swollen heat, seeking an end to the sweet torture he was creating in her. His hands slid over her belly and down her legs, discovering those secret places that made her shiver and writhe in torment and pleasure. Her legs fell open, welcoming him as he slid down to find the hot core of her desire.

Then he was caressing her with his hands and mouth, his tongue relentless as it stabbed repeatedly into the molten core of her. Her fingers dug grooves in the hard flesh of his shoulders as a velvety whisper of a moan drifted past her lips. Suddenly the moan turned into a wail as rapture seized her and she dissolved into a blinding release of heat and pleasure. Then Robin was arching above her, coming hard inside her, lifting her with each thrust as she tightened about him and quickened again with escalating passion. Higher, brighter she burned until she exploded a second time. Moments later Robin lost control and joined her in a world of dazzling splendor.

"Do you think 'tis an unnatural thing for me to—to lose control when we make love?" Kate asked once her breathing returned to normal. "You have only to touch me and I go up in smoke. I'm not sure it's right."

Robin rolled his eyes heavenward. "Lord deliver me from what is natural and right," he said reverently. "I wouldn't have you any other way. I love you just the way you are."

"And I love you. I'm finally able to admit it. Father was right all along. He was wise enough to see what neither of us realized. We're perfect for each other, love."

"I knew you loved me all along," Robin said with typical male conceit. "The problem was that it took you too damn long to realize it."

"Thank God you never gave up on me."

When they returned to the parlor a short time later, Serena and Silas were still sitting on the couch, talking earnestly. Only now Serena wasn't shaking her head quite so determinedly. Nor was she so obviously contemptuous of Silas. She appeared to be quietly thoughtful, considering his words carefully. When Kate and Robin entered the room, Silas raised his head, his expression somewhat startled, as if he hadn't realized they were gone.

"Have you two settled things between you?" Robin asked as he settled into a chair and pulled Kate onto his lap.

"We're getting married," Silas said with quiet determination. "But first Serena has something to tell you."

Robin arched a well-shaped eyebrow. "I'm all ears."

Serena had the grace to look uncomfortable. "You—" she licked her lips nervously. "You never—never made love to me that time."

"I never believed I did."

Serena started to say something, changed her mind, and looked away. Silas jumped into the void. "Is it all right if I leave Serena here while I go to Parramatta for the preacher?"

"Certainly," Robin agreed with amazing control. He had every reason to hate Serena, but right now he'd agree to anything to get the little minx out of his hair. "You've made a wise decision, Serena."

Serena slanted Robin an oblique glare. "I've been given no choice," she claimed, offering a defeated shrug.

"Don't look so glum, Serena," Kate advised. "Your baby will have a father who loves him, and you certainly can find no fault with what Silas has offered you. Obviously the man is crazy about you. Marriages have been built on less."

"Like your marriage?" Serena snapped harshly. "Everyone knows why Robin married you."

"I married Kate because I loved her. I still love her; nothing will ever change that."

"You don't—"

"Serena!" Silas warned sternly. "I won't have my wife acting like a shrew. 'Tis over with Robin. From now on I'll be the only man in your life."

Kate silently applauded Silas's words. Once Silas found the courage to stand up to Serena he had become a different man. Perhaps he could keep the little hellion in her place after all.

The wedding took place at seven o'clock that night in the parlor. If the bride didn't look radiantly happy, no one noticed or complained. She repeated the marriage vows at the proper time, though they came out stilted and wooden, and dutifully raised her face for Silas's kiss at the end of the ceremony. Robin offered them the use of one of the spare bedrooms for the night, for Silas expressed his wish to leave the next morning. His business demanded he return with utmost haste.

The brief ceremony was attended by Kate and Robin, who acted as witnesses; Jack Dent, the station boss; Maude, Lizzy, and Big John. Kate nearly burst out laughing when she saw how captivated Lizzy was with Big John. Her head came only to the middle of his massive chest and he was thrice her weight, but obviously Lizzy thought him magnificent for she could keep neither her hands nor her eyes off him for more than two minutes at a time.

What Big John thought about all that devotion was unclear. He had loved only one woman in his life, and she was dead. Yet Lizzy was undeniably lovely and obviously smitten with him. What would come of the unlikely attraction remained to be seen. Big John had never before been the recipient of the kind of rapt attention lavished on him by Lizzy. The result of the meeting between Lizzy and Big John was that when Lizzy learned that Big John was going to Bathurst she expressed her eagerness to accompany Kate and Robin to the new settlement.

Later that night Kate and Robin laughed over the way everything had turned out. Big John was being offered a huge boost toward emancipation, Lizzy was so fascinated by the gentle giant that she was unlikely to interfere again in their lives, and Serena now had a husband who adored her and a baby on the way, both of which would soon put an end to her wicked ways.

"Things have a way of working out, love," Robin observed sagely. "I have a wife whom I love more than my own life, and our first child will be born in a matter of months. A year ago, I sincerely doubted that happiness existed for me in this world. Funny, but I never visualized marrying a woman so stubborn, so obstinate she'd make my life a living hell for a while. Until I tamed her and turned her into a purring kitten."

"Purring kitten!" Kate repeated with mock horror. "When have I ever purred, Robin Fletcher?"

"When I touch you like this, Kathryn Molly McKenzie." His hands drifted beneath her nightgown, taking it with him in an upward caress that ended between her thighs. The fingers of one hand slid into her with effortless ease as Kate's eyes opened wide.

"Oh . . ."

"And like this." His other hand pulled the nightgown over her head and tossed it aside before fluttering down between her breasts. He caressed her with light, teasing strokes, gliding over the swollen curves of her breasts, then splaying over the sweet mound of her slightly distended stomach.

He chuckled when a noise that sounded suspiciously like a purr rumbled past her lips.

"I've never asked you, are you happy about the baby?"

"Aye. Having your children will make our marriage complete. Are you happy?"

Wild Land, Wild Love

"Ecstatic."

"Make me purr, Robin."

"Ah, Kate, hearing you purr is music to my ears. I loved the way you hated me, but I'm going to enjoy the way you love me even more."

Epilogue

"Bloody hell, Dare, how could you have gone through this twice?" Robin tunneled his fingers through his hair in a nervous gesture that conveyed his frustration and worry.

"I wasn't with Casey when she had Brandon, but I didn't leave her side when she had Lucy. And you're the first to know, I'll be with her again when she bears our third child. But this one is absolutely the last. I didn't marry Casey to turn her into a brood mare."

Dare and Casey had traveled to Bathurst to lend support to Kate and Robin when Kate delivered her child. Casey attended Kate now as she labored to bring forth the baby, having gone into labor the night before. The children had been sent outside to play while Dare tried to calm Robin's fears. Since

Dr. Proctor was temporarily practicing medicine in Bathurst, Kate had the best of care. But that fact still didn't keep Robin from pacing back and forth across the kitchen floor where he and Dare had spent most of the night.

"Three children," Robin said with considerable awe. "As far as I'm concerned, this will be our last. I won't put Kate through this again."

Dare smiled indulgently. "I imagine Kate will have something to say about that."

Suddenly a muted scream drifted down to them from abovestairs. "Bloody hell, she's dying! I'm going up there!" Ignoring Dare's amused chuckle, Robin sprinted toward the stairs.

Robin had been with Kate for hours, holding her hand, talking softly to her, sharing her pain yet not really able to help. As the hours passed, he grew frantic with worry, although Dan Proctor had insisted everything was progressing normally. Finally, Casey had sent him downstairs to join Dare. Unfortunately, Robin was unable to cope with the sight of Kate suffering, and both Casey and Proctor felt Kate would fare better without Robin hovering over her, disturbing her with his excessive worry.

Robin flung open the door to the bedroom, his eyes going immediately to the bed where Kate lay white and limp. "My God, she's dead!"

"Kate's fine," Casey assured him, hurrying over to intercept him. "You have a beautiful daughter. If you'll be patient a few minutes, I'll clean her up so you can view her properly."

Sending Casey an exasperated look, Robin pushed past her to kneel beside Kate. Proctor was still working over Kate, but Robin saw nothing except Kate's pale face and the erratic rise and fall of her breasts beneath the bedsheet. She didn't look fine to him. "What's wrong with her?"

"She's exhausted," Proctor said, removing something from the foot of the bed and walking away. "Kate came through like a trooper. Your daughter is healthy and promises to be as great a beauty as her mother."

Kate opened her eyes, saw Robin's face contort into a grimace of worry, and smiled. Immediately Robin's features softened and his eyes grew misty as he bent and placed a tender kiss on Kate's brow. Casey brought a small bundle and placed it in Kate's arms.

"We have a daughter," Kate said. Her eyes were so filled with contentment and intense with maternal pride, Robin was amazed. Had she already forgotten the pain and travail she'd suffered in order to bring forth this child? "Are you disappointed we didn't have a boy first?"

Finally assured that Kate was indeed fine, Robin spared a glance at the tiny scrap of humanity he and Kate had produced. She was beautiful, and for the second time in his life he was consumed with a love so intense he nearly burst from it.

"I'm not disappointed at all. She's wonderful. I'd be perfectly satisfied if we never had another child."

Despite her weariness, Kate smothered a grin. "As lusty as you are, I doubt she'll be our only child. Do you mind if we call her Molly?"

"'Tis a perfect name for our perfect daughter."

Wild Land, Wild Love

"Perhaps you should leave, Robin," Casey suggested as she took the baby from Kate's arms. "Kate is exhausted, and there is still much to do to make her comfortable."

Robin rose reluctantly. "Aye. Rest, love, I'll return later."

"Robin?"

"Aye, love."

"I was wrong. I'm not too old to have your children."

"Old? Whatever gave you that idea? You'll always be young to me. Even when we're both gray-headed and bouncing our grandchildren on our knees. A love like ours is ageless."

Taken by You

CONNIE MASON

English nobleman Morgan Scott pillages the high seas. When he and his crew attack the *Santa Cruz*, he sees the perfect opportunity for revenge: an innocent Spanish nun whose body he can ravage to spite her people. But Morgan quickly finds himself torn between this act of vengeance and the passion incited by her fiery spirit.

Even as Luca Santiego fears her fate at the hands of the powerful privateer, she fights the feelings of desire he inspires with his sparkling eyes and muscular contours. She may be posing as a nun, but the emotions she feels in his strong arms are anything but pious, and she soon longs to be taken by him.

Lionheart
Connie Mason

Lionheart has been ordered to take Cragdon Castle, but the slim young warrior on the pure white steed leads the defending forces with a skill and daring that challenges his own prowess. No man can defeat the renowned Lionheart; he will soon have the White Knight beneath his sword and at his mercy.

But storming through the portcullis, Lionheart finds no trace of his mysterious foe. Instead a beautiful maiden awaits him, and a different battle is joined. She will bathe him, she will bed him; he will take his fill of her. But his heart is taken hostage by an opponent with more power than any mere man can possess—the power of love.

SURRENDER
to
the FURY

CONNIE MASON

Five years after Nick Drummond swindled her father out of everything he owned and left Aimee LaMotte with an illegitimate child, he reenters her life a Union soldier as the South lies in flames. And though the beautiful belle's heart cries out for revenge, she is undone by the unexpected gentleness and nobility of the man who wronged her years before. She cannot deny the irresistible desire that draws her into the powerful, loving arms of her enemy, and forces her to surrender to the fury.

___52266-7 $5.50 US/$6.50 CAN